ASCENSION

NATE TEMPLE SERIES BOOK 13

SHAYNE SILVERS

ARGENTO PUBLISHING

CONTENTS

The Nate Temple Series—A warning	1
Chapter 1	3
Chapter 2	8
Chapter 3	12
Chapter 4	17
Chapter 5	22
Chapter 6	28
Chapter 7	31
Chapter 8	36
Chapter 9	42
Chapter 10	48
Chapter 11	53
Chapter 12	60
Chapter 13	66
Chapter 14	73
Chapter 15	78
Chapter 16	83
Chapter 17	90
Chapter 18	96
Chapter 19	104
Chapter 20	110
Chapter 21	117
Chapter 22	124
Chapter 23	130
Chapter 24	136
Chapter 25	141
Chapter 26	146
Chapter 27	150
Chapter 28	157
Chapter 29	162
Chapter 30	169
Chapter 31	175
Chapter 32	180
Chapter 33	184

Chapter 34	189
Chapter 35	196
Chapter 36	200
Chapter 37	204
Chapter 38	210
Chapter 39	214
Chapter 40	220
Chapter 41	227
Chapter 42	233
Chapter 43	239
Chapter 44	245
Chapter 45	252
Chapter 46	257
Chapter 47	262
TRY: UNCHAINED (FEATHERS AND FIRE #1)	268
TRY: WHISKEY GINGER (PHANTOM QUEEN DIARIES BOOK 1)	274
MAKE A DIFFERENCE	277
ACKNOWLEDGMENTS	279
ABOUT SHAYNE SILVERS	281
BOOKS IN THE TEMPLE VERSE	283

This is a work of fiction. Names, characters, businesses, places, events, and incidents are either the products of the author's imagination or used in a fictitious manner. Any resemblance to actual persons, living or dead, or actual events is purely coincidental.

Shayne Silvers

Ascension

Nate Temple Series Book 13

ISBN: 978-1-947709-29-4

© 2019, Shayne Silvers / Argento Publishing, LLC

info@shaynesilvers.com

ALL RIGHTS RESERVED. This book contains material protected under International and Federal Copyright Laws and Treaties. Any unauthorized reprint or use of this material is prohibited. No part of this book may be reproduced or transmitted in any form or by any means, electronic or mechanical, including photocopying, recording, or by any information storage and retrieval system without express written permission from the author / publisher.

THE NATE TEMPLE SERIES—A WARNING

Nate Temple starts out with everything most people could ever wish for—money, magic, and notoriety. He's a local celebrity in St. Louis, Missouri—even if the fact that he's a wizard is still a secret to the world at large.

Nate is also a bit of a…well, let's call a spade a spade. He can be a mouthy, smart-assed jerk. Like the infamous Sherlock Holmes, I specifically chose to give Nate glaring character flaws to overcome rather than making him a chivalrous Good Samaritan. He's a black hat wizard, an antihero—and you are now his partner in crime. He is going to make a *ton* of mistakes. And like a buddy cop movie, you are more than welcome to yell, laugh and curse at your new partner as you ride along together through the deadly streets of St. Louis.

Despite Nate's flaws, there's also something *endearing* about him…You soon catch whispers of a firm moral code buried deep under all his snark and arrogance. A diamond waiting to be polished. And you, the esteemed reader, will soon find yourself laughing at things you really shouldn't be laughing at. It's part of Nate's charm. Call it his magic…

So don't take yourself, or any of the characters in my world, too seriously. Life is too short for that nonsense.

Get ready to cringe, cackle, cry, curse, and—ultimately—*cheer* on this snarky wizard as he battles or befriends angels, demons, myths, gods, shifters, vampires and many other flavors of dangerous supernatural beings.

~

FEATHERS AND FIRE   **THE NATE TEMPLE SERIES**   **THE PHANTOM QUEEN DIARIES**

TEMPLEVERSE

DON'T FORGET! VIP's get early access to all sorts of Temple-Verse goodies, including signed copies, private giveaways, and advance notice of future projects. AND A FREE NOVELLA! Click the image or join here:
www.shaynesilvers.com/l/219800

FOLLOW and LIKE:
Shayne's FACEBOOK PAGE:

www.shaynesilvers.com/l/38602

I try to respond to all messages, so don't hesitate to drop me a line. Not interacting with readers is the biggest travesty that most authors can make. Let me fix that.

CHAPTER 1

I stood beneath a rusted steel awning, anxiously shifting from foot to foot as I mentally prepared myself for the worst possible outcome. It was early December, but the temperatures still hovered in the mid-fifties, so I hadn't needed to dust off my bulky winter coats.

It also made the pouring rain a lot more tolerable.

A tugboat drifted down the nearby river—the only potential eyewitness, but only if they had a pair of binoculars and happened to be staring toward the mostly abandoned warehouses occupying this forgotten stretch of riverbank.

If things went south here, my Horseman's Mask wouldn't help me.

Because a wise man once said that it was generally considered unwise to wear a bomb vest to a wrestling match. Me. I was the wise man who once said that.

Rain poured down mercilessly—as if the old gods had woken up in a shitty mood and wanted to further punish the foolish mortals for how far they had fallen since the time when their lives were managed by the older, harsher, tough-love, creation gods. Like old war vets on a porch, the old gods saw their successor new-age gods as nothing more than hipsters, treehuggers, and unconditional love gurus.

Mortals these days! When we were running things, those flea-infested meat-

sacks knew how to properly respect our Names, devoting their every meal to us through prayer and worship.

Both at the beginning AND at the end of the meal! Hell! They even thanked us at funerals!

Instead of wearing their Varsity Lettergod's jackets with pride, the old gods had been placed into retirement communities and now wore dirty undershirts, kicked back on their recliners, chugged cheap manna-mead, and shouted obscenities at the static on the glass-tube television screen of humanity.

Because humanity had gotten all intelligent and evolved and didn't feel they needed to worship the new gods, let alone the old gods. They had lost their fear of the higher powers. Now, humans worshipped—and made fortunes off—technology.

All because the new gods had phoned in their duties, focusing more on their petty dramas and politics than policing the evolving bacteria known as humanity down on Earth.

Like I was writing a screenplay, I imagined the cranky old titans, giants, and celestial beings—the parents of the modern-day gods—grumbling unhappily to any who would listen. *The new-age gods never even made their own universes for crying out loud! They'd just inherited—*

I blinked slowly. Then I wiped rain from my forehead, muttering under my breath as my imagined godly soap opera struck uncomfortably close to my own upbringing. I'd inherited much, too. And I often bitched about my parents not doing enough for me.

"Where are you?" I growled, now agitated by my own inner psycho-analysis as well as my partner's punctuality.

No matter where I tried to stand, my feet squelched into puddles, unless I stepped out from the rusted, aluminum, tetanus umbrella—which would only serve to get me soaked *and* put me in full view from the lone, flickering streetlamp illuminating the worn-down shipping yard.

"Come on," I murmured again, glancing about uneasily. "You good for nothing—"

A Gateway ripped open a few feet away, and Alucard leapt through before it had even finished opening all the way. He landed in a puddle but managed to roll at the last second, holding up a large object wrapped in plastic.

"You found it!" I hissed excitedly. "Hot damn!"

"Listen," Alucard urged, rolling to his feet with a panicked look on his face. "We need to get out of—"

From inside the Gateway—but still sounding far away, as if they hadn't located the opening Alucard had made with his Tiny Ball—a familiar woman's voice rolled over the sound of pouring rain. "Where did the bastard go?" Callie Penrose demanded. "There's only the one exit." My eyes almost bugged out of my head.

"I will slice him into slivers," a grim, foreboding, male's voice growled in response.

"I will fuck him," another man's cold, dusty voice—sounding as if it had emanated from a long-forgotten corpse—promised.

"Hopefully not in that order, freaking psychos," a third man chuckled. The third man's voice sounded familiar, although I couldn't immediately place it. "He probably has a good reason for stealing it."

I rounded on Alucard as his Gateway winked out, thankfully cutting off the voices. "They *saw* you? What the hell, man? No one was supposed to know!"

Alucard shrugged. "How the hell was I supposed to know Starlight had a goddamn alarm system hooked up in his cave?"

I frowned. "The bear's name is Starlight?" I asked, momentarily shaken at a thought that should have hit me long before now. Because that had been the song Pan had left behind in his own cave—*Star light, star bright, first star I see tonight*. Since coincidences were conspiracy theories in my experience, I didn't even bother analyzing it, going straight to the assumption that it had to be related in some strange way.

But *here*, right the fuck *now*, I didn't have time for a reunion with the Kansas City death-squad.

But my happiness just wasn't meant to be—and I imagined those old gods excitedly leaning closer to their static-plagued television set, eager to watch humanity fuck itself.

Because at that exact moment, another Gateway erupted into existence, and a woman wearing white canvas pants and top—almost like military BDU's—stepped out. Her white hair shone in the dim glow of the streetlamp as rain plastered down her stunningly beautiful, ruthlessly cunning, face. Callie Penrose. She held a fox in the crook of one arm, but it appeared to be sleeping. Two more figures jumped through after her, and I froze, staring in disbelief as I momentarily forgot all about my plans for the evening.

Because a damned skeleton with a crimson hood-scarf glared at me, and his eyes were smoking pits of shifting shadow. Also, his ivory bones were marbled with silver streaks in a striated fashion—as if all the cracks of his prehistoric youth had been infused with chrome. He had apparently been a pirate in his glory days, because he also wore a wicked pair of leather boots that looked to have once belonged to Jack Sparrow.

"Skeletor," I breathed.

"Don't mention apples. He gets twitchy about apples," the second man murmured. I turned to look at him and felt my shoulders relax ever so slightly.

"Cain," I said. He was an asshole, but a familiar asshole. And I knew he had a modicum of common sense. Somewhere. "Haven't seen you around town for a while. Welcome back."

He smirked, raking an amused hand through his shaggy hair as he took a deep, nostalgic breath. "Better women in Kansas City," he chuckled. Then he snapped his fingers as if recalling something important. "Remember that joke you once told me that I didn't appreciate? I think I've matured since then, and I'd really like to hear it again."

I frowned. The last time I'd seen Cain in St. Louis had been at Fight Club, and I'd accidentally made an inappropriate joke about his origin story. In my defense, I hadn't known he was even present. I'd been telling the joke to someone else and he'd overheard it.

Alucard was shaking his head adamantly. "Do *not* tell any jokes," he warned me.

I'd already decided as much, reading the eager look on Cain's face, even though I didn't quite understand what he was trying to set me up for.

Callie waved a hand at Cain, silently commanding him to shut up. He obliged with an amused chuckle. Skeletor faced me full-on, ready to react violently if I did anything he deemed threatening. He must be the new guy to be so suspicious of me. Callie turned back to me and rolled her eyes in annoyance, her shoulders relaxing in mild relief. "What the hell, Nate? This was your doing?" she demanded, blindly pointing at the plastic bundle in Alucard's arms. "I thought you were in Cairo?" She shot a dark look at Alucard, who instantly averted his eyes. "I'm certain someone told me—this morning—that you were in Egypt."

I shrugged with mock guilt, allowing myself to sink into a deeper, calmer state. I relaxed my vision so I could view them all at once, focusing on none of them in any specific manner whatsoever, just like Alice had taught me. "I don't know what you're talking about, Callie," I said slowly.

Skeletor had a crude red balloon drawn on his upper arm bone, and the words *well done* were written underneath it. As I kept him in my peripheral vision, I realized that I was sensing a strange familiarity with him. I detected a similar bond between all three of the gang from KC. Like a strange trifecta that was tentatively reaching out to me, inviting me into their apparent club. But I didn't allow myself to focus on it or acknowledge it.

I was busy.

"You could have just asked, Nate. I would have said yes," Callie muttered, shaking her head as a bemused smile finally split her cheeks.

"Hypothetically," I began, "theft would indicate that I didn't want anyone else to know about it," I said in a distant, hollow tone. Then, without warning, I spun.

Cain cursed and Skeletor roared. I slammed down my hand—which was suddenly encased in my Horseman's black diamond armor—and I latched onto the end of a silver katana that was about an inch away from my lower spine. The form holding it was just a shifting haze of shadows. Before it could flee, I grabbed its shoulder with my free hand and tore the Shadow Skin away with the sound of ripping cloth.

CHAPTER 2

The figure hissed as if suddenly doused with boiling water. A buff Asian man materialized before me, wearing clothes similar to Callie, only in black. He dropped to his knees at the sudden pain of me tearing away his Shadow Skin, his flesh now red and agitated.

I didn't dare drop the Shadow Skin. When not bonded to flesh, Shadow Skins were notoriously dangerous. I wondered if this man even knew that. I hadn't really known anything about Shadow Skins until I'd fully accepted my lifetime in Fae as Wylde. I'd relearned a great many useful things, like how to sense and trap the trickster Shadow Skins before they fled to cause cataclysmic mischief. I still gripped the tip of his katana in my other hand, so I knelt down before him, using my Fae magic to fling up a dome of air around us so that Callie and her pals couldn't interrupt.

The man's blade began to glow red, then orange, and then white. I didn't let the extreme heat travel through to the hilt, but I could tell that it was growing uncomfortably warm in his hands, nonetheless. I stared him in the eyes. For his part, he didn't look subservient. He also didn't look angry. He looked…disciplined. Determined to draw in the pain of the obviously burning hilt. Willing to learn from this lesson if he survived, and willing to die if that's what came of his mistake.

I ignored Callie and her dogs railing against my defensive dome.

"Just you and me, child," I murmured dispassionately. "Give me your

Name or I will *take* it from you." I was very careful to only use my Fae magic rather than my wizard's powers. That was very important for what Alucard and I had planned after this farce.

The warrior gritted his teeth, fighting me. I allowed the blade to grow hotter, and it began to actually warp and drip molten droplets like a melting candle. One of the droplets landed dangerously close to his thigh, hissing and steaming as it struck the wet gravel.

He did not flinch.

"Your Name, or I will take much, *much* more. I will consume your *soul*," I warned in a soft voice, leaning closer to stare into his proud, determined eyes.

"Protecting. Her..." he hissed through clenched teeth, ignoring the stench of burning flesh from his palm.

The dome of power around me abruptly shattered and Callie shouted at me frantically. "Let him go, Nate! He's overprotective. That's not a crime!"

"Still," Alucard drawled dangerously, "we've got a major situ-Asian here."

Cain burst out laughing, repeating the phrase a few times as if trying to memorize it.

"Shut it, Cain," Callie snapped.

I silently reminded myself why I was really doing this, using it as motivation to maintain my glare with the overzealous bodyguard. But I did allow the hilt of the blade to instantly cool—no longer burning him.

"He held a blade to my back, Callie," I said, not breaking eye contact with the man. "He *will* give me his Name or things are going to get ugly. I don't care who he is to you. If one of my friends had done this to you, I would have been *first-in-line* to put him in his place. And you know it."

"He's right, Callie," Cain quickly cut in. "Nate is still an asshole, but he's got a point."

I slowly glanced over my shoulder and dipped my chin at Cain. Callie's face was a thunderhead of anger mixed with bitter understanding. She opened her mouth to talk, but I cut her off.

"I don't want to hear *your* apologies. I will hear *his*. When you bring a sword to the warriors' table, be prepared to die by the sword," I growled, turning back to the man. "I want to make sure that he remembers that lesson."

The man stared at me, seeming surprised by my words. His eyes were deep and wise, as if he was genuinely considering my words rather than trying to reassure me so he could flee the torture. I saw no fear in his eyes, for he was fearless. I saw pain in those eyes, but he acknowledged it no more than he acknowledged the rain pouring down upon us.

Finally, he nodded intently. "I am Ryuu. I lead the Shinobi now policing Kansas City for the White Rose. I ask your forgiveness for my disrespect," he said, lowering his eyes. Surprisingly, I thought I caught a faint flicker of amusement in those eyes before he lowered them. "Ironically, your response to my disrespectful act has earned you much respect in my eyes—if that matters to you. I accept full responsibility for my actions," he said, keeping his eyes lowered.

I lifted his chin with my finger. He grimaced at the sensation of diamond-crusted skin touching his chin, but he did meet my gaze. "My name is Master Nate Temple. Welcome to St. Louis, Ryuu. And welcome to the warriors' table. I'll save you a seat."

A slow smile stretched across his face, as if he had found great honor in my words—which only proved he was a lunatic. Luckily for him, I liked lunatics.

I yanked the katana from his grip and flung it into a puddle. "No need to keep showing us how tough you are, Ryuu. I already smell your burned skin. See to it before I decide to play doctor, which will both heal and hurt. Most patients say that my healing feels worse than the injury."

He nodded, his eyes flickering to the sizzling, warped katana. "Would you be opposed to me keeping that? As a reminder of your lesson?"

I blinked at him and then let out a laugh, shaking my head. "Fine." He smirked back, and I extended a hand, pulling him to his feet. I held out his squirming Shadow Skin. "Scale of one to ten," I asked him.

He took the Shadow Skin, frowning down at it thoughtfully. "Eight."

I grunted. "That's…hardcore, man. I heard it feels exactly like being skinned alive."

He met my eyes and finally nodded. "Accurate." Then he began walking back towards Callie, scooping up the ruined blade on the way.

"For the record, I heard it hurts more putting it back on. Maybe let the pain fade before replacing it."

He stared down at it for a long moment. Then he closed his eyes and held a corner of the folded shadow to his skin. He gasped and hissed as it whipped back around him, smoking as it settled back into place. His knees wobbled and he almost fell, but he caught himself with a groan, and slowly straightened. His fingers were shaking as he met my eyes. "Right again," he rasped.

But he was smiling.

Okay. He was *definitely* bodyguard material.

Alucard had strategically placed himself off to the side, perfectly positioned to counter any attack on my person.

I turned to address Callie, Cain, and the bone guy, hating myself for this next part. It needed to be said for multiple reasons—one of them I couldn't afford to talk about. The fox was still sleeping, seemingly totally unaware of the drama that had taken place. I cleared my throat, "You three stood there, talking to me like old friends, and silently watched—even distracting me with conversation—as you waited to see if the new guy could pull a fast one on me. If Ryuu had attacked me *before* we began speaking, that would have been a different matter. An instinctive reaction to a theft, I would have tolerated. But we had already moved beyond that point. That makes you *all* complicit. And I've got enough on my mind already without having to be concerned about my friends testing me."

Even though I was partially right, I hated to say it so harshly. Especially to Callie.

But…

I was the leader of the New Horsemen, and all our lives might one day depend on the chain of command. Potentially, a day that was sooner than any of us hoped.

CHAPTER 3

*R*yuu spoke up. "They don't always see me when I use my Shadow Skin."

"Callie did," I said.

Callie nodded almost imperceptibly. Her eyes flicked to Ryuu as if to make sure he was alright.

He waved a hand dismissively. "Injured pride and crippled ego. Both build character." He turned to me. "For what it's worth—and definitely not to diminish my apology—I was only taking a defensive position."

I smiled approvingly, nodding at him.

Callie studied me, definitely not pleased by my tone or the situation, but also knowing that she had brought the extra drama on herself. The moment she'd seen it was me, she should have called off Ryuu, but she'd let him creep up behind me. What the hell was that all about?

Ryuu had positioned himself closer to her than the others, not even seeming to be aware of it. He also no longer seemed to be paying attention to our conversation but keeping his eyes vigilant to our surroundings.

"Why was all of this necessary, Nate?" Callie asked, her eyes drifting to Alucard's package.

"Again," I muttered, trying to fortify my defenses under her frustrated—and guilty—stare. "We aren't going to talk about it. In fact, it's best if you leave. No offense, but I'm in the middle of something important."

Callie studied me thoughtfully, reading between the lines. Despite her obvious frustration, I could see the intelligence in her gaze as she attempted to remove her emotions from the equation and see the situation from my perspective. Knowing how intelligent she was, I was certain she picked up on the multiple layers of the conversation. That I wasn't just speaking as Nate, but as her new boss—the Horseman of Hope chastising the Horseman of Despair.

She finally nodded. "Understood. Next time just ask. I am vigilant in my protection of Kansas City. Just as you are here in St. Louis. Open communication would have prevented Ryuu from overreacting," she said calmly.

Unfortunately, that wasn't the right response, and I hated myself for what I needed to say next. Ryuu had accepted his guilt with honor, not attempting to justify himself before his apology. Callie needed to do the same.

I shook my head, keeping my face calm. "Ryuu was just doing his job. He's a stranger and acted accordingly. Others should have known better and called him off. Open communication," I added—repeating her choice of words—feeling like I had just pulled the trigger on a loaded pistol.

Callie's lips thinned and she nodded very, *very* slowly. "I see. I apologize."

And right there, I knew certain dynamics of our relationship had just changed between us. Not significantly, but noticeably. I could tell that Callie knew I was both right and wrong—in different ways. Similarly, I knew I was both right and wrong, in different ways.

Cain's eyes looked about ready to pop out of his head. "Anyone else smell that?" he asked gently, sniffing at the air. "Smells like awkwardness..." he murmured.

Alucard murmured his agreement, much quieter.

Skeletor sniffed at the air, his face somehow shifting as if it wasn't made of bone.

The ensuing silence was pregnant with tension. I sighed, relaxing my shoulders as I refocused on Callie, wondering how much I could safely say without ruining my secret operation with Alucard—because that was the primary motivation between my choice to dismiss the Ryuu situation and to make a glaring spectacle out of it.

The Horseman angle *was* important. But I could have given her a private, verbal warning without an audience.

But...handling it the way I had served multiple purposes. I had chosen to use the opportunity like a blade for a very important reason. And now I had to figure out a way to tell her enough that she would stay far away from St. Louis without jeopardizing my plans with Alucard and his package.

"Odin doesn't want anyone learning it was stolen," I lied, indicating the plastic package Alucard held. "He asked me to *discreetly* retrieve it." I shot Alucard a pointed look. "I obviously picked the wrong man for the job."

"I do not think discreet means what you think it means," the bone guy suggested somberly.

I turned to look at him, and I instantly found myself biting back a smile as I realized how adorably innocent he actually was. He didn't even understand how snarky his comment had been. How precious. "Sweet tattoo."

He dipped his chin at me, and I thought I caught a faint spark in the air, but the rain made it hard to be certain. "Balloons are badass."

I blinked at him, wondering if he was joking. He stared back, the dark smoke in his eye sockets shifting and twisting of their own accord. "Right."

This guy and Carl, I thought to myself, *would probably make the best buddy-cop movie ever.*

I turned to Callie, unable to find a way to continue my conversation with the skeleton without snarking him to death. "If it was for anyone else, I would have asked. Now, I really do need you guys to leave. I have a meeting I can't be late for," I said, shooting a glance at the plastic covered book Alucard was still holding.

Callie studied me silently for a few moments. "Sure. I'll let Starlight know. I'm sure he will understand, but he might want to talk to you later about theft."

I sighed. "Fine. But you might want to let him know why I kept it under wraps. Probably in his best interest, too. Plausible deniability."

Callie shook her head. "I'll let you handle that. I would hate to get involved in something over my head. Plausible deniability."

Then a Gateway screamed open behind her. She didn't even look at it. Ryuu leapt through before her, making sure the other side was clear. Callie calmly stepped back, staring me in the eyes the whole time.

Then that little fox in her arms suddenly lifted its head and stared at me. The hair on the back of my arms stood straight up. The thing had no *eyes!* Just craters caked with crusted silver as if someone had melted them away with a soldering iron.

But that wasn't what shocked me. I felt an ancient, merciless power within that eyeless gaze, and I instantly knew what it was.

A Beast.

Callie was walking around with a Beast. Holy crap.

"Those things are dangerous," I warned, not taking my eyes off the creature.

Callie smirked, petting the fox. "I think they're cute," she said. Cain and the skeleton hopped through after her and the Gateway snapped shut, leaving Alucard and me alone in the rain.

"What the hell, man?" I demanded.

"Yeah. I forgot to tell you she picked one up at the shelter," he said, shivering at the thought of the Beast. "Why do you think I so wisely kept out of your little lover's quarrel?"

I blinked. "No! I was talking about your fumbled robbery. And that was not a *lover's quarrel*. I'm trying to keep my ass in one piece."

He arched a dubious eyebrow at me. "By attacking her invisible ninja and almost burning his hand off? Or was it provoking her new skeleton friend, Xylo? Or maybe it was when you talked down to a fellow Horseman in front of non-Horsemen? Which one of those was you trying to keep your ass in one piece? Because it looked like you were floundering, trying to find any way you could keep Callie out of danger." He leaned forward, jutting out his jaw. "Newsflash. We're fucking Horsemen. It's probably the most dangerous job in the world. And even before that, Callie was doing just fine kicking ass and taking names."

I scowled at him. "I wasn't trying to keep her *safe*. You—*and only you*—know what I was really doing and why I had to make a scene. Was I wrong to trust you with my secret?" I snarled.

He shook his head. "No, but I can still call you on your bullshit. I know what you did was necessary, but that was way more than you trying to keep her away with a lie. That was deeper. And I think you know it. I think that's why you're clenching your fists right now and turning into a human glow stick."

I frowned, opening my mouth. Then I realized that he was right. I *was* turning into a human glow stick. My veins were glowing with golden light beneath my skin—either a sign that a god was nearby or that I was losing my grip on my self-control. It was probably the latter, but I suddenly wished it was the former. Some creature I could really sink my fists into—

an immortal being who was designed to withstand a long, drawn-out beating.

Because Alucard was right. Seeing Callie had...well, it *had* been different. I wasn't exactly sure what it was, but it wasn't the same between us—and I was pretty sure that was even before our little spat. Granted, I was under a lot of pressure at the moment, and lying to Callie that I had stolen the Bioloki on Odin's behalf had been necessary, but...

Something *was* different about Callie. Or about *me*. And I hadn't particularly liked the way I had seen Ryuu looking at Callie either. Not necessarily in a predatory way or anything, but in a very...intimate way. Professionally intimate, but still.

I shook off the thoughts. My love life could wait until I took care of this other crap. I needed to hurry before I got caught up in my own lies. Or before my lies grew too deep too fast, causing irreparable fractures between me and my friends, who I trusted and respected more than I openly admitted.

I wasn't trying to keep Callie safe by lying. I was trying to prevent Ragnarök.

If such a thing was possible.

"Follow me. We're set up inside the one closest to the water. Everything is ready."

Alucard nodded, following my brisk pace. "Why that one?"

I shrugged. "It's close enough for us to make our next appointment without anyone getting suspicious. And it's closer to water in case we start a fire."

"You expecting a fire?"

I glanced at him. "How the hell should I know? I've never tried to snare a god."

CHAPTER 4

Alucard stood back near the entrance to the warehouse, playing lookout.

I sat before a ring of candles—since fire was an element of my target's lore—sipping an energy drink. The Bioloki that Alucard had stolen from Starlight—Loki's prison for the last few centuries—sat beside me with a stone now stuck to the front by a wad of packing tape.

The ring of candles was interspersed with other items as well. Two glass jars of spiders, a wolf figurine, a garden snake coiled up in a small aquarium, a combination lock I had picked up at a convenience store, a fishing net, a knotted hemp rope that I had found in the back of the warehouse, and a perfectly intact spider's web stretching from two pegs glued to a small wooden base. The web had taken me the longest to acquire, since I'd had to set up a moveable apparatus in a place where spiders typically lurked, hoping one would choose my wooden posts to make a web.

Like I'd told Alucard, I'd set the place up ahead of time, knowing I had to get this over with as fast as possible—before anyone thought to ask questions about my absence. The Callie situation had eaten up a chunk of that time, so I had to wrap this up quickly.

I couldn't afford any of my well-intentioned friends asking too many questions. Because I would be forced to lie to them, and I wanted to limit that as much as possible. Only Alucard knew the full story, and I'd put him through rigorous oaths before deciding to accept his help.

It was time.

I took a deep breath and pulled out a piece of paper from my pocket. I had no idea how authentic the scribbled prayer was, but after hours of research, I decided it suited my needs. If it wasn't accurate, at least it matched my intents. I'd also tweaked it to make it more personal. I opened my mouth and began to read the prayer out loud.

"Hail Loki. Trickster. Web-weaver. Father of beasts.

Odin-kin and fortune-bringer.

Word-smith and fire-singer.

You know the songs that shall remain unsung.

You do not mince your words, bite your tongue, or promote kindness over honesty.

For you are the master of lies, and speaker of harsh truths.

And your songs reveal that which we would wish to hide from ourselves.

We are all chained to the masks that we wear,

Slaves to the sheep that our society commands us to be.

I pray to you, Loki, Black Sheep, chaos-bringer.

May your fires of change set us free."

My words echoed in the space of the warehouse, and I waited a few moments.

"And I'm sorry for kicking you in the balls," I added for good measure, recalling our last encounter during my fight with Mordred. "It was a dick move," I admitted, smirking at the double entendre.

Dark laughter suddenly erupted from the center of the ring of candles, and a tall, dark-haired figure suddenly materialized before me. Unlike the last time I had seen him, he was not a portrait of burned, melted skin. He had healed in the weeks since then, and my stomach was eternally grateful for that. Unless…he really was still burned and merely using an illusion to disguise his injuries from Mordred's fire.

Loki stared at me, shaking his head as his laughter slowly began to subside. He spent a few moments considering the objects surrounding him, nodding pensively.

Then he turned to look at me, and faint flames danced in the depths of his blue eyes. "I hope you know this circle cannot protect you, Nate Temple."

I nodded, shrugging carelessly. "I never use protection, Trickster." He cracked a toothy smile, shaking his head. "I wanted to show you some respect. You've been imprisoned for a long time, so I thought a prayer would be appreciated."

He cocked his head suspiciously, as if wondering whether or not I was lying.

"Are you actually healed, or is this an illusion?" I asked.

He smirked, and between one moment and the next—with no noticeable effort on his part—he was suddenly Alucard. Not just mimicking Alucard, but a hauntingly uncanny doppelgänger. Then he was suddenly Ganesh. Then Achilles. Then Callie.

He smiled wide at the reaction on my face. Each transition had been seamless and terrifying.

"I am healed," Callie's double said, "but don't take my word for it, Temple."

I shuddered, waving a hand. "Great. But it's going to be hard for me to focus if I'm staring at a beautiful woman. And you will want to hear my plan."

He shrugged easily, switching back to his normal form in mid-motion. His eyes took in the book beside me, but he didn't appear to recognize it or care much about it—likely assuming it was the source used for my prayer.

Perfect.

"I have a few questions, first, if you don't mind. It will dictate how our conversation goes—whether or not I think we can help each other."

He smiled, looking amused. "How fascinating."

I ignored his sarcasm. "You made it very obvious that you wanted to kill Odin, or at least hurt him as much as you possibly could. You were willing to kill your own mother to get to him."

He yawned, shifting slightly as if working a kink out of his back.

"Why, specifically, do you want to hurt Odin so badly? I know he's been a shitty father and locked you away for a long time, but what is your *biggest* grudge with him? What pushed you so far that you were willing to kill Freya in order to get to him?"

Loki stared back like a caged tiger. "Because he will stop at nothing to kill my son now that he is free. Odin pitted father and son against each other, using extortion to force me into my prison to protect Fenrir, and threatening Fenrir with my death if he rose up against the Allfather. Except now we are both free," he said hungrily.

I tried to keep my face neutral, having a hard time imagining my butler being so ruthless. I knew very well that the Odin from the stories had been a tough, often cruel, bastard. Pairing that legend with the strict butler I had grown up with was hard to fathom. Like accepting your neighbor was actually a serial killer.

"Mordred broke you out of prison, promising to give both of you freedom in exchange for Gungnir," I said, wanting to confirm their arrangement, because I still had a lot of questions about what Mordred had been involved in behind the scenes. "But Mordred betrayed you when you didn't escape Niflheim fast enough, keeping Fenrir for himself."

Loki nodded, his eyes glinting with fire. "All I wanted was to go far away and spend some time with my son in peace. Odin took *everything* from me. Mordred was just an opportunist."

"You're welcome for the Mordred thing, by the way. I did it for you."

He rolled his eyes. "Right. The only way you can help me is to give me Gungnir, give me Odin, or give me Fenrir. Those are my cards," he said, waving a hand. "Now, show me yours."

"In a minute. I have a few more questions, first."

He sighed impatiently. "Then by all means get on with it," he muttered.

"Why did Mordred want Gungnir?"

Loki grew very still. "That is not a question you want to ask, and that's all I'm going to say."

I frowned, caught off guard. But it was obvious that he meant it literally. "Okay."

Loki grunted. "I will not be threatened into a bad bargain a second time, Temple," he said, gesturing at the items in the ring. "Although impressive, I don't rightly care how strong you are, or that you are a godkiller."

I scoffed. "Don't bother threatening me over Thor, Loki. It will not even remotely intimidate me or make me feel guilty—"

But I cut off as he suddenly started clapping loudly. "*That's* for Thor. The shit-crusted, electron fucker," he cursed, spitting on the ground. "I was talking about the godkiller aspect in general. I'm sitting here talking to a mortal, and I don't have a headache."

I cocked my head, sensing that he was speaking literally, not insulting me. "You get headaches talking to mortals?"

He nodded. "If we try to discuss important things, yes. Why do you think none of us gods ever 'prove' ourselves to our people, or why we only visit them when we are disguised as some fucking hairy animal? It's to be more relatable. And to avoid the headaches."

I narrowed my eyes at the hairy animal insult but managed to stay on task. "You're saying the reason a god doesn't actually answer prayers is because it's painful for them to do so?"

"I can visit them without a problem but proving that I am Loki—to most humans—gives me an instant migraine. We are not compatible with most of humanity. That's what magic is *for*—to permit lines of communication between different levels, or flavors, of power."

I stared at him, recalling something Pandora and Alice had mentioned a few times—something Callie apparently knew already. "The Omegabet—"

"Don't fucking say that out loud, you goat-sucking fool!" Loki hissed, glancing about frantically. "Fuck! Are you trying to get us killed?"

CHAPTER 5

I blinked, caught off guard by the god's sudden anxiety. "That's a secret? I only just heard about it."

"Of course you only just heard about it! You're on a new level of power, apparently. You can talk to us gods about more important things. In a way, you *are* a god."

I arched an eyebrow, seriously doubting the simple assumption. "I highly doubt it. And if so, this is a pretty shitty onboarding process."

Loki shrugged. "Everyone gets all hung up on the title, *god*. Or godly powers, for that matter. Sure, we have them, but to us, it's just normal." Sensing my confusion, he gazed upwards, trying to think of a better explanation. Or maybe I was managing to give him a headache, after all. "It would be like someone running up to you in the street and declaring how incredible it was that you could swim."

I studied him, kind of understanding his bad metaphor. I…actually hadn't thought about it quite like that. It was similar to my wizard's magic. To me, it was normal, but to everyone else…

"Listen," I said. "No offense, but you're the God of Mischief. Not really Mr. Honesty."

He nodded wearily. "I've had this conversation about a billion times. Literally. This is a perfect example of why we don't often bother speaking with your kind directly. We might visit for a one-night stand, but that's about the extent of our interest."

Wow. "Okay," I said, realizing we were getting nowhere productive. "Here's where I stand. I called you here because I can't have you running around stirring up shit. I don't particularly care about the Norse pantheon —other than the fact that I'd rather delay Ragnarök, and I'm certain that a large number of the Aesir gods feel a certain way about me killing Thor."

Loki shrugged. "I imagine it's an even split, but I doubt those cheering you on will keep you safe from those cursing your actions. Loyalty is not a common commodity in Asgard."

I nodded. "Who should I be concerned about?"

He gave me a very frank look. "All of us, you idiot. You should be concerned about all of us. Especially me. I lie for a living. The fact that you are a godkiller makes you a threat even to those who applaud you for killing Thor. I would not go to Asgard without an army, if I were you. It's safer to all of them if you simply die."

"You sure don't seem to care that I killed Thor. You two were brothers, of a sorts, right?"

He shrugged. "I don't have any fucks left to give. Well, for my kids, but that's about it. Thor was not a kind person. Not even remotely. He was all about his name, fame, and claim. He got drunk from his notoriety. Imagine my surprise to find that pop culture now paints him as some kind of superhero. Read the old stories. They aren't entirely accurate, but they're pretty damned close. I've been gone for a while, but I know he spent a lot of time removing the worst of the stories from circulation. And I thought *I* was a good liar," he laughed.

I nodded, considering his words—how Thor's image had gone through a rebrand. "Like the Brothers Grimm."

Loki grunted. "I'm sure glad we got rid of that problem. Sent them across the damned ocean. By the brief looks of things, it seems you guys eradicated them."

I nodded, keeping specifics to myself—that my own ancestor had been the one to banish them. Then I'd finished the job hundreds of years later when I accidentally brought them back.

"Okay," I sighed, brushing my hands together. "I'll admit that I'm a fan of you taking Fenrir and getting the hell out of here. Mainly because without

Gleipnir—and in the likely event that he's heard you are also free—he might throw a tantrum and kick off Ragnarök. So…it seems our interests align."

"That's great—"

"Until they don't," I said, cutting him off. "I'm not buddying up with you out of necessity. I'm trying to prevent a future mess, because I have plenty of other things to worry about already. I want you and Fenrir out of sight, just like you said. I also want you two to leave Asgard alone. At least for a while. Let the dust settle a little over the whole Thor thing. Is there some way I can get an oath from you on those terms?"

He smiled cheerfully. "Not a chance. Not one that you could trust anyway. But I can shake your hand if it makes you feel better. Just be sure to count your fingers after," he chuckled.

I sighed, smiling faintly. "Damn."

"In all honesty, though," he said, his eyes growing distant and serious. "What your pal has with his pups…" he trailed off, smiling sadly. "I never got that with my kids. I'd sure like to try it. I want to be a better father than Odin was to me."

He was talking about Gunnar. I knew Loki wasn't to be trusted, but what other option did I have? If I wanted Fenrir out of the picture, who else was going to be able to help me? Odin was missing, and I didn't know any other Aesir that I could trust, other than Freya. But she was Odin's wife, so I wasn't sure what obligations that entailed.

The worst Loki could do was send Fenrir after Odin—although terrible, that was between him and his son. Odin had made his bed and had to lie in it.

And if I did nothing, it was only a matter of time before Fenrir broke free on his own and did what he wanted anyway. Or if whoever Mordred had seemed to be working for succeeded in using Fenrir as a weapon—which would likely be even *worse* than letting Fenrir do what Fenrir wanted. That was a scary scenario to contemplate.

And…I had a soft spot in me for kids and Beasts, and absent fathers wanting to make amends.

That didn't mean I trusted Loki. About as far from it as one could get. But it was my best option.

"Since we can't trust handshakes, how about this?" I asked, holding out the Bioloki. "Do as I ask, and you can keep this."

His eyes widened in disbelief, not having sensed it until I held it up for him to visually inspect. Sitting beside me, I'd turned it so that it looked like any other book. And since I'd taped a Sensate—a stone that blocked all magical auras from detection—to the front, he'd dismissed it earlier. "Clever," he mused, smirking at the Sensate.

I nodded. "Thank you. But I'm not finished."

He cocked his head curiously. "Pray tell."

"If anything happens to me—even if it's not your fault—this book goes up for auction. Absolutely *no one* has the authority to cancel the auction if I am dead. Even if you threaten to kill everyone I've ever met, this book will still go to auction if I die." He stared at me, perfectly still, and I could tell that he believed me.

Which was good, because I was telling the truth. It had been the only way I could find to guarantee his cooperation. To remove all loopholes. To call his anticipated bluff about extorting me with threats against my friends, and to call that bluff so openly that he believed me. Because, if I was being entirely honest, Loki could decide to hunt them down anyway, so I wasn't increasing the dangers. I was simply telling him that any temper tantrums he tried to throw wouldn't change anything.

"I spent my early years as an occult bookseller, and I personally know all the whales in the business. Many of them are reclusive and keep their purchases discreet. But something like this…" I mused, tapping the book as I shook my head. "Will easily fetch nine figures. To have a god trapped on their bookshelf? Hell, it could even sell for a billion. And you will be powerless to stop it if anything happens to me. The only way to get your prison off the open market is to work with me."

He stared at me, his eyes glittering darkly. "I'm impressed," he admitted in a soft tone.

I nodded. "Of course, you could always bid for it yourself, thwarting my clever plan."

He smirked absently. "Naturally."

"Which is why I have set up a second auction for Gleipnir—the only leash strong enough to restrain your son, Fenrir. He will live out his days as a domesticated dog, paraded in front of the other pantheons like a chihuahua. Same rules apply—if I die, auction goes live."

He gritted his teeth. "Unless I won that auction, too."

I nodded. "Naturally. Which is why I've spelled both items. Only I can safely touch them. Even if you used illusion to pretend to be another buyer or tried to use a proxy you controlled from behind the scenes, you will *never* be able to touch or own either item—directly or indirectly."

He frowned. "That's...impossible."

I shook my head. "You left a hair behind in your coffin. I used it to make a ward."

He scoffed in disbelief.

I shrugged, holding out the Bioloki. Then I lobbed it to the god. His eyes widened, and he held out his arms to catch it.

The book touched his flesh, and he abruptly flew backwards, slamming into a pile of wooden boxes and blowing entirely through them. The book had already returned to my hands, just as I'd designed the spell to do.

Loki climbed to his feet, his eyes wide and his hair sticking straight out. "What the hell?" he wheezed, staring at the book in my hands.

I nodded. "It returns to my possession if you try to touch it or own it in any manner whatsoever. You could bundle it up in a lead chest and try to hide it in your basement, but if you try to acquire it in any other way than through my permission, it will simply return to my possession. You are quite literally the only being in the universe who is unable to touch your own prison, or your own son's leash. It's called insurance. My spell is unbreakable, so now it's time to make a deal."

"I assume Gungnir is similarly enchanted?" he cursed.

I shrugged. "It has gone missing, but if I had it, I would have enchanted it," I admitted. His eyes widened to hear that Gungnir was missing. I nodded. "Why do you think I'm in a shitty warehouse, suggesting we team up? If Odin gets his hands on Gungnir, I can pretty much guarantee that his first trip will be to show it to Fenrir—personally."

Loki's lip curled back murderously. "Okay. You've officially caught my attention, godkiller..."

I nodded. "Great. Now, I'm being watched by a lot of people right now, and not just the Norse pantheon. I can't do my own research on this without drawing unwanted attention to it. So, you're going to be my spy for the next twenty-four-hours, or so. I need you to find out where Mordred stashed Fenrir. Meet me back here tomorrow just after sunset." He nodded, following along. "Once we know where he is, we can proceed with the rest of my plan..."

And I made a deal with the God of Mischief, fully expecting that he would attempt to double-cross me at least a dozen times. But I'd hopefully anticipated all of that.

Our relationship was not one of allies.

It was of schemers trying to outmaneuver one another. The real game was betrayal, and I was playing with the master.

I'd entered into a battle of wills with the God of Mischief. Neither of us trusted the other, but our interests currently aligned.

But for how long? And who could out-bluff whom?

CHAPTER 6

Now that my business with Loki was finished, I felt both relieved and on edge. I couldn't afford the distraction, because I had another task to accomplish tonight.

Maybe a little adrenaline, mayhem, and murder would help clear my head.

"Okay. They obviously haven't noticed anything or we would be fighting for our lives right now. I'll put the book in my bag so we know it's safe," I told Alucard, slipping it into my Darling and Dear satchel. No one else could take things from my satchel, no matter how hard they tried.

"Was all that lying to Callie really necessary?" he asked. His tone wasn't accusatory, more frustrated.

I shot him a frank look. "You know it was."

He sighed. "I know, it's just that bad stuff always happens when we aren't honest with each other. Yet here we go again."

I nodded my agreement. "It keeps things interesting, that's for sure. We can come clean afterwards. If we succeed." And I began creeping down the length of the building, keeping my eyes on the shadows as I observed our target. This building was on the opposite side of the deserted warehouse district from where I had spoken with Loki—which had been intentional. Close enough to sneak in our secret appointment, but far enough away for our second appointment to remain unaware of our presence.

The rain continued to pour, masking our approach towards the spacious two-story warehouse building. The upper level was all leaded, grimy windows—one of those old factories that had been renovated too many times from its origins, when natural daylight had been an important factor for the workers.

The cracked parking lot was surrounded by a chain-link fence that was warped, rusted, and collapsing, reminding me of repurposed chicken wire—how it never quite took the shape you wanted it to on the second usage.

Tall weeds grew from the cracks in the aged pavement, proof that no one used the place regularly—not any upstanding business owners, anyway. I knelt behind an old rusted-out car with no tires.

"What's the play?" Alucard whispered, studying the building.

I glanced down to see him clutching a small voodoo doll in his hand, fidgeting with it. "You're more than welcome to use your Horseman's Mask if you want any practice, but I think that's excessive and frivolous."

Alucard pursed his lips and shoved the doll back into a pocket, buttoning it up carefully. I bit back my smile to see how protective he was of it. It had taken him a while to figure out how to conceal it as anything other than a Mask, and he'd seemed just as surprised as me to find the object he'd chosen.

"Where did this lead come from again?" he asked.

"The same nefarious woman as the last few."

He shot me a grim look. "And we're trusting this to not be a trap? Don't we have enough paranoia already?"

I shook my head. "Oh, no. I'm definitely thinking it's a trap. And this paranoia is the perfect cover for our other...mischievous activities. Anyone asks what we were up to tonight, we have an alibi," I said, pointing at the warehouse.

He studied me with a resigned look. "As long as we're on the same page, I guess."

"Go team—what the fuck?" I hissed, abruptly pointing at the entrance to the warehouse.

A bear cub was ambling up to the door, seeming to have appeared out of nowhere. It plodded up to the door, lazily weaving back and forth before it swiped a small paw at the door. The door exploded into the building and the bear casually turned to look directly at us.

Then it winked at me. Shouting and cursing rolled out from the dim interior and I cursed, jumping to my feet. The bear blinked out of existence, and I realized he hadn't been wet, despite the heavy rain.

"You are fired from the team's asset acquisition department," I snarled at Alucard. "That was a goddamned magic bear."

Alucard's jaw was clenched in concentration as we ran towards the open door. So much for stealth. "Starlight's cave was empty. This is probably a result of your lover's quarrel—Callie showing you how pleased she was to be so highly respected by her new boss."

I grunted. "After I just told her how important and discreet I needed to be? She wouldn't do that."

Alucard snorted. "All's fair in love and war. What's the plan to deal with this newest batch of assassins?" he asked, eyeing the open doorway.

"Hurt them indiscriminately but try not to kill them. Not yet. We need answers. These assholes keep dying on me before I can question them, but they'll be Freaks of some sort."

"Number one stunner," Alucard murmured. Before I could ask what he meant, he suddenly kicked the side of my ankle hard enough to tangle my feet together so that I cartwheeled and splashed into a puddle and then the side of the goddamned building with a loud, heavy bang on the aluminum siding. It sounded exactly like a struck gong.

I whipped my head around and wiped the water from my eyes only to see Alucard disappear through the open doorway. He was singing at the top of his lungs, but he put real effort into it, like he was trying out for a part in a play rather than taunting those inside the building.

"This little light of mine, I'm gonna let it shine!"

The shouting intensified, and I heard Alucard laughing before a blinding flash of light erupted within, blowing out a dozen of the windows on the upper level.

CHAPTER 7

I ran for the door once I was certain Alucard's blast of light was finished. I didn't want any friendly fire to blind me.

I flung up a shield, in case any of the alleged assassins had guns or projectile magic, as I tried to gather my bearings. I stood in a wide-open space with crates, pallets, and long-defunct machinery collecting dust. I saw warning labels on the equipment—peeling and covered in cobwebs—but they were all written in symbols that resembled Chinese or Japanese. The warehouse looked like it had once been some kind of fabrication shop where they made metal parts for boat engines, but I was no mechanic so that was just a guess. It had obviously been abandoned a long time ago, and hastily enough for the workers to leave behind their valuable tools and half-finished projects. And they hadn't returned later to reclaim them.

Alucard stood near a long conveyor belt that led to a large machine press of some kind that was at least twenty feet tall. He had one foot firmly planted on an unconscious man's back, pinning him to the ground. Another slumped form lay sprawled across the conveyor belt—dead or unconscious, I couldn't tell.

Because my attention was drawn to Alucard—he was pointing at a man about twenty feet away who had his back to us, staring attentively at the burning warehouse wall.

Alucard grinned at me and then motioned for me to watch as he lobbed a wrench over the wizard's head, striking the far wall with a metallic *clang*. The man instantly responded by screaming and hurling a trio of fireballs at the sound. I blinked incredulously, realizing that the pyromaniac was still blinded by Alucard's night light impersonation and that he was trying to use his hearing to locate the invaders—us.

I rolled my eyes and waved a hand at Alucard to knock the wizard out before he hurt himself or burned the building down over our heads. The man beneath Alucard's boot suddenly shouted and squirmed—obviously *not* unconscious—as he attempted to spin into an offensive position. Alucard instinctively picked him up and bodily threw him at the pyromaniac—who had turned around at the sudden sound, already lifting his arms to light us up. The blinded wizard let loose a roiling ball of flame that engulfed his airborne ally in an instant. Except the suddenly-screaming, now-burning body slammed right into him, sending him hurtling into the aluminum wall where he struck head-first, his neck letting out a sickening *pop*. He crumpled limply to the ground, landing in the inferno he had created near the wall, his arm extended in the air like a flag of surrender.

My eyes widened as a sudden weaker ball of fire squealed pathetically up into the air in a sad arc from his outstretched hand—like when you thought a firework was finished, only to see it unexpectedly let off a surprise dud round that scared the hell out of everyone.

"Whoops," Alucard mumbled.

The man on the conveyor belt—apparently stirring awake from the brief encounter—began unsteadily climbing back to his feet, blinking wildly as if still blinded by Alucard's initial flash of light. I saw magic begin to form around his fingers, and Alucard instantly picked up a threadbare bag of metal parts from the ground, flinging it at him in hopes of knocking the guy down from his perch before he let loose with his magic. It worked like a charm, except the bag ripped, sending the contents hurtling like buckshot. A large object struck the man in the forehead, but a rusty pipe stabbed into a nearby circuit panel with an eruption of sparks.

The conveyor belt kicked on—much faster than it probably should have—like a rug yanked out from beneath the man's feet, sending him crashing onto it with a pained grunt. And it was a one-way ticket that swiftly carried the poor bastard towards the suddenly active metal press that rattled and groaned as loud and as rapid as automatic gunfire. I was sure it had initially been designed to crush large hunks of solid steel into flattened disks without ever slowing down. But right now, it sounded ready to implode as it picked up speed, its rusted parts squealing and groaning in protest against the cold start without any lubrication whatsoever.

Which could get a man brutally killed in multiple other situations.

Before either of us had time to react, the Murder on the Orient Press came to its last stop for the man, and the machine pulverized him with a sickening squelch that sounded like a crushed melon, painting the interior compartment of the press in blood and gore.

I realized, with a disgusted thought, that the press no longer squealed as loudly. In fact, it practically purred in comparison, its parts freshly oiled and primed with wizard innards. Still, it was loud enough to make me think we were at a military firing range.

"Jesus!" I hissed, shaking my head at Alucard. "Stop *killing* them, man!" Three dead in less than a minute.

"I'm not trying to!" Alucard snapped, sounding baffled at the man's unfortunate luck. I swallowed audibly, careful to keep the contents of my stomach where it belonged, but the smell was impossible to ignore. The man hadn't even had time to cry out before he was transformed into industrial paste.

Alucard ran up to the circuit breaker and simply tore it from the wall, disconnecting the power. The press kept on running, though, obviously on a different breaker. He next slammed a large door closed over the machine's opening, leaving only a small window for items on the conveyor belt to enter the press. The noise-dampening doors worked like a charm, cutting the noise down in half.

Gunfire abruptly opened up on me in continuous triplets, striking the shield I had thankfully left up. Bullets hammered into it, ricocheting everywhere, and Alucard and I ducked down behind the shield as I strengthened it in case the bullets packed more punch than my initial defenses could handle.

I saw a man's pockmarked face under the brim of a plain black cap. He was wielding some kind of semi-automatic rifle, clenching his jaw as he calmly walked closer, squeezing the trigger in good form rather than in an erratic onslaught. He was experienced. I readied myself to counter his assault the moment his clip ran empty, but the shooter suddenly gasped as one of his own bullets ricocheted back to hit him in the face, painting the wall behind him with crimson gore as he stumbled and fell backwards.

Before I could take a breath, two more men popped up from behind an adjacent stack of pallets, holding out their hands, ominously. Rather than wait for Alucard to continue murdering the men I wanted to question, I flung out my hand, hurling a percussive blast of air at them. One man flew into a large pile of trash bags, but the other slammed into an ancient forklift—the pointed end—and was instantly impaled.

By *both* forks, for crying out loud.

I blinked incredulously. The place was a deathtrap. No wonder everyone had abandoned their tools, refusing to come back even to salvage and pawn the equipment. I know I wouldn't have, in their shoes. After what I'd personally seen, I knew I had no intention of coming back.

I glanced around warily, verifying that no more attackers were about to pop up. The fire still blazed at the far end of the room, but we had time before it became a concern. The space remained quiet and I let out a breath of relief. At least one of them had survived—the one I had knocked into the trash bags. He lay motionless, obviously unconscious.

Alucard grunted, shaking his head as he walked over to an impromptu desk shoved up against an interior office wall. Taking one last look at the crime scene, I joined him, watching as he shuffled some papers stacked in messy piles. They all looked old and were covered in more foreign symbols. But the desk was littered with half-empty sodas and fast-food wrappers.

I saw no hint of what they had been doing here.

Alucard turned to look at me, letting out an annoyed sigh. "You see the scars on their faces? These guys were killers. Hitmen."

I nodded. "This was the largest squad I've run into. Six of the bastards."

Alucard shook his head angrily. "I'm still trying to wrap my head around this—that you've been taking out these hit-squads without telling any of us. I just thought you were hitting the bars more often than usual or doing some weird magic stuff."

"This *is* weird magic stuff," I said, waving my hands dramatically. "And I couldn't talk about it without all of you wanting to form a posse. I'm not some vigilante. It started out as me trying to catch one of them to interrogate. But they keep getting themselves killed when I show up." I grimaced at the glistening crimson press.

"You see," he began, "you say that like it's totally normal. That you aren't bothered by them wanting to murder you, but more that they had the audacity to die before you could question them. That's not normal, Nate."

I shrugged. "Normal is relative. If I would have thought we were walking into something like this, I would have brought backup. Sorry."

He waved off my concern. "And this *nefarious woman*, as you call her, just keeps sending you tips?" he asked suspiciously. "You don't find that curious? That maybe she's lying to you, sending you out to be her hired killer—one who works for free?"

I sighed, nodding. "Yep, I've considered that. But she gets upset when I kill them. She tried to kidnap me, too, but she failed. She apologized for that, saying that she had only tried to kidnap me to interrogate me before one of these groups found me. I asked for proof, and she told me where to find one of these supposed groups. But they all died in the exchange, so she told me about another one. Rinse and repeat." I held out a hand, gesturing at the dead bodies. "None have been as intense as this, and all of the other groups were trios."

"Wait. Gunnar told me about that—the person who tried to abduct you outside Chateau Falco. *She's* the one giving you these tips?" he demanded angrily.

"Yes. And your reaction is *exactly* why I haven't told anyone about it. Rather than simply killing her, I wanted to see if she was telling the truth." I locked eyes with Alucard. "And she's been right every time. It's not her fault they keep dying on me."

"Did they all have this bad of luck?" he muttered, speaking over the steady purr of the press.

I shook my head, pointing at a nearby crate that had been used to collect trash. It was half-full. "They've obviously been here for a little while. They were perfectly safe until we showed up, so it seems their bad luck came with us," I said, frowning uncomfortably. "Maybe it's just because they were all half-blind."

Alucard nodded unconvincingly. "Yeah. Maybe you're right."

I turned, scanning the rest of the warehouse for any other desks or maybe a helpful map on the wall that pointed to Chateau Falco with a date and a time written in angry red ink.

And I saw the damned bear cub sitting on a pile of old wood. He slowly lifted a paw to point at a stack of pallets, and then drew a line across his neck.

CHAPTER 8

Alucard opened his mouth to shout out in alarm at the silly old bear, but I slapped a hand over it to silence him. He stared at me, his eyes still wide, but I mimed taking a deep breath for him to compose himself. He did so, and then gave me a reassuring nod. I released his mouth, and he carefully bent down to pick up a wrench without making a sound.

I faced the indicated hiding spot and spoke. "I think we're all done here. No one else to—"

A grizzly man jumped out from behind the machinery, and Alucard flung out his hand, underhanded, as I swiftly sidestepped. A blast of dark green power slammed into the spot where I had been standing as Alucard's wrench clocked the wizard right in the nose, knocking him down to the ground with a gurgling shout. A second ball of flame in his hand immediately splattered to the ground, catching him and a pile of wood scrap on fire.

Alucard grunted. "Henchmen these days," he muttered, shaking his head in disappointment. "How do they expect to move up in the ranks if they can't take a wrench to the face?" he complained, shambling over to the fallen man. He began stomping on the flames while I turned to face the bear. The bear nodded at me, and then began chewing on a stick clutched in his paws.

"That it?" I demanded, not entirely sure whether or not I could trust him. This had to be Starlight—the mysterious wizard bear from Kansas City. I heard he had a penchant for drugs and mischief, but that he was generally a likable…creature. Being a local celebrity, I didn't believe everything I heard, so I highly doubted he was an actual druggie.

Except I couldn't afford to play the trust game right now. And I'd just indirectly robbed him.

He nodded placidly. "Seems that way, Catalyst. Seems that way."

I waited for him to reprimand me for thievery, but he just continued to watch me and gnaw on his stick, angling his jaws to get a better angle on the slobber-coated end. "Well, I appreciate the warning. You must be Starlight," I finally said, hoping to strike up some dialogue and find out why he was here if he wasn't going to chastise me.

"Oh, heavens, no," he said, plucking the stick from his mouth. "I'm a bear, Manling."

I nodded stiffly, attempting to rein in my impatience. "A bear named Starlight, then."

He shrugged, opening his jaws wide as he prodded at his mouth with his stick as if he was trying to clean his teeth. "Sure. Sometimes, Tiny God," he admitted.

I narrowed my eyes suspiciously. "I get it. You're referencing my various titles and names to prove that *Starlight* is just a shirt you sometimes wear. Is there a point to this?"

"I'm sure there is, godkiller. Somewhere. There usually is."

"Okay. So…"

He studied me thoughtfully, cocking his head. "Did you hear that?" he suddenly whispered, leaning forward interestedly.

I steadied my breathing, concerned by his sudden focus. "Hear what?"

He cocked his head. "They're stuck at the bottom of a well, praying. They have answers, but they're scared of the questions," he whispered, one of his ears twitching.

I felt the hair on the back of my arms stand up. "Who?"

"The Elders…"

And the hair stood even straighter, my pulse suddenly quickening. "What's wrong with them?"

"They miss their chains. Life was better, then."

I stared at him, confused. "Slavery was better?" I asked, not having known they had been slaves. Carl had never mentioned it.

"Chains gave them freedom. Independence gave them banishment. Their temples grew dark and drafty, their prayers unanswered when their masters abandoned them."

I stared at him. "Do they need help?"

He suddenly snapped out of it, shuddering. "Who dares help the Elders? Who dares wear the bone crown? Not me. Not any god I know. Too risky."

I nodded in understanding and, perhaps, agreement. "What is the point of this, Starlight?"

"Bear. Call me bear. It's easier with you. Starlight can mean so many other things when it comes to you." I narrowed my eyes to hear my suspicion confirmed—that Starlight's name might not be a coincidence, or that Pan's parting message may hold a deeper meaning.

"This is very interesting, but I have one question before we continue," Alucard drawled, interrupting our conversation.

Starlight—bear—turned to look at him. "Go ahead, Morningstar, Horseman of Absolution, Daywalker—and whatever other Names you've scooped up. With all due respect."

"How high are you right now?" he asked, straight-faced.

"Dude. Not cool," I hissed. "He's a magic bear."

Starlight chuckled good naturedly. "I don't even know where I *am* right now, man. This might be a new level for me. For anyone. I can *taste sound*." He glanced over at the hammering press and lifted a paw. "Quiet, you."

The. Press. Stopped.

And I neither saw—nor sensed—any magic whatsoever, even though that was obviously what he'd just used.

Starlight licked his lips happily. "Ah, much better." He began chewing on his stick again, and I caught a faint hint of maple in the air. No wonder he was gnawing on it.

"You're actually high right now?" I asked incredulously. Alucard must have known him very well to ask such a rude question and then get such a straight-forward answer.

"So high," Starlight murmured, grasping with a paw at nothing in particular. I began to feel suddenly cheated, his strange comments about the Elders carrying less significance. He was high out of his mind, and I'd almost bought into his farce. He was obviously powerful and respected—Callie had mentioned Starlight only in passing, but I knew they saw him as a sort of revered Shaman within their Cave, which was what they called their pack of shifter bears. Although he looked to be the size of a young cub, the fur and whiskers around his mouth were gray and old.

He also didn't look like much of a fighter. Callie had said that the other bears were all muscle heads, the kind of beings you didn't want to meet in a dark alley at night—or anywhere else for that matter. So his magic must be significant. The fact that Alucard hadn't been surprised about how high he was—and that he'd still had no problem using his strange magic despite his impairment—actually spoke volumes.

That didn't ease my frustration, though. If anything, it increased it exponentially. What the fuck was I talking to right now?

He glanced over at me, as if sensing my growing frustration. "Did you know—"

"I don't care, bear," I snapped. "Be gone. I have important things to look after at the moment. Come back when you're sober."

"Heh. You said carebear," he said, giggling. "Mischief managed." I flung a blast of air at him, but he was simply gone, leaving my power to shove over the stack of rotten wood. It hadn't been enough to harm him, but I'd wanted to see how he reacted—wanted to see if I could sense him using magic.

For the second time, I hadn't. I spun, lifting up my hands defensively in case he retaliated. "Be helpful or leave. This is not a joke."

He laughed, and I found him sitting atop the forklift, propping his rear paws on the impaled wizard's shoulders. "It's all a joke, if you know the punchline. Loki is clever. Are *you* clever Master Temple?"

I flung another probing blast of air, and this time I noticed a shift to the air before he disappeared. I still didn't sense any magic, though. I took a steadying breath. "What do you *want*, Starlight?" I demanded, spotting him seated upon a small pallet jack.

"To warn you about Mordred, of course."

I froze, staring at him. "Mordred is dead."

Starlight shrugged. "Dead men give better warnings than living men. Mordred was clever. He almost had Loki, but you messed all of that up. Mordred might have kept him busy, but now he's out of the game, and you're surrounded."

I growled angrily. "Who am I playing against if Mordred and Loki were just pawns?"

"Great question, Master Temple. Great fucking question. It seems you know how to use your head when you get out of your own way. That's worth knowing. If I was here searching for anything," he said, sounding slightly puzzled. "I can't remember why I came here," he said, staring down at the stick in his hands as if surprised to see it.

"I stole your book," I reminded him. "I think that's why you came. It would be incredibly helpful if you didn't tell Odin about that if he comes looking for it."

He scoffed. "Nah. That's not it. Mordred wanted you to find the Bioloki, and I'm not about to tell Odin diddly squat. I accepted the Bioloki from Mordred so that you wouldn't waste precious time looking for it later. Mordred wanted Loki at your throat, not in your pocket. And Thor. And the Knightmares." He glanced up at me. "That was a particularly splendid bit of Naming on your part. You have no idea." And he clapped his paws softly. "Knightmares!" he cheered, grinning over at Alucard.

"Mordred wanted me dead," I growled. "It didn't work out that way."

Starlight shook his head. "No. He didn't want you dead. He liked you. Respected you, even."

I grunted. "I have enough friends. And if he wasn't trying to kill me, he sure came close."

Starlight snorted. "None of them tried to kill you. Not Thor. Not the Knightmares. None."

I opened my mouth, but no words came out. Because as I played through my encounters with them, I realized he was right. The Knightmares had wanted to abduct or imprison me, but none had tried to kill me. I'd confronted Thor numerous times, and he'd always managed to escape, only choosing to confront Gunnar directly. "He wanted me busy," I said, frowning thoughtfully.

He nodded. "He wanted you not to rise up any further than you already had. He wanted your star to fall, so his could shine as bright as it should have against any other sky. Your existence made his achievements pale in comparison, despite his prestigious lineage."

My phone rang, making me jump. I glanced down, fumbling to silence it. When I saw who it was, I cursed, looking back over at Starlight. But he had disappeared. Damn it.

Alucard grunted. "Grateful Dead groupie," he muttered unhappily.

"I think I've had enough of these games."

"Does that mean you're finally ready to meet me in person?" she asked hopefully. Her voice was naturally smoky, making it hard to focus.

"No. I think I'm just going to find the person funding their field trips and introduce them to extreme violence."

"I've offered to help you do that, but you keep turning down my advances. What's a girl to think?" she teased.

I smirked. "I honestly thought they would have just given up by now. And I don't see how turning myself in to your care is going to help. In fact, it sounds like a great way to set me up."

"You're a suspicious person by nature, Nate. I get that. I am, too. That has served you well so far. But if I meant you harm, why would I waste my time by giving you guys forewarning about this squad, or any of the other squads? If I was trying to kill you, I wouldn't have used one of your Shadow Stones to try abducting you at Chateau Falco. I would have used about a dozen RPGs and a fleet of drones."

I grew very quiet. That…yeah, that might have done the trick. Then something she had said suddenly made me pause. *You guys*, she had said. She could see us. Right now. She was *here*. Maybe I could trap her, but I couldn't risk giving away my awareness.

I had to handle this very carefully. Because if she had seen us with Loki, I would need to shut her down. Fast.

CHAPTER 9

I walked over to Alucard, considering my options. If she could currently see me, she wouldn't have asked how many assassins were in the warehouse, or if they had been wizards. She would have seen it all. So she must be outside.

I hit the mute button on the phone. "Get Othello to run a trace," I told Alucard hurriedly, and then I immediately unclicked the mute button. "So where does that leave us?" I quickly asked her, hoping to cover up the brief silence. Alucard began furiously typing on his phone, texting Othello, the best hacker I'd ever met.

"Where does that leave us?" she repeated, sounding thoughtful. "How about this. Go grab one of their phones. Look for an app called *Lullaby*. Or you can just download it on your own phone. I'll wait."

I frowned, and then motioned for Alucard to toss me Wrenchface's phone. He used the man's thumb to unlock the screen and then lobbed the phone at me. I scrolled twice before I saw the app and opened it. "Okay. Looks like a shopping app," I said, after a brief glance.

She chuckled. "Click *Hot Deals*."

I did, and several listings popped up. I opened my mouth to tell her to get to the point when the top offer caught my attention.

"Let me know when you're finished reading," the woman said, as if she knew exactly what I was seeing.

I read through to the end and my eyes widened. I grunted. "One billion dollars to clean a temple," I muttered, shaking my head. It had been worded carefully, but there was no question I was looking at the assassination contract placed on my head.

"All the mercs use it, but that's definitely the largest payout I've ever seen," the woman said. "Congratulations."

I handed Alucard the phone, letting him read it for himself. "If you were trying to convince me of our friendship, you only succeeded in giving me a billion reasons why we probably won't ever be friends."

She laughed lightly. "I've made it perfectly clear that I'm not making a move until we talk in person."

"Why?" I demanded. "This is a billion dollars."

"I gave up blood money a long time ago—" she cut off abruptly, and I heard a clicking noise on the other end of the line.

"Hello?" I asked, wondering if she had dropped the phone.

"You do know that I'm not hiding from you, right?" she finally asked, sounding annoyed and disappointed. "All I want to do is sit down with you. I've made that abundantly clear. I'm smart enough not to approach until you agree to a truce, that's all."

"What are you talking about?" I asked. Alucard was staring down at his phone with a predatory smile.

She sighed. "Please. Show me a little professional respect. I doubt it's a coincidence that the nastiest virus I've ever seen just tried to hack into my laptop. I would have told you I was in Colorado if you had just asked me. Othello's trace was unnecessary."

I blinked, shocked to hear her mention Othello's name so casually. Alucard suddenly held out his phone for me to read. *Trace complete —Colorado.*

The fact that this woman had so calmly dismissed Othello's hacking skills was...absolutely terrifying.

"You're a hacker?" I finally asked.

She scoffed. "Hell no. I knew you worked with Othello, so I hired her through about a dozen proxies to build me a foolproof computer. She will realize that shortly—when her own countermeasures snap back at her. Might want to warn her. She's literally hacking against herself right now."

Alucard held up his phone, smirking as he showed me Othello's newest text. WHO THE HELL IS THIS BITCH, AND WHERE DID SHE GET ONE OF MY COMPUTERS?!

I shook my head, waving at Alucard to get it out of my face. "Might as well calm her down," I told him. "Tell her I'll explain it later.

"Niko," the woman said.

I frowned, thinking I had missed something she'd said. "Pardon?"

"Othello will find out eventually, so I figured I would just tell you. My name is Niko."

"Oh...how, um, did you see us if you're in Colorado? You let slip that you knew I wasn't alone. That's why I had Othello run the trace. I thought you were here."

"Drones, caveman. Drones," she said dryly.

"Right. That was my first guess," I lied, trying to wrap my head around the storm of surprises Niko was hitting me with—an assassination app, her name, her hiring Othello. Who the hell was Niko? I was suddenly glad that she hadn't tried to kill me yet. "I had to be sure this wasn't an ambush on your part," I explained.

Alucard had apparently finished texting Othello, because he now had his hands on his hips and was nudging Wrenchface with his boot, as if trying to wake him. He wasn't being gentle about it.

Niko sighed. "I know. I obviously don't expect you to take my word for any of this but ask yourself if I've done anything to make you doubt my word. I've warned you about every single squad who took this contract—and I warned you before they had time to make their move. Without my warning, they would have come for you at any time of day, any location, innocent bystanders be damned. This is a *billion* dollars, Nate. That much money can easily clean a conscience. Dozens could have died, and they wouldn't have cared as long as they fulfilled the contract on you. Instant notoriety. Instant wealth. This is a dream job. The phrase *too good to be true* comes to mind, which was one reason that I decided to try talking to you first."

I grunted. "Look. I appreciate your help, but Good Samaritans are mythical creatures in my world. Trust really isn't a virtue of mine."

"I'll say," Alucard grunted, planting a boot in the wizard's ribs. I scowled, but he wasn't paying attention, the bastard.

"How many were there this time?" Niko asked.

"Seven."

"All wizards?"

"As far as I can tell," I answered, thinking back on their apparent terrible luck.

"And they took the contract when it was only seven-fifty. The really big hitting crews are about to start popping out—the ones who typically get hired to take out countries and organizations. Think black ops wizards. What if a crew of a dozen Freaks attacked your school to draw you out? Or *any* school for that matter. As the reward goes up, morals go down."

"What about *your* morals? One billion dollars is very persuasive…"

She was quiet for a few moments. "My morals go up at an exponential rate when I see prices even a tenth of this size. Only dangerously powerful people offer to pay this kind of money for one man's head. And since multi-billionaires are a rare breed, I'm thinking this is an *organization* footing the bill. Which is why I've been helping you more and more. How long until the price on your head is so high that they take bigger risks? Maybe they attack you when you're at a big public event like a baseball game? Or they attack a hospital? You start throwing magic around to keep yourself and everyone else safe, and suddenly you become Public Enemy Number One to the authorities—all of them. They might not kill you, but you'd be a wanted fugitive—typical hunting tactic. Put you on the run so you're easier to pick off. That's what I would do. Except this annoying little conscience of mine won't let me."

I realized my head felt like it was spinning, even considering the possibility of a group of supernatural assassins attacking me in such a way. Not just at the repercussions of revealing that I was a wizard in a flagrant display of magical carnage, but at how many innocent bystanders might suffer for it.

All because some bag of assholes was willing to pay a billion dollars to ruin my day.

"On a related note, make sure you don't leave any evidence behind at the warehouse. You've already got enough bad press without the police finding your DNA at a murder scene."

I grunted. "Thanks. I was thinking of writing my name on the ground to really mess with them."

"What a novel idea," she chuckled.

I let out a breath, trying to think through it all. "Alright, Niko. Tell me your story. When we first talked, you admitted you were contracted to kill me, so you're a reformed assassin. Why haven't you pulled the trigger, so to speak? How did you get mixed up in this if you have such a pure heart?"

"I became a wizard to help people, but the Academy soon learned that I had a knack for combat magic. My intended career took a detour."

I processed that in silence. "You're working for the Academy?" I asked. Then I stared at the dead wizards. "They all work for the Academy?" I growled, feeling my rage building up. I'd given them an ultimatum in the past. I thought I had been perfectly clear with their Grandmaster. It seemed that they needed a reminder on our relationship status.

"No. That was where I was *trained*. Where *every* wizard is trained. Except for you, of course, which isn't suspicious at all. Our instructors used to talk about the Temple family dynasty—and it wasn't flattering."

I waved a hand, feeling my anger dying down. Her words made sense. "I already know all about the Academy trash-talking my family. That's what happens when you don't grovel and lick their boots. You get blacklisted," I muttered.

"That's why I left before they could recruit me into the Justices. Needed work, so became a merc," she admitted. "The pay was good, and I got to pick my own targets. Be my own boss."

"You realize how that sounds, right? That you're a killer, and you think you have the moral integrity to judge me? Hell, I didn't get paid for any of my kills, so I'm pretty sure I'm already winning that contest. How about you come to Chateau Falco and I'll put you behind a ward to interrogate you on your past crimes?"

Niko was silent for so long that I thought she might have hung up.

"That's what I thought—"

"Okay," she said. "We'll play judge, jury, and executioner for each other. I'll even answer your questions first. But you have to agree to answer mine immediately after. Killer will judge killer, and a twenty-four-hour truce will follow as we deliberate and then come to a verdict. If I decide you're guilty, I'll give you fair warning before I begin hunting you down."

I blinked, surprised. "Just like that?" What was her freaking angle here? If I was truly as corrupt as she seemed to fear, why would she agree to such a thing?

"Sure. Fair is fair. With an oath that you will release me after I answer your questions, of course. Let's say one hour's worth of questioning each."

Alucard was shaking his head. "Bad idea, man. Whenever a man walks into a police station asking for handcuffs, he's scheming. Think Keyser Söze from *The Usual Suspects*."

I had an altogether different fear, but I didn't dare voice it. Anyone I encountered could be Loki in disguise. I'd just backed him into a corner, so I was running under the assumption that he was actively searching for a way to get the Bioloki and Gleipnir without having to fulfill his part of our agreement. So to agree to walk into a warded circle with a stranger who might actually be Loki? No way. Even if she wasn't Loki, I didn't have time to play cross examination with Niko.

"First impressions matter, Niko, and yours was an abduction attempt. Tell me you only have my best interests at heart, and I'll agree to your terms."

She sighed. "How can I promise that? Everyone paints you as a monster. Offering you a truce when you might actually be the narcissistic sociopath that the Academy preaches is more than fair. If our roles were reversed, would you make that promise?"

I let out a resigned breath. "Not a chance in hell," I admitted, unable to argue her logic.

"Exactly."

"I'll consider it, Niko, but right now, I really have to go."

She sighed disappointedly. "Stay sharp, Nate. I think things are only going to get worse with the increased payout. I'm ready to handle this quietly whenever you're ready to come in."

"I never come quietly," I growled instinctively.

Alucard burst out laughing, and it took me a moment to realize how my words had sounded.

"Well," Niko murmured, sounding amused. "That's something."

"Goodbye, Niko," I said, my face beet-red.

"One more thing—" I hung up before she could finish.

CHAPTER 10

I rounded on Alucard. "Did you kick him to death?" I demanded, pointing at Wrenchface as I stormed over, pocketing my phone as I moved.

He was too busy laughing to answer, taking deep breaths to compose himself.

I glanced down at Wrenchface and blinked. His nose was destroyed in a cringeworthy manner, and blood covered his face. I stared at him, shaking my head in disbelief. Although the strange twist in luck had worked in our favor, it was still concerning. Because luck could turn on a dime, as any lifelong gambler well knew.

I might slip on a banana peel and cause a ten-car pileup or choke to death on a feather.

But nothing unlucky had happened to *us*. Had Loki done something to me? To Alucard? Some kind of insurance policy, maybe? Since nothing bizarre had happened until we entered the warehouse, I couldn't rule Niko out of the equation either. Maybe she'd helped me more than she had admitted. Maybe not.

Without further evidence, I couldn't do anything about it other than pay close attention over the next few days. I'd ride Lady Luck as long as I could and hope I got off in time.

Alucard finally regained his composure and joined me. "Crazy. I think the wrench broke his nose and sent the cartilage right up into his brain. Like that movie where the dude outside the bar accidentally killed that guy."

I turned to give him a flat look. "That describes every action flick circa 1985."

"It had Ghost Rider in it."

"Nicholas Cage? Are you talking about *Con Air?*"

He snapped his fingers. "That's the one. I've been thinking about that for ten minutes," he complained. Then he eyed me pensively. "Man, you lead a sad life to remember crap like that."

I rolled my eyes, staring down at the guy. It really had been a one-in-a-million shot.

"What about the trash bag guy? He survived, right?" I asked, shooting a glance at my watch.

Alucard winced. "Broken bottle of whiskey sliced his inner thigh. Bled out."

I ran a hand through my hair and let out a curse.

"With all the other stuff we have going on, how important is it that you talk to one of these guys?" Alucard finally asked, his voice rough.

I turned to look at him, frowning. "What do you mean?"

He pointed down. "How badly do you want answers about this girl and the apparent billion-dollar contract on your head?" he asked. "Scale of one to ten."

I frowned at the bizarre hypothetical. "Seven?" I finally said, shrugging. "I have no idea. And I don't see how that's relevant—"

"Seven?" he sputtered.

I shrugged. "Eight?"

He closed his eyes and took a deep breath. "I know some voodoo."

I blinked, and then slowly turned back to him. "You know voodoo," I said flatly. "And I'm just hearing about this now, why?" I asked incredulously.

"It's dark stuff, Little Brother. I try to keep the past where it belongs, but I was raised in New Orleans. Kind of an obvious connection."

I frowned. Now that he put it *that* way...

"You're a necromancer?" I asked doubtfully.

He smirked. "Neck romancer, *definitely*. But necromancy..." he shrugged. "I've been known to dabble."

I grunted. "Alright. Pick one who looks important. We'll take him back with us."

"What about the other bodies?" he asked, grabbing the broken nose guy by the ankle. I frowned at his hands, a stray thought coming to mind. I let out a tired sigh, lifting my hand to remove all the evidence in one blazing inferno.

My phone vibrated in my pocket and I frowned, plucking it out. I read a text from Niko.

There should have been eight of them, not seven. Next time don't hang up on me.

I stared at it for a few seconds, not comprehending. Then it hit me. "Son of a—"

The wall on the far side of the warehouse blew inwards in a shower of flame and shrapnel. "You're all dead!" a large, hairy man bellowed without even looking our way, blindly hurling fireballs ahead of him. They struck a pile of pallets not even close to us.

"We missed one," Alucard murmured, looking confused by the man's target.

"Protect him!" I snapped.

The eighth wizard spun in surprise, momentarily pausing to frown at my words.

And that's when I saw the sheet of flaming metal begin to fall down from over his head, perfectly angled to decapitate him. I flung up a hand to catch the debris with a blast of magic.

He, on the other hand, lifted his arms to unload fireballs on me.

I gritted my teeth, tossing up a weak shield as I continued to hold the roof up over my attacker's head. "Maybe you could hurry the hell up and knock him out before something kills him," I growled at Alucard. "I think this place is cursed with bad luck."

He muttered unhappily, glancing at his fists. "Play shield for me."

"Sure. I'm not already doing that or anything!" I snapped, flicking my eyes towards the wall of air currently being pelted by balls of fire.

"Well, make more of them. I can't knock him out from over here," he growled, already running away so that I couldn't snark back.

I very seriously considered letting one of the fireballs clip him, but with our luck it would somehow kill the wizard I wanted to take alive.

So I began flinging out more magic—surgical blasts of cold air to freeze his flaming projectiles, sending balls of ice ricocheting up into the rafters, walls, and—

I grinned as one clipped Alucard in the shoulder. "That's what you get, Sparkula!" I hooted.

Alucard took it like a champ, ducking under a fireball I missed in my celebratory taunt, and closed the rest of the distance in a blur.

He slid under the last blast and uppercut the wizard in the jaw, knocking him up on his tiptoes. Alucard immediately grabbed a fistful of the man's hair, yanking his head back, and sank his fangs into the wizard's neck. It lasted only a moment, but I watched as the wizard's eyes rolled back into his head and he went limp. Instead of catching him, Alucard took a quick step back so that the man crumpled to the ground.

Alucard turned his head to spit out a mouthful of blood, grimacing in disgust.

I released my shields and used my magic to shift the collapsing roof to crash a safe distance away. Then I jogged over, studying the wizard to make sure he was still breathing. "You don't like blood? At all?" I asked Alucard, remembering that even with his Daywalker powers, he still hadn't minded blood on occasion.

He spat again. "His blood tasted foul. Like licking the handle on a slot machine in Vegas."

I frowned. "That's both incredibly nasty, and ridiculously specific."

He nodded, spitting out a third time. "First thing that came to mind. Can I have some of yours to wash this nasty taste out of my mouth?" he asked eagerly, and I could tell that he was being completely serious.

I shook my head. "That's a monumentally stupid idea. We're both Horsemen, now. I don't even want to *think* about what could happen." I glanced down at the unconscious wizard. "No more voodoo, at least," I suggested happily. "Silver lining."

"Fine," he muttered unhappily. "Let's just get out of here. I need a drink. Anything to wash this out of my mouth." He reached down and grabbed a hold of the wizard's legs and stared at me, waiting. The building was burning nicely now—thanks to the eighth wizard's additional fire—and I knew the growing flames would be enough to withstand the rain and delete all evidence on their own.

I opened a Gateway back to Chateau Falco, but I didn't immediately step through. Alucard was still pouting. "Hey, you see that propane tank?" I asked, pointing at a small tank sitting near the wall where the fire was stretching closer.

"Yeah. Looks like a hazard," he murmured, sounding amused. He dropped the wizard's leg and cracked his knuckles. "You ready?"

I counted to three in my head and then shouted at the top of my lungs. "PULL!"

Alucard lunged forward, snatched the propane tank by the handle, and flung it up into the air. I formed a ball of fire in my palm and hurled it at the tank in mid-arc. It exploded on contact with a concussive thump and I grinned, finally stepping through the Gateway.

CHAPTER 11

Ashley began cursing me out the moment we were through, calling me nine flavors of idiotic for blowing up a propane tank with the Gateway open.

Apparently, she and her pups had been playing a short distance away from the Drop Zone—an area beneath a giant willow tree that I had designated for Gateways—and Calvin and Makayla had abruptly bolted towards us, knowing that a sudden portal of sparks meant that their godfather was back home—and he usually carried snacks. Luckily, Ashley had caught them before they hopped through into the unlucky warehouse of death. I let the Gateway wink shut before they got any fresh ideas.

They were yapping excitedly at me, wagging their tails so hard that it began throwing off their balance, causing them to stumble and trip. They were both about the same height, although Calvin looked broader in the chest and shoulders. Calvin was white like his dad, and his eyes were so bright and pale that they took my breath away when he really focused on me.

Makayla was solid black, taking after her mother—other than the white socks up her paws. The pups suddenly stopped and cocked their little heads, their eyes latching onto the unconscious wizard Alucard was dragging behind him. Bubbling growls soon rolled out of their throats, making them sound like nothing more dangerous than tree frogs.

Alucard dropped the wizard's feet and grinned at the curious pups. "Snack."

The pups began circling the body from a safe distance, their hackles rigid as they tested their curiosity.

I shot him a disapproving look for Ashley's sake and reached into my pocket to pull out two strips of jerky, tossing one to each of them. They momentarily forgot about the wizard and attacked the jerky like piranhas, growling at each other in warning.

I let out a sigh, hiding my usual anxiety to see them. Despite how mellow and accepting Ashley and Gunnar were about the whole thing, I still wasn't sure what to make of their kids being born as wolves rather than babies. Pandora has promised me that they were completely healthy and that it had been necessary for Freya to save their lives, but beyond that, I had been given very cryptic and vague assurances. Gunnar had even demanded that I leave it alone and not worry about it. I'd temporarily agreed to stay out of it, but I was coming dangerously close to hunting down Freya myself to demand real answers.

"What if the shrapnel had flown through and hit them!" Ashley demanded, planting her fists on her hips.

I looked her in the eyes. "That would have been a valuable lesson for Lady and the Tramp," I said in my best wizardly voice, using the nicknames I had given her pups.

Ashley cleared her throat. Actually, it sounded more like a very hostile growl, but I gave her the benefit of the doubt. "Pratchett is not an acceptable excuse."

I grunted. "Pratchett is *always* an acceptable excuse. Hogfather is the shit."

She met my eyes, and they were definitely hostile now. "Mentioning harm and my pups in the same sentence will get you an ass whooping. And I told you not to call them that."

I nodded, wondering why she was so on edge. "Take a breath, Ashley. You know I wouldn't let anything bad happen to the furballs, and it's my right as godfather to spoil them, toughen them up, and tease them. It's in the by-laws." I glanced around, frowning. "Where's Gunnar?" Then I narrowed my eyes, noticing an anomaly. "And who the fuck is that?" I demanded, pointing at a strange Dodge Charger in the drive, parked up near the fountain by the front door. With the sudden puppy onslaught and angry mother wolf, I hadn't immediately noticed the car through the screen of hanging willow branches, even though they offered very little cover.

"You have guests," Ashley said. My shoulders instantly tensed in alarm. She was only just now telling me this? What if they'd seen my Gateway? No wonder she was on edge! "Gunnar is entertaining an old FBI friend from Quantico and his partner. They used to be sparring partners, and Gunnar is using that to keep them busy."

"Gunnar is boxing the FBI guy?" Alucard drawled in disbelief. "Most people just make a pot of coffee or something."

Ashley waved a hand, cutting him off as she turned back to me, shooing me back towards the trunk of the willow tree as if to get me out of sight. "They're definitely Regulars, but the old friendship bought Gunnar some time. They have questions about a sighting of you near Stonehenge—before you destroyed it. Then the message carved into the parking lot outside that bar in East St. Louis, courtesy of Thor. You are supposed to be globetrotting. It would look very strange for you to suddenly be here when Gunnar is inside telling them you are *not* here."

I grunted angrily, wanting nothing more than to stroll inside and tell them to get off my property, but Ashley was right, so I followed her advice and began walking out of sight from the entrance and all the windows, grumbling unhappily.

"Why is Alucard dragging a dead body?" Ashley asked, leaning down over the wizard and sniffing audibly.

Alucard cocked his head, glancing down. "He's not dead. He's happy," he said, kicking the wizard in the ribs. The man groaned but didn't wake. "See? He laughed."

Makayla, having already gobbled down her jerky—yipped and tripped over her own paws in an effort to tear the dead wizard's shirt.

"Girl, you're built like an improper fraction," I said, shaking my head with a chuckle.

"Nate!" Ashley hissed. "You cannot say things like that to a lady!"

"Heh. I got you to use my nickname." She folded her arms, her eyes practically blazing. I sighed. "Life is suffering. I'm strengthening her princess claws—"

I cut off as the front door to Chateau Falco opened. Ashley and Alucard turned to look, crouching low so as not to be seen. Gunnar walked out, wiping a bloody lip with a grim smile. Shit. I felt an icy chill roll down the back of my neck. Had he *eaten* the FBI?

Seeing blood on Gunnar's lip, the rest of the Randulf clan suddenly went berserk, threatening to give away our presence. Ashley, being the sensible, responsible mother that she was, suddenly exploded into her werewolf form in a shower of shredded fabric and let out a vicious snarl. In her fury, she stomped down with one of her paws, directly onto the unconscious wizard, hard enough to crack a few ribs or maybe his spine. He lurched up with a gasp.

Which, of course, immediately sent the pups into a frenzy of barking and yapping.

In the span of one or two seconds, I realized I had a fucking situation on my hand as two FBI agents strolled down the front steps after Gunnar, their heads already turning to find the source of the barking. I flung up a hasty illusion shield between us and Chateau Falco and latched onto all three werewolves with my magic.

Gunnar's eye had widened in horror, obviously sensing Ashley hulking out and hearing the pained gasp of the wizard over Calvin and Makayla's barking. Werewolves had enhanced senses, and to feel so much sudden anxiety from all three of his family members, it was all he could do not to hulk out and kill everything within a one-mile-radius. Especially since my illusion was blocking the real situation and he had two FBI agents walking directly behind him.

All three of them stared in our direction, and I held my breath, hoping my magic had been good enough to hide us, because I was already seeing stars at juggling so many different flows of power right after juggling so many flows of power in the warehouse.

My wizard's magic was out of practice these days, which I was beginning to realize was a fucking problem.

The FBI Agents frowned thoughtfully, looking directly at us. Since it would be even more bizarre to suddenly silence the pups barking, I focused on just keeping them still until the FBI Agents left.

"Our puppies must have found a rabbit," I heard Gunnar tell the FBI Agents in a loud voice, smiling strangely. "Ashley is probably trying to chase them through the brush."

The two men were pure stereotypes, one blonde and the other dark-haired, but both were clean cut, freshly shaved, and sturdy in the shoulders.

The blonde guy was slightly taller, but other than that, they could have been created in the Quantico factory for all the individuality they displayed. The taller one held his jacket over a shoulder, and his shirt sleeves were rolled up. I thought I noticed blood on his knuckles, and the beginning of a shiner under his left eye.

Gunnar really had been boxing with him.

Unfortunately, my hostage wizard from the warehouse picked up on Gunnar's voice, saw the three men in the distance, and gasped excitedly. I kicked him in the nuts on pure reflex. "Gag him," I hissed at Alucard.

The vampire quickly slapped his hand over the wizard's mouth, his eyes as wide as saucers as he checked on the FBI Agents. Gunnar had drawn their attention and was now standing between them and us as he guided them towards their car. I could see the tension in his shoulders, and I knew he was probably only a millisecond away from shifting himself—thanks to sensing Ashley freaking the fuck out. They were all spiraling together, feeding off each other's energy and growing more manic by the second.

Jesus.

Ashley was snarling in a low, ominous growl, straining against my unseen bonds, fighting with every drop of strength she had as she snorted loudly—inhaling the scent of her bleeding Alpha. I felt sweat beginning to pop out on my brow from having to juggle several things at once.

That's when the hostage wizard remembered he had magic of his own, and I saw weak sparks growing around his fists.

I hit the wizard with a shield, blocking him from using his power and wondering if it was wise to try using a Gateway to get him and Alucard the hell out of here. Then again, with him being conscious again, Alucard would likely be forced to kill him to get him to listen—which didn't work for anyone, historically.

He would need my help to block his magic. Which meant I would need to drop the illusion, suddenly revealing a goddamned werewolf and two puppies who looked hellbent on hurting the bad G-Men who had bloodied their daddy's lip.

So I had to keep this shit show together right here.

Then the hairy wizard bit Alucard's palm and the vampire hissed loud enough to make a flock of birds burst from the tree branches above us. Goddamn it!

The pups suddenly stopped barking and dove for the wizard. I bent down to try to catch one, but she tripped over her own ears and rolled clear, scuttling sideways in an awkward tumble.

The two of them managed to reach their target, and each of them sunk their teeth into the wizard. Everything changed as the skies immediately darkened with rapidly gathering storm clouds. Thunder rumbled hungrily, deep enough to feel in my very bones, and flickers of lightning began dancing across the sky as torrents of rain suddenly fell from the ominous clouds.

The wizard had instantly stopped fighting against Alucard, his limbs locked rigid as if he was being electrocuted. Blood began to ooze out from beneath the pups' muzzles as they breathed loudly through their nostrils, tugging and growling and whipping their heads back and forth. It might have been my imagination, but lightning seemed to crack louder and closer each time they snapped their heads left and right. One thing that definitely wasn't my imagination was the faint fog now pouring out from their nostrils and rolling over the wizard. The pups dug their paws into the earth, tearing harder at the wizard, who was still stiff as a board.

I gasped to see that with each strike of lightning…

The pups were growing stronger, larger, and more developed. As if a few months were passing before my very eyes, tripling their size.

As they matured, their fangs and claws stretched longer, their muscles grew denser, and their balance and footing grew sturdier, decreasing the odds that our hostage was going to survive long enough for interrogation.

I saw the two FBI Agents frowning up at the skies as they dove into their car. Gunnar held a beefy hand over his eye in order to deflect the rain from obscuring his vision. As the rain soaked his white shirt, the curves and swells of his muscular frame only grew more pronounced, highlighted with each brilliant strike of lightning. He didn't flinch, even as one of the strikes sounded as if it hit the looming mansion behind him.

The car pulled away, probably thinking Gunnar had lost his mind.

I let out a breath of relief and was surprised to notice a puff of vapor as I exhaled. I realized that my fingers felt like ice—almost numb. Ashley was shivering, staring down at her pups in alarm as her growl turned into a nervous whine. The grass and puddles around us were now covered in frost or frozen over entirely.

I gasped to see that even the wizard was slowly turning to ice. Frost inched outward from where the pups held him in their jaws, slowly covering his entire body. His eyes also looked to have a film of ice over them, and he was no longer breathing.

But the pups...

As their fur grew thicker and longer, new muscles rapidly forming over their chests and shoulders, they slowly began to turn into smoke, only their fangs and claws remaining solid. With one final cracking sound, the wizard froze entirely solid.

The misty pups suddenly broke free from their grip, wobbled unsteadily as they shuffled into one another, and then promptly collapsed to the ground. Their eyes fluttered and they promptly passed out on top of each other in a cute, misty, puppy pile. Their hazy forms slowly returned to physical bodies, but a ring of fog hung around them like a protective barrier. Thankfully, the thunder and lightning petered out, and the torrential rain lessened to a mere heavy downpour.

The wizard's frozen form abruptly shattered with another sharp crack, cascading into a human silhouette of crushed ice, making all of us jump. In those frosty meat-cubes, I saw absolutely no blood. Calvin and Makayla's puppy stomachs, on the other hand, looked suspiciously full.

Gunnar suddenly raced over to us, white fur sprouting up from his forearms as I noticed the Gate to Chateau Falco finally closing behind the FBI vehicle. He skidded on his knees and snatched up a puppy in each fist, lifting them to his face by the ruffs of their necks. They hung limply, but they both let out weak whines as their dad nuzzled his nose against theirs, one at a time.

I stared at their plump bellies, imagining the sloshing wizard's blood within.

Then I stepped back, grabbing a stunned Alucard by the shoulder as I released Ashley from her restraints and dropped the illusion spell. My head spun for a moment and I shoved Alucard behind me, prepared to Shadow Walk if Gunnar and Ashley attacked on pure instinct. It wasn't that they might actually think we had done anything to their kids, but we were in close proximity to their suddenly vulnerable family, and these were hyperviolent werewolves.

Not rational, objective, aware-wolves.

I wasn't about to become a statistic, thank you very much.

CHAPTER 12

I had no explanation for whatever the hell had just happened, but I knew the pups had done it all on their own. Alucard was shaking his hand, gritting his teeth in pain. I glanced down to see that his fingers were white and looked stiff, signs of superficial frostbite.

"I couldn't let go," he whispered, staring at the werewolf family. "My fingers got stuck to his mouth. Like sticking your tongue to a metal pole in the winter. What the hell did you hit him with?" he asked.

I shook my head. "I didn't do anything. I just blocked the wizard from doing magic, restrained Ashley, and held up an illusion so the FBI wouldn't see us." I stared at the pups—at Gunnar holding them in his lap. Ashley had shifted back from her werewolf form and now sat beside her husband, resting her head on his shoulder. Tears fell down her cheeks and she was shaking with adrenaline. But I could tell everyone was healthy and unharmed—just frightened.

Gunnar slowly lifted his head to stare at me. His eye was a storm of unspent fury, and his lips were set in a murderous frown, emphasized by his thick beard. "I think you need to go talk to Freya. Right the fuck now. It is safer for her if we remain here," he added in a throaty growl, letting me know that he wanted nothing more than to join me so he could rip her limb from limb.

I nodded my agreement, not bothering to tell him that it might not be so healthy for her to see me right now, but that was what godfathers were for —to plug their godchildren full of candy and to plug their godchildren's foes full of hot lead.

I was pretty much designed to be a godfather.

"I need to know if you have ever seen them do anything even *remotely* like that before. Any questionable behavior, because if Freya is innocent, she will need to know every symptom and behavioral anomaly."

He stared at me, forcing himself to calm down. Ashley seemed to be regaining her composure as well, and only just now noticing their sudden growth spurts. They'd aged at least six months, looking well into that awkward stage for large-breed dogs—all lanky bones and legs. Because even with their new slabs of muscle, it was obvious they would get much, much larger.

As I studied them, I noticed their bellies seemed to be slowly shrinking, their bodies digesting the wizard's blood to grow stronger and develop faster. I'd never heard of such a thing.

Alucard was staring, too. "Vampire werewolves?" he suggested, staring at their bellies and then the pile of bloodless wizard cubes.

All three of them turned to me with various reactions of panic, alarm, and curiosity. I shrugged. "Maybe?" I admitted, frowning. "But that doesn't explain the ice thing."

"Are Odin and Freya tied to ice powers of some kind?" Alucard asked, scratching at his chin.

I frowned, but finally shook my head. "Not particularly."

"Well, my calendar just cleared up. Our answers are now puppy slushy," Alucard muttered, toeing the pile of wizard chunks. "I can't voodoo whatever this is."

I grunted, realizing our whole soiree with the assassins had been pointless. Maybe his bad luck had carried with him through the Gateway. I shuddered at the thought, dismissing it since I had no facts to back it up.

"Are the FBI going to be a problem?" I asked Gunnar.

"Yes. But I think I stalled them for a few days, maybe a week. We'll talk about it later." He glanced up at me. "You do realize that I let him hit me in the face to buy you time," he said in a low growl. Ashley was concerned enough by his tone that she placed a calming hand on his knee.

I nodded uneasily. It wasn't necessarily a threat, but a stern warning. He was an Alpha werewolf, and he'd let another man hit him in order to buy me time.

That was the equivalent of a man letting a stranger slap his wife to buy a friend some time.

He had also lied to them, which was a felony, and Gunnar used to be in the FBI.

Essentially, I owed him one. More than one.

I swept my gaze over the puppies, and then the remains of the wizard. "Is Freya still in Asgard with Alice?" I asked. I'd sent her along with Freya to learn as much as possible about her powers. The two had grown very close while spending time together in the Armory, and I'd given Alice a Tiny Ball to give her an emergency escape option if she ever felt in danger.

They shrugged. "Odin has been traveling a lot, bringing news of Thor's fall to the Nine Realms and explaining his long absence. Freya and Alice visited a few days ago for their weekly checkup," Ashley said, petting Makayla absently, "but they didn't stay to chat. Freya is due back in a few more days, but I'd rather you get answers right now."

"No problem. I was just hoping to save some time if you knew exactly where she is." I studied Chateau Falco, thinking. "You guys going to be okay here by yourselves, or are Drake and Cowan lurking around somewhere?"

Gunnar shook his head. "They failed me."

"Pffft," Ashley suddenly piped up, shoving his shoulder forcefully. "They asked to work with Alex in Camelot, and you granted them permission. It wasn't a punishment of your choosing, *Mr. Big Bad Wolf*," she laughed.

He narrowed his eye. "I would have," he argued stiffly, obviously embarrassed.

I smiled at their banter. "So, why did you agree to let them leave? They're your lieutenants," I said, frowning. I'd wondered why I hadn't seen them around much, but I'd been spending a lot of time in the Sanctorum, researching dozens of different topics, histories, myths, and gods, and familiarizing myself with my inventory of legendary weapons in the Armory. A war was brewing on the horizon, and I wanted to be prepared.

Gunnar shrugged. "Odin's wolves are with me." He pointed towards the giant white tree—still oozing blood—and I saw Odin's wolves dozing near the trunk, blatantly unconcerned about the heavy rain.

The tree had been damaged in a fight with Thor and some Knightmares. I wasn't entirely sure what it meant that the tree was bleeding, but the crimson stain down it's white, scaled bark was ominous and impossible to ignore. Another alarming fact was that Geri and Freki were in their much scarier, monstrous forms—not even attempting to pass themselves off as friendly pets.

"Why didn't they come over when the pups went all misty?" I asked, frowning.

"I told them to guard the tree with their lives. It's oozing about seven pints of blood a day. That seems important. When the FBI showed up, I told them to make themselves scarce and to not interfere."

But Gunnar and Ashley both looked uneasy as they stared at the mythical wolves. So did I. Even with Gunnar's commands in place, I found it highly suspicious that Geri and Freki hadn't freaked out at the sudden storm and haunting mist powers the pups so suddenly displayed. Unless…it wasn't surprising to them. Like…if they had known about it already.

If that was the case, it meant Odin or Freya had known about it already, too.

I frowned at the wolves. "And they just happened to stay with you…" I mused. "How very generous of Odin. Convenient, even."

Ashley nodded, catching my deeper meaning. "Gunnar bargained for it. So long as our pups are actual wolves, we keep Geri and Freki."

I slowly turned to face her, my forehead furrowing in disbelief. "And you're only just *now* telling me this?" I demanded.

"It's not like you've spent much time with us. Other than the bedtime stories, we've hardly seen you. Then you hit the bar every night."

I kept my face blank, willing Alucard to keep his mouth shut. The longer they believed I was at the bar every night, the better off they would be. I now had a billion-dollar price tag on my head, and I wasn't about to get them roped into that. Not when they had pups to look after. Definitely not now that those pups were developing strange powers.

I needed answers. Now. I'd fully intended to talk to Freya anyway, but I'd hoped to deal with the assassin thing, first. That obviously wasn't getting resolved anytime soon—especially not with the fee increasing.

And I wanted Othello to do some digging on both this Lullaby app and Niko. Too many loose ends, but godfather duties came first—

Geri and Freki suddenly let out bone chilling howls, making me jump. I spun to see them on their feet, staring at the upper branches of the white tree. Two inbound large, dark blurs caught my attention, aiming straight for the shelter of the white tree. Hugin and Munin. They didn't attempt to slow as they drew close, and they struck the branch hard enough to snap it from the tree in a shower of splinters.

Then they began to cartwheel down towards the ground.

"RUIN!" I shouted desperately at the top of my lungs. I was already racing through the rain, intending to use my magic to break their fall if my Baby Beast wasn't home. My friends stayed behind to protect the pups.

My Baby Beast swooped down from the treehouse high above and caught the two large ravens right before they hit the ground. He silently set the two huge ravens down, bobbing backwards to give me some space. "They're exhausted," Ruin said. He sounded exhausted himself.

Like Geri and Freki, the ravens looked similar to how I had seen them in Niflheim—monster ravens. Had they been too big for the branch?

"You two okay?" I demanded, staring down at them. Geri and Freki loomed behind me, whining softly as they stared at their Norse fraternity brothers.

"Tired," one of them wheezed. "Trying to catch up on lost time." The other raven had simply passed out already.

I crouched down, nodding slowly. "Okay. Take a breath."

"Odin sends a message for you," he practically whispered. "Do not go to Asgard. Danger..."

I gritted my teeth angrily. "Where is he?" I growled.

The raven was already unconscious, his head lolling to the side. Without a word, Ruin scooped both of them up and carried them into the treehouse high above. I had tasked him with guarding the bleeding tree, not knowing Gunnar had done the same with Geri and Freki. "Don't let them leave, Ruin."

"Sure thing," he murmured tiredly, closing the door softly.

Maybe he'd been working too hard. I glanced down at my watch, trying to control my breathing as anger threatened to consume me.

"Nate," Alucard warned, suddenly standing behind me. "This might not be—"

"Nope. We're going to Asgard." I turned to find that Gunnar had followed Alucard over. "Hold down the fort," I told him. "Keep the FBI busy and your kids safe. Alucard and I are going to go get some answers."

Gunnar stared back grimly. "I want answers, Nate, but remember that without their help, my pups wouldn't have even been *born*, and Ashley might have *died*. Instead, I have a family. I want an explanation but think before you bloody your knuckles."

I gritted my teeth. "I'll try."

"We'll meet at Achilles' Heel in a few hours," he said. "The boys are playing poker all night. Wanted me to invite you if you stopped by," Gunnar said.

I nodded, masking my frown. This was going to be a long night. "Okay. I'll call you when we're finished."

I had spent a considerable amount of time reading back up on the Norse pantheon, memorizing the different players, rivalries, powers, and the parts they would play in Ragnarök.

Because we had killed Thor, and he had a big role in their take on Armageddon—to fight the world serpent, Jörmungandr. Which meant that the events of Ragnarök had already changed. For better or worse was yet to be determined.

One thing I knew for certain was that I didn't have many friends in Asgard. The Aesir gods had watched as Gunnar and I executed Thor in their own throne room. Even if they had agreed that Thor had been an asshole, my actions had disrespected all of them. A human killing a god in their seat of power. If I could do that to Thor with impunity, what did I intend for the rest of them?

I was just as curious about that answer.

"Let's go ruffle some feathers, Alucard."

"They better have drinks," he complained, spitting again. I rolled my eyes as I ripped open a Gateway to Asgard, right to the royal chambers. Thinking on Norse mythology, a very interesting plan began to emerge in my mind, so I was smiling as I stepped through the Gateway.

CHAPTER 13

Alucard jumped through after me and we found ourselves in the center of the royal chambers—or whatever Odin called his throne room. The Mead Hall, perhaps.

Conversation suddenly halted, and I realized we were surrounded by what felt like the whole pantheon of Aesir gods, a smattering of warrior einherjar, and a trio of armor-clad Valkyries. The dwarven armorer had obviously relished the opportunity to work on female armor, taking particular care in traversing the pleasant slopes of fresh, previously unexplored new challenges.

To protect—and accent—the boobies at all costs.

I could stand behind that.

Their golden armor gleamed brightly, decorated with sinuous, layered plates, and meticulous, silver filigree that, when combined, served to both emphasize and distort the Valkyrie's silhouette like an optical illusion—which would be absolute hell in a fight.

Each set of armor—and the weapons they carried—were unique as well. Some were accented with gems, feathers, strips of cloth, and other design accoutrements that were likely intended to further distract opponents. Or maybe they just liked looking lovely *and* lethal. They exuded auras of overwhelming violence, and they studied us like cats spotting mice in a barn.

No. More like black panthers spotting a pair of deer. I wisely dipped my chin at them, specifically. They smirked approvingly.

Because although I had respected them, I had chosen to respect them before *anyone else*.

Odin was standing before his throne, speaking to a few men and women. Freya and Alice stood off to the side, and the blonde-haired child leapt forward with a bright smile as she let out a squeal of delight that threatened to shatter glass. "NATE!"

I smiled, but held out a hand, urging her to remain where she was—where less projectiles could impale her if my reception was less than warm. Freya got the message and placed a firm hand on Alice's shoulder, keeping her close. I nodded at Freya. She shot me a very calculating look, shuddering slightly. I had sent Alice here with her to hopefully learn more about her Seer powers, but also so Alice might pick up some information I could later use if the Aesir decided they wanted me off the playing board.

I hadn't tricked Alice into doing this. In fact, it had pretty much been her idea to begin with. Tactically, it made perfect sense—help her get better at using her powers, and be a spy on my potential enemies. But as a father figure—or at least, an adult—I didn't feel quite so noble. Still, Alice would have found her own, likely more dangerous, method to get here and be angry if I had tried to stop her, so I decided that it was better to be on her good side and know what she was up to.

Odin cursed to see me, looking exhausted. "Damn it all, boy. What do you want?" he snapped.

"You promised me a meeting," I said, smiling brightly. "I have some questions, and answers will require a field trip," I added, making an impulse decision to act upon my vaguely outlined plan that I'd first considered about one minute ago.

Odin placed a hand on his forehead, closed his eye, and took a deep, calming breath. He'd picked up a replacement eyepatch on his travels, because I'd refused to get his old one back from Grimm. He probably had dozens of them lying around. "Give me a few minutes, and I will be right with you," he finally said. "I also have things to discuss with you," he added.

I nodded absently. "We will just mingle," I said, smiling pleasantly at all the hostile faces. "I love meeting new friends and catching up with old friends," I said jovially. I glanced around the room and settled on a familiar face near a table laden with finger foods. "Hey, Heimdall!" I crowed, waving at the manager of the Bifröst. He had been kind to me when I last visited with Gunnar. Whether that had been genuine or not, I had no idea.

He smirked, waving back at me. "Welcome to Asgard, Temple," he said. Several pockets of Asgardians began talking in hushed tones, shooting Heimdall thoughtful glances. Perfect. Sow seeds of discord—achievement unlocked.

Odin pursed his lips unhappily, but finally nodded. "So be it."

"Is there anything to drink behind this rippling wall of man meat?" Alucard asked, loud enough for all to hear as he winked at a trio of einherjar who were lined up before a different table that appeared to hold pitchers, drinking horns, and metal goblets.

One of the leather-armored warriors cocked his head to study Alucard, his chiseled jaw like a slab of hairy granite. "Are you sparkling, little man?" he asked in a gravelly baritone, squinting at Alucard's skin.

"Not as much as your eyes, Mr. Dimples," Alucard fired back, grinning as he took a cue from my approach, "but maybe that's just the love in the air."

The three warriors stood in stunned silence for about five seconds. Then Mr. Dimple's two pals burst out in laughter, clapping him on the shoulder. His face gradually morphed into a smile when he saw that Alucard obviously wasn't trying to offend or challenge him personally, but was simply defending himself with wit over brawn.

Odin continued speaking in low, private tones with the dozen or so people surrounding his throne. He didn't look happy that we had free reign among his people, so whatever he was talking about must have been very important.

I wondered who he was talking to, but since old mythology books rarely had accurate profile pictures, it was impossible to guess.

But I could sense the waves of power radiating from each of them. They were definitely gods. Some of them might even be god-like representatives from other Realms—dwarves, elves, or giants. Although I saw no pointed ears, and I doubted any were giants, because they looked no larger than any of the other gods in attendance.

I turned to see Alucard now strolling around the room, flipping a coin and humming to himself. He walked right in front of some Valkyries, smirking rakishly. His three new einherjar pals cheered him on, daring him to compliment the warrior maidens. I hoped he didn't. Well, kind of. Part of me was right beside the einherjar, cheering him on.

Odin continued to watch me out of the corner of his eye, looking suspicious. The tension in the room was incredible. The gods all knew I had killed one of their fellows in this very room no more than a few weeks ago. Even though the consensus was that Thor had been an asshole, I was still an outsider who had killed one of 'them.'

Group think. Herd mentality. Safety in numbers.

To ease the tension, I walked over to the exact spot where Thor had died and leaned my back against a pillar, eyeing my fingernails as I cocked my leg to anchor my boot against the wall for support.

My gesture, unsurprisingly, did not ease the tension in the slightest.

I stared down at the ground, noticing a faint impact crater from where Gunnar had used Mjölnir to pulverize Thor into the ground. I stood right in the center of the area where Thor's blood had pooled. Back then, my Horseman Mask had been broken—fractured. I had known that a god's blood might be powerful enough to heal it completely, and I had briefly entertained the idea of dipping my Mask into Thor's blood to heal the fracture.

But the more I had thought about it, the more certain I had grown that I simply couldn't make myself do it. Thor had almost killed Ashley.

Using his blood to heal my Mask would be a constant reminder of that act—of him—every single time I needed to put it on. His blood would forever taint my Mask of Hope.

Thor's essence would touch my *face*. The man who had almost *murdered* my friend.

I knew I could have looked at it another way—that it was a constant reminder of his evil and greed, and that I could use that fiery, emotional reminder to make sure I never walked the same path.

But I was pretty sure all I would imagine were two puppy paws kicking my fingers from Ashley's womb. It would taint the whole job of being a Horseman, disgusting me every time I had to put the Mask on. No matter what I told myself, my cause would be tainted—literally powered—by Thor.

There were lines. I had fewer than most, but that was one I just couldn't make myself cross.

So I had used his blood in an entirely different way. And that choice had saved my life with Anubis. I still had reservations about that—about why Anubis had wanted his blood so badly. It hadn't really been just his blood, but his soul. Still, Anubis was a schemer, and I was confident that he hadn't been saving my life out of charity. Given recent developments, I had reason to take a trip to Hell and talk to an old friend—

A large, imposing figure suddenly loomed before me. He was tall and wiry, but he radiated danger. His gray eyes were as cool and calm as a winter pond—and just as lethal beneath that thin layer of ice. They weren't directly threatening, but fate lurked in those depths for any brave enough to take a swim. He smiled politely. "I am Tyr. God of War," he said, his hands clasped behind his back.

I'd read about Tyr. In some stories, he had been the leader of the Norse pantheon long before Odin, so I needed to tread very carefully.

I remained calm, waiting for some attack or threat. When nothing happened, I held out my hand to shake his. He smirked absently and lifted a nub from behind his back. His hand was entirely missing. "I appreciate the gesture, Master Temple."

I winced, remembering another part of his story too late. "Sorry. I completely forgot," I said, kicking myself.

He shrugged. "It happens. Fenrir has a wicked bite," he said softly, shooting a thoughtful look at Odin. I nodded, keeping my face blank. Because Fenrir was prophesied to defeat Odin in Ragnarök, and Fenrir was currently being held in a minimum-security prison. At least, that's what I feared, because Mordred had abducted him, and now Mordred was dead.

Which was the whole point of me working with Loki on the sly. Since I no longer had to worry about powerful beings easily being able to read my mind, I didn't have to fear accidentally giving away that sneaky secret. But my face could still tell on me if I wasn't careful.

Gleipnir, the legendary ribbon that restrained Fenrir, was currently being used to hold Mordred's once brain-washed Knightmares in custody with Alex until I had time to do a final check-up on them.

Not because I was a good guy who cared about their well-being, but because I wanted Gleipnir *back* for when Loki and I found Fenrir.

Until we figured out the ramifications of murdering Thor, I couldn't risk Fenrir being free and deciding to kick off Ragnarök early. We didn't have a substitute for Thor to fight Jörmungandr.

Which was probably one of the things Odin was working so diligently on right now.

Unfortunately, I also couldn't risk releasing the Knightmares until I knew they were healed. They were nigh-immortal warriors, and there were nine of them. Even with Mordred dead, those nine Knightmares could cause unbelievable harm if I didn't approve their general mindset and cleanse their armor.

Hell, Alex might not even want them in his employ after what they had done—even if it had been against their will.

Long story short, Gleipnir was needed in multiple places, but since I didn't yet know where Mordred had stashed Fenrir, Gleipnir would stay with the Knights.

Camelot was one of my next potential stops, with or without locating Fenrir. I needed to at least finish cleansing their sets of armor. But it wasn't a priority, because I knew it would leave me exhausted, my power depleted, and I couldn't afford being out of commission right now. Not when I was working with Loki.

Priorities. That was what this was all about.

Which was why I had finally decided to recruit Alucard to help me. Gunnar and Ashley needed to stay with their pups—especially after the whole mist-pire ability they'd displayed—so I'd chosen the Daywalker and fledgling Horseman of Absolution. I'd learned that I could sense the other Horseman Masks, which was something Loki would not be able to duplicate. He could walk and talk like Alucard, but he couldn't fake that.

I hoped.

Because Loki was fucking good at illusions. Even gods couldn't see through them. So I had spent the last few weeks lying my ass off, laying false trails, only trusting Alucard with my true plan. Like Alucard telling Callie I had been in Cairo, and Gunnar telling the FBI I was out-of-town. Essentially, I was running my own rumor mill to hide the truth, and anything I could do to make things even more confusing was a positive. Like here in Asgard. I needed to play this close to the chest in order to keep myself as safe as possible, but I was humble enough to know that I needed an ally—not just to protect myself from Loki, but also to potentially play dogcatcher for Fenrir.

Tyr dipped his head. "It's not every day one meets a godkiller. Or two Horsemen." He eyed the ground beneath my feet. "Nice introduction. Well, nice *reminder*, I guess. You're first introduction spoke volumes, but your encore..." he trailed off, winking. "Imagine me doing the world's longest slow clap," he said, lifting up one palm and holding it in front of his face.

I burst out laughing. "Wow. That...okay."

He smirked. "Remember, not all who wander are lost. You have allies here, even though we may hide in the shadows. Crowns are not permanent," he mused. "Thank the gods."

Then he was walking away. I studied him thoughtfully, keeping my face blank since everyone was watching me from a distance. Had he been hinting that he was against Odin, or humbly referring to how he had lost the crown of the Aesir? And what did he know about Fenrir? I knew Thor had been working for—or with—Mordred, but I also suspected him to have had other allies…

Maybe those allies were present right now. I'd need to stay on my toes, be tough as nails—

A mongoose suddenly latched onto my leg, raking at me with wicked claws, and I jumped in alarm.

CHAPTER 14

A heartbeat later, the creature hugged my leg tightly, and I realized it was just Alice, too impatient to wait any longer before running over to me. I smiled, patting her on the head and discreetly checking to make sure I hadn't squealed like a little girl. No one was laughing at me, so I must have played it cool. "Hey, Bones. I'd hoped the diet here would fatten you up more," I murmured disappointedly.

She scoffed, swatting at me while giving me a toothy grin. Freya approached with a much more reserved smile, and I could tell she was as tense as wire. Odin discreetly angled himself so that he could observe us in his peripheral vision, and possibly catch a snippet of our conversation.

"Hey, Freya." Rather than dancing around the topic and acting polite for the crowd, I dove right in, leaning close to speak unobserved. "I need you to explain what went down with the pups. If I said they turned to smoke and drained a wizard of all of his blood to grow stronger, would that surprise you?"

Her smile faltered, and her face went pale. "What?" she whispered. Her eyes grew distant, and I could tell she was self-conscious about the eyes in the room watching us. "May we walk, or are you particularly invested in this spot?" she asked, swallowing audibly.

I straightened, holding out my elbow. "When a woman asks me to walk, I walk."

She rolled her eyes. "Doubtful, but I'm not here to quarrel. Things are... not what they seem in Asgard. My husband is not receiving the reception he had hoped for. In fact, he has been absent these past weeks. It is coincidental that you arrive on the same day."

I grunted. "He sent the drumsticks with a message. Told me not to come to Asgard. Naturally, I chose to disregard that."

She missed a step, but kept her face blank. "Is that so..." We walked onwards, and I realized she was leading me behind the throne to a large balcony overlooking a courtyard that was blooming with frost and winter flowers of some kind. They weren't quite as strange as Fae, but they were close.

"Regarding the wolves," she began, checking that we were indeed alone, "I had feared that some element of Niflheim would remain, which was one of the reasons I birthed them as wolves rather than babes. I had hoped to strengthen them by using their wolf forms. It seems that it did not work."

I gritted my teeth. "And what exactly does that mean, Freya? Are they in danger from this Niflheim element?"

Freya thought about it and finally shook her head. "If anything, I believe it makes them stronger, but I have no way of knowing."

I clenched my fists until my knuckles popped.

"Maintain your calm," she urged, flashing me a hollow smile. "There are those who seek opportunities of emotional imbalance here. I understand your frustrations and fear, but I refuse to lie to you, even knowing your penchant to punish the messenger for harsh truths."

I took a calming breath and nodded. "I'm listening."

"I did not impregnate Ashley," she said dryly. "I was handed a difficult task—delivering babies who were premature and also past-due. Tell me of another midwife in all of existence, living or dead, who has done such a thing. I can assure you that the babes were healthy when last I saw them."

Alice was watching the two of us, keeping her back to the crowd so as not to draw attention with the look on her face. She nodded her agreement. "I played with them. I saw no danger," she said carefully, letting me know she hadn't sensed anything with her powers.

I smiled at her. "Thank you, Alice." Then I turned to Freya, keeping my face devoid of concern. "They didn't seem unhealthy when I just saw them, either, but the sudden abilities I mentioned were a shocker. I fear what it might indicate. After their birth, Ashley explained that with their heightened ability to heal as wolves, they would grow healthier in that form then as human babes. But that it will only last a year or so. That's all I've been told."

Freya hesitated, but finally nodded. "Yes and no." Alice, sensing the conversation was growing serious, suddenly skipped away to intercept some Valkyries. She began touching their weapons and speaking with them excitedly. The warrior maidens gobbled it up, instantly falling victim to her wiles. Within moments, they were playing with her hair and showing off their weapons, allowing Freya and I to walk further from the main hall.

"Alice has them wrapped around her finger and they don't even know it. Or they don't care," Freya said, smiling to reassure me. "She's a bright child—smart enough to know she needed allies other than me."

I smiled, nodding my head. "She found the toughest inmates in the prison yard and made an alliance," I said approvingly. "Atta' girl."

"Precisely."

"Speak plainly, Freya. We don't have much time for privacy, and I need to know that the pups are safe. Gunnar and Ashley need to know. They placed a lot of trust in you to deliver their babes safely. They even went along with the idea to deliver the children as pups—which is strange as all hell, Freya, even for werewolves. So to suddenly have this growth spurt and mist ability..."

Freya nodded, not taking offense by my words as she leaned up against the balcony.

"Let me ease your concern in the simplest manner first," she began, checking that we were out of earshot from any other gods. "I gave them some of my own power to keep them safe. To make them stronger. And to shield them from accessing those godly powers, birthing them as pups added a second layer of protection—for themselves and everyone else."

I blinked, slowly turning to glance at her. "You did *what?*" I whispered, stunned.

She nodded, not looking at me. "I have been known to go overboard when it related to protecting those I care about," she said in a haunted tone.

I didn't offer a comment, knowing all about the story of her son, Baldur. After a seer told Odin of his son's untimely death, Freya visited every living and non-living entity she could find, and made them all swear an oath not to harm her son, making him impervious to harm. With those oaths in place, the Aesir soon made sport of it, hurling spears, sticks, rocks, and anything else at him. But nothing harmed him—every projectile simply bounced off the shining god's chest. Loki, annoyed by the attention his brother was getting, eventually tricked Freya into admitting that the only entity she did not obtain an oath from was mistletoe, so he carved a spear from it and tricked the blind god, Hod, to throw it at Baldur during the next display of Baldur's invulnerability.

The mistletoe spear killed Baldur on the spot, and the gods freaked the hell out.

Because Baldur's death was the first presage to Ragnarök.

Obviously, Ragnarök hadn't actually started, so I was betting Baldur was still alive and well. In fact, I had based my entire research of the Norse pantheon on the assumption that all of the gods still lived, so that I would only have pleasant surprises when I learned some stories were actually true.

"Seeing how devoted you were to protecting them..." she trailed off, dragging a nail across the railing. "It was inspiring. So I chose to give up some of my godhood, whatever that is worth these days," she added, her eyes flicking my way to reference my godkiller power—a constant reminder that gods were no longer safe from recrimination for their actions.

I nodded, wondering if Gunnar and Ashley knew anything about this. "Does that make them demigods?" I whispered, my mind racing with both concerns and excitement.

She shook her head. "I do not believe so. But it will help them remain strong in the event that there are complications as a result of Ashley's... unprecedented pregnancy, and her time in Niflheim."

I thought about her words, thinking furiously. "That sounds like you used rocket fuel to gas up a lawnmower..."

She blinked and then let out a series of coughs, masking her smile with her hand. "How...visual. But yes. The metaphor sounds accurate. We are uniquely bonded."

"Uniquely bonded, how?" I asked, frowning.

She discreetly pulled back her sleeve to reveal a dozen tiny bite marks on her wrist—the size of puppy teeth. My eyes widened and I looked back up at her.

She nodded, lowering her sleeve. "They are teething, and Makayla likes to bite her brother's paws when she's losing."

Without warning, I gently grasped her hand in mine and bowed as I held her wrist to my lips, feigning chivalry. Rather than kissing her skin, I took a deep, discreet inhale. Then I lowered her wrist and smiled at her. "My lady is too kind," I said, loud enough for anyone nearby to hear—so they would think I was merely being polite to the Queen of Asgard.

Then I held out my elbow again. She took it, smiling as we continued to walk. "Fresh blood," I told her. "Had to be sure it wasn't an illusion of some kind. I hear that's going around." My mind was racing with the implications. She was bonded to the pups. If they were harmed, she was harmed. And vice versa. Which meant I needed to make sure Freya didn't come to any harm.

It also meant that she would do everything possible to keep those pups—and herself—safe. And the way Asgard was looking with all the secretive looks and muted conversations, I could see any number of people taking out their frustrations on Freya in Odin's absence.

CHAPTER 15

Freya smiled at my gesture, shaking her head. "Paranoia makes the heart last longer."

I grunted my agreement. "If you saw something alarming in the pregnancy, why didn't you simply use magic to heal them as they came out. Why give them a gift that lingered?" I asked carefully.

She glanced over at me with a suddenly cool look. "Because my son tried to stab me while I was delivering the babes. That cost me five precious minutes at a time when every second counted. I did not know what might happen post-pregnancy, so I gave them the best protection that I could afford. Thank you for saving my life, but be careful when judging something you know nothing about."

I dipped my chin, acknowledging her answer and silently apologizing. "Perhaps you should consider that my entire life has been riddled with interference from gods, and that it has given me justified biases on their actions."

She studied me thoughtfully, and finally nodded her head. "Then we are both wiser for seeing our lands from different mountain peaks. I know your words come from the heart, and that you are interested only in keeping the pups safe."

I nodded, and even gave her a faint smile. I saw that Odin was still speaking with the gaggle of gods, but he continued to glance at us curiously, looking as if he wanted to split himself in two in order to find out what we were discussing while still managing his underlings.

"Please give the situation some thought and get back with me."

"Of course," she said haughtily. "I didn't go to all that trouble for them to die prematurely—especially not now," she added, absently rubbing her wrists. "You are being very secretive."

I nodded. "You're going to see me do some crazy things soon, but I need you to back me up, no questions asked. And not to tell anyone—anyone—at all. Unless you trust them with your life. Because if my plan goes tits up as a result of loose lips, I'll trace it back to the source and kill everyone." I met her eyes. "Everyone."

She studied me, looking a little pale.

I nodded. "I mean it, Freya. You don't know me that well, but I don't fuck around when it comes to my friends. And everything I do is for my friends, believe it or not."

She nodded. "I think you're actually telling the truth. Even when it benefits you as well, the underlying motivation is always them, first."

I smirked. "I have it on good authority that I've made one or two selfish decisions in my day. I'm not perfect. But lately…yeah. Friends first." I waited patiently. "Can I count on you? Even with my threat?"

"Gods help me, yes," she finally murmured.

I nodded in relief. So far, my plan was going smoothly. Even with Freya's revelation about being bonded to the pups. In fact, that might have just solved a separate problem for me.

I flicked my gaze towards Odin. "Where has he been? You said he hasn't been here much, but you and Alice have been here the whole time, right? Why would he warn me not to come? Is something specific happening?"

She shrugged, not looking over at her husband. "We love each other fiercely, but we do not always act as husband and wife. He is in a position of power over me, speaking authoritatively. Taking love out of the equation, he is king, and I am queen. In that respect, some of the other gods are technically higher in authority than I am."

I nodded, thinking of Callie for some strange reason. "It must be hard to have a working relationship with each other…" I said, sincerely.

She grunted. "You have no idea. If you love someone, never work with them. Especially not if you are on different authority levels. At some point, the duties will collide, and you will be forced to pick obligation over affection. Or, worse, affection over obligation. The victim changes depending on which you choose."

I nodded, licking my lips. I realized I had stumbled into a conversation I suddenly didn't want to have. I'd rather talk about the mating habits of the common Draccus at this point. "Noted."

She leaned out over the balcony, pointing to a section of blue flowers as she spoke in barely a whisper. "He has been obsessed with finding Gungnir and Fenrir. I'm not sure which he fears more, but they are close for his full affection. He hasn't slept, and I hardly ever see him, but when I do, he is exhausted. Hugin and Munin haven't rested for weeks." She glanced over at me. "I do believe he will have harsh words with you for losing his spear," she warned me.

"Understatement," I murmured.

"Of course, he has also been traveling the Realms to reconsolidate his power, address Thor's death, and formally announce his return. But like before, he does not have Gungnir at his side. There has been word that some doubt his claim. That he might not truly be the Allfather, but Loki in disguise—since it is whispered that Loki has escaped. Mordred's doing, most likely. Or Loki's for that matter."

"He's panicking," I mused, wincing at the term since it reminded me of my old friend, Pan.

Freya nodded. "To put it mildly. And following Thor's death, you make a surprise visit to Asgard—the scene of the crime, as it were. It puts Odin in a difficult position." She slowly turned to look at me. "I know you have the best intentions—for that of your friend and their babes—but you rarely make things easy for anyone, including yourself."

I grunted. "Yeah. But it's just so much more fun this way. There's nothing quite like starting off your day by ruining someone else's."

She smirked, smiling absently. "I will take your word for it."

I spotted Alice seated on a Valkyrie's knee, fiddling with a dagger as big as her head. "I hope Alice is progressing well with you. She's safe, right? And pulling her own weight?" I asked.

Freya laughed. "You would be a good father, Nate. You asked if she was safe in a pantheon brimming with vengeful, petty killers. But you followed it up with making sure she was earning her keep. Most fathers would have stopped at protection, but you don't value protection in and of itself, do you?"

I frowned, not having actually broken it down like that. "Um…"

"You know that learning to arm your underlings is more important than keeping them safe. Both are needed, but one trumps the other."

I nodded, understanding what she meant. "Definitely. There will always be a big bad wolf who can blow your house down. Simply learning how to improve your defenses is not enough. Not in the long run. Not in our world. Brick-layers die, but brick-throwers thrive."

She smiled. "Well put. It's endearing to see a man arming a child rather than placing her on a safe pedestal. Children need to embrace danger, to learn to face their fears with their chins up."

I arched an eyebrow, slowly risking a glance at her. Freya's eyes glittered, and I could tell she was deep in her own dark thoughts. "Maybe dial down the crazy a little bit," I suggested politely. "The message stood on its own. The homicidal smile was overkill."

She blinked, slowly turning to face me. "I think the Valkyries will like you very much."

I grinned. "I sure as hell hope so!"

"I am in charge of them, you know. Everyone thinks it is Odin, but I was technically the first Valkyrie, and I, alone, command them. I let Odin take the credit, preferring anonymity."

I blinked at her. "Really?"

She shrugged. "Recognition is for rejects. Real power is quiet. You should remember that."

I nodded, remembering reading a snippet about her leading the Valkyries, but I hadn't been certain it was truth. "Wow. This whole conversation just turned terrifying. We're cool, right? Because you're scarier than I thought you were, and I'd like to make sure we're cool."

She laughed lightly, swatting at my arm. "I had a wild, misspent youth. But we are *cool*, as you put it," she murmured, rolling her eyes. "And I will teach Alice as if she were my own. No one knows that she has a flight of Valkyries watching her every move. I pity the fool who tests their vigilance."

I burst out laughing. "A-Team reference—check."

She glanced over, frowning. "Asgard Team?"

"Never mind," I said, chuckling as I recalled her lack of pop culture references. She hadn't known about the Lord of the Rings, so cable television was hopeless. "Human thing."

"What are you really here for?" she asked. "It wasn't just about the pups. I sense schemes in those green eyes."

I shrugged innocently. "I'm just trying to change the world, I guess."

"For the better?"

I remained silent.

"Answer me, wizard."

I shrugged again. "We will see." She studied me thoughtfully, and finally gave me a slow nod. "I should probably mingle," I told her. "I have a few others I want to talk to. Remember what I told you. Things are going to get weird, soon."

She nodded. "I stand ready."

I bowed politely and then turned away to walk around the room, fishing for conflicts or friendships.

I would use either to my benefit.

CHAPTER 16

I spotted Alucard chatting it up with more of the einherjar, but I could tell he was keeping a very close eye on me as I moved about the room. Good.

I saw Heimdall chatting with Tyr, so I dipped my head at the pair of them, silently wondering where they stood on the trust spectrum.

I saw a blur of motion out of the corner of my eye, and I instinctively lashed out with my Fae magic to slow the projectile down as I leaned just out of harm's way. With time slowed ever so slightly, I snatched the weapon out of the air, and used its momentum to spin in a full circle and throw it right back at my attacker. The hatchet slammed into the crotch of a giant statue with a loud cracking sound, missing my attacker's ear by about three inches.

A Valkyrie.

I stormed towards her and planted a quick kiss on her cheek before she could stop me. Rather than killing me on the spot, she burst out laughing, confusing everyone who had stopped to stare at me.

"The heavens are stained with the blood of men," I quoted.

"As the Valkyries sing their song," Kára purred. She held her fingers to her cheek where I had kissed her, not even seeming aware that she was doing so. "It's good to see you again, Nate."

"Better here than that shithole bar you own," I teased. I jerked my chin at the hatchet beside her ear, nodding proudly. "That was pretty badass, eh? I've been practicing."

"I can tell," she laughed, eyeing the castrated statue. "I hate feeling like there is a threat lurking over my shoulder. Thank you for saving this damsel in distress."

I scoffed. "Damsel *of* distress, more like." She beamed proudly, as if I had called her the most beautiful creature mankind had ever beheld.

In all honesty, she *was* stunningly beautiful. Kára had long, blond hair that trailed back into a tight braid, and the sides of her head were cleanly shaved. She had one blue eye and one green eye, so I frequently felt a sense of vertigo when talking to her, finding myself focusing on one eye over the other. She was tall and lithe, with plenty of curves to balance out her ridiculously ripped muscles.

She was even more dangerous than she was beautiful, and I'd spent quite a bit of time with her over the last few weeks. Initially, I'd heard about her and her hatchet-throwing bar from Achilles. It was where I'd first encountered Thor, so I'd made an effort to visit her and make sure we were on good terms after I destroyed her parking lot.

Four pitchers of beer later, and we'd become fast friends.

So when Gunnar thought I'd been hitting up the bars a lot, he hadn't been wrong. I had quickly found that I rather enjoyed spending time with the deadly warrior maiden. Her name meant *stormy one*, and she had the temperament to prove it. She was snarky, afraid of nothing, she knew how to take care of herself, and she was entirely detached from my history in St. Louis. She also had a wealth of knowledge on the Norse pantheon.

She knew all the juicy stories, and I'd eventually talked her into being my eyes and ears in Asgard.

I wrapped my arm around her shoulder, winking at one of her fellow Valkyries—who smirked, rolling her eyes. Alice still sat on her lap, inspecting the same wicked dagger from earlier, utterly mesmerized by it. I doubted she'd even noticed the commotion or my near death.

"What's the real story around here?" I asked Kára softly. "Roll with my flirting. I'm putting on a show."

"I could forsake my vows for one of your shows," she mused playfully. "Until I grew bored. You men all grow wearisome after a short time."

"Some last longer than others," I argued, grinning.

"Not those who openly talk about the length of their lasting."

I gave her a mock scowl. "Damn. You've learned about overcompensation. My plans to make you swoon are destined to crash on rocky cliffs."

She nodded. "Owning a bar—even if it's just a cover—teaches you a lot about the depraved nature of men. You haven't evolved much over the centuries."

"I don't doubt it," I said, chuckling.

"You're quite good at this," she said, leaning into me and resting her head on my shoulder.

I grunted. "You are a poor liar, but as long as they buy it, I'm satisfied."

She spoke in low tones, catching me up on all the latest gossip—which wasn't much. At least it matched what Freya had said, though. Odin had been absent until now, and his ravens had been spotted throughout the Nine Realms in the past weeks, carrying messages back and forth. "That is what he is doing now," Kára murmured, "making sure his messages were sent or received, and that his missives were followed and obeyed."

I nodded, smirking as if she'd said something particularly naughty.

"And what's the verdict on goat-boy?" I asked, referring to Thor.

She tensed marginally, so I squeezed her shoulder in warning, reminding her to stay in character. "Fuck him," she whispered, her shoulders relaxing. "He would have doomed us all. You did what needed to be done. You made enemies and allies, but I imagine both will remain hidden until it's too late to make a difference."

I grunted. "They'll wait on the sidelines until they can back the winner."

"Yes. They are cowards," she said firmly.

I sighed, giving her shoulder one last squeeze before parting with another kiss on her cheek. "Vigilance," I whispered in her ear.

She kissed me on my cheek, catching me off guard. "It's what I do, Temple," she purred. Then she was walking back to her position, smiling approvingly at the hatchet sticking out of the statue's groinicus minimus. She extracted it with entirely too much pleasure, and in my opinion, the statue looked sad.

I kept the grin on my face—which wasn't too hard to do—for everyone to see as I let my eyes linger on Kára's back for a few moments. Then I let out a dramatic sigh and turned away.

It was time to talk to Odin. Whether he was ready or not.

I spotted Alucard a dozen paces away, drinking from a gnarly horn with a contingent of cheering einherjar.

They cheered louder as he finished it off in one pull and slammed it down on the table. "Nate!" he hooted. "This stuff is *amazing*!"

"And strong, man. How much have you had?"

"Just a few," he admitted. "I was careful."

Judging by the amused looks on the Asgardian faces, I was betting he had severely underestimated the alcohol content of the godly beer. "Right. We should move this along."

I motioned him ahead of me, back towards the center of the room.

I shot a look at the einherjar who seemed to be in charge, a tall, bearded, bald man with two scars down each of his cheeks. His chest was hairier than my head. "How long have I got?" I asked, smirking.

Realizing that he had a comrade rather than a reprimand, he grinned back. "If he lasts longer than five minutes, I'll give you my best knife," he said, chuckling.

"Deal," I said. And I pulled out my phone to start the timer. I slipped it back into my pocket and stuck out my hand to shake on it.

The man blinked at me, caught off guard, and then he grinned wide, shaking my arm firmly. "I'll stick by my word, godkiller. My name is Ragnar."

"Nate," I said, shrugging. "Sounds much scarier."

He grinned. "As you wish, Nate."

"Five minutes," I mused, scratching at my stubble. "That should be long enough. You and your men mind giving me the benefit of the doubt here? I'm going to make things interesting, and I always thought loud and angry was more fun. If he's got less than five minutes, I need to get their attention fast."

Ragnar considered that, combing his beard with scarred, calloused fingers. He finally nodded. "You just had a private conversation with Freya for longer than five minutes and the Valkyries didn't impale you. Then you got Kára to kiss you. I believe you've earned more than our trust. Me, I think it's time for my men to scout the halls for about, oh…" he scratched at his beard thoughtfully, "five minutes or so."

I grinned, dipping my head gratefully. "Thank you, Ragnar."

"Good luck."

"I've never turned her down before. Not going to start now. Take your time out there, Ragnar."

He chuckled, shaking his head. "Oh, I'll be staying. We have a wager, after all." He lifted his arm, and the einherjar around the room slowly began slipping out the doors. The best part was that no one else seemed to notice —or they just weren't paying attention, because they were all staring at Alucard who had his hands on his hips and was glaring up at Odin.

Well, the shit show had apparently started. "Polish that dagger for me, Ragnar."

He laughed as I turned my back on him, hurrying over to Alucard.

The gods still huddled in small groups around the perimeter. A larger congregation stood near the entrance, all seeming to huddle towards someone speaking in the center.

I shot a glance up at Odin, really getting a clear look at him this time. He looked incredibly tired, with deep circles under his eye and eyepatch. I knew that thoughts of Fenrir loose had to have him on edge, not even counting the fact that Gungnir was also missing.

I began to feel a prickling sensation in my shoulders, sensing a growing hum of tension, and it seemed to be centered on that same knot of godly gossip behind me. Odin was nodding to a god who was talking to him, but his eye was focused on me, and he looked as if he was waiting for a trap to spring. He had good intuition.

"I'm feeling unappreciated," I finally said.

Odin leaned forward, suddenly dismissing the god speaking to him. "Perhaps it would be best if we reschedule. There is a lot of work for me to do here—"

"Can we reschedule, Alucard?"

"Nope. You've got that thing with the masseuse later. They book a year in advance. Tardiness means no happy ending."

I frowned. "I do love my happy endings," I admitted.

"Then there is Ganesh and Shiva. Meditation practice—which you sorely need," Alucard said.

I sighed wearily, staring Odin in the eye. "Anger management. Or as I like to call it, problem-solving." I cleared my throat before speaking in a flat, monotone, "Woo. Sah."

I spotted Ragnar about ten feet away, pretending to stroke his thick mustache, but really concealing his grin. The rest of the gods and Valkyries seemed to be tightening the circle, as if not wanting to miss this spectacle.

"Then the Fight Club with Achilles, Leonidas, and Asterion," Alucard reminded me.

The Valkyries perked up at that, looking suddenly interested.

"We can't *talk* about that," I said tensely, shooting him a dark look.

"An unspecified violent altercation with unidentified friends at an undisclosed location. Allegedly," Alucard corrected himself.

"Better."

"Then you need to visit the Fae Queens. They both owe you favors."

I nodded, glancing back up at Odin. "Seems like I'm booked up."

"Tomorrow is even *worse*," Alucard said. "You've got that extermination thing to deal with. What was the pest called again?" he asked, frowning over at me. He stumbled slightly, but no one else seemed to notice. Well, no one but Ragnar, who looked to be salivating with anticipation.

"The Academy of Wizards," I said, knowing Alucard was on borrowed time. That Norse booze was about to send him into a coma.

Odin, of course, did not have a happy face. His friends mirrored his visage, amplifying it, even. With so many gods surrounding us, it was very hard for me to keep my skin from bursting into a golden glow and showing off my godkiller powers.

Odin gritted his teeth, and he seemed to be trying to impart a subliminal message directly into my brain via the throbbing vein on his temple. "Again, I am busy cleaning up a mess—"

"Cool. Finish that later. You made a promise, so we're leaving. Unless I need to make another mess," I suggested, smirking.

The crowd grew tense and angry at my flippant tone. But with my reminder of Odin's promise, and blatant lack of concern that I was surrounded, they grew hesitant. Well, all but the Valkyries. They looked anticipatory.

"You talk a big game, but from what I hear, you weren't the one to make the mess you keep bragging about," someone taunted from the larger knot of Asgardians that I had noticed. "Where is your big friend?" His fellows were all staring deeper into their midst, but I couldn't see the speaker.

I glanced away dismissively. "You didn't raise your hand, boy. The adults are talking."

The room grew brittle with silence. "Do you have any idea who I am—"

"I *said*," I interrupted in a low, warning tone, turning back around. I was surprised to find a tall, solidly-built man with short blonde hair stepping out from his crew of fellow gods. I stared, unable to finish my sentence.

He was surprisingly handsome, rather than scarred and battle-proven.

But that wasn't why I found myself at a loss for words. He stood out like a sore thumb, not wearing anything even remotely conducive to battle. Unable to help myself, I burst out laughing.

"Who is *this* ass clown?" I hooted. "He's dressed like the CEO of a watermelon patch!"

He wore a flannel dress shirt and a tan *Carhartt* jacket with jeans and boots. He'd also buttoned his shirt all the way up to the collar, and tucked it into his jeans.

His face purpled, and I caught muffled laughter from throughout the room—except from those in his cheer squad. They looked suddenly livid.

Alucard nudged me, speaking under his breath. "I'm feeling kind of tipsy, Nate. We should probably wrap this up."

Shit.

CHAPTER 17

I waved a hand at the god, dismissing him. "You look fun, but I really don't have time to play with you right now."

I turned my back on him, ready to get Odin to our next destination. I still had a long night ahead of me, and I didn't feel like carrying Odin and Alucard. Freya suddenly appeared in my peripheral vision, but she shoved me to the side before I had a chance to open my mouth.

And she let out a cry of pain.

I spun to see everyone shouting at each other, but all I cared about was the red cut on Freya's arm. A gash that would have also affected Gunnar's pups. It wasn't fatal or anything, but it was the intent that mattered. Someone from Watermelon Patch, LLC had thrown a knife at my back.

And Freya had taken the blow meant for me.

Kára was suddenly on the fringe of the crowd, hoisting a man up into the air.

With a freaking trident through his gut.

He didn't die, but he looked like he really wished he could have, rather than remaining impaled by a Valkyrie.

Odin settled a hooded glare on the helpless offender. "You will wish you never did that. You will wish so for a very, *very* long time." Then he began shouting at the mob of arguing gods, doing his best to calm them all down.

Kára handed her trident to a fellow Valkyrie, who began carrying him from the room, keeping him hoisted up on the trident like a flag. She was also clumsy, because she bumped him into the doorframe about three times on her way out, eliciting all sorts of cringeworthy squeals and gasps.

Rather than involve myself in that hot mess, I sprinted up to Freya and gripped her by the shoulders. "Thank you, Freya. I won't forget this."

She grunted. "It's barely a scratch."

I leaned in closer to inspect it, and told her what I needed her to do. In all the chaos and confusion, there was no way anyone else could have overheard.

"Are you out of your damned mind?" she hissed.

"You can't tell a soul. When it's time to go, I'll say *applesauce*."

She sputtered incredulously, but I was already turning away. "Someone help her. I've got an ass to kick," I growled, rolling up my sleeves. I locked eyes with Mr. Watermelon. "You'll do."

Alucard was shadow-boxing thin air, huffing and puffing as he worked on his combos while a crowd of baffled Asgardians watched. Ragnar held his massive arms out wide, urging the audience to give Alucard some space. "Let him work it out of his system. He'll pass out in a minute."

Alucard, for his part, kept going like a machine, turning any drunken stumble into a bob-and-weave move, never ceasing his punching combos. I shook my head, focusing back on my own foe.

I flung a blast of air at him—with the exact same motion I would have used to cuff an upstart teenager on the head. It struck his chest, sliding him back on his feet a few inches, but that was the extent of it. He brushed off his shirt and scowled at me. I grunted, having anticipated a slightly more dramatic effect. "You must be Baldur."

He nodded proudly. "Do your worst. Nothing can harm me."

I lowered my arms and stared at him. "You're a special kind of stupid, you know that?"

He narrowed his eyes angrily, but he didn't speak.

"When Freya went out to make everyone promise not to hurt you, was there a second group of Horsemen walking the earth?"

The room suddenly grew silent—my words serving to silence the crowd better than Odin's furious shouts. "A Horseman is a Horseman," he snapped.

I shrugged. "When I first put on my Mask," I said in a calm tone, "all Four Horsemen—the originals—almost died. They couldn't even remain in the same city as me without getting deathly ill in a matter of minutes. So… evidence seems to say all Horsemen are not alike."

My words echoed.

"Even if your mother—who *still* hasn't heard an apology from you or your friends—*had* earned an oath from the original Horsemen…I'm a different, darker breed, champ. And that's not even considering my party trick," I added, smiling as my arm began to glow with golden light. Gasps rose around the room, eyes shooting towards Odin as if begging him to stop me.

But Odin remained silent.

I let out a slow, menacing laugh. "The real question is how lucky you feel right now. Do you feel as lucky as Thor?" I asked sweetly.

Heimdall was suddenly there, holding Baldur back a heartbeat before he lunged. "Leave him be, Baldur! Trust me. You were not there to see—"

"His *friend* killed my brother, not *him*!" Baldur snarled furiously.

"And he *deserved* it!" Odin said, his voice booming over our heads.

Baldur froze in Heimdall's grip, turning to stare incredulously at Odin. "What?" he asked, in probably the coldest tone I'd ever heard.

Odin nodded. "Thor overstepped, and look what it cost him. He would not be dissuaded from pestering Nate Temple. Learn from your brother's mistake."

Baldur clenched his fists, outraged. "You would sit *there*, on your throne," he snarled, pointing, "and stand for this *wizard* against *me*? To spit on your dead son's name?" he asked incredulously. "It seems the rumors are correct. The Allfather has left us for good."

Odin opened his mouth but I lifted my hand, cutting him off. The room instantly silenced as my veins began to glow brighter. "This has nothing to do with Odin, other than the fact that the only disrespect I've seen is yours. Thor attacked a pregnant woman. Her husband brought swift justice. Odin could not have intervened without taking honor *away* from Thor."

Tyr slowly stepped forward, holding up a hand. The God of War cleared his throat, turning to face me, and I suddenly remembered that he was also considered the God of Justice, the Lawgiver. "Temple speaks the truth. Odin's intervention would have shamed Thor deeply—making it seem as if Thor was incapable of solving his own problems without his father stepping in. It would have made all of Asgard appear weak." Then he dipped his chin at me, and I saw respect in those deadly eyes.

The crowd began to murmur thoughtfully, not having thought about it in that way. Baldur gritted his teeth, furious.

I turned to everyone else in the room, holding out my hands as I slowly turned to address them all, one of my arms glowing brightly. "The only disrespect I've seen today is how this spoiled child thinks he can treat his mother and father. And I *still* haven't heard him apologize for drawing his own mother's blood, even if it was through a proxy." I slowly turned back to Baldur. "Odin is not speaking as *your father;* he is speaking as the *Allfather*. But you are stomping your feet too loudly to hear common sense. I tire of your presence. Go see to your friend. I think I can hear him screaming from here," I said, cupping my hand up to my ear and smiling. "Yes. I can."

Baldur's face purpled, but he spun on a heel and stormed from the room. A small retinue of gods joined him, mildly muttering unheard curses over their shoulders—for Baldur's benefit, of course, since none protested loudly enough for anyone still in the room to hear.

Odin held up a hand, glancing out at the gathered faces. "Please leave us."

Like children sent to bed, they looked crestfallen, but after the show they'd seen so far, no one looked ballsy enough to challenge Odin, and they all began filing out in groups, murmuring softly to each other.

The doors finally closed, and the only remaining Asgardians were Kára, Odin, Tyr, and Freya. Alice was attached to Freya's leg like a leech, making me smile.

Odin let the silence build, studying me warily. "It would seem I have another mess," he said tiredly.

"This one is less bloody."

"Perhaps that makes it a worse mess, long term."

Tyr nodded his agreement, but he did so politely and respectfully, giving me an idea.

"We are both busy men," Odin said, leaning forward from his throne, as he stared at me very intently. "I respect my previous oath, but I implore you to reschedule," he said meaningfully.

I sighed. Then I turned to Tyr, the God of Justice. "He promised to answer some vitally important, time-sensitive questions for me. Weeks ago. Understanding that he has obligations and duties to perform, I have not pressed the issue until now. I have respected his time, but I believe it's time for him to respect mine."

Tyr nodded pensively, turning to Odin. "Is this true?"

Odin sighed tiredly. "Yes."

Tyr nodded. "Then I agree with Temple, Allfather. We all know how important it is to value our oaths."

Freya stepped forward, and I noticed that she now had a clean bandage wrapped over her arm. Alice still clung to her leg, attempting to look invisible, but not wanting to be more than an inch away from her mentor. "I wish to accompany them," Freya said. "Tempers have flared often between these two, and I can make sure cooler heads prevail. Even though he has proven himself a friend of Asgard, and is apparently more honorable than my own sons, he is *also* a godkiller."

Tyr turned to me, arching an eyebrow. "Is this acceptable?"

I grunted. "Lady just took a knife for me," I muttered. "Of course, it's acceptable. And for the record, if I wanted to harm Odin, I would have said so the moment I set foot in Asgard. I'm not one to bite my tongue, if you hadn't noticed," I admitted, smiling. "But Freya's request is perfectly reasonable. And it's better than a flight of Valkyries ready to impale me if I sneeze too loudly."

Kára grinned approvingly.

Tyr nodded. "Then it is settled."

I very discreetly pocketed the black marble I'd been palming—having fully intended to throw it at Odin before I thought to use Tyr as my secret weapon. Overall, it worked out much better than my last-resort abduction plan.

I realized everyone was looking behind me, so I glanced back to see Ragnar carrying Alucard with both arms, holding him like a baby. I had been too distracted to notice. "Little guy is all tuckered out," Ragnar said, grinning.

"You owe me a knife," I replied. "He definitely lasted longer than five minutes." I ripped open a Gateway back to Chateau Falco and pointed my hand through it. "Just throw him over there somewhere," I told Ragnar.

He arched an eyebrow at me. Then he shrugged. "He won't feel it anyway." And he promptly tossed Alucard onto the dark lawn outside my mansion. Alucard didn't even flinch or groan upon impact. Ragnar held out a gleaming dagger, handing it to me hilt-first. "He's welcome back anytime," he said, chuckling.

I rolled my eyes and accepted the blade. It was a thing of beauty. I turned to find Odin had descended the raised dais, and was standing beside Freya and Alice, looking annoyed and ready to answer my questions as fast as possible. "Let's go, Asgardians."

I tucked the dagger into my waistband and stepped through, wondering how long it would take me to make Odin angry.

With what I had planned, it wouldn't be very long, that was for certain.

CHAPTER 18

Gunnar, Ashley, and the pups had been cooking marshmallows over a small fire, so our sudden arrival had surprised the hell out of them, but Alice had immediately calmed them down with her terrifying war cry. "PUPPIES!"

Calvin and Makayla tackled her much easier than in the past since they were much larger now, suffocating her with slobbery wolf kisses, wagging tails, and overexcited whining sounds as they steamrolled her. I noticed gauze bandages wrapped around both of their front left legs, and shot Freya a considering look, motioning her over to the werewolf parents with a grim frown that spoke volumes—*your problem*.

Freya obliged, speaking to them in soft tones and showing off her own matching bandage. I watched as Gunnar and Ashley's faces grew concerned and thoughtful.

Odin, for his part, had stared at the wolf puppies with surprise, looking confused about how much they had grown in such a short time. Hearing that his wife was lecturing the parents about the pups, he drifted closer, close enough to hear the explanation. Gunnar, although listening attentively, nudged Alucard with his boot a few times, frowning down at the snoring vampire.

Calvin and Makayla soon tired of Alice and raced over to me, hopping and whining as they attempted to lick me to death. Alice climbed to her feet, brushing the debris from her dress before walking over to me with a smile.

"How's your training going, Bones?" I asked.

She beamed. "Freya has started showing me seiðr magic, but it's difficult to understand."

I nodded. "Practice makes perfect." I waited a beat, speaking softly. "I'm going to need you to stick extra close to Freya for a while. I can't go into more detail right now."

She studied me thoughtfully. "Okay. You've been lying a lot lately. To everyone."

I nodded. "Necessary, but I haven't lied to you."

She smiled faintly. "You can't lie to me. You promised, and I know your tells."

I grunted. "I already regret teaching you that. Don't rub it in," I growled.

She grinned, nodding as she studied the puppies with a distant look in her eyes. "They're fine, you know," she said. "They are more powerful than before, but I don't sense any direct danger from it."

I waited to make sure she didn't see anything else concerning before sighing in relief. "That's good to hear. It's not some kind of affliction, then? A sickness?"

She shook her head firmly. "No. That would be like saying your magic is a sickness. This is simply a new ability of theirs. A part of them."

I didn't bother explaining that abilities could be just as dangerous as diseases.

"But I do see grave danger in their future. I don't know what it is, but it's not related to their new powers," she whispered softly. "And it won't happen soon."

I shivered. Would my plan be enough to keep them safe, or did I need to go back to my original idea? "Thank you, Alice. I'll figure it out."

Calvin and Makayla no longer emitted fog from their paws or mouths, so it was difficult for me to see them as anything other than happy, energetic puppies. Still, with their bond to Freya, my mind was already racing with plans and ideas—any way for me to keep them safe from indirect harm.

They curled up at my feet, only consenting to remain still after I'd planted a hand on each of their heads and dutifully began petting them. Like a dead man's switch on a bomb. Release it, and *boom*.

Freya was now leaning down over the pile of crushed wizard ice, and I was surprised that it hadn't thawed or grown goopy and noxious. In fact, the cubes hadn't melted at all. Like the pups had frozen them on a molecular level, or somehow dehydrated them into frozen jerky cubes.

I used my chin to indicate the pups as I locked gazes with Freya. "They bit him and turned him into that, freezing him with sudden mist and draining him of all his blood. Like they sucked out his soul and froze him." I stared at them. "In related news, they are now bigger."

Odin still looked decidedly uneasy about the whole situation. I'd only spoken with Freya about it in Asgard, since he'd been busy entertaining the godliticians.

Finally, he turned to me. "I understand that I promised to speak with you, but you've had weeks to meet with me. Why stir up trouble in Asgard now, and why are we here?"

His eye flicked to the pups, and the look on his face told me that he definitely considered that to be Freya's problem—which was absolutely correct.

"I needed a Guber."

He narrowed his eye. "What did you just call me?"

I waved a hand. "I needed a Godly Uber. You are taking me to Yggdrasil."

"Why would I do that?" he asked guardedly, seeming as if he was searching for any excuse to get the hell out of here—one that wouldn't result in me chasing him down and embarrassing him in front of another crowd.

"I want to see the three wells. We can go to Urðarbrunnr, first." He stared at me flatly, entirely motionless. "You know, the Well of Urðr. I want to meet the Norns and hear my destiny." This time, I realized everyone was staring at me, unmoving. "But I will settle for Mímisbrunnr—the Well of Mímir—the one you threw your eyeball into so you could learn a thing or two. We can save Hvregelmir and its resident dragon for last," I said, grimacing. "Really, it doesn't matter which one we visit first. I want to see all three of the wells, eventually." Dead silence answered me, so I shot Odin a sober look. "I won't leave you alone until you take me. I'll follow you to the end of the Nine Realms, chasing you down like…say, a giant wolf," I said, winking at him. "You'll have to kill me to get rid of me."

He stared back at me, looking stunned at both my request and my instant descent into threats. That I was willing to die for this when I'd never expressed an interest in the wells before now. That was exactly what I wanted him thinking about. "Yggdrasil doesn't exist in the physical realm," Odin finally said.

I shrugged. "I've Astral Projected with Shiva before."

He grimaced. "Why the sudden interest in Yggdrasil?"

I smiled. "I want to carve my name into the trunk, of course." Freya cursed under her breath—an instinctive response to my sacrilegious comment. I waved off her concern. "A joke. Seeing Yggdrasil is on my bucket list."

Odin frowned pensively. "No. We never agreed to that. It is a sacred place, and you are obviously lacking in respect," he said, turning his attention to Freya as if hoping she could speak some sense into me.

"You know, I figured you would say that," I said calmly. "How about this. If you ever want to see Gungnir again, you're going to make this a fun field trip for me."

He stiffened, slowly turning his head back to face me. "You said that you lost Gungnir."

I shrugged, grinning back at him. "I've found it. Or maybe I never lost it. Or maybe I'm lying right now."

Alucard surprised us all by groaning musically, but it was obvious that he was still unconscious—like he was singing in his dreams. The best part was that he was humming Kenny Rogers' *The Gambler*.

Gunnar scoffed incredulously, covering his mouth to stop from bursting out laughing. That was the definition of a wingman. Even black-out drunk, Alucard was backing me up.

I turned to Odin. "So, do you know when to hold 'em and when to fold 'em?" I asked in a sing-song voice.

"Where is it?" he hissed, taking an instinctive step closer.

I shook my head. "It's safe. I'll decide when you get it back. You already offered it to me once. I'm keeping my options open."

Odin shuddered, gritting his teeth. "You're doing this just to vex me. With Fenrir unbound, I must have my spear!"

"Whine all you want, but I'm not handing it over until things are a lot more stable in Asgard. That's like handing over a nuclear bomb."

"There is unrest specifically *because* Gungnir is missing!" he seethed.

I shrugged. "You know how stubborn I am, Odin. I'll happily carry the secret to my grave, so your only chance at getting it back is to calm the hell down and work with me. Trust me. Because if you challenge me, you will lose and Gungnir will be lost forever. Also, Fenrir will have a much easier time without me around to keep you safe."

"You intend to keep me safe from Fenrir?" he asked, sounding shocked.

I shrugged. "Not sure yet. Things have changed. Maybe he doesn't want to eat you. We will never know if we don't find him first, because Mordred was working with some bad people."

He studied me warily. Then he let out a deep, resigned breath, and drew a vertical line in front of him from the ground to up over his head like he was unzipping a tent.

The air shimmered slightly, but that was about it.

Then Odin walked through what looked like a gossamer, translucent curtain, and into a much greener version of...Chateau Falco.

"Fuck me," I breathed in disbelief, hopping to my feet to follow him through the opening. "Yggdrasil is *here*?"

I stared at the raw land where Chateau Falco had first been constructed —as if we had gone back in time a thousand years. If the slopes and valleys had changed in any way, I wouldn't have even noticed it, but the land was surprisingly identical, and I saw shimmering holograms of Chateau Falco flickering into hazy existence before evaporating again—as if showing me what would one day be built here. What was being built here. What had once been built here.

Future, present, and past.

Odin grunted indelicately, shaking his head. "Yggdrasil is everywhere. And nowhere. It is at the beginning and at the end. If I stepped over from a Hooters restaurant, you would see the land as it was before Hooters was ever constructed. And as it would be thousands of years after the Hooters restaurant had disintegrated to dust. Yggdrasil is in the spirit realm. Your mind is simply processing it over our current location, and removing all modern civilization from the depiction."

I grunted, feeling deflated. "Oh. Well, that's not as cool." Internally, my thoughts were racing. The Alpha and the Omega—as the world was in the beginning, and as it would be at the end.

He rolled his eye, pointing ahead of us.

An ash tree, seemingly made of white light and shards of crystal, stood before us. And when I say before us, I mean that it stood where Carl's tree now stood at the real Chateau Falco.

Exactly where Carl's tree stood.

Even creepier, this tree was slightly smaller and oozed blue blood...

Exactly where Carl's tree oozed *red* blood at the real Chateau Falco.

The tree didn't quite seem real, and it was slightly smaller than Carl's tree. It flickered with veins of rainbow sap across the aged white bark, zaps of every color slowly coursing down or up the trunk like a mouse down a snake's digestive tract. I watched as a yellow orb drifted up the tree towards an intersection where a blue orb would cross its path. The two collided at the intersection, and a new green orb branched off into a third vein as the yellow and blue continued on their initial paths—as if they hadn't just created a new blossom of life.

White flowers grew from the bark, waving in a wind that I couldn't feel. The air was pregnant with crisp life, an aromatic perfume of wildflowers, and I heard a faint chiming sound coming from the upper branches.

Crystal and bone wind chimes hung from the branches, and they were decorated in painted whorls and runes. Some of them glowed, and some of them shone with dark light, if that made any sense. Or maybe they just projected shadows.

Faint curls of bark peeled off the tree trunk, drifting up into the air like dandelion puff, making the tree look as if it was disintegrating before my eyes. But at the same time, I watched as new bark grew across the surface, rejuvenating even as it died.

Although the tree itself seemed slightly smaller than Carl's tree, there was also a hulking, ominous strain to the air, as if it couldn't quite be constrained to one particular size. To that effect, I noticed a faint hologram around the tree—stretching thousands of feet higher than the physical tree, as if the tree's spirit or soul was simply too large to be contained in any physical manifestation.

And that soul stretched so high that it appeared to reach the moon, with ephemeral branches stretching across the sky for miles.

I slowly turned to stare at Odin, hoping for answers. But...he looked just as enamored as me. Noticing my attention, he plastered on a faint smile. "It is a mesmerizing sight to behold, no matter how many times I see it. Tied to each of the Nine Realms, it often reflects them at various points, shifting from one to another as it so chooses." He frowned slightly at the oozing trunk. "Although I will admit I've never seen it bleed before."

"Ragnarök..." Freya whispered, her voice sounding haunted. I glanced over to see her clutching Alice close to her hip. Gunnar had apparently hopped through with us and was also staring at the tree, his mouth hanging open wordlessly. I could see Ashley and her pups on the other side of the shifting curtain. Alucard was still unconscious.

I frowned uneasily as I stared back through the curtain. The pups went from moving in slow motion to suddenly racing around Ashley's ankles at the speed of light. Then back to moving slowly, and then fast again, switching back and forth in no discernible pattern or logical rhythm.

Odin waved a hand unconcernedly. "They are perfectly fine. Yggdrasil is, in essence, time—both past and present. It is also every location and no location. It is a spear stabbing the wheel of time, if you want to think about it that way. The axle that lets time spin. The spokes are each of the Nine Realms."

He stared up at the tree wistfully, breathing deeply.

"Do the gods still come here every day to discuss stuff?" I asked absently, also staring up at the tree, realizing just how small I was in the larger scope of things.

Odin scoffed. "No. The lazy bastards—when they can be bothered—always vote to stay in Asgard. We only come here for War Talk. It's more ceremonial than anything."

I nodded. "Just curious. It's too beautiful to ignore."

Three roots as thick as the physical tree stretched out across the earth before sinking into the ground. Near each root, an earthen tunnel led deeper underground, parallel to the root, allowing one to walk under the world to see where the root led.

I already knew the answer to that.

The three roots led to the three famous wells in Norse mythology:

Urðarbrunnr, or the *Well of Urðr*, as it literally translated, was where the Norns lived. They were three powerful women who controlled the destiny of all creatures of the Nine Realms, and their names roughly translated to past, present, and future.

Hvergelmir stretched all the way to Niflheim, where a serpent-like dragon named Níðhöggr gnawed on the roots of Yggdrasil.

Mímisbrunnr, or the *Well of Mímir*, stretched to Jotunheim, the Realm of the giants. It was where Odin had chosen to offer his eye in exchange for prophecy and knowledge, proving his belief that no sacrifice was too great for wisdom.

"What are we doing here, Nate?" Freya asked, holding Alice close. The small blonde child was staring at the tree with eyes as wide as saucers, murmuring wordlessly under her breath. From here, it reminded me of a GPS unit endlessly saying *recalculating...recalculating...recalculating...*

I forced myself not to laugh out loud as I turned back to the tree.

"I like it here," Gunnar finally said, smiling brightly as he absently stroked his beard. "It's peaceful. Tranquil—" He suddenly jerked his attention upwards, gesturing adamantly with one finger to indicate a spot higher up the tree, making him look like a dog on point. "SQUIRREL!"

I had flinched at his sudden shout, but I quickly masked my reaction by following his gaze up the tree. My jaw fell open and I instinctively clenched my fists, ready for a fight.

CHAPTER 19

Gunnar's observation skills were uncanny. A fucking red squirrel the size of a freaking SUV stared down at us with his chin resting in one of his large paws. His other paw was absently gouging out strips of bark from the World Tree in a bored, defiant gesture, but he was resting horizontal on his stomach, obscuring the rest of his body behind the tree trunk. He had tall, pointed ears, with long red fur sprouting from the tips like tufts of grass.

What I could see of him was covered in more of the same long, sleek, red fur, and it flowed out around his paws like a Clydesdale's hooves. His velociraptor-like claws were easily strong enough to support his massive bulk. He stared at me with eyes as black as the deepest, loneliest corner of the universe—a place where all suns had died. His long, stained front teeth were etched with golden runes that glowed, and they looked tough enough to bite through steel. He was easily the size of a luxury sedan or small SUV, and it was pretty damned obvious who he was.

Ratatoskr—the squirrel who ran up and down the World Tree, delivering messages between a wise, unnamed eagle at the top, and the serpent Níðhöggr at the bottom. Except Ratatoskr was known as a troublemaker, and usually modified the messages into harsh insults, fueling animosity between the two. He was the original gossip artist or tabloid reporter of the Norse pantheon.

"Who is the primordial pap smear?" he asked in a bored, almost lazy drawl that reminded me of Scar from *Lion King*. He looked directly at me as he asked it.

He didn't actually have a British accent, but the *way* he enunciated his words made him *sound* like he did. It reminded me of the stereotypical British nobility who were often depicted as posh, snooty, elitists—capable of silencing their foes with condescending inflections and a rapier wit that sliced so deep and fast that the combination often left their verbal opponents bleeding out before they knew they had even been cut by the linguistical ninjas.

It was a talent as powerful as magic, and I envied those who wielded it. Ratatoskr had apparently mastered it long before humans.

He had just called me a primordial pap smear, and it was a clever enough insult that I couldn't even be that offended. In the grand scheme of things, he wasn't necessarily wrong. I memorized the line instead.

Also, he looked naturally equipped to murder all of us as easily as a squirrel could bust a nut.

Well, you know what I mean.

I glanced back at Gunnar, not even bothering to point out the dog versus squirrel eternal rivalry. "Ratatoskr is not a fucking squirrel, man," I began. "Well, he is, but—"

"The bacterium has evolved enough to speak," Ratatoskr mused, shifting his bulk as if preparing to pounce.

Gunnar turned to Odin, squaring his shoulders. "Mine. Ratatoskr is mine."

I slowly turned to stare at him. "He's not a soda. You can't just *have* him." I turned to Odin. "Can he?"

"Of course he can't!" Odin snapped, looking bewildered. "What the hell is wrong with you people?"

"Yeah, Gunnar. What the hell?" I demanded, folding my arms.

But Gunnar was no longer looking at us. He snarled as he took an aggressive step forward, and then he snapped a bone bracelet off his wrist. It instantly shifted into his Horseman's Mask, and he slapped it on his face without warning anyone. His forearms erupted with long, white fur as diamond claws sprouted from his fingertips, and I realized I was holding my breath, wondering if he would finally reveal his true Horseman of Justice form.

I waited a moment longer, and let out my breath in disappointment. Just his Alpha werewolf form, but wearing a golden Mask that seemed to be made of quartz, glittering with thousands of facets. It had taken me several times before I fully adopted my own Horseman form.

He pointed a claw at Ratatoskr. "MINE!"

Ratatoskr launched himself from the tree, landing before Gunnar in an explosion of soil and gravel. Golden runes were branded into his fur, and they seemed to glow with power. His tail was a massive club as long as his body, doubling his size. And instead of typical fur, the hair on his tail looked more like bone spines. He flicked his tail into the air and slapped it down on the ground three times in rapid succession, flattening the earth around him, sending shrapnel to ricochet off Gunnar's Mask and…

The Horseman of Justice didn't move a millimeter. The squirrel lunged at him, snapping his long yellow teeth at Gunnar's face, a hair's width away from contact…

And still, Gunnar did not flinch. "Mine," he snarled in a lower, more primal growl.

He slowly lifted his claws, extending them towards Ratatoskr's face.

Ratatoskr snarled, his curled claws digging into the earth as if he was trying everything in his power to pull away, but finding himself unable to retreat. Then, inch-by-inch, the great squirrel began to kneel, hunkering lower and lower until he was crouched down before Gunnar, and he let out a long, shuddering breath.

I shook my head in disbelief, feeling more confused than ever. Gunnar—the Horseman of Justice—had just picked his figurative horse. Damn it all.

"A fucking squirrel!" I snapped, throwing my hands into the air. "No one is *ever* going to take Team Temple seriously with this kind of shit happening left and right." I altered my voice into a high, frightened pitch. "Oh, no! Here comes the New Horsemen! Hope rides on his unicorn. And wait! He rides alongside the Horseman of Justice on his squirrel of death! Don't worry, the other two Horsemen are coming, but one is passed out drunk and the other is at church with a skeleton and a ninja." I kicked at a rock on the ground, sending it flying into the trunk of the World Tree. "I can't *wait* to see what Alucard and Callie pick."

Gunnar studied Ratatoskr thoughtfully, completely ignoring me. "It is an honor to earn your respect."

Ratatoskr rose, climbing to his full height. He studied Gunnar thoughtfully. "I...believe we are going to cause a lot of trouble, Horseman." He appraised Gunnar, his black eyes seeming to see through the Horseman. "Justice," he mused, sounding anticipatory. "That pleases me immensely," he said, curling his lips back to brandish the true length of his fangs. "I have work to do here, but speak my name and I will answer the call—as long as there are things to eradicate, of course. I will honor this duty. Thor is dead and Fenrir is loose. Ragnarök looms, and my home will soon be dust in the wind. I think you may have just saved my life, Horseman. Thank you for choosing me."

Gunnar nodded, peeling off his Mask. It snapped back into a bracelet and he clipped it back onto his wrist, turning to look at me. He clasped his hands behind his back and nodded proudly. "So cool." Ratatoskr slammed his club tail into the ground, nodding his agreement.

I closed my eyes and counted to ten, breathing slowly. I finally opened them, and turned back to Odin. "I think we're done here."

Odin turned from studying Ratatoskr to frown at me. "I thought you wanted to see one of the Wells," he said, looking as if he didn't have any idea what to do about this recent development.

I shrugged. "I just walk into one of those holes, right?" I asked, pointing.

He thought about it and finally shrugged. "Well, yes...but that sounds ridiculous when you put it like that."

I shrugged. "Good enough for me." And I turned away, walking back towards the gossamer curtain leading home.

"Wait! What was the point of all of this? It couldn't be to acquire Ratatoskr. He just happened to come down at the right moment."

I glanced over my shoulder. "I, myself, don't believe in coincidences," I said mysteriously, enjoying the darkening shade his face was turning. "And I just needed you to take me here, to Yggdrasil. I can find the Wells later."

He went entirely still. "What do you mean, later?"

"Once I visit a place, I can Shadow Walk there at a later time of my choosing." And I winked at him. "Thanks."

"Oh, shit!" Ratatoskr crowed. "The Horseman wizard played you, Allfather!" He turned to study me excitedly. "This new job is going to be *way* more fun."

I grunted, amused by his enthusiasm. "Don't get too excited. He's the boring one," I said, pointing a thumb at Gunnar.

Gunnar frowned. "I am wild when I want to be," he muttered defensively.

"Oh, don't get me wrong," I reassured him. "You're a raving lunatic on the battlefield, but you're not as crazy as me."

Gunnar arched a brow. "You realize how stupid that sounds, right? I just need to make sure you understand how you come across to other people."

Ratatoskr watched us with an amused expression. "You're bloodthirsty, eh?" He turned to me. "You sure you don't need a mount?" he asked. Gunnar glared at him.

I shook my head. "I ride a unicorn. Well, an Alicorn, technically."

Ratatoskr grew unnaturally still, his tail suddenly standing straight up. "Just to clarify," he said, sounding uneasy. "What's your unicorn's name?"

I faced him fully, trying to translate the strange look on his squirrelly face. I hadn't ever really studied a squirrel's face before. You could take anyone in the world and show them a picture of a squirrel and then ask them what it was, and they would probably all get it right. But if you took an equal number of people and asked them to describe a squirrel to you—or better yet, draw one—you'd get a bushy-tailed pigeon, rat, cat, and probably any other number of land-based mammals.

None of them would resemble a squirrel.

So staring at Ratatoskr, a talking, violent, mischievous, legendary, monster squirrel…was unsettling.

"Grimm," I finally told him.

He hopped back a step, slamming his tail into the ground hard enough for me to feel it in my toes. "Sweet Idunn's tits!" he cursed incredulously.

Freya squawked indignantly. "RATATOSKR!" Alice was hiding behind her, poking her head out to stare at the squirrel with wide eyes.

He wilted instinctively at her mom voice, but he wasn't deterred. "Grimm is still around? I thought he was banished to the—"

Odin cut him off with a violent gesture. Surprisingly, Ratatoskr obeyed, even flinching involuntarily. Then he simply leapt up into the tree and began scrambling away as fast as he could move, his bushy, spiny tail hammering into the bark hard enough to rain down white twigs and small branches. "Fuck this damned tree. Fuck this nerdy eagle. Fuck this gothic serpent. I get to hang out with Grimm again!" he chittered excitedly, his voice trailing off as he disappeared up into the apparition-like portion of the World Tree, seeming to become ephemeral himself.

Gunnar joined me after a final wave at Ratatoskr—who had forgotten all about Gunnar.

I shared a long look with him, wondering what the squirrel had been about to say regarding Grimm and his supposed banishment. How the hell did Ratatoskr know Grimm? Did terrifying monsters have a weekly poker game or something?

I was about to step through the curtain when Odin called out. "Wait!"

I hesitated, debating whether or not I should make him follow me, but I decided I'd put the old man through enough hell for one day. "Yeah?"

"What deal did you make with Anubis?" Odin asked carefully. "When you were fighting Mordred. You were on the ropes, boy. At the end, even I thought you had already lost. Then you were suddenly back."

I turned to look at him, studying his face thoughtfully. "Temples don't fall. We just stumble," I told him, quoting my dad.

He grunted. "Every Temple falls. Eventually."

I narrowed my eyes dangerously. "That a threat, old one?"

"It's a fact, you hot-headed fool." He pointed at the crest branded into my palm. "Why do you think they keep building new ones?" I knew he was referring both to my last name and the construction of a temple, but I wasn't that impressed. I'd heard much better double entendres.

"Maybe they were just waiting to build the best one. The design for the Sistine Chapel took years to master. Millennia, technically, if you look at it from a human existence perspective."

"You think you are the Sistine Chapel, boy?" Odin snapped.

I shrugged. "I think I'm what comes after the Sistine Chapel," I admitted, biting back a grin.

"You can't possibly be that arrogant."

"Watch me be this arrogant," I said dryly.

He cursed. "Your father fell. His father fell. All fathers fall down eventually. No matter how glorious we are in life, we all enter our crypts the same way at the sunset of our lives. Very few ever leave."

I was already walking away, stepping through the curtain.

"Where are you going now, boy?" Odin demanded.

I didn't turn around this time. "I'm going to go eat some applesauce and drink some beer. Then, I'll probably go kill the Academy."

Gunnar missed a step, but recovered it well.

CHAPTER 20

So far, my plan was moving along nicely. I had visited—and caused a noticeable ruckus in—a broad swath of locations in a relatively short period of time, leaving behind a confusing trail for gossip. And that wasn't even counting the blatant lies and rumors I had started about my recent activities and sightings all across the globe. I still had more to do, but I was pleased with myself.

And sitting at the bar with a drink in hand, I couldn't help but feel like an international man of mystery.

I could only hope that Loki was holding up his end of the bargain.

After visiting Yggdrasil, Gunnar had driven me and an extremely grumpy and hungover Alucard to Achilles' Heel to see if we could catch the tail-end of their poker game. We'd missed it by an hour but had arrived in time to find a few stragglers hanging around and shooting the shit over beers.

We found War, Death, Shiva, and Achilles sitting around a table, drinking, when we arrived. Alucard had promptly laid his head down on the table, preferring nap time to nightcaps.

We'd been casually catching up with Death and War for the last twenty minutes, hearing about their recent travels—a forced vacation since being near me had almost killed them. Now that I'd named the rest of my band of Horsemen, they'd finally been able to return to town.

Well, Famine and Conquest were away on business of some kind, but War and Death had been eager to see Gunnar and Alucard—to congratulate them on their new part-time jobs.

Which, thankfully, had left little room for me to talk about anything. Until the nosy bartender had asked me to come help him grab refills for the table.

Achilles popped the tops off a few bottles of beer, setting them down on the tray as he counted under his breath, his eyes briefly flicking over to the loud table behind me and back again. "What have you really been up to lately, lizard?" He finally asked, not looking up.

I arched a brow. "I am a *wizard*, ignorant barkeep. The W stands for winner—an L is for loser."

Achilles snorted at me. "Alright, wiener-lizard."

"*Winner*," I corrected him. "I didn't ask about your depraved fetishes for male reptiles."

He rolled his eyes. "You're friends with an ancient reptilian race that the rest of the supernatural community is terrified of. You are now a lizard. Like those conspiracy nuts talking about lizard men really running our country from behind the scenes. Hell, maybe they are referring to Elders, too."

I rolled my eyes, deciding it was better to just answer his question. "I saw Cain earlier. You ever heard of a skeleton guy walking around Kansas City?" I asked, remembering Xylo, as Alucard had called him.

Achilles frowned. "Nope to the bonehead, but I wouldn't mind getting Cain to jump into the fight schedule every now and then. He's good with a crowd."

"You might want to visit Kansas City. It seems they have ninjas, now." He glanced up at me thoughtfully, sensing the hint of annoyance in my tone, but picked up a rag and began wiping the counter rather than pressing me on it. "I just hung out with Odin."

Achilles stopped wiping down the bar to look up at me. "Where did you find the bastard? Was he in Kansas City, too?"

I frowned. "Asgard, of course."

Achilles frowned. "Strange. My Valkyrie friend said no one had heard from him in quite some time."

"*Your* Valkyrie friend?" I teased, rolling my eyes. "Kára is way too cool to associate with *you*, tool."

Achilles smirked shamelessly. "I'm not going to tell her that."

I laughed. "Odin's been running around a lot, reassuring the Nine Realms about his absence. And calming them down about Thor's murder. The whole giant snake thing is probably a concern."

Achilles scratched as his scruffy jaw. "I tried calling Kára, but her phone went straight to voicemail."

"I saw her in Asgard. Maybe her phone doesn't work there."

He shrugged, nodding dismissively. "She's not the kind of girl that I should need to worry about being in danger," he chuckled. "Still…"

I laughed. "She would kill you for thinking she is weak. She recently tried to kill me with a hatchet, by the way," I added, hoping to reassure him about her self-defense capabilities.

He smiled, letting out a breath of relief. "Oh, good," he said jovially. "Even if she's losing her vision in her old age, at least she tried. It's the thought that counts, right?" He scooped up a trio of beers and pointed at the tray. "Carry that for me."

I grunted. "Do I look like a butler?"

"You look thirsty, and only working men drink at my bar."

"Then I will surely die of thirst," I sighed miserably.

He rolled his eyes, chuckling. "Trust-fund brats—wouldn't know honest work if it hit them in the face."

"Dishonest work is so much more rewarding."

"Cheers to *that*," he muttered, laughing. "Now grab the tray. Consider it community service, my lord. The peasants will love you for it," he said, walking past me without a glance. I sighed and picked up the tray of beers before following him over to the table.

Death glanced up at me as I reached the table. "Ah, the beer wench is here," he said, eyeing my tray.

I curtsied, setting the tray down. "Don't forget to tip," I said, taking a seat. "A real tip, not the heat you guys *think* you're packing down south."

Shiva grinned, slapping the table with two of his four hands. "So quick with the words. It really is a pleasure to see you again, even if it has been brief. Too bad you missed Ganesh. He often asks about you. And Asterion regaled us with the tale of you topping him."

I chuckled. "*Tipping* him," I corrected, not wanting to try explaining *topping* in any manner whatsoever. "And I wish I could have been here sooner."

Shiva shrugged, sipping at his drink. "Remember that time you astral projected to my hut on my mountain?" He asked, laughing loudly. "I thought my bull was going to kill you!"

"Now *that* would be a fine steed," War interjected, nudging Alucard. "Much better than a damned squirrel." Gunnar swiped up a beer and began guzzling to hide his scowl.

Alucard groaned, not bothering to lift his head from the table as he blindly swatted back at War. "Go away," he said, his voice muffled from the table.

We'd managed to get him vertical and coherent, but he was both hungover and drunk at the same time—a terrible combination. Norse mead was no joke.

I smiled, turning back to Shiva. "I have my own mountain, now, and it's got a killer view. You should swing by sometime. I need to learn how to build a hut, though. All I have is an igloo."

Shiva nodded. "It would be my pleasure," he said. "On that note, I must depart. They already took all of my money anyway." He scowled at the two Biblical Horsemen and their stacks of Tootsie Rolls—their chosen form of currency for their weekly poker games.

No currency exchange needed this way, they'd told me. Which kind of made sense, since they all called different parts of the globe home.

Shiva bowed formally, waved with all four hands—at different people with each—and then simply vanished.

"It's a bad idea to travel like that when you're drunk," Achilles murmured, sitting down on an adjacent table, and propping his boot up on the chair. "Be responsible. Don't drink and rip holes in reality."

I grunted. "How would you know?"

"Believe it or not, I have known other, more reputable, wizards in my many, many years," he muttered.

I rolled my eyes. "Prove it."

He smirked back at me. "They wouldn't like you much."

"Then I've saved you from bad influences."

He rolled his eyes back at me and sipped his beer.

"You do understand that you're a Horseman, not a Squirrelman, right?" Death asked Gunnar, his face entirely serious.

Gunnar had his arms folded across his chest and he was not bothering to hide his scowl any longer. They had been giving him a hard time, off and on, for the last ten minutes, now.

"He's a terrifying, mythical beast," Gunnar argued.

"He's a squirrel," Death clarified.

"And you're a *werewolf*," War added, shaking his head. "It's like you're *asking* to be mocked."

Gunnar narrowed his eye. "I think he's cool. And you haven't even seen him. He's a nightmare, and he has a mouth like a sailor."

The two Biblical Horsemen shared a silent, considering look and finally shrugged. "I'm not nuts about it," War finally said.

Gunnar's face turned purple and I burst out laughing.

Achilles shot a brief glance at Alucard, who was still face-down, dozing on the table. Achilles grinned wickedly as he raised his beer to us. "Skol."

Alucard whimpered. "Screw all of you…"

We all grinned at our pitiful friend, and then shouted at the top of our lungs, "SKOL!"

Then we all dumped a generous portion of our beers on the back of Alucard's head, drenching him in the last thing he wanted right now. He spluttered, jumping away from the table and cursing up a storm.

He finally lifted his head to glare at us, beer dripping steadily from his hair. "I'm done. Unless you have any more energy drinks in the back," he asked, turning to Achilles.

Achilles shook his head. "Still restocking from my temporary shut-down. No blood yet." True to his word, crates of liquor and beer surrounded us, forming a labyrinth of booze since he hadn't put them all away yet. "I might have some actual energy drinks in the back fridge."

Alucard sighed dejectedly and then stumbled over to the bar in search of the liquid heart attacks and a towel to dry off. Achilles took a big pull from his beer, polishing it off, and then set the empty on the table.

"I'll be back," he said, heading towards the restroom. "Don't wreck the place while I'm gone," he added from over his shoulder.

Gunnar had gone strangely silent, angling himself to watch me in what he thought was a discreet manner. But he only had one eye, so he often-times didn't realize how blatantly obvious he came across.

Death climbed to his feet, brushing his hands off. "I better get back, too. Othello is in a feisty mood." And then he cast a withering look my way.

I grunted. "Not my fault. She's the one who sold Niko the laptop."

Death waved a hand. "Just giving you a hard time, Hope." He glanced down at War, who was leaning back in his chair, balancing on the rear legs as he nursed his beer. "You in charge of the shit-show tomorrow morning?"

War didn't look up but stared at me instead. "Nah. I think I have something else going on. You can teach the squirrel."

I frowned. "What?" Gunnar had leaned forward as well.

"Grimm and I need to teach Ratatoskr the ropes. General rules and bylaws associated with being a Horseman's mount."

I smiled crookedly, assuming they were teasing again. But they didn't even blink. "What do you mean? *They* have training? Why the hell didn't *I* ever get any training?"

"We didn't think about it, to be honest," Death said. "And don't forget that we couldn't come anywhere near you until now—until you picked the rest of your Horsemen."

He had a point. Even being in the same city that I was in had nearly killed them—something about the extreme imbalance of power as a result of Horsemen needing to work in groups of four. It was also why my Mask had fractured. Since I'd picked Callie, Gunnar, and Alucard, my Mask had healed and, apparently, *training* could commence.

"Training for the *mounts*, not for the actual *Horsemen*," I said, just to clarify.

Death nodded. "We'll figure out what to do with you guys later."

I glanced at Gunnar, thinking of his new 'horse'. I was undecided on how I truly felt about it, but I was more concerned by Ratatoskr's apparent acquaintance with Grimm.

My unicorn had been spending a lot of time with Pegasus, lately.

Deep down, I knew he was still upset that he now had a rainbow firmly attached to his forehead. Although grateful to me for me saving his life, he was surprisingly self-conscious about his new horn.

"Unless you wanted to take a stab at training them," Death said, sounding hopeful.

I sighed, grumbling under my breath. "No. It's just that I'd hoped to have Grimm on hand over the next few days. I might need the backup."

I felt Gunnar eyeing me again. He'd been doing it all night when he thought I wasn't paying attention.

"Okay. Let's get this over with," I said, turning to face him. "Have you forgotten what it's like to hang out with non-dads? You don't need to stare at me like you're waiting for me to chew on the furniture or pee on the carpet."

He didn't react, continuing to stare at me. "I've just been wondering about something you said. You didn't eat any applesauce."

I kept my face calm, ignoring War and Death's sudden interest. "It was a figure of speech, Sherlock."

"No," Gunnar said confidently. "It was not."

"Whatever," I muttered. My phone vibrated in my pocket, so I pulled it out to see Niko's phone number on the screen. I ignored it, set my beer down, and stood from the table. "I'm going to go hit the head. Go home without me. I'll make a Gateway."

"Why?" Gunnar asked. "Did I really just piss you off?"

I waved a hand. "No. I just need to take a walk." I glanced over at the bar, not seeing Alucard. "If he doesn't ride home with you, I'll take him with me."

And I continued on towards the restroom. I was considering making a pit-stop, based on something Starlight had said in the warehouse. I didn't actually understand any of the weird things he had told me, but every time I thought about it, my mind immediately wandered, and I found myself recalling the last thing my father had ever said to me.

In the security feed at Temple Industries, he'd looked up at the camera and said something very specific—fully aware that he was moments away from his last breath. To be honest, I hadn't thought about that message for a very long time. Maybe that had been a subconscious coping mechanism my mind had thrown into place.

Or maybe recent events were making me feel nostalgic—seeing how dysfunctional Odin's family was, and finding similarities to my own upbringing. So, I didn't have a specific reason for wanting to make my quick detour, but the more I thought about it, the more convinced I was that I needed to pay my respects to my ancestors.

"Don't chew on the furniture!" Gunnar snapped as I was rounding the corner. I flipped him off without turning to look, ignoring their laughter.

But I did catch War's faint voice before I reached the restroom door. "What do you think *applesauce* means?"

CHAPTER 21

I found Achilles at the urinal, and I grinned nostalgically, reminded of one of our first encounters. "Just like old times, eh?" I asked casually.

He flinched and turned to glare at me from over his shoulder. "Hell of a thing to say to a man at the pisser."

I nodded. "Yeah. I've got a dagger for you."

He looked at the ceiling, letting out a breath. "And you somehow made it even *weirder*."

I grinned, whipping out the dagger that I'd won from Ragnar. I held it out for him to inspect. Achilles finished up, and then walked over, reaching out for the blade.

I pulled it back. "Wash your hands, first. That's disgusting."

He rolled his eyes and quickly washed up, drying his hands before walking back over and snatching the blade away with a slight growl. He held it up to the light, twisting it back and forth and grunting his approval. "Hell of a piece," he said, handing it back.

"No. It's for you to keep."

He frowned suspiciously. "Not sure I can afford it."

"I just want to ask you a personal question. I didn't want to do so in front of everyone else."

"Okay," he said, obviously hesitant.

"I met Baldur tonight—total prick, by the way—and I got to thinking about how far his mother was willing to go to keep him safe after hearing a prophecy about his death. She traveled the world, obtaining oaths from every living and non-living entity that they would not harm her son. The only one she forgot to ask was Mistletoe—which obviously became his sole weakness."

Achilles lowered the dagger to his side and grew very still, not seeming to breathe as he listened.

"Then I remembered that your story isn't so different," I said. "That your mother, Thetis, dipped you in the River Styx to keep you safe from all harm—except she missed your heel. Both mothers made a small mistake, and now everyone knows about your weaknesses."

He slowly nodded, watching me like a hawk. "And?"

Reading his rigidly tense body language, I decided to lean my back against the wall in a slight slouch, breaking eye contact as if I was having trouble searching for the right words. In actuality, I was psychologically manipulating him in order to put him at ease.

I shrugged. "Freya *extorted* everyone else to play nice, putting her son in a safe bubble. Your mother gave you armor, essentially *daring* everyone else to test themselves against you. But both were forms of *defensive* protection."

He nodded thoughtfully. "I don't know much about Baldur, but it sounds accurate. I'm still waiting for you to get to the point, though."

"It's kind of the opposite of my story, you know?"

He casually tucked the dagger into his waistband, as if he suddenly realized that he didn't need to be holding a bare blade in his current mind-state. He folded his arms. "How so?"

"My parents littered my future with objects of power, even though they never openly explained any of that to me. In fact, they lied their asses off about it. But they put people and events in place that were designed to kind of bump me in the right direction. Like a series of tests. I bitch and moan about all of their secrets and lies, but despite my frustrations, I'm pretty fucking pleased to learn that they had good intentions in mind."

He nodded, listening. "I see your dilemma. It's all about which wolf you want to feed—anger or gratitude."

I snapped my fingers, pointing at him. "Yes! That. It's taken me a long time to really wrap my head around it all. To get my emotions out of the way so that I could actually see the benefits to what they did rather than wallowing in my own self-pity." I shrugged, letting out a breath and lightly bumping the back of my head against the wall. "Just curious if you went through some shit that others wouldn't understand. From a different perspective than me, but kind of similar."

He studied me warily, likely surprised that we had spoken so long without me pranking him, harassing him, or otherwise delivering some news that was guaranteed to give him a migraine—which was a fair point. I found immense pleasure in tormenting Achilles, but only because I respected him so much.

"Sure," he finally rasped. "Every single person in the world knows that my fucking heel is made of glass, figuratively speaking. Every single time I get into a fight, guess where they always attack first? Every time I get into an argument, guess what joke they always resort to? It's goddamned embarrassing for everyone to know your greatest weakness. I damn near had an anxiety disorder about it, to be honest. But back then, no one knew what the hell an anxiety disorder was," he grunted, chuckling mirthlessly. "So, I forced myself to train harder, fight more ruthlessly, anything to make up for my weakness. Anything to get them to stop laughing at me. Then, at night, I drank and fucked myself to oblivion to hide from my shame."

I glanced over at him sidelong. "How do you fuck yourself to oblivion?" I asked seriously.

He blinked, and then burst out laughing. "Okay, I screwed as many women as possible, and drank as much as my body would allow," he clarified, rolling his eyes.

I nodded, thinking about it. "That sounds shitty."

Silence stretched between us for so long that I finally glanced over at him. He was grinning, and the moment my eyes met his, he shook his head in disappointment. "You missed it. I bet myself five bucks that you, of all people, would catch it."

I sighed, glancing down at my feet. "Five bucks? That's it?"

He shrugged. "The bar hasn't been open for a while."

I nodded. "Okay. I was trying to see if *you* understood it, but I can explain it if you want. For five bucks."

He narrowed his eyes doubtfully, his smile fading. "Deal."

I took a deep breath. "With everyone knowing what your weakness was, you actually had the biggest goddamned advantage of any other warrior on the field. Every opponent you faced was essentially crippled—with false overconfidence—and they didn't even know it. I wouldn't be surprised if you told me that every single fight you've had was ridiculously easy."

He was dead silent, proving that my words had struck a chord, but I didn't look over at him.

"Not easy because your combat skills were so superior—which I know they are. And not easy because their combat skills were so inferior—which I know they weren't. But because when they faced you, all they saw was a shining glass target, something they could easily shatter, and that made them all ridiculously *predictable*. In essence, all you had to do was master the ability to counterattack any offensive move aimed at your heel, and your legendary reputation would have probably still been as good as it is now. Because each opponent faced you with only one thing on their mind—break the heel. And since you *knew* that, you always knew what they were going to *do*. They might as well have been blind, first-year trainees, no matter how strong or badass they were against any other opponent on the field. Against any other warrior, they would have been forced to think, but against you…their eagerness and emotions took over, leaving you an easy victory." My words echoed in the room, and I could sense Achilles staring at me incredulously. "Now, where is my five bucks?"

He grunted. "I'll apply it to your tab, asshole."

I dipped my chin graciously. "Thanks."

He studied me warily, leaning against the counter. "You didn't come in here to tell me that. What's really on your mind? Because I know the look in a man's eyes when he's taking a calculated gamble—the eyes of a general. I've seen what those men can do. How every domino is purposely set up, waiting for that last flick to put it all into play, even though his own soldiers doubt him until he makes that last move."

I nodded. "In essence, my parents strengthened me offensively. You and Baldur were strengthened defensively. So all those 'lucky' moments I just said that you experienced…well, I have those too. Just from a different perspective. Everyone is always looking at me to do the big, loud, obnoxious hocus pocus stuff, and they always act surprised when I win against opponents who should have handily beaten me. They don't understand that I never *just* do the big loud magic. I usually have a dozen aces up my sleeve that are specifically designed to counterattack what I already know they are going to do. Now, that doesn't mean I'm doing it all on purpose or that I'm that much of a badass. I've been really fucking lucky. No question. I should have died a dozen times over by now. But I am starting to believe that some subconscious part of me has always known about my figurative glass heel. I think it's just taken me longer to learn about it than it took you."

He shook his head. "That's not all of it. Spill, or the boys are going to wonder why we're taking so long in here."

I snorted, wondering how to phrase my thoughts as carefully as possible while still getting the answers I wanted...

"Given the pros and cons of our polar-opposite, but similar, backgrounds, would you want to change anything? If you could go back and tell your mother to make a different choice, would you?"

He thought about it for almost ten seconds. "No. It was worth it. And not just because it made me a badass. I've spent centuries fighting other warriors, and it was very rare that I encountered anyone who knew their own flaws and strengths as well as I knew mine. My mother's curse was a blessing in a way she never intended. Without that obstacle of overcoming my own legend, I might have just skated by, drunk on my own victories—winding up as just another dead soldier on the pages of history. My mother's overprotectiveness *directly* failed, since everyone knew of it. But *indirectly*, it saved my life."

I nodded. "I'm not sure Baldur is so enlightened. He seems dead set on taking Odin down, and I had a really nasty feeling about him the moment we met. To be honest, I purposely pressed his buttons, hoping that he would be more like you, but I'm entirely certain he is nothing like you. He celebrates his invulnerability, thinking it makes him better than everyone. He's an entitled know-it-all, and does not respect his own weakness."

"You picked a fight with him, didn't you?"

I shrugged. "Best way to test a man."

Achilles nodded. "True," he admitted. "Well, whatever it is that you're doing, I can tell that you don't want to talk about it just yet. I'll admit I'm damned curious, though. If there is anything I can do to help, just ask."

I nodded. "Thanks. But I do have one other question."

"Shoot."

"Did your mother really do it?" I asked.

He stared back at me for a few moments, and then a wolfish smile split his cheeks. "I've been waiting my entire life to hear someone ask that..." he whispered, shaking his head.

I shrugged. "Kind of seems like an obvious question. So many people know about your heel…and they also know how successful you've been in battle—each backs up the other. It almost seems like propaganda." I swiped my hand in a gesture that encompassed the building we stood in. "Exhibit A—look at what you called your bar. Another reminder for everyone to see. A subliminal reminder."

He smirked. "Allegedly."

"Hypothetically, I could argue that if you had won a few big fights, and then started a rumor that your *only* weakness was your heel…that would be a pretty good way to turn fiction into fact, or myth into history. Each successive victory would only further cement your claim and, pretty soon, everyone would take it as fact. The more that legend grew, the hungrier the other warriors would become—the more *emotionally invested* they would become—to take you down, meaning every single one of them would be gunning for your heel, even if only to disprove the legend. And as long as you knew how to protect your heel, defeating them all would be like stealing candy from a baby." Achilles nodded, grinning from ear-to-ear. "So. Is it true? Did your mother really dip you in the River Styx?"

He took a deep breath and finally sighed. "That's the irony of it all. Whether she really did it or not doesn't even matter—the rumor alone *made* it true." He chuckled, shaking his head.

I smirked. "And there is only one way to prove it."

He grinned boyishly. "Also true. But since we're being honest with each other, and you gave me this fancy knife, I won't string you along. I swear on my Name that it's the truth—my mother dipped me in the River Styx."

"But the rumor would have had the same effect."

He nodded. "Absolutely—as long as I won those first fights in an epic fashion. As long as I put on a good show."

I nodded along, straightening from the wall. "Thanks, Achilles. You didn't have to tell me any of that, and I'll keep it in confidence. We better get back."

"No problem, Temple. No problem. Felt good to talk about it, as a matter of fact." He winked. "Or fiction."

I grunted, rolling my eyes. I exited the restroom first, only to find War leaning against the wall, holding a cigar cutter to a thick, aromatic cigar. "A word, Hope."

"As long as that cutter is only for your cigar, sure."

He smiled, looking me in the eyes as he chopped the tip off.

Achilles walked out a few moments later, pretending to dry his hands. He saw War, dipped his head with a curious frown, and then kept on walking. "Smoke out back, asshole. I'm closing up and going home."

War grunted and motioned me to follow him out the back exit.

This ought to be interesting, I thought to myself, as I followed him out the door.

CHAPTER 22

War lit his cigar with an old-school Zippo lighter, puffing contentedly for a few moments. Then he leaned against the brick wall, staring up at the dark sky. The streets were damp, but at least it wasn't still raining. It was definitely chilly, though. It was December, and Missouri could be surprisingly cold one day, and alarmingly warm the next.

It was late, but we still had a few more hours until dawn. Surprisingly, I didn't feel as tired as I thought I should have. I'd slept in until late afternoon today, anticipating that the warehouse fiasco and my summoning of Loki would take a while.

They hadn't, but a slew of other things had filled up the time.

"I heard you talking to Achilles," War said without preamble.

"Oh?" I said, as casually as possible. I leaned back against the wall beside him. "Achilles probably wants that to remain private, which is why I spoke to him privately, where people wouldn't overhear," I said, shooting him a pointed look. "Or eavesdrop."

War chuckled, licking his lips and then spitting out a few flecks of tobacco. "That wasn't the part I was most interested in, but your analysis was very clever, and spot on. You did well. So well that he didn't even realize your true purpose. You made him think it was all about him, or all about you, when neither was true. Bravo. That is the second interesting thing you've done to catch my attention tonight."

I arched an eyebrow, keeping my face blank. "I don't know what you're getting at, but I'm all ears."

"The second thing was applesauce, by the way."

Inwardly, I cursed Gunnar, but nothing showed on my face.

"I pressed Gunnar a little bit, and I unearthed a treasure trove of glittering, golden lies."

I sighed. "Gunnar is strung out these days, but especially tonight."

War nodded. "His pups. He mentioned it. Never heard of such a thing, for what it's worth." He glanced over at me, taking a few deep puffs of his cigar, staring deeply into my eyes. I was pretty sure he inhaled. Hardcore. "You don't know me as well as you know Death. We've only really talked the one time, and that was on the eve of your war with the Greeks."

I nodded, remembering it well. He'd given me some advice that had been hard to digest. But it had been good advice, in the long run.

"I think we should spend some time together, Horseman to Horseman," he suggested. "A large part of training is just camaraderie. Brotherhood. So you can call this training, or you can call it hanging out."

"And if I don't want to hang out right now?"

"Then you can call it training," he said, puffing on his cigar.

"Maybe you've just had too much to drink—"

"Maybe I'm not really War. That would be alarming, wouldn't it?"

I froze, taking a sudden step back. Loki. Shit.

He puffed on his cigar, not having moved a muscle. "That's called a bluff and a tell. I'm pretty good at poker, you know. Most Generals are."

I studied him suspiciously. "Prove it."

He shrugged, resting his boot up against the wall. "You can sense my Mask if you try hard enough. They resonate with each other. Well, they kind of repel each other."

I focused on my Mask, and then focused on the man beside me. After a moment, I felt a faint magnetic attraction. Except he was right, it was almost how two magnets repelled each other if the wrong polar ends were close—not as strong, but as if a faint buffer existed between our Masks.

With Alucard's Mask, it was the opposite feeling. They hardcore attracted each other.

I leaned back against the wall, letting out a breath, realizing he'd gotten me with his bluff, which meant he purposely referenced the illusion comment, knowing that it meant something.

"How did you know?" Then I frowned uneasily. "Does anyone else know?"

He shook his head. "I don't even think Death noticed, but he was too focused on getting home to Othello. And he already trusts you, sees you as a friend. We haven't bonded like that yet, and I usually look very closely at people—especially my friends."

"You want to chaperone or something? Is that it?"

He coughed, laughing mid-inhale. "No," he said, coughing a few more times. "I want to hang out. I'm intrigued in how you chose to handle this. Your first conflict after naming all four of your crew, and you only let one of them into your inner circle. I guess you could say I'm curious." He spat again, clearing his throat. "And you need training," he suggested. "Since you don't have Grimm at hand, I figured one of us old dogs might be of assistance."

I sighed tiredly, trying to think of a justifiable excuse. The fewer people who knew about my plans, the better. That was the power behind my deal with Loki. Utter chaos.

"What do you think you know?" I finally asked.

He thought about it for a few moments and finally grunted. "I won't say any names, of course, but I think you're playing magician."

I frowned, feeling the hair on the back of my neck stand up. That was... exactly how I'd come up with my plan. "Meaning?"

"It's all about the distraction. Look here, look there. Oh, you're right next to me? Then look over here. Oh, you're far away, then look at the flashing lights and smoke machines. In fact, why not just look at all the distractions while I do my trick right in front of you." He glanced at me, gauging my reaction, but I kept my face blank. "You're making smoke like your life depends on it. All so that no one sees the obvious. In fact, you've even done a few obvious tricks—also as misdirects—to catch the overconfident members of the audience. And you're hiding tricks within other tricks, sending everyone off in different directions. You've got several distractions and several tricks for every individual who might be watching. The only person who knows the truth is the magician's assistant, and I'm pretty sure even he doesn't know *everything*."

I sighed, nodding. "I didn't realize it was so obvious. It seemed to be working."

He grunted, turning to face me directly. "Oh, no. You're killing it. They don't have any idea. Hell, you even had me baffled for a while. Until I heard about the applesauce and your talk with Achilles." He chuckled. "And I'm impressed enough to admit that you may even be pulling the wool over *my* eyes, making me think I have you figured out. Which is why I'm insisting that I tag along until your performance is over."

I realized I was smiling, nodding along. "Applesauce gave it away?" I asked, surprised.

"A General—the good ones anyway—are magicians, too. We're also gamblers. Applesauce led me down the proper path, but there is only one way to see if I'm right. But I will openly admit that you might be a lot more dangerous than I ever thought—and I thought you were plenty dangerous back when I first saw you in this bar," he said, pointing a thumb at Achilles' Heel behind us. "When you sucker punched that Angel right out the goddamned door! But then when you were completely out of magic, all your allies gone, and you somehow convinced Death to let you borrow his *horse*? Fuck *me*!" he breathed, his eyes twinkling excitedly. "The balls on this guy! You fucking *died* to save his future girlfriend. And then you came back and roasted your enemy's soul on a fire! Yeah, Temple, you're fucking dangerous. You're the fucking *Omega*, in my opinion."

I stared at him, stunned. I…wasn't sure if I had ever felt so proud to earn another man's respect.

"Thanks. And I'd appreciate your help. I might need it more than I first thought, to be honest."

"I'd recommend caution in your trust," War said, puffing on his cigar. "Not that you need to hear that or anything. But I'd check that Horseman bond each and every time you see us. If one of us—Alucard or myself—even steps away to piss, you better check who *really* comes back. I know I will. We can't afford any mischief," he said meaningfully.

I nodded. "You read my mind. I've been doing that with Alucard already, but I should make sure he's doing the same in case someone tries to impersonate *me*."

As if on cue, Alucard walked out the back exit to the bar. The door slammed shut behind him, followed by the sound of a dozen deadbolts slamming into place. Alucard muttered darkly under his breath before he spotted us leaning against the brick wall. He sauntered over, looking more alert than before.

I took a moment to sense his Mask, verifying it was the real Alucard. I let out a faint sigh of relief and smiled at him.

"I think that beer shower did the trick," he said. "Or the three energy drinks. Either way, I feel much better. Achilles made me help clean up before he would tell me where you went."

I chuckled. "Where is everyone else?"

"Gunnar and Death already left. Told me to hitch a ride with you."

He glanced at War, discreetly shooting me a look when the Horseman wasn't looking. I nodded. "He's clued in."

Alucard arched an eyebrow. "Oh. I thought—"

Out of nowhere, a glass bottle struck the wall behind us, and I felt a dull thump deep in my chest—like a shockwave rolling out from the point of impact.

And with the sensation, my power was immediately sucked out of me— all magic of any flavor whatsoever.

I gripped my necklace on instinct and froze. "Holy shit," I breathed, spinning to glance at War and Alucard. Their hands had also shot to their Horseman Masks. Alucard's face went slack and he shook his head. He abruptly opened his mouth wide, and I saw the muscles on his neck straining. But his fangs didn't pop out.

"Um. I can't get it up," he said, his eyes darting about the parking lot. I hadn't really noticed, but there were a dozen or so cars parked nearby. An adjacent building looked like some kind of apartment complex, so I was betting Achilles shared the lot with the tenants.

Nothing moved in the darkness, the area only illuminated by one dim yellow streetlamp.

I reached into my satchel, and my hand struck the bottom, finding it empty. My eyes widened in disbelief. "That's…not possible," I hissed, scraping my fingers across an interior I had never felt before—because the Darling and Dear satchel was bottomless.

War narrowed his eyes, gritted his teeth, and flexed his fists at his side. He shook his head minutely, letting me know that his Mask was also useless as his eyes tracked the parking lot. He sniffed at the air, and I noticed a strong earthy smell. For some reason, it made me think of a cold…spiciness —like that sensation from those muscle rub ointments but not minty.

"Motherfucking witches," War cursed.

As if amused by his words, cackling laughter suddenly surrounded us from the perimeter of the parking lot, resembling a pack of hyenas.

They definitely outnumbered us, which was always fun.

CHAPTER 23

𝓐lucard grunted. "Damn. No sparkle power either," he said, glaring at the shadowy lot, suddenly noticing just how many hiding spots there were. "What do you think they want?"

"I doubt they're selling cookies," I muttered. Then I remembered the call from Niko that I had ignored. "Pretty sure they want me dead," I growled. "If they were anything but assassins, they would have made their demands after safely nullifying our powers."

"I agree," War said.

"He's a clever boy, isn't he?" one of the cackling voices taunted in a strange accent—definitely European, but I couldn't place it. And I didn't see her anywhere, obviously hiding from us to make sure we didn't have any weapons or guns.

"Assassins," Alucard muttered. "Creepy Euro assassins."

I nodded. Then I turned to War, speaking low so as not to be overheard. "Crews like this have been hunting me lately, but the group we took down earlier tonight had incredibly bad luck. Maybe the witches heard about that and are trying to even the playing field."

"Let's not rely on their bad luck," War said dryly. "I always assume that half of my plans will fail. Then I incorporate those anticipated failures into a *new* plan."

I nodded, remaining vigilant in case any of the witches grew bold. "Let's find a way out of their death trap or we will be stuck playing defense while they pick us apart. I bet they used an expanding circle, but I have no idea how big of a radius it has," I said, thinking out loud. "If we can get out of it, we can fight back. We just need to make it to the SUV—"

"Gunnar took it, remember?" Alucard interrupted. "Said he had an early meeting with the FBI guys tomorrow. Which is actually only a few hours from now."

"Shit," I cursed, having forgotten all about that. "If we can get out of their spell, I can make a Gateway."

"We're either ass-hauling or car-stealing," Alucard said.

"Car," I said, scanning the abysmal selection before us—half of the vehicles were damaged or broken down with slipshod repairs. One was even on concrete blocks. A food truck stood at the back of the lot, and I noticed a large circular object on the roof, but I couldn't tell what it was since the dim streetlight didn't reach it.

Achilles' Heel wasn't in a necessarily thriving part of town, but I did see a few promising potentials. "I bet they have more of those nullification brews to throw at us once we escape *this* area," I said, waving a hand. "They'll just keep moving the trap on us. That's what I would—"

"Duck!" War shouted, shoving me into Alucard as he dove the opposite direction. A glass vial struck the ground in an explosive *thump* that shattered the glass in every nearby vehicle and sent me and Alucard slamming into the side of a sedan.

I climbed to my knees, ignoring the piercing ringing sound in my ears, and then used the bumper of the car to pull myself the rest of the way up. The force of the blast had tricked open the locking mechanism on the trunk so that it had sprung up, and I found myself staring at a long duffle bag full of sports gear.

Lacrosse sticks stuck out of the unzipped end, and I wasted no time snatching them up. I shoved one into Alucard's hands, startling him.

"Catch and counter!" I snapped, holding my stick up.

He blinked at me, shaking his head. I saw a drop of blood hanging from his earlobe and cursed, checking my own. Yep. Same.

He said something to me, snatching up the lacrosse stick, but I couldn't hear his voice over the ringing in my ears.

The blast had deafened us. Hopefully, not permanently.

I spotted War waving his arms at us to catch our attention. Once we turned to look, he shoved his head inside the broken window of a car, and I watched him frantically checking for keys. It only took him a second before he extracted himself, glanced up to check for any inbound witch bombs, and then he moved on to the next car.

I turned to see Alucard nod at War's suggestion before checking the front seat of the red sedan I'd just pillaged. I kept my eyes out, ready to catch anything else they threw at us, and hopefully throw it right back up their warty noses. I hadn't realized how much I relied upon my hearing until it had been taken away. So my gaze darted back and forth frantically, terrified that I might miss something.

I caught motion out of the corner of my eye and lunged out with the lacrosse stick to catch it.

I missed.

The blast sent me into a coughing fit, but at least it didn't physically throw me anywhere or burn me to ashes. Although I did suddenly feel ridiculously dizzy, having to focus all of my attention on not falling down as the parking lot tilted crazily.

Which was when the *second* glass vial hit the car behind me—only missing me because I'd stumbled forward, almost tripping over my own two feet as I fought to remain upright.

This time, the blast sent me flying through the air, but not before washing over me in an icy splash that felt like I'd been hit with the world's coldest water balloon. The chill leeched into my very bones so fast that when I hit a hard metal surface a few seconds later, I didn't feel that much pain—just a sudden halt to my aerial flight.

I sat on the ground, slightly dazed, but thankful that my balance was more easily managed with my ass firmly rooted to the ground. The frigid chill began to fade, so I assumed it had been an area spell, no longer affecting me the moment I left the impact zone. Alucard came sprinting up to me, but he dove over my shoulder rather than helping me to my feet.

I now heard a distant roaring sound combining with the ringing sound in my ears, and I found myself hoping that it was a positive development—because I still couldn't hear anything that was actually happening around me.

I looked up to see that War stood out in the open with his cigar firmly wedged between his teeth, looking like a lunatic as he violently shook a lacrosse stick in one hand. He then began to spin in rapid quarter-circles, swiping his stick spastically as if he was trying to swat down an elusive bumblebee.

The ringing in my ears seemed to be slowly fading, but the lack of voices made the whole thing strangely surreal, like I was watching one of those old silent black and white films.

War abruptly lunged to the side and caught an unidentified flying object, bringing his lacrosse stick back to ride the momentum so the fragile glass didn't explode in the net on the end of his stick. Then he whipped it forward with a suspiciously smooth grace, flinging it at—

I blinked.

A goddamned quidditch player was hovering on a broom about ten feet above a car. She wore leather pants and a flowing top, and she was hauntingly beautiful—with harsh cheekbones and long blonde hair. She looked like she should have been starting her first year of college.

War's return-volley struck her in that perfect *face*—again, with absolutely no sound that I could discern—and she instantly erupted in flames, her mouth flaring wide in a noiseless shriek. She crashed atop the car, thrashing and flailing, burning brighter and brighter before simply exploding into smoke.

War was waving his lacrosse stick victoriously and puffing on the cigar still clamped in his teeth. He suddenly whipped his head around to stare over my shoulder, and I noticed an unhealthy splash of unrepentant madness in those Horseman eyes. Then he pointed his stick over my shoulder, pumped his fist, and began pounding my way, the tip of his cigar glowing brighter as he drew closer, trailing a thick streamer of smoke behind him like a coal—burning train.

Something suddenly grabbed my shoulder, yanked me back, and lifted me up. I instantly began swinging my fists, startled by the sudden movement since I still couldn't hear anything but the ringing and roaring sound in my ears.

My foe swatted my hands away before shoving me in a new direction. I slid on my ass along a cold metal surface before bumping into a cheap wall that gave slightly under my weight. Boxes rained down on top of me, burying me instantly, and my sense of hearing continued its slow return.

I started kicking my feet, desperate to break free of my prison and kick some witch ass, but the ground suddenly shifted, sending me and the boxes sliding forward to strike yet another wall.

"Hold on!" Alucard shouted, sounding like he was far away.

I swatted at the boxes, trying to get a look at what the hell kind of carnival ride I was on. A moment of clarity showed me that I was in the back of what looked like the food truck, Alucard was behind the wheel, and War was clambering up through a large hatch in the ceiling.

Then Alucard floored it, and I went tumbling into the back of the food truck again, smashing through some of the boxes.

"This is fucking ridiculous! Let me fucking get my bearings!" I shouted, swinging wildly to get free of the boxes and boxes of…

I froze, blinking.

"Donuts?" I asked, staring down at the pink frosting covering my fingers and hands. More frosting covered my jacket and jeans in a rainbow of fingerpaints and smudges. I even had a few smashed donuts stuck to my sleeve.

Alucard swerved, but I managed to catch my balance this time, kicking my way clear of the rest of the baked goods. War was entirely out of the food truck now, surfing up top to battle the witches with his lacrosse stick, apparently.

I tried to use my magic, but it was still no use. We must not have gotten very far yet. My hearing was coming back with a vengeance, because I could hear sirens, shouting, cackling laughter, and War screaming from beyond the open hatch. I stumbled towards the massive windshield and crouched down beside Alucard, slapping him on the thigh.

"Hey! Can you hear me?" I shouted.

"God damn!" he hissed, swerving sharply in surprise. "I'm right next to you!" he snapped, getting the truck back under control.

"Good. What the hell happened?"

"I was running over to help you when I saw the fucking keys just hanging from the ignition. I jumped over you to make sure the engine actually worked and then I hauled your ass inside." He glanced down and snatched at my sleeve, plucking off a semi-squished chocolate glazed donut. "My favorite!"

I swatted it out of his hand right as he tried to take a bite. "Donuts are for closers, and you haven't gotten us out of this mess yet."

He hissed at me—which was remarkably un-frightening since his fangs still weren't working.

"How many witches are left?" I asked, not spotting any through the windshield, but still hearing their cackling laughter all around us and War's shouts as the truck roared along at a blazingly fast forty miles per hour.

"I think there are three more, but I didn't get a good look. Why don't you go up top or lean out the door so you can start throwing magic as soon as we get out of this damned anti-supernatural zone."

I nodded, choosing the floor-to-ceiling entrance and stairs that Alucard had used to haul me inside in the first place—which resembled the sliding, folding doors and stairs on most public buses. It was better than risking my life up top with nothing to hold onto for support.

I found a lacrosse stick on the floor and scooped it up. While I gripped a support rail with one hand, I descended the stairs and wedged my feet firmly into place for additional security.

Then I leaned my head out the open bus door for a quick glance and froze, ignoring the cool wind whipping at my hair.

A witch sat on her broom, hovering about six feet to my right and a few feet above my head, keeping pace with the food truck. She, too, was beautiful—and practically a spitting image of the one who had caught fire outside the bar—except she wore a dated black dress with striped tights. She hadn't seen me yet, and her feet hung low enough for me to reach with my lacrosse stick.

It was my lucky day.

CHAPTER 24

I watched as she glared hatefully at War on top of the truck, hurling a small glass bottle and instantly cursing as she obviously missed.

But hitting her with my stick wouldn't be enough to get rid of her, so I hesitated, trying to think of something helpful I could do without my magic.

I watched as she tugged on a strap hanging across her chest, and a freaking Kalashnikov plopped into her hands. Without thinking—and before she could bear down on War—I snagged her foot with the net on my lacrosse stick and yanked down as hard as I could.

She shrieked, releasing the weapon to snatch onto the broom, which thankfully remained level with the top of the truck. I'd expected it to swoop underneath her to save her.

I craned my neck towards Alucard. "I snagged one!" I shouted. "Find something to hit! They have freaking machine guns!"

He grinned wickedly. "Construction zone!" he laughed, pointing ahead through the windshield. And he began slowly angling the truck towards a bunch of cones, concrete dividers, and heavy machinery parked on the shoulder.

But bullets suddenly peppered the windshield as a second witch noticed her partner's plight, darting ahead of our truck and maintaining the same speed. Another identical clone. What the hell? She sat backwards on her broom, grinning darkly as she continued to fly in front of—and a safe distance above—our food truck, taking careful aim with her machine gun...

At me.

Rather than freak out, I very pointedly blew her a big fat kiss. Her smile faltered, and she whipped her head around just in time to get a very close look at the huge, green, overhead traffic sign.

It decapitated her without even suffering a dent, but her blood splattered across the passenger side of the windshield, making it impossible for me to see anything without looming over Alucard's shoulder. A moment later, the truck ran over something big and squishy, and I had to fight to keep hold of my lacrosse stick as my witch screamed bloody murder, cursing in a strange language.

"This truck isn't passing a health inspection anytime soon," Alucard murmured.

I held on tightly to the lacrosse stick and the squawking witch I'd snared, frowning uneasily as I realized that we were no longer the only ones on the road. I spotted a baseball cap on the dashboard and cringed at the slogan.

Show-Me Your O-Face.

The logo was a crude stick figure with arms and fingers outstretched, its body shaped like the State of Missouri, and it had a large frosted donut for a head.

I would never be able to read our state's nickname—*The Show-Me State*—with the same level of pride I'd once had. The logo and slogan were forever imprinted directly onto my brain.

But as I considered the growing number of cars, the fast-approaching police sirens, the wide-open door that gave every passing vehicle a full-body glamour shot of Nate Temple restraining a helpless woman with a lacrosse stick, and the fact that Gunnar had just told the FBI that I was overseas...

I snatched up the hat and slapped it on, tugging the bill down as low as possible. The witch began to fight harder, kicking her feet wildly as she began to lose her grip on the broom. I tugged right back, hoping to dislodge her and send her crashing to the asphalt and directly under one of our tires, but she was resilient.

Alucard suddenly switched lanes, almost sending me falling out the door, but I managed to catch myself and maintain my grip on the stick. I stared out the door, confused to suddenly see us slowly passing a starter home sitting on a trailer.

"Shit. Police coming in hot behind us," Alucard cursed. "We might have a minute before they're on top of us."

And that's when my magic suddenly woke back up inside me.

Jesus. That had been one hell of a potion to cover such a large area. These witches hadn't been messing around. I heard War shouting excitedly, obviously getting his powers back too. I also heard more gunfire from the other side of the food truck.

I stared back out at the yellow starter home and a truly sinister thought slithered into my brain. "Pace this truck. Don't pass it!" I snapped at Alucard.

I ignored his sudden protests as I wedged my hip up against the end of the lacrosse stick, pinning it between me and the frame of the truck's opening. Then I drew deep on my magic, filling myself to the brim. Once confident that I held slightly more than I thought I would actually need—just to be safe—I flung out a hand towards the starter home, latching onto the roof with a cord of air stronger than a hundred ropes of braided steel.

The beautiful young witch stared at me in horror and I grinned, lifting up my other hand to aim at the tires on the side of the trailer.

"Show-Me Your O-Face, witch!" I screamed at her.

And I let loose great balls of fire at the tires, rocking the house downward at a sharp angle as the tires exploded and the rims slammed into the pavement with a shower of sparks. I simultaneously yanked down on my cord of air, using the momentum from the tilted trailer to bring the starter home crashing down onto the witch, squishing her onto the pavement.

"What the fuck!" Alucard screamed.

I hurled a razor-sharp blast of air at the tow-hitch connecting the truck to the totaled trailer, not wanting the driver to crash, and let out a sigh of relief as the truck wobbled dangerously but maintained control. He did slam on his brakes, though.

I slapped a hand over my hat and leaned out to look back and witness the results of my hard work.

And—I shit you not—I saw a pair of witch legs sticking out from beneath the house as it came to a grinding halt.

War suddenly leaned over from the roof to stare down at me, his red hair whipping in the wind. "Did you just drop a house on her?" he asked incredulously.

"Damn right I did!" I said smugly.

He burst out laughing. "I took mine out, but those cops are awfully close. The house will slow them down, but there's no way we can outrun them in this hunk of junk."

"If you give me a minute, I can make a Gateway and get us the hell out of here. That house thing was a doozy."

He disappeared for a moment and then leaned back over from the roof to stare down at me. "There's a giant donut on top of our truck. It's barely hanging on after one of those witch bombs hit it."

I grinned, imagining sending a giant donut rolling down the street towards a cavalry of police vehicles. "Perfect. Break it free in ten seconds, and then get your ass down here as fast as you can!"

He disappeared, and I quickly turned to Alucard. "Are you flooring it?" I asked him, counting down in my head.

He nodded stiffly. "I'm giving it all she's got."

"Okay. Keep it up but be ready to stop as fast as you can without killing us in the process."

He shot me a panicked look, but nodded, tightening his fingers on the wheel.

Three...two...one...

I heard a metallic *clang*, the sound of tearing metal, and then a heavy scraping sound across the roof.

And then a crash as the donut struck the road.

War dropped through the roof with a big grin on his face. "It's rolling right for the police! Between the house and the donut, they don't know what to do!" he shouted, laughing so hard that tears were leaking down his face—or maybe that was from the wind as he fought up top, because his mess of red hair looked like a second-hand batch of cotton candy.

"Stop the truck, Alucard. I'm making a Gateway to get us the hell out of here."

The truck was heavy, so it took a few seconds to come to an uncomfortable, but manageable, stop, and I hopped out of the truck, making sure to keep my hat tugged low as I urged the others to hurry. I ripped open a Gateway as fast as I could, hesitating only a moment before I chose a safe destination.

The cars all around us had already stopped to stare at the insanity we had caused—some of them had even gotten out of their vehicles.

But the moment that ring of fire erupted in the middle of the road, they gained a whole new level of respect for the food truck's slogan.

"Show-Me Your O-Face," I chuckled, and then I stepped through my Gateway with Alucard and War hot on my heels.

I let it wink shut and sank to my butt, laughing so hard that I quickly decided to fall all the way down and spread my arms wide.

War and Alucard sat down beside me, and my laughter must have been contagious, because soon we were all laying in the grass, staring up at the Temple Mausoleum in the Bellefontaine Cemetery.

I licked my lips and tasted frosting, sending me into another giggling fit. I glanced down at my chest to see a chocolate glazed donut stuck to the collar of my jacket.

"Hey, Glampire. Donuts are for closers," I said, holding it out to him.

He grunted and snatched it from my grasp.

"That's disgusting," War said, trying to catch his breath and stop laughing.

"I don't even care," Alucard said, his mouth obviously full. "Mmmmmm. It's so fucking delicious."

"SHOW-ME YOUR O-FACE!" I crowed, throwing my hat up into the air. My shout echoed through the darkened garden of the dead, fertilizing it with a little bit of laughter, a little bit of luck, and a whole lot of life.

After a long silence, War cleared his throat. "I hope you guys wear a large," he said, "because I picked up some t-shirts."

Alucard choked on his donut.

CHAPTER 25

I had told War and Alucard that I wanted to clear my head and get some fresh air, leaving them to explore the inside of the mausoleum for themselves. I'd tried calling Niko to apologize for not answering my phone and to thank her for trying to warn me about the witches.

But my call had gone straight to voicemail. I shot her a text instead, hoping she'd see it whenever she turned her phone back on.

I had wanted to lay low for a while before returning home or parting ways with my crew to get some rest. Because I didn't want to lead any other witches back to Chateau Falco if there had actually been more than the four we killed. And with the FBI coming to my mansion in the next few hours, I couldn't very well walk through the front door.

Regardless, I felt surprisingly energetic, bolstered by the extra sleep I'd gotten the day before. If I tried to go to sleep right now, I'd probably just stare up at the ceiling for a few hours and have a stagnation-induced panic attack.

It had been a last-second decision to come *here*, though. With the FBI so interested in speaking to me, I also hadn't wanted to risk going to my bookstore, Plato's Cave, assuming that it was likely under surveillance. Also, Othello and Death were shacking up there since they'd essentially moved into my old loft above the store.

Hello, plan B—boys sleepover in a cemetery. The Temple Mausoleum was as safe as a castle, and it was highly unlikely that any of my enemies would think to search for me in a cemetery. I was essentially hiding in the place where my enemies wanted to *ultimately send me*.

Heh. How genius was that?

But I couldn't deny that I also had another reason for wanting to come here. Starlight's comments about Elders had gotten under my skin, even though he'd admitted to being stoned when he'd said them. Because the tree at Chateau Falco was a Gateway to the Elders' realm and it hadn't stopped bleeding for weeks, which seemed like a bad omen of epic proportions. And suddenly Yggdrasil had a matching owie—only with blue blood.

So, what were the Elders up to, and what did it have to do with Yggdrasil?

Unfortunately, I couldn't place my finger on exactly what it was that had bothered me about Starlight's cryptic comments. They had been so abstract and vague. Still, the fact that he'd chosen to say them at all made me think that time was of the essence.

Which was why I'd come outside for fresh air—to think.

In my opinion, thinking often required drinking, and a particularly fine libation was my favorite lubrication for stubborn frontal lobe rejuvenation.

Braining was a demanding science, not for the faint of liver.

So I had opened a tiny Gateway back to my office in Chateau Falco—large enough to reach through and grab a bottle of Macallan that I remembered placing on my bookshelf.

As I took a healthy swig straight from the bottle, I replayed Starlight's words about the Elders in my mind, analyzing them from various angles.

They're stuck at the bottom of a well, praying. They have answers, but they're scared of the questions...

The only wells I had stumbled across were the three beneath Yggdrasil, and given how terrified the Norse pantheon was of the Elders, I doubted the Aesir would lease out one of their sacred pools to the scary reptiles.

Chains gave them freedom. Independence gave them banishment. Their temples grew dark and drafty, their prayers unanswered when their masters abandoned them.

The Elders seemed to have been slaves at one point, and freeing them from bondage had gone poorly for them—and everyone else in the supernatural community. I noticed the obvious reference to Temples and

Masters, but I didn't know what to make of it. Had an ancestral Master Temple once been their slave owner?

But that sounded doubtful, because I'd met some of my ancestors, and they'd practically soiled their pants upon hearing about my friendship with Carl.

But Carl *did* seem to worship me to some extent. Was that a result of *me*, personally?

Or my *bloodline*?

Who dares help the Elders? Who dares wear the bone crown? Not me. Not any god I know. Too risky.

I let out a frustrated sigh and took another swig from the bottle in my hand. Then I began to walk the perimeter of the two-story, architectural masterpiece.

The Temple Mausoleum.

The marble colossus was austere and imposing, but also breathtakingly mesmerizing. It had been designed in a way that equally represented the beauties of life, both the good and the bad, and it was a stark declaration that the Temple family didn't discriminate against other faiths. The upper tier was held aloft by thick Corinthian columns. Both levels were lined with exquisite carvings and statues of mythological and religious significance— from all cultures, faiths, and creeds. Fairies, monsters, gods, humans, and even symbols from just as many tongues—portraying a timeline of human history.

I squinted my eyes as I took the time to study each face, wondering which other gods might be currently hiding out in my city. Like a magnet, something in my city was apparently drawing every major pantheon to St. Louis, and I was pretty sure I was that magnet.

The Catalyst.

But I didn't have time to worry about that right now. It was high on my list of priorities, but preventing Ragnarök was slightly more important.

I saw a carving of Odin clutching his legendary spear, Gungnir, and I shook my head. There was not a kind feature on that face—not even a line of compassion. As much as he was revered in pop culture, Odin had a solid reputation for being an absolute prick. He'd seemed to mellow out some in recent years, but how far beneath the surface was the old Odin?

Athena—now dead—stood tall and strong, a portrait of wisdom and intelligence. She'd been corrupted somehow, and I'd been forced to kill her.

It felt like it had happened ten years ago. Still, I dipped my head in a respectful manner, honoring the goddess she had once been.

Anubis sat on a throne, holding a scepter of some kind, and I saw two jackals resting at his feet. I squinted my eyes, wondering if it was a clever way to depict Cerberus, the guard dog of the Underworld—three separate canines as opposed to one huge canine with three heads.

Zeus sat on a cloud, seeming to be studying a bolt of lightning in his lap with a puzzled frown on his face. I was pretty sure he'd watched me kill Athena, but I hadn't heard a single word about their pantheon playing present-day politics.

Maybe they had learned their lesson.

I continued walking, my thoughts drifting as I scanned more of the statues and carvings.

I'd learned a lot since I'd last been here. Met more gods and monsters. Learned more secrets.

And my parents were always hiding things out in the open. They'd revamped the security on the building to a ridiculous degree. I already knew that they'd hidden the Hand of God and the Hourglass here—two deadly artifacts that had saved my life on several occasions.

The Hourglass had just recently saved my life in Fae, allowing Pandora to give me the help I needed at the exact right time.

My parents had stolen it from the Fae Queens back before I was born, and it had the ability to control—to some extent—the time fluxes between Fae and Earth.

It was how I'd had the unique opportunity to grow up in Fae—spending an entire childhood there—before coming back to Chateau Falco to experience a *second* childhood on Earth, entirely unaware of my dual upbringing.

Until recently.

So, yeah. The Hourglass was powerful, and definitely worth an exorbitantly expensive security upgrade to the Temple Mausoleum where my parents had hidden it.

On that note, Pan had been very adamant about always keeping the Mausoleum safe and protected, even once choosing to stay behind and guard it when the door had been damaged in a fight that had left Tory injured and possibly dying. The mausoleum had been more important to him than my friend's life.

And Conquest had hinted at secrets within the mausoleum as well, but I wasn't sure if he had been speaking in a general fashion or specifically about *my* mausoleum.

The fallen always have lessons to impart, if one knows how to speak with the dead...the dead keep secrets, he had told me.

And then he'd very helpfully disappeared on me, the painfully beautiful bastard—the handsomest doctor the world had ever seen.

Given all these strange occurrences, I couldn't shake the feeling that there was some other secret to uncover here. Something big.

Because...bulletproof windows and a bank-vault entrance were more than *security*. They were *defenses*—intended to protect against an *assault*. Lethal booby traps would have made more sense if my parents were just wanting to guard some treasure. Maybe.

I sighed, taking another swig of liquor to prevent my brain from squealing and overheating.

A metallic flash in the air caught my attention and I instinctively jumped back a step. A coin landed in the grass by my feet, and I recognized the familiar gleam of Olympian gold.

CHAPTER 26

I scanned the statues before me, still twitchy about projectiles after my recent close encounters of the witch kind. "What is this?" I growled.

"A coin, naturally," a disappointed voice said from behind one of the statues.

I narrowed my eyes, trying to get a clear view of my guest. A pair of golden eyes gleamed back at me from one of the shadows, and a man slowly stepped forward in a way that signified no threat. And he was absently rolling a golden coin back and forth across his knuckles, making me think of a tiny golden Slinky toy—but without the penchant to spontaneously choose to operate according to the mysterious laws of quantum mechanics, and somehow get tangled up into a knot without human contact of any kind—like mine always had when I was a kid.

Was the Slinky tangled up beyond repair, or was it perfectly fine? Because *both* realities were simultaneously true until you looked down at it to manually check.

Not today, Schrö-Slinky.

He stepped entirely out from the safety of the statues and onto the grass, the wings on his sandals fluttering as fast and soft as a hummingbird's wings as they assisted his descent, allowing him to float down to the ground rather than merely *step*.

Hermes, the Greek Messenger God.

He was a tall, tan man with wavy, golden hair that brushed his shoulders, and he wore a pristine white toga with a gold metal belt around his waist. His golden irises glinted in the light of the moon like a reflection on a still pond. He was strong and ripped, but no one would have ever called him bulky. More like an endurance athlete who lifted more weights than most.

"Sweet purse," he said.

I narrowed my eyes, instantly ready to kill him as I proudly straightened it on my hip. If anyone should have called it by the right name, it was Hermes.

"It's a *satchel*, asshole," I growled.

"You're goddamned *right* it is!" he growled back, with an almost feral conviction to his tone as he clenched a fist and hoisted it in the air.

I took a deep breath and smiled, shaking my head. "You have no idea how annoying that gets," I finally said.

"You're kidding me, right?" he said dryly. "I was the first one to *name* it a satchel."

"You're satchel Jesus?" I whispered reverently, lifting a hand to my chest as if to calm my racing heart. "Oh, blessed be!"

He nodded in a saintly manner. "Peace be upon you, child."

I chuckled, happy to have a little easy banter, but deep down I was wondering why he was really here. After I'd killed Athena, the Greek pantheon of gods had gone radio silent—while it seemed that every other pantheon had suddenly chosen to rear their heads.

"Why are you here?" I asked, discreetly clenching my bottle of liquor in order to use it as a weapon in case he was here with bad news. I'd killed his sister, after all. He'd seemed understanding at the time, but I didn't buy into the old, oft-repeated adage—*time heals all wounds*.

In my opinion, *time opened old wounds*, was a more accurate assumption.

At least that was *my* take on it.

"You are gearing up to do something particularly dangerous," Hermes said, continuing to roll the coin across the backs of his knuckles the same way someone might drum their fingers atop their desk without realizing it. "I wanted to get an idea where your head is at."

"Why now? I've done plenty of dangerous things these last few years. Where have you been since Athena?" I said, not wanting to admit to whatever *particularly dangerous something* that he was referring to.

"After Athena, we were commanded to leave the Temple boy alone. To observe from a safe distance. Too many Greeks have forgotten their oaths after moving to St. Louis. They now seem to worship the godkiller."

"That's a management problem."

He shrugged. "That is your opinion. Zeus holds another."

"What is *your* opinion?"

He smiled, looking amused. "It is no secret that I have frequently favored mortals over my own family. Perhaps I am doing so right now. Or perhaps I am doing as I was told. That is for you to decide. My words cannot be trusted, after all."

I grunted, finding the irony in the truth of his statement.

"You obviously found it worthwhile to visit me." I glanced down at the coin thoughtfully. "And to pay me for my time," I said suspiciously, bending down to pick it up.

"Time," Hermes mused, the coin on his knuckles suddenly halting, "is such a fickle mistress—deceptive and almost impossible for you to grasp, even though *she* always has a firm grasp on *you*—steadily grinding your bones to dust, aging you with every passing hour. And what do you do? You keep begging for more!"

I nodded thoughtfully, processing his macabre metaphor. *Time* had been a vital element in my fight against Mordred. "I've got a wild idea. How about you give me something useful and I'll act surprised. I can even cover my eyes while you count if that sounds more exciting."

He smirked. "I have already done what little I could to aid you, but ascension is another matter entirely. That is where true divinity and depravity lies—two sides of the same coin."

"I've heard that word before," I said, frowning. "Ascension. What exactly is it referring to? My promotion to godkiller?" I asked.

He smiled sadly. "Perhaps. Perhaps not," he replied, shrugging.

I studied him, wondering how far I could trust him, and why he was dodging my question.

"Know that if you proceed with your newest idea, there will be repercussions for you. I'm not trying to threaten you or sway your decision. In fact, I applaud it. But you do need to understand the consequences. I have it on good authority that some Olympians are still quite...agitated about that particular legend becoming common knowledge," he said, winking at me again. "Further agitation could carry unhealthy side-effects, or repercussions. It was always considered a hallowed place—not available for public use."

I grew very still, wondering how much he actually knew and how the hell he knew it. I'd literally told no one. Not even Alucard. "Then maybe they should have put up a fence to keep the riffraff out."

Hermes grunted, shooting me an amused grin. "I would say that the fence we placed around it was quite *substantial*," he said dryly.

I shrugged, not bothering to hide my arrogant grin. "Obviously not." But I was very troubled by how he had discovered my plan—because he obviously had, judging by his responses.

"I think I like you, Temple. You made good use of the coin I entrusted to Asterion, long ago. My family is still rather upset about that, when they think no one is listening. But I'm always listening, you see, pressing my ear against the keyhole, in a manner of speaking."

I nodded. "You're the Messenger God. Makes sense."

"The thing about listening through the keyhole is that—if you're not cautious enough—you run the risk of them opening the door on you." And he snapped his fingers, making me jump. "I truly do wish you the best of luck," he said, winking mischievously. And with the flap of a hummingbird's wings, he was simply gone.

I narrowed my eyes. *Best of luck*. And he had claimed to have already aided me as much as he could.

The assassins. Had he been the source of their bad luck? But...

Why?

With a muttered curse, I decided I'd had enough fresh air and quantum Slinkys.

CHAPTER 27

War had his hands on his hips, shaking his head as he surveyed the dome-ceilinged nave from top to bottom. "Magnificent," he murmured to himself, sounding awed. Then he turned to look at me. "How long did it take to build?"

I shrugged. "Long time."

"Reminds me of home," Alucard said. "But the Cities of the Dead in New Orleans have nothing on *this*," he admitted, lifting his head to gaze at the bulletproof, stained-glass window high above.

"A true mausoleum is a rare sight these days," War explained, "unless you visit one owned by the government, but those have become glorified museums. They were originally built as a celebration of life rather than a convenient place to bury their dead."

I nodded along distractedly, turning away from them to study the two-story, Temple family tree that occupied the tiled, back wall of a wide, shallow pool. A fountain gurgled in the center—emitting a soothing, bubbling trickle rather than an overbearing geyser.

The main difference between typical family trees and mine was that the names of my relatives weren't located on the branches—they were on the roots. Sapphires marked each woman, and rubies each man, their names etched with silver into the tiles beside each gem. My name was the last and lowest part of the root system, having no other relatives to share the nutrient production for the massive tree.

I was the last Temple.

As I glanced at the waterline below my name, I noticed that the tiles simply ended rather than continuing down into the water. That seemed strange. I stared harder, thinking that the tiles might just be obscured by the rippling surface of the water. Or perhaps the light was reflecting strangely under the surface. But as I continued to lean forward, I realized it wasn't a reflection—

"You're welcome," Alucard said. And then he shoved me into the pool. I went completely underwater and instinctively sat back up with a gasp, lifting my hand to make him pay with a helping of excessive force.

But…

The water felt surprisingly refreshing, and since I was already wet, I figured that I may as well take a closer look at the wall. So I turned around, ignoring the baffled look on Alucard's face, and submerged. Thankfully, the pool was only a few feet deep, and the water was clean and clear, so I had no problem studying the back wall.

I froze to see that not only was there no tile, but that there were faded lines carved into the surface. It made me think of three roads branching out from the waterline to extend to different points at the base of the pool, forming a triangular shape when taken as a whole.

Occasionally, the indentions seemed to flare brighter, as if reflecting the electrical lights from the ceiling outside the pool.

Maybe the indentions had been painted with metallic flecks at one point in time.

I lifted my head from the water and wiped at my eyes, staring down at where I had seen the lines. Seeing them combined with the tree above, they actually kind of looked like…roots—but not a part of the tiled tree. More like the tiles had covered something up.

"No need to play it cool, Nate," Alucard said, sounding annoyed. "You still had frosting in your hair, so I was trying to be helpful."

I waved a hand for him to be quiet as I frowned at the three underwater roots.

I reached back under the water to trace them with my fingers, seeing if there were any kind of hidden levers or buttons, or if any of the lower tiles were loose, but I found nothing.

I let out a sigh, scrubbed my hands through my hair, and dunked one more time, figuring I might as well put some effort into my bath.

War and Alucard watched me in silence, looking concerned by my strange behavior.

"What were you doing?" War finally asked, peering past me.

"Nothing. I thought I saw something odd, but I think it's just some old etchings on the wall—beneath the tiles."

He nodded. "I was just asking Alucard about the increased security. The automatic sensors that turn on the lights, the vault door, the bullet-proof windows..." he trailed off, watching me nod along. "Was all that to protect this Hourglass and Hand of God?" he asked, indicating the items I'd set down on the lip of the pool. I'd been checking over them—for the thousandth time—a few minutes ago, looking for any kind of missed secret. I'd even tried dipping them in the water and scrubbing them with my shirt.

And I'd found nothing.

Frustrated by my lack of new discoveries, I'd set them down and resorted to studying the tree. I'd had no new epiphanies or revelations regarding the things Starlight or Hermes had said. I hadn't even *told* War and Alucard about Hermes' visit, as a matter of fact—because that might have led to questions about my secret plan. The one that the Messenger God had somehow figured out. His warning hadn't necessarily deterred me. In fact, it had kind of motivated me, but I had a few other things to check on before I did anything rash.

"My parents hid them here," I explained, "so they upped the security on the place. They were hidden in such a manner that only I could have ever found them anyway, so I don't know why they even bothered. Adding the hardcore upgrades made the place look more suspicious, as if they were *trying* to lure burglars here."

War nodded. "Unless there are still more secrets to find."

I shook my head at the echo of my own thoughts. "Been there done that. No levers or trap doors. No trick walls. I even hired an Archaeologist to come check it out, using every tool at his disposal—thermal imaging, ground penetration devices, metal detectors..." I waved a hand, implying that the list went on and on. "And I didn't sense any magical secrets either. The place is as quiet as...well, a tomb."

Alucard patted War on the shoulder consolingly. "It was a good theory.

Nate's spent many a drunken night here, trying to bust that particular nut," he explained.

I groaned at his phrasing, which seemed to make him happy.

War shrugged. "I was thinking about a magician, for example..." he mused, casting me a meaningful look. "How they use sleight of hand, letting you think you know what's happening, when they are really leading you by the nose."

I grunted. "I wish. I fucking hate mysteries. Trust me. The only other things of value are these gems," I said, pointing at the family tree. "And although they are indeed valuable, they don't warrant *this* kind of security system."

War let out a sigh before glancing back up at the domed ceiling and then out at the cavernous halls branching out from the pool. "Despite her mysteries, this place is a hall of victory," he mused. "I can practically feel your ancestors' achievements." He turned to look at me. "You come from a noble family, Temple. And I'm not referring to their monetary wealth."

I sat down on the edge of the fountain, not bothering to take my feet out of the water as I stared up at the colossal family tree and the multitude of gems indicating different ancestors. I nodded to War's statement, careful to keep my face neutral. Some of my ancestors hadn't been quite so noble. "For the most part, yes."

"Every family has its share of black sheep," War chastised, waving a hand dismissively. "Why are you making that face?"

I sighed, wishing I'd hidden my emotions better. "I was just thinking about something my dad once said to me," I told him.

Because I was remembering the last thing my father had ever said to me on the night that he'd died—the video recording from Temple Industries. I'd read his lips.

Dynasty is not destiny.

It had infuriated me, making me think that he had been alluding to my forced role as CEO of Temple Industries—which had been brief and incendiary, just like I'd warned him.

Because my dad had said that stupid little phrase every morning while shaving in the mirror—like a good little corporate automaton. It was his self-motivational go-to.

"Were you going to share with the class?" Alucard asked, and I realized I hadn't spoken. Instead of telling them the snippet from the recording, I decided to share the whole quote. A quote I'd often found scribbled on various slips of paper on my dad's desk—right alongside his second favorite quote.

I'd never once heard him say the whole quote out loud—which I'd found rather strange. Not even when I had asked him about the full quote after seeing it on his notepad. Like he considered it blasphemy to do so.

Because he'd had no problem saying his second favorite quote out loud.

I cleared my throat, glancing at my friends. "*We flip our glass to ancestors past. Dynasty is not destiny. Nobility is not class.*" My words echoed in the vast mausoleum. "You mentioned nobility," I explained. "It reminded me of that quote."

War was frowning. "Who wrote it?" he asked.

I shrugged. "One of our ancestors. My dad never told me which one," I admitted with a slight frown.

War reached down to the Hourglass and flipped it over, staring at it curiously.

I furrowed my brows and blinked at him. "What are you doing?"

He turned away from the artifact to look up at me. "You said your father gave you this," he explained as if I was daft.

I slowly nodded. "And? We already passed that point of the conversation." I eyed my liquor bottle with a frown. "Have you been sneaking sips or something?"

He looked at me very strangely, even turning to Alucard as if to ask for some support. Alucard held up his hands in a *don't ask me* gesture. "No, I haven't been drinking," War muttered. "I was wondering—other than the obvious reasons—why you would flip this. It doesn't fit the theme of your father's quote. I assumed it was a riddle."

Not having the faintest idea what he was talking about, I mentally reread the quote. And then I finally understood what he was getting at.

"*Our glass,*" I said, clearly enunciating my words, "not *Hourglass*—" I stiffened, finally hearing how similar it sounded when spoken out loud. I'd always seen it written down. The only part that my father had ever said out loud was *dynasty is not destiny.*

But audibly...

Hourglass, not *our glass*...

No way.

But nothing had happened when War flipped over the Hourglass like the quote suggested. War now had his eyeball pressed up against the glass as if trying to peer inside for a secret message.

I dismissed his primitive approach, and instead wracked my brain, trying to find a new path to explore. Anubis had once told me that the artifact was a Key…but a key to what *lock?*

I repeated the quote in my head, breaking it down. It didn't take me long until I was suddenly staring at the family tree.

"Ancestors past…" I murmured.

I turned towards War to find that he had suddenly stiffened, slowly pulling the Hourglass away from his eye with a frown. Then he lifted it to his nose and sniffed it.

I stared at him, frowning. "What the hell are you doing?"

He looked at me with a very somber expression on his face, carefully holding it out to me with one hand. I took it, unable to break eye contact with him.

Because War looked shaken to the core.

"That isn't sand, Nate," he said pointing at the powder within the Hourglass. "That is bone dust. And it smells like *you*…and *them*," he rasped, gesturing vaguely at all the statues filling the mausoleum.

My eyes widened in disbelief. *"What?"*

He nodded. "Trust me. I know bone dust."

"That…is really fucked up," Alucard murmured. "Bone dust is fucking *dangerous*. Even voodoo priests are wary of it. And you're saying it smells like *all of them?*" he hissed, his shoulders tightening.

War nodded firmly. "I would bet my Mask on it. Don't ask me how. Maybe it's their ancestry that I'm smelling."

I stared down at the Hourglass as if it were a venomous snake, wondering what to do with War's new information. Finally, I stood to my feet and waded up to the wall. As I drew closer, the three vines beneath the surface began to glow with blue light.

"Holy shit," Alucard hissed.

I took a deep breath and flipped the Hourglass, tensing my legs in preparation for anything.

A previously nonexistent hatch flipped open on the uppermost base of the Hourglass, exposing the bone dust to the air, and I felt my heart suddenly racing for multiple reasons.

Alucard's warning about the dangers of bone dust…

And because I remembered the *second* quote my dad had always written in tandem with the unspoken one. The quote he'd had no problem saying out loud.

Maybe I needed to say *both* of them out loud—like a prayer.

Was my dad really one of those guys who had written his password down and left it on his desk where anyone could find it? Othello would be appalled.

I cleared my throat and stared at my family tree—at my ancestors. "We flip our glass to ancestors past. Dynasty is not destiny. Nobility is not class."

Every gem on the wall began to glow with an inner light, pulsing in sync like a single beating heart.

I took a careful, steady breath—not wanting to accidentally become a cannibal by snorting my ancestors' remains—and then I poured some of the bone dust into my palm. The tiny hatch abruptly snapped shut as if rationing my dosage.

"I will show you fear in a handful of dust..." I whispered—the *second* quote from my dad's notepads.

And then I sprinkled the bone dust into the water.

The gems on the wall suddenly flared brighter, and my vision wobbled as a sound like a struck tuning fork the size of a car filled the halls of the Temple Mausoleum. Even my teeth vibrated at the intensity of it, forcing me to clench my jaw.

Then I felt a deep *thump* in my chest, and the goddamned floor of the pool dropped out beneath me, flushing me down the world's darkest, scariest, water slide.

I wanted to scream—but I didn't dare open my mouth for fear of ingesting any of the bone dust in the water.

CHAPTER 28

I splashed into a deep pool of water, still protectively clutching the Hourglass to my chest to keep it safe. I hadn't wanted to risk breaking it on my ride down the slide.

I breached the surface and stared incredulously at my surroundings, treading water with my free hand. Flickering, blue-flamed torches set into the walls illuminated a vast, red-stone cavern. I heard Alucard and War shouting at me from up above, so I glanced back at the slide to see—

"Motherfucker," I cursed.

A wide flight of stairs ran parallel to the slide, climbing all the way up to an opening in the ceiling that was obviously my mausoleum, because Alucard and War were running down them as fast as they could manage.

"Goddamned slide," I muttered as I swam my way over to the edge of the pool. I set the Hourglass down first, and was hoisting myself out when War grabbed me firmly under my arms and simply pulled me to my feet, showing off his ridiculous strength.

He stared at me, patting my shoulders to make sure I was alright.

"I'm fine," I told him. "I may or may not have peed in the pool, though," I admitted, bending down to scoop up the Hourglass and shove it into my—"Damn it! My satchel is still up there—"

Alucard slapped the satchel against my chest, not even looking at me. "I grabbed it. In case there was treasure down here," he admitted shamelessly. "They always forget to take a bag with them in the movies. Rookies."

I chuckled at his expectations for treasure as I shoved the Hourglass into my satchel and settled the strap over my shoulder and across my chest. Then I finally took a real gander at my Batcave.

"What *is* this place?" Alucard breathed, shaking his head in disbelief.

For some strange reason, an endless supply of water still poured down the slide from the mausoleum above, and it had already begun to overfill the landing pool, causing it to spill out into a wide channel that continued down the center of a tunnel of stygian darkness. But beyond that I could see dim gray sky—the entrance to the cavern.

I estimated it was a little over fifty yards away.

I took a few steps closer to get a better look at the new stream, but I instantly froze as more blue torches suddenly flared to life on either side of me, pushing the darkness further back. A resounding *clang* made me jump, expecting a wall of spikes to spear me to death.

But instead of instant death, two new streams of fresh water suddenly burst from the walls—one on each side of me—as if an unseen dam had been lowered. The new streams merged with the center channel, tripling its force and size.

I sucked in a breath to suddenly notice that a statue was pressed up against the left wall of the tunnel, and it was straddling the new stream. A quick glance showed me the same thing on my right—the streams of water flowing directly out from beneath the hauntingly familiar statues.

"It's just like the mausoleum," Alucard grunted, pointing overhead to the twenty-foot ceiling.

He wasn't wrong, but he wasn't entirely correct. These statues were very different from the ones above. Although they still portrayed couples in powerful, triumphant poses, these looked savage and sinister. The crisp blue light definitely didn't make them look friendlier.

I stepped closer, studying the statue on my left. It depicted an armored man and woman screaming as they crouched atop a pile of bones, their empty palms held out as if hurling magic at unseen foes. Wizards. Battle wizards, judging by the lack of physical weapons.

"Now I understand," War said excitedly, stepping up beside me to stare at the statue with an awed expression on his face. "I knew I sensed warriors here, but every single statue above was a celebration of the mind, representing their more…civilized accomplishments. Their public face, you could say." He pointed at the statue before us, his excitement growing. "But these are their warrior sides. How they became the men and women we saw above," he explained, pointing at the woman's jubilant, screaming face. "This shows them as *soldiers*—before they ascended to *scholars*," he said, shifting his finger to point at the mausoleum above.

I nodded woodenly. "As above, so below," I said absently. "This is Florence and Malachi Temple," I told him, recognizing them from the mausoleum. Up there, they'd been holding books and smiling at one another.

"War," the Biblical Horseman said, stretching his arms wide as he began to spin in a slow circle, looking like he was about to break out into a heartfelt musical number.

"And Peace," Alucard added with an amused grin, pointing his finger up at the ceiling.

I hesitantly took a few more steps towards the darkness, and was almost instantly rewarded with more blue flames crackling to life. Just like before, a metallic clang reverberated from beneath newly illuminated statues, birthing new streams to flow into the center channel.

I pressed on towards the cavern's entrance, choosing to take only cursory glances at the statues that emerged with each flare of light and clang of opening floodgates. The center channel grew wilder and louder with each step I took until all I could hear was the roar of a raging river that grew stronger with the unveiling of each new Temple ancestor. And I suddenly saw the symbolism in the cavern's design. The blood—or stream—of each ancestor merging together until there was a singular, unstoppable force screaming out to reach the light—the open sky.

It was both chilling and inspiring.

Each statue revealed a similar fight or battle pose, but the armor or clothing would change depending on the historical and geographical fashions of their day. I saw ancestors who I recognized and many who I did not.

Those who I didn't recognize could have stemmed from our origins in Europe. But even when I didn't know their faces from the statues up in the mausoleum, I recognized their names from the roots of the family tree.

Roots, I thought to myself.

The answer had been right in front of me. Our names were on the roots, not the branches—in this cavern, not the mausoleum. Real strength came from your roots, not your accomplishments.

Accomplishments were the rewards, the trophies.

The roots were what *earned* you those accolades.

I shook my head as I continued to walk, realizing that I was grinning proudly.

The stream was now a deep, frothing, unstoppable force, seeming to shine like mercury in the glow from the blue torches. Where was all this water coming from, and why hadn't the water from the pool in the mausoleum run dry yet? Opening up the slide must have unlocked another floodgate.

We were almost at the cavern's entrance, and I could feel waves of heat from the open sky.

And that's when I saw the statue of my parents. I skidded to a halt and stared, not having really thought about my parents being a part of this experience, even though it made obvious sense. They were standing back-to-back in front of a startlingly familiar cave in the Land of the Fae. They were cut and bleeding, screaming defiantly at unseen foes. They each held balls of flame in one hand and a sword in the other. A Fae arrow pierced my mother's thigh, but you wouldn't have known it from the ecstatic look on her face.

I was unable to move as I studied every feature of their faces. The cave in Fae behind them was perfectly accurate, not a boulder out of place. The cave where I had been born.

I saw the Hourglass hanging from my mother's belt, and my knees suddenly felt weak. They had stolen it from the Fae Queens. But if the Hourglass was full of bone dust from our ancestors…

How did the queens ever get a hold of it?

My parents hadn't been *stealing* it. They'd been *retrieving* it!

Holy shit. How did nobody know that?

War and Alucard stepped up beside me, staring at the statue in respectful silence.

"From nothing to nobility," Alucard said, pointing at the wall behind my parents. The words were carved into the stone, and the Temple Crest stood just above it. I'd been so transfixed with the statue that I hadn't even noticed the message.

I turned to look at the statue on the opposite side of the tunnel and saw another Crest with different words below.

"From Alpha to Omega," I said, reading it out loud.

Seeing that we practically stood at the entrance, I walked towards the sky, eager to see where we were. The onslaught of water roared past me right over the edge of the cliff, forming a new waterfall.

I stared outward, shaking my head wondrously. We were on top of a huge mountain overlooking a valley of sizzling stone. Luckily, we were facing west with the rising sun on the opposite side of our mountain. Even still, it was hot enough to make my throat feel dry. I couldn't imagine how it would feel in direct sunlight.

The waterfall I had accidentally birthed appeared to be the only water for miles in any direction. Perhaps even hundreds of miles.

As I stared down at the valley far below, I saw what looked like dozens of tiny figures pointing up at the waterfall, but it was hard to tell what they looked like since they stood in the shadow of the mountain.

I noticed movement and realized that just as many figures appeared to be fleeing from the new waterfall—

"Fucking Carl!" Alucard suddenly hissed, grabbing my shoulder and spinning me to the left.

CHAPTER 29

The ledge extended around the side of the mountain in a dusty, rocky, boulder-strewn path that gradually led down to the valley below. And sure enough...

Carl was no more than twenty feet away from us, dozing before...a giant white tree, like the one at Chateau Falco. Its roots clutched onto the side of the mountain like desperate fingers, refusing to let go for fear of plummeting down into the valley.

"Your family is seriously fucked up, Nate," Alucard said, frowning at Carl. "Why isn't he moving?" he asked uneasily.

A pit of dread settled in my stomach as I sprinted over to him. I knelt a safe distance away so that he didn't kill me on instinct the moment he woke up and found a wizard looming over him. "Carl," I murmured, wincing at the bloody bandages wrapped around his forearms. They weren't a little bloody. They were a lot bloody, and the claws on his hand looked chipped and gouged, as if he'd used them to climb up the mountain. But he was breathing steadily through his nostrils—

I froze in horror. His mouth was sewn shut with what looked like silver wire. "What the fuck?" Alucard whispered, grimacing.

War had wisely taken up a defensive position, glaring down the path in case anyone else tried to join our party. Like all those people we had seen in the valley. Except I now realized that they hadn't been *people*. They had been

Elders. The Elder realm had been sitting under the Temple Mausoleum all this time, and I had never known.

I used my sleeve to wipe the sudden sweat from my brow, feeling like I was in a desert. The puncture wounds from the silver wire over Carl's mouth didn't look infected, and there was no fresh blood to speak of, so it wasn't recent. "Carl," I urged, cautiously shaking his clawed foot, wondering why he wasn't waking up. How much blood had he lost, and why was he up here all alone?

I glanced over his shoulder at the tree and I blinked to see a familiar, bleeding hole in the trunk. A dozen broken blades littered the ground around him, looking like they'd been used to inflict the damage on the tree. I even noticed a few jagged, ivory splinters in the hole itself.

"Carl!" I hissed, louder, and I leaned closer to shake his shoulder. His eyes fluttered open dazedly and his nostrils abruptly flared.

I swiftly leaned away so as not to threaten him, and I let out a relieved gasp. He blinked rapidly, staring at me in bewilderment before suddenly averting his eyes from mine.

"It's me, Carl. I found you."

His shoulders trembled violently, and I realized he was overcome with emotion, but unable to open his mouth to speak. Instead, he let out a deep breath through his nostrils, his shoulders going slack as he sagged against the tree in a sign of exhausted victory.

And I watched a tear rolled down his scaled cheek.

"What happened, Carl?" Alucard whispered, pointing at his bandaged arms. "Are you okay?"

Carl nodded wearily. He clasped his palms together and held them to the side of his head like a pillow, closing his eyes theatrically. "Tired? You're tired?" I asked.

He nodded firmly, lowering his hands.

I slowly reached my hand up towards his face, speaking calmly, "I'm going take this crap off, Carl. You don't have to be scared. We'll get you out of here—"

He ducked his head and rapidly scooted away from my touch before climbing to his feet and holding out his hands in a panicked gesture that said *stop*. Seeing that we had understood, Carl shook his head and clapped his fist to his heart like a salute. Then he tapped his lips and nodded firmly.

I blinked at him, not understanding his explanation. The *don't touch my kickass braces* message was loud and clear, though.

Carl's chest, I suddenly realized, was also decorated with over a dozen shallow gashes, all looking old enough to have begun healing over with fresh white scales. He'd taken a beating recently, but he was still here. "Are you being punished?" I asked, confused. "Is that why you're up here?"

His nostrils flared and his eyes narrowed dangerously as he stared at the ground. Then he clapped his fist to his chest even harder, like some kind of military salute.

"He feels honored," War suddenly said, cocking his head thoughtfully. "I think he considers this a duty. Or a traditional penance?" he added, finally shrugging. "I'm just guessing here."

Carl thought about that for a moment and then shook his head, obviously frustrated. I had a sudden thought. "Is there some other way you can communicate with us? Through my mind, maybe?" I asked, remembering his people had an affinity for mind magic of some flavor.

He nodded uneasily, so I stepped forward, motioning for him to try. He stepped back, making me halt. Then he slowly lifted a claw to point in my general direction, and shook his head.

Why wasn't he making eye contact with me?

Alucard stepped up. "I volunteer as tribute," he said with mock solemnity, quoting the girl from *The Hunger Games*.

Carl whipped out a bone sword I hadn't noticed hanging from his belt, and he did it faster than I've ever seen, lifting it high overhead as if to decapitate Alucard—who suddenly looked like he'd dropped some cargo in his pants, jumping back with a panicked shout and a feral hiss.

I quickly lunged between them, holding up my hand. "Stop, Carl! It was an expression," I explained.

The moment I jumped between them, Carl had dropped his sword and darted back from me, crouching and dropping his gaze in shame. What the hell was wrong with him?

I blinked down at him and then risked a look at War. He was scratching his head in confusion. "Is he always like this?"

"No," I said—at the same time that Alucard said, "Yes!"

War looked from me to Alucard, even more confused. "Your team needs to learn some Yoga or something. You guys need to calm the fuck down every once in a while, if this kind of shit is normal."

I sighed before turning back to the Elder. "It's okay, Carl. Alucard was offering to let you communicate with him—"

"Not the fuck anymore!" Alucard snapped. "The lizard just tried to kill me!"

Carl's tail began to whip back and forth, not appreciating Alucard's tone.

"See what I mean?" War suggested helpfully. "Yoga."

I ignored him, crouching down before Carl. His body went rigid and I could tell that he wanted nothing more than to get away from me. I used two fingers to gently lift his chin, but he kept his eyes averted, his nostrils flaring like a panicked horse. It was almost as if he'd lost what little domestication he'd gained from me over the years. "Hey. It's only us, buddy," I said soothingly, hoping to calm him down. "I don't know what you've been going through since you left, but we're here now. Why don't you try talking to Alucard? I've gone through some...changes recently," I explained. "The whole mind-talk thing doesn't work on me like it used to."

Carl nodded stiffly, still refusing to make eye contact with me. I straightened and took a few steps back, gesturing with my hand for him to proceed. "Thank you, Alucard," I said in a tight, warning tone. "It is so helpful of you to do this."

War chuckled at the dark look Alucard shot my way. "No swords this time," he demanded.

Carl stretched to his full height and approached Alucard with his sharp claws outstretched, showing no timidity as he locked eyes with the vampire. Alucard looked suddenly less certain about his decision, but he stood his ground as Carl set his claw on Alucard's shoulder, staring deep into his eyes.

Alucard's face suddenly went slack and he sucked in a sharp breath. Carl simply stepped back, dipping his chin at Alucard and clasping his hands behind his back.

Alucard blinked several times, staring at Carl as if at a ghost.

Then he slowly turned to me. "Um. I...can hear him now. For a second there, it felt like he was scraping a claw across my brain, but...it didn't hurt," he tried to explain, shaking his head. "I think he established some kind of bond."

Carl nodded.

Alucard turned to look at him thoughtfully before turning back to me. "He doesn't want to talk about it, but he's adamant about joining our party."

War grunted. "Party," he said flatly.

"What do you mean he doesn't want to talk about it? About his wounds? What he's been doing since he left? His parents? Why he's bleeding, or why his mouth is sewn shut?" I demanded, listing a handful of topics that we definitely *should* be talking about. "Which one does he not want to talk about?"

Alucard licked his lips uncertainly. "Yes. All of that," he said. "Look, I'm just the messenger. I can't read his mind or anything. He's like a voice in my ear or something."

I studied Carl, folding my arms, assessing the whole situation. Starlight had said the Elders were at the bottom of a well, praying. That they had answers but were scared of the questions. Had he been referring to this? Because it was obvious that Carl didn't want to hear questions, and the pool that had brought me here was kind of like a well...

The rest of Starlight's comment whispered in my ears.

Chains gave them freedom. Independence gave them banishment. Their temples grew dark and drafty, their prayers unanswered when their masters abandoned them.

Was that what the wire on his lips represented? Some kind of figurative symbol?

Because the Elders sure seemed to know my ancestors, even placed a shrine on the top of their mountain to worship them. And that cavern of *Temple* ancestors had definitely been *dark* and *abandoned*. And Carl looked like he had been working on some kind of ritual here by the tree, or maybe standing guard for something.

"Were you waiting for me?" I asked Carl.

He nodded slowly, keeping his eyes lowered.

"He's scared to talk to you," Alucard said uneasily. "He's been waiting for a while. He saw Thor break the tree," he explained, "but he couldn't reach through the hole to help," Alucard said, pointing at the bloody hole in the tree.

I blinked incredulously. "It's the same tree?"

Alucard was silent for a moment. "It's an anchor. A Gateway of some kind, but it's not active. They've been waiting for the waterfall to come back. It's very, very important, but he won't explain why," Alucard said, glancing over his shoulder. He turned back and smirked crookedly. "And that's all from the Fucking Carl podcast. No more questions."

I muttered under my breath. "Grab your weapons, Carl. We were about to go pick a fight. Maybe that will snap you out of...whatever this is."

"Oh, he *liked* that," Alucard said, shuddering. "Too much, in my opinion.

Carl, for his part, had shown absolutely no emotional reaction to my words. Instead, he walked over towards a nearby boulder and pointed behind it.

"Um. You need to hand them to him," Alucard said, frowning in confusion.

"What?"

"He won't touch them until you do," Alucard said. "You have to *give* them to him."

"He had no problem holding a sword a minute ago," I muttered.

Alucard shook his head. "That was different. That was intended for the tree. He only raised it against me because he thought I wanted him to—" he scowled incredulously at Carl. "What the fuck, Carl? You thought I *wanted* you to decapitate me?" he demanded.

Carl nodded, shrugging his shoulders. War burst out laughing.

Alucard folded his arms, shaking his head. "Whatever," he muttered. "Anyway, the weapons back there are for murder. *Only* murder. They are weapons of war."

I sighed, deciding that it was easier to just go along with it. I walked over and glanced behind the boulder. Sure enough, I found a belt loaded with blades and two long swords—as well as a shoulder harness carrying a ridiculously large number of daggers. They had been back there for quite some time, judging by the thick coating of dust. Carl hadn't worn them for...*months*, it looked like.

I scooped them up and unceremoniously tossed them to Carl, feeling ridiculous. "Prepare for war, Carl." Even though he was unable to speak, I suddenly recalled how absolutely terrified most gods were of him. He was ruthless with his blades as well, so this accidental detour might have made my negotiations with Loki a lot simpler.

Carl dipped his head, his tail twitching back and forth like a dog wagging his tail after thinking he heard the word *walk*. He strapped on his belt and harness with swift familiarity and a hungry sigh of anticipation.

I turned to Alucard, shaking my head and wiping more sweat from my brow. "Remember when we used to call you Alu-Carl?" I asked, smirking. "Good luck ever getting rid of that nickname *now*."

I heard him muttering darkly under his breath as I walked past him towards the cavern.

"We're leaving?" War asked, sounding surprised.

I didn't turn to look as I continued on, nearing the waterfall. "Nope. We're going down to the valley," I said sarcastically. "I just want to ride the waterfall because it looks faster."

"Maybe we *should* explore!" War argued, not appreciating my tone.

"Carl says that the valley is certain death," Alucard cut in. "The sun here would burn us alive. Literally. And judging by how much Nate is already sweating, I don't doubt it."

I stopped, turning around to look at Carl, dismissing his knee-jerk reaction of averting his eyes. Lizards liked direct heat, but hot enough to burn us humans alive? Where the hell were we? I doubted that it was a pocket realm in Fae, because it felt…alien. Different somehow. I glanced at War, seeing he was also sweaty, but Alucard…looked fine.

He noticed my attention. "New Orleans blood. I could walk into a steam room and not need a towel," he said smugly.

I finally shook my head and continued on. "No valley. We have enough problems back home to deal with, first."

I wasn't going to explore the Elder Realm until I got some real answers from Carl. If he wanted to play the silent game, I would wait him out. Whatever reasons he had for his current actions, they were obviously important to him, but I also had important things on my mind.

I noticed an unfinished statue near the entrance and slowed. On our initial walk through the cavern, I'd vaguely noticed it and promptly dismissed it as a boulder, my attention drawn to the waterfall instead. Looking at it now, I realized that it was another statue—a work in process.

Jagged, unfinished wings sprouted out from a vaguely human silhouette, and enough work had been done on the face that I knew it was a man, not a couple. It looked to have been started with crude tools in order to first break off the larger, unneeded chunks of stone.

I frowned, recalling the chipped and scored texture of Carl's claws…

Nah.

CHAPTER 30

We had rested up in the Armory, not wanting to risk running into anyone at Chateau Falco and then having to explain where we had found Carl, or why War was with me, or why we smelled like donuts, cigars, whiskey, and sweat.

Pandora had taken one look at our sad state of affairs, sighed, and then left the room without a word. She'd come back a few minutes later with blankets, bars of soap, towels, robes, and ordering me to tell my friends where the healing hot tub was—which she repeated three times. Meaning we must have looked rougher than I'd thought.

She had cocked her head upon seeing Carl's mouth wired shut, but she hadn't asked any questions. She had locked her door, though, which made me feel incredibly trustworthy and appreciated.

I'd encouraged everyone to sleep through the afternoon, knowing that we might need our rest, depending on what Loki had found since last night. If he hadn't found anything yet, I had enough other drama going on to keep me busy for one more day. In fact, it might even be preferable, but that all depended on how my next conversation went.

So I'd left the gang behind, telling them to meet me in an hour at the same warehouse we'd used to summon Loki. Carl had seemed agitated to let me out of his sight, but I couldn't very well walk him around Chateau Falco without drawing attention—even without his shiny new braces. Alucard had calmed him down, reassuring the Elder that they would both come hunt me down if I was late to the rendezvous.

Which was how I found myself sneaking up from the tunnels outside the Armory and through the magical, secret door that led to my office. I stepped out and froze.

"I already told you what our budget is, Felicia," Othello said tiredly into the phone, but her eyes did widen to suddenly see me appear out of nowhere. "Yes, yes, I understand, but…"

I turned away to see Gunnar seated in a leather armchair, staring up at me with an arched eyebrow, his quartz-like eyepatch glittering as it reflected the glow from the fireplace.

The exact two people I wanted to talk to but I needed to talk to them separately, damn it!

"Pop quiz time," I said to both of them, recalling War's warning about not knowing who I could really trust—that anyone I encountered might be Loki in disguise.

"Hold on," Othello said into the phone, sounding annoyed. "My boss is doing that eccentric thing I told you about." I narrowed my eyes at her. "Yes, I know it sounds endearing. But much like the first time a sleeping baby wakes himself up by farting too loudly, the humor fades when the habit continues on into adulthood."

Gunnar burst out laughing.

I pointed a warning finger at him. "Silence."

"No, I'm not saying he—" Othello took a deep, calming breath, slapping her palm against her forehead. "Just fix the budget before tomorrow morning, and pay the rest of the vendors for crying out loud. I'll talk to you tomorrow. Bye, Felicia." And she hung up the phone.

Judging by her conversation, I was pretty sure it was really Othello, even if I didn't know what vendors she was talking about. Was there some event for Plato's Cave?

Still, I had to be sure. I wasn't letting her get off that easy. "What was my nickname in college?" I asked her.

She arched her eyebrow at me, looking puzzled. "Pharos."

"Where did we study Russian?"

She grinned wickedly. "Somewhere deep within a knot of sweaty, tangled sheets—"

"Okay," I said, cutting her off. "You're good."

"Oh, I *know* I am," she purred.

I rounded on Gunnar, hiding my blush. "What was our fort called?"

He didn't hesitate. "Chateau Defiance."

"What happened at your bachelor party in New Orleans?"

"I was a perfect gentleman and caught up on my sleep," he said as if reading a teleprompter. Othello snorted doubtfully.

I nodded. "What do they now call us in New Orleans?"

"Beerlympians." Gunnar grinned proudly. "Allegedly."

I let out a sigh. "Good. You both passed. Now, what are you doing here?" I asked Gunnar.

"Yes, Gunnar. Tell Nate what you're doing here," Othello said in a sickly-sweet tone.

Gunnar sighed. "Apologizing for bringing the FBI here without warning her. Begging for her forgiveness," he said in an overly shamed tone, glancing past me at her with one sad puppy eye.

She snorted. "Fine. Apology accepted."

"Thank you, Othello." Then he turned to me. "Good call on wearing a hat last night. It just barely did the trick of masking your identity. Agent Murphy and his partner, Agent Glass, even brought the picture to our meeting this morning," he said dryly.

I sighed guiltily. "Yeah, about that—"

"But what I *really* want to know is why you roped *War* into your games rather than asking *me*," he interrupted in an angry growl, and I could tell that deep down, my choice had actually hurt his feelings on a personal level. I knew this because he was subconsciously thumbing his new bone bracelet —his own Horseman Mask. But I also knew he was concerned about his pups, resulting in a conflict of desires. The angrier he was with me, the less it would seem he cared about his pups—a shitty thought to have, but I knew Gunnar well. That was exactly why he hadn't ripped my head off yet. "What are you really up to? You and Alucard have been thick as thieves, and now you show up giving us a pop quiz?" he demanded, pointing at his chest and then Othello.

I nodded. "I was going to tell you, but then Calvin and Makayla showed us their new trick," I explained, fibbing a bit. "I also need someone I can trust to look after Chateau Falco for a little while longer. And, to be completely honest, I wasn't too crazy about the whole *my kids are wolves* thing. I wanted you and Ashley both here to keep an eye on them. Which is actually what I came to talk to you about. Want to go for a walk?"

His eye stormed over at my last sentence—me asking him, a werewolf, if he wanted to go for a walk. Shaking a leash in his face would have been less subtle.

I grinned, holding up my hands. "That wasn't even on purpose. Damn."

Gunnar relaxed and set his hands on the arms of his chair, preparing to stand.

"If you two leave, I'm telling him all about Lullaby, Nate," Othello warned.

I spun to glare at her. "What the hell?" I demanded.

"Okay, I'm going to tell him either way. I shouldn't have tried to extort you."

I began to growl at her. "No, Othello. You don't know what you're talking about."

She leaned forward daringly. "I don't think *you* know what you're talking about. I've been doing some digging into our new pal, Niko, and her friends," she explained, and I could actually *feel* Gunnar's attention latching onto her words. "Chateau Falco may be in grave danger. I, for one, would encourage Gunnar—a Horseman—to stay here and hopefully keep us all safe."

I studied her and saw the genuine fear lurking in the depths of her eyes. She wasn't bluffing.

"Gunnar," I said, staring Othello in the eyes, "I can't tell you what I'm doing with Alucard and War, and I need you to promise that you won't pry or you could jeopardize everything and put the entire world in danger. Sound like something you can manage?"

"Yes," he said without hesitation, but I knew he was holding back about a hundred questions.

"Good. In return, I will come clean on something else I've been hiding from *everyone*—until last night when I roped in Alucard and Othello. I even lied about it to *Callie*—which cost me something big. In fact, I'm pretty sure I irreparably broke something between us in doing so. *That's* how dedicated I am to keeping some things private."

The two of them stared at me in shock, not sure how to respond.

"You both need to accept that I had my reasons for leaving you in the dark, and that it had nothing to do with your skills or abilities or anything like that. It was a tactical decision. Just like I'm not asking why you're *really* meeting behind closed doors, or what budget Felicia is working on, because I sure as hell am curious. You two are scheming as well, but I trust your judgment. Let's just leave it at that. Agreed?"

They both nodded, looking shaken by my rapid-fire commands. And my suspicions were confirmed, judging by the purple spots on their cheeks. They are up to something as well.

"From here on out, this is a feelings free zone. Facts only." I glanced up at a clock on the wall. "Because I have very little time, so let's get started." I leaned against the fireplace so they could both see me as I ran through a quick history. I turned to Gunnar, first. "Remember that abduction attempt on me a few weeks back? With the black marble prototype from Grimm Tech?"

Othello growled territorially. "I do *now*."

"Yes," Gunnar said. "She called you right after, but you never explained or brought it back up, so I just assumed you killed her."

I frowned to hear that his first assumption had been that I murdered her. "I didn't kill her, Gunnar. Her name is Niko. She used to be—or might still be—an assassin. There's an app called Lullaby that mercenaries now use to list their assassination contracts. Niko has been helping me avoid early retirement by giving me forewarning about any assassins who accepted the billion-dollar price tag on my head." His eye bugged out at the dollar amount, but I pressed on. "But she won't help me find who posted the contract until I agree to meet with her in person, which I've obviously been reluctant to do. That is why she tried to abduct me in the first place. She thinks I'm dangerous, but she also has a conscience and says she doesn't kill for money. As doubtful as that may sound, her actions so far have been consistent with it."

Gunnar nodded, his lips pursed tightly together, and he was forcefully gripping the arm of the chair, outraged to hear that his best friend had been in constant danger and that he hadn't been informed.

Othello looked equally shaken, but feelings were denied entry in this room.

"Okay," I said, turning to Othello. "Now that the facts have all been laid out, tell me what you found, and why you think Chateau Falco is in danger. Your news may impact what I was going to talk to Gunnar about."

She nodded, gathering a small stack of papers on her desk and straightening them like a lawyer preparing a case.

CHAPTER 31

Othello cleared her throat delicately. "I've been playing around with that Lullaby app. Pretty clever stuff. Apparently, even I had a contract on my head for a while, but it was archived years ago."

I grunted, wondering who wanted Othello—one of the world's greatest hackers—dead. I also wondered what her boyfriend, the Horseman of Death, had to say about it. Maybe *archived* meant that the person who had originally posted the hit had been permanently *archived*—by her boyfriend murdering him to death.

"Here is what set off my alarm bells. I found a new contract for someone who sounds suspiciously like Niko. It was posted late last night after you spoke with her. So I did a little research on the phone trace I did for you, wondering where in Colorado she was hiding out. This is from a satellite I hacked last night in order to get a visual."

I didn't even bother reprimanding her for her felony. She laid out a picture on the desk. I walked over to inspect it.

It showed an aerial view of a long, rectangular building surrounded by woods, and I could easily read the familiar words painted on the roof, as if they had been intended for a satellite picture: NATE TEMPLE WAS HERE.

I grunted. "She anticipated your move." Othello sniffed primly. "And it's the same message Thor wrote in the parking lot of Buddy Hatchet," I muttered, remembering the first time I'd met Thor—when we'd destroyed the Bifröst. I'd also teased Niko on the phone last night, telling her that I was considering writing those exact words down at the warehouse for the cops to find later. I handed it to Gunnar without looking at him.

Othello nodded, her eyes now twinkling excitedly for some reason. "I was going to send a team there later today to remove it, so I took some more pictures this morning to get accurate directions for them, since the first image showed only woods and no roads."

She dropped another photo on the table, and this one showed a flickering green fire, the building already reduced to charred rubble and smoldering coals.

I felt the hair on the back of my neck stand up. "This morning?" I hissed.

Othello nodded. "Mere hours after a contract for her head was posted to Lullaby. I think her fellow assassins figured out that she turned snitch. That she's been helping you waylay their teams. And they went to Colorado to remedy that."

"I tried calling her early this morning but she didn't answer," I said, feeling sick to my stomach.

Othello nodded. "I know. I saw."

"You've been watching my phone?"

She waved a hand dismissively. "Don't act so surprised. I stalk everyone I care about. Especially when they're talking to people like Niko. Anyway, when you called her, she was here in St. Louis. Not Colorado." Othello noticed my sudden frown. "Exactly. Way too convenient. Someone must have warned her that she'd been compromised. So I did some more digging and found that someone else did call her before you, but the conversation was too short for me to trace the origin." I shook my head. Was Niko that good, or incredibly lucky? "And that's not even the strangest part," she said. "Guess what her first stop was in St. Louis," she said, leaning forward eagerly.

I shrugged. "Purple."

"What?" she asked, her excitement deflating.

"I hate it when people ask me to guess something. I'm going to guess wrong either way, so I've decided to start giving random bullshit answers. No offense." She began tapping her finger on the desktop, not even remotely amused. I sighed, waving a hand for her to continue.

"Niko went to...*Buddy Hatchet*. That axe throwing bar where you first fought Thor—the same place where he left the message that she duplicated on the roof in Colorado. That is one hell of a coincidence for that to be her backup safehouse."

I grunted, trying to process it all into a story that made sense. Because Kára, the Valkyrie, *owned* Buddy Hatchet. Were they friends? If so, was that a good thing?

Was Kára telling Niko how great I was?

Or was Niko warning Kára how *dangerous* I was?

Or maybe Niko had simply been trying to send me a message in Colorado, using her painted roof to tell me where she was going next—a direct reference to the conversation we'd had only hours before, using it like a coded verification phrase.

No matter which reason was true, one major priority had just jumped to the top of my list. Because if Freya had followed my secret request—codename *applesauce*—Kára was now in a perfect position to hurt me and someone I cared about very deeply. If Kára was actually an enemy, of course —which wasn't yet known.

"Thanks, Othello. This helps more than you know. But what did you mean about Chateau Falco being in danger?" I asked, too focused on the Niko situation to think about much else.

Othello slowly tapped her finger onto the second picture. "The same people who tried to kill her are likely after you. They firebombed this place with only a few hours' notice. And green fire also suggests it's from your side of the fence. Not your typical fire."

Then she leaned back in the chair, folding her hands over her waist.

I slowly turned to Gunnar. "Um. Looks like you have a new job, Smokey, because only you can prevent wizard fires," I said, pointing at the picture.

He curled his lips menacingly and nodded one time, not even catching the reference.

"It also segues into what I wanted to talk to you about," I added. He frowned but urged me to continue. I took a deep breath. "I want to dip Calvin and Makayla in the River Styx and make them immune to harm like Achilles."

He stared at me incredulously.

Othello let out a nervous breath. "Fuck me," she breathed.

Gunnar studied me, not blinking as he processed my idea. But he didn't shout, and he didn't yell at me. He understood the need—that something very strange was happening to his children. "I will need to talk to Ashley, of course. And based on Othello's news—in addition to everything else we've recently seen—it *would* grant me peace of mind."

I grunted. "That's an understatement."

He nodded soberly. "And I know you wouldn't suggest such a drastic measure lightly. You are their godfather, Nate. We trust you on these sorts of things…"

I nodded, licking my lips as I tried to consider any factor I might have overlooked. None came to mind.

"Would you do it if you were in my shoes?"

I'd been expecting the question. Still, hearing it sent butterflies through my stomach. I took a deep breath and nodded. "Yes. I would."

Gunnar nodded thoughtfully. "Barring Ashley's outright refusal, I will agree if you promise to meet with Agent Murphy and Agent Glass tomorrow night."

Othello coughed suddenly, making me smile. She would somehow be conspicuously busy.

Gunnar shot her a warning glare before turning back to me. "The longer you delay, the worse it looks. They just want to talk. I've already gotten them to largely back down and they believe that you're not a criminal. Meeting with you in person would seal the deal. Or this dark cloud is going to loom over your head—and ours—for a long time. The government will send everything they can at you, even if it's only to smother you in legal cases. You have enough enemies to deal with already." He glanced at the picture of green flames. "Obviously."

I sighed, grumbling unhappily as I realized that he was right. "Fine. Where?"

"Here. Chateau Falco."

"Okay, but that means I *really* need to get out of here and go deal with my other problem. Now."

"I'll talk to Ashley about your proposal, but I'm sure she will agree with your verdict," Gunnar said, and I could tell he was actively preventing himself from grinning excitedly.

Othello chimed in. "It's so weird how your flight from Stockholm lands tomorrow morning. Almost like I knew you were going to agree."

I narrowed my eyes. "It's a conspiracy, I tell you."

She waved a hand. "The benefits of you owning a company jet."

I frowned at a new thought. "How are the ravens doing?" I asked, knowing that it probably wasn't wise to talk to them, but still wanting to make sure they were okay.

"Ravens?" he asked, blinking rapidly.

I arched an eyebrow, suddenly curious. "Yeah. The big scary ones. Not all those other ravens we have around here," I said sarcastically.

"Oh, yes," he said, looking embarrassed. "They're still sleeping, actually, but Ruin said they are fine. No injuries. I was just going to go check on them."

"Good." I wasn't sure why he was acting weird about it, but I wasn't going to fault him for keeping secrets. "Once all this crap is resolved, we need to talk about Ratatoskr."

He nodded. "They began training this morning, apparently."

I nodded, seriously hating that fact. Grimm would have been a big help for my upcoming plans. "Well, keep me posted if you hear from our ponies. Death can be a real hardass."

Othello growled protectively, but I ignored her as I turned to leave.

"Ruin wanted to talk to you about the tree," Gunnar said as I was turning away. "It's stopped bleeding, apparently, but he found what looks like tiny bone fragments in the latest batch of blood."

I nodded. "I know. Tell him to stay vigilant, though. Just in case."

"What do you mean, *you know?*" Gunnar sputtered, sounding angry. "You—"

I Shadow Walked to the warehouse before he could finish his sentence.

Because I'm petty.

And because I didn't want Carl and Alucard to come looking for me because I was late.

CHAPTER 32

The moment I entered the warehouse, I discreetly checked the bond between me and the other Horsemen, making sure that they had their Masks and weren't actually Loki in disguise. They had dragged some wooden crates together to form a circle, and were all sitting down, looking bored.

Thankfully, their Masks checked out.

Carl turned his head to catch me in his peripheral vision, and I saw his nostrils flare as he scented me. But he still didn't make eye contact. With War and Alucard verified—and Alucard somehow brain-bonded with the Elder—Carl earned default verification status.

War glanced over at me and smiled, nodding his head to let me know he'd checked my Mask as well. He'd chosen to sit on the crate closest to a taller stack of crates so that he had a backrest. Pro-tip—when lounging around an abandoned warehouse, grab the best seat. "I already showed Alucard how to do it."

Alucard looked up with a grin. "Checked you the moment you appeared," he said smugly. "I even had a nasty surprise waiting, just in case."

"Good. Is everything ready?"

They nodded. Well, Carl just watched us in silence, turning his head back and forth like he was watching tennis.

I walked up to them and sat on an empty crate, wondering how much I needed to tell War and Carl. They hadn't asked a single question so far, which I found rather strange. "How much do you two know about all this?" I asked.

Alucard grunted. "Carl says he just needs to know when and who to kill. Probably ought to add who *not* to kill."

Well, that made things easier.

War shrugged. "I've got theories, but all I really know is that we're meeting Loki. Like Carl, it's better if you don't give me too many details. If I have too much information, I'll start making decisions out of habit. It's kind of nice to sit back and let the dice roll. To be a soldier again. I like surprises, and I'm watching how you handle things. That's good enough for me. Just consider me the muscle of the team. You're the brains."

"That sounds like a very poor training system."

War chuckled. "The analysis will come after. You handle some things very differently than I would, so it's fun to watch. I may have even learned a few things from you. But a team needs a *single* leader. Anything else results in division. I'll back your plays, and follow your lead—like a good soldier. I don't need any special treatment. I want to watch how you think, to see firsthand why everyone is so afraid of you. Maybe I can learn some of that," he chuckled, winking at me.

Alucard grunted. "I guess I'm the flashlight guy, but I can be a minion if necessary. I know it's probably safest that way, since we're dealing with Loki. Compartmentalize the information."

I nodded. "What's Carl?" I asked, amused by his flashlight comment.

"He's the mysterious psycho with a shadowy past. And he doesn't *speak*," Alucard said in a dramatic tone.

Carl nodded agreeably, still refusing to meet my eyes

"Alright. He should be here just after sunset, so make yourselves comfortable until then." I turned to Carl, trying not to take it personally when he suddenly dropped his gaze to the ground. "I'd like to save your presence as a surprise in case Loki starts being difficult. But we *cannot* kill him. We *need* him. Okay?"

Carl nodded.

"For what it's worth," Alucard said, "Carl offered to scrape Loki's mind and get whatever answers we need."

War's eyebrows practically jumped off of his forehead.

I shook my head firmly. "No. We need him alive. My whole plan rests on him being alive. Otherwise we have failed. Okay? I *really* need everyone to understand that."

They all nodded.

War took my advice to get comfortable, leaning back against the wall of crates and crossing his ankles.

We sat in silence, thinking private thoughts, waiting for the sun to set. Carl began sharpening one of his swords, and it wasn't long until Alucard gagged noisily. "That's disgusting, Carl. Do you really just casually think about things like that?" Carl looked up to stare at him, and the ridge of his mouth formed as much of a smile as the silver wire would allow.

And Carl never stopped sharpening his sword as he did it.

"It's…just not right," Alucard muttered, looking away. He didn't even try to tell us whatever Carl had thought about either.

War lit up a cigar and began to hum an old, haunting campfire song that sounded hundreds of years old—all between puffs of his cigar that filled our circle with the strong scent of sweet and spicy tobacco, reminding me of my father's beloved Gurkha Black Dragons.

I realized that I was staring at him, transfixed by his tune, and that the hair on the back of my arms was sticking straight up. Without words, it sang of loss and pain and sorrow, of a people banding together against all odds, knowing they stood no chance.

I'd never felt emotional from a mere tune before. Not anything as dark and foreboding as this, anyway.

I had to force myself to walk away, unable to think clearly with it distracting me.

I exited the building and stared up at the darkening sky, thinking of what I had told Othello and Gunnar about Callie—how I'd caused irreparable harm by lying to her. The words had been off the top of my head, but they had sounded worse when said out loud.

More…final.

Was I being overly dramatic? I still knew that I had been right in my decision, but likely wrong in my delivery.

I wasn't sure if I would have changed anything if given a second chance. Was that because I was thinking like a leader rather than a lovestruck fool? Freya had warned against the perils of working with someone you loved—especially if one had authority over the other.

And I definitely had authority. Like War said, when more than one leader tried to emerge—even accidentally—division ensued. I sighed, straightening my satchel—the one Callie had gotten for me from Darling and Dear. It was time to get my head in the game. Callie would have to wait until later, when we had the chance to talk in person. In private.

Judging by the creeping darkness, it wouldn't be very long until Loki arrived, and I'd finally know what our next step was.

Regardless of the outcome, I knew I needed to meet up with Kára, first. For multiple reasons, but primarily because of codename applesauce. On a whim, I tried calling Niko, but it went straight to voicemail again. Maybe she'd ditched her phone after her fellow assassins turned on her.

I couldn't do anything until I got an update from Loki. I wasn't about to let him slip through my fingers on a technicality.

I walked back into the building, ready to remind Carl to hide—

He was already gone.

Alucard noticed the look on my face and nodded. "We're good," he said, seeming to emphasize the word *we* to indicate Carl.

We waited the next ten minutes in silence, and I was about ready to prepare my ritual circle from last night and drag his sorry ass here against his will—

Boom. Boom. Boom. A fist banged on the door.

War exhaled a thick ring of smoke. "Showtime."

We turned as the door slowly opened with a chilling squeal.

CHAPTER 33

Rain poured in through the open door, instantly puddling on the concrete floor. Wind screamed and whistled, fighting to follow a large cloaked man as he walked into the building.

The wind made his cloak whip and snap, and he wore a folded, pointed hat on his head to balance the long, pointed beard down his chest. Lightning cracked from the sky, limning him in the doorway as a dark nightmare made flesh.

The Wanderer.

Odin.

"Shit," Alucard muttered.

I stared back defiantly, holding my ground.

"Where. Is. Gungnir?" Odin growled, his lone eye seeming to crackle with its own inner lightning.

I waited five seconds.

And then I burst out laughing—the most condescending laugh I could manage on demand.

"Overkill, Loki," I finally wheezed. "The lightning was way too much."

The figure stared at us in silence. Then he threw his hat on the ground and stomped on it for good measure. A second later, an entirely different man stood before us—the Loki I had met here last night. The puddles and rain were simply gone, and there was no lightning outside.

"Really? I thought I nailed it," he grumbled unhappily. "I had him fooled," he said, pointing at Alucard.

"Oh, it was good," I reassured him. "I just expected it. And I was outside a few minutes ago. Clear sky. The real Odin would have let the storm start before he even knocked. It's all about the foreplay."

He sighed. "Everyone's a critic," he muttered, walking towards us. "Let's just get this over with."

I held out an arm invitingly. "Pick a seat, as long as it's that one," I said, pointing at the shortest crate. The rest of us sat down, giving him no other option.

He grunted, shaking his head. "It's better than the Bioloki. Even the worst of days up here can't compare to the best of days in that cursed book," he said, sitting down with a contented groan.

I nodded. "I bet."

Loki studied War openly. "Hello, stranger. You smell like horse."

War blew an impenetrable cloud of smoke in his face without cracking a smile.

Loki smirked, waving it away. "I like him. But I was really hoping for the wolf with the hammer."

I leaned forward, placing my elbows on my knees. "If I was the kind of guy who cared what you hoped for, that would be worth discussing. But I'm not. Now, with every second you waste, your son's chances grow slimmer. Tell me what you've learned, Loki."

He nodded. "If you can't say something nice, say something clever but devastating. Don't half-ass two things, whole-ass one thing. And never camp out in an unlucky warehouse by the riverfront."

I had been about to cut him off for his flippant answers, but he had stopped after the last sentence, grinning mischievously. I frowned.

"I knew that one would tickle your fancy," he said. "When I felt that wave of unluckiness last night, I simply *had* to take a look for myself."

I grimaced, hoping my friends didn't start asking questions about it, because I didn't want to tell them about Hermes. Also, he'd just confirmed my assumption that it *had* been Hermes.

"You were there?" I asked, frowning.

He nodded. "Why do you think that idiot kept hurling fire against the wall? I was throwing things at it."

Alucard muttered darkly under his breath, obviously feeling guilty because he had been the first one inside the building.

"I watched as chance was distorted, turning your little brawl into a bloodbath. It truly was a thing of beauty. Was that your doing?" I just stared at him, keeping my face blank. He pursed his lips thoughtfully, reading entirely too much into my non-answer. "I used an illusion to make *you* think the wizard on the trash pile had died," he explained, pointing an accusatory finger at Alucard. "He was banged up but alive. I think he caught the only luck in the building, other than you two, of course. He heard your whole conversation, though, so I just *had* to have him."

I stared at him, not entirely sure where to start or where he was going with this. Since it was his son's life on the line, I decided that he had to have a good reason for bringing it up. "Why?"

"A.B.L."

I frowned. "What?"

"Always. Be. Leveraging."

I frowned. "How would taking that worthless wizard help you? Or Fenrir, for that matter?"

Loki shrugged. "Ah. Well, you said you wanted to question one of them. He was the only one of them still breathing, so I took him." He leaned towards Alucard as if to tell him a secret. "That's what leverage means, by the way," he said in a loud whisper.

Alucard looked like he was reconsidering my command to let Loki live. I didn't blame him, but I held a palm out to tell him to calm down. He gave me a faint nod.

"You wasted your time. He didn't know anything about me," I told Loki. "Just that I needed to die."

Loki nodded in understanding. "I needed to know more about you. Why these assassins wanted to kill you, and why they had…such an unlucky time trying," he said, winking. "Found that answer outside your precious mausoleum, even if I couldn't figure out how to get inside the cursed place."

War and Alucard both glanced at me, but I pretended not to notice.

"Awkward…" Loki said, grinning. "Anyway…I promised to let the lucky wizard go if he told me the full spiel. Turns out, he was hired by the Academy. Total assholes, right?" Loki asked, holding a palm out to Alucard. He ignored it entirely, watching me instead.

So *that* was how Niko had been targeted so quickly. Loki's survivor from the warehouse had snitched on the snitch.

Then my brain registered what he'd said about the assassination contract on me, and I was seeing red in a matter of seconds.

The Academy.

Those sleazy, pathetic, good-for-nothing hypocrites had a very bad day coming their way, and I very seriously considered making it a priority over Loki's son if he kept this up much longer. But I kept my face composed, showing nothing—pretending like this wasn't anything newsworthy.

Because that was exactly what Loki wanted. I didn't know why trying to get under my skin was a bigger priority than saving his own son, but he had to have a reason. Maybe it was nothing more than petty pride—knowing that I had him by the short hairs, and deciding to do everything in his power to make me pay for each second I held him hostage.

"You almost got a friend killed," I said in a warning tone, thinking of Niko.

"Almost makes the heart beat longer," he said brightly. Seeing none of us sharing his enthusiasm, he sighed. "I kept his electronic raven and let him go," he said, pulling out a phone and tossing it to me.

I caught the phone—or electronic raven, as he'd called it—and pulled up the contacts. Sure enough, Niko was listed, and the number matched the one I had for her. It even showed that the phone's last call was to Niko. I frowned, glancing up at Loki in confusion.

He nodded proudly. "I knew he would instantly hunt down this Niko person for betraying him and his pals. So I used his electronic raven to summon her and tell her I was coming for her in Colorado. Then I hung up!" he said, chuckling. "Since you said I *almost* got a friend killed, I'm assuming she took my advice to heart."

I cringed at his twisted sense of delight. "What the hell is wrong with you?"

He frowned. "I saved her life. Right after you abandoned me at Yggdrasil."

That film of red rage I'd just suppressed was back in a nanosecond.

Whips of white fire suddenly exploded from my hands. War and Alucard fell backwards off their crates, cursing in surprise. Loki had moved the fastest, already standing five feet away with his hands held up above his head in a gesture of surrender.

"What did you just say?" I whispered, letting my whips scorch the concrete as I began to walk towards him. "You were supposed to be finding Fenrir, but now you tell me that *you* were the Odin we met up with? Give me one good reason why I shouldn't rip you in half for wasting my time. I thought you wanted to save your son, but it seems I was mistaken."

Loki waved his hands dramatically. "This still means surrender, right?"

Seeing that I hadn't slowed my advance, he took another step back. "Oh, fine. I've known where Fenrir was for a while now—days after you killed that lying sack of shit, Mordred," he cursed, spitting on the ground.

I stopped and stared at him, my whips still crackling and burning.

"This better be good, Loki…" I warned.

CHAPTER 34

Loki shrugged, but I heard the desperation in his voice. He'd found my line—how far he could push me before I snapped.

"I've been checking in on Asgard a few times here and there, sending out false reports for Odin to chase down. He hasn't actually set foot in Asgard since the Mordred thing. Not once. Poor leadership in my opinion. Even Freya hardly wanted to remain in the same room with me, if that tells you anything. When she saw me—Odin—I saw true fear in her eyes."

I knew Freya was wise enough to fear Odin—the god, not her husband—but she had obviously downplayed that fear when we'd spoken in Asgard. Maybe she feared that if she said too many bad things about him that I would simply kill him for her. Which…hurt, to be honest. That she'd been scared to tell me the full truth for fear of what I might do with it—like she thought I couldn't control my emotions.

She hadn't said many nice things about him either, though—lending truth to Loki's claims.

Loki was nodding eagerly, realizing that he'd struck a topic that walked me back from the edge. "And to hear what some of the other gods are openly saying these days about Odin…he has no shortage of enemies, that's for sure." He shook his head slowly. "Which makes me deliriously happy, if I'm being honest. He was, and always will be, a frost giant's dick."

I ignored that, still wondering what the hell his goal was with all of this.

"If you already knew where Fenrir was, then why didn't you just tell me last night?" I demanded, cracking a whip dangerously close to his face. "We could have already gotten your son back!"

And I could be dealing with any other number of important things.

Loki frowned at me, urgently brushing a live spark from his shoulder "I'm the only one in the world who knows where my son is, and I'm not Mimir. Chop this handsome head off and we're *all* unhappy."

I took a deep breath and let the whips wink out. "You're right. Decapitation is way too good for you. Talk or we are going to take turns beating your head against the wall."

Loki's face paled as War loudly cracked his knuckles, clenching his cigar between his teeth with an eager grin. "Oh, I like that plan." Alucard nodded excitedly.

Loki stepped closer to me. "The reason I've been dicking around with you for the last ten minutes is because we don't stand a chance. None. I know *where* he is, but I don't know *who* runs the compound. That's one major reason I went to Asgard—to try and get some real answers—but your little stunt cut that short."

"Did you want War or Alucard for the first round of head-smashing?" I asked.

"Judging by the security at the compound," he said hurriedly, "I knew I stood no chance at breaking in. So I tried sneaking in, pretending to be one of the guards. But the alarms went off the second I tried to open the door—like not even the *guards* are allowed inside. They have these gargoyle things..." He shuddered. "The only other time I ran that fast was ten minutes after I first tasted something called Indian curry. Luckily, I made it away from danger...*this* time."

Alucard grimaced, shaking his head. "Oh, that's *foul*."

"Oh, you have *no* idea," Loki agreed. "I was so embarrassed that I pretended to be a different person when I left the restroom. Then another identity when I left the restaurant. Never again."

War grunted, shaking his head. "This is incredibly unhelpful. Let's just do a couple head smashes. I'm having a hard time focusing on what he's saying because I keep envisioning how much better his whiny bullshit would sound if he was lisping through a few missing teeth."

"Think about it, Temple!" Loki pleaded. "They're holding Fenrir hostage —*without Gleipnir*. You know how many chains Asgard made to try and restrain him before finding one that worked? These are scary fucking people."

He wasn't wrong. In fact, I almost suspected Odin was behind it all, and that maybe he'd commissioned a new Gleipnir while he searched the globe for his stolen spear so that he could come back and kill the wolf at his convenience. But that would be a side of Odin I hadn't yet seen. I knew he'd been an asshole in the stories about him, but if he had Fenrir restrained in some hidden bunker, the problem was already taken care of.

In fact, he probably would have announced it to all of Asgard, parading Fenrir down the streets to prove Odin was back and in charge—having successfully recaptured Fenrir without having to use Gungnir. It would make him look all the more impressive.

It just didn't make sense for Odin to be behind it.

I pointed at my chest and then at Alucard. "You had two Horsemen volunteering to help last night! You're telling me this compound is *that* secure!?"

Loki nodded somberly. "Absolutely. That is exactly what I'm fucking saying. It's why I've been visiting Asgard disguised as Odin. I've been trying to figure out which one of the throne-hungry bastards is behind it all. Because whoever runs the compound with Fenrir, I think they're Asgardian, and they fucking hate Odin more than Thor ever did. More than even I hate him, and he locked me in a *book* for a few centuries! Any other god or pantheon would have turned him in and demanded a ridiculous award, knowing Odin would gladly pay up." I nodded thoughtfully, and Loki pressed on. "I have three suspects so far. Baldur—for the obvious reasons you saw during your visit. Tyr—because Odin took the throne from him. And Heimdall—because he's too perfect. And I've never much liked him, to be honest. But that's just petty spite. We're destined to kill each other at Ragnarök, so I propose we kill him just to be thorough. Hell, let's just kill them all."

I threw my hands into the air. "This is ridiculous. I'm going to put the Bioloki up for auction. You could have bitched and moaned about this last night and saved me some time."

"Let's not be hasty," Alucard said, holding his hands out in a calming gesture. "There was talk of head-smashing." War nodded, punching his fist into his palm.

Loki ignored them without fear this time, his eyes glittering with anger and disdain as he leaned forward. "You just don't get it, do you? I've fucked with every single Asgardian, and now they finally have a chance to stick it to me. Or Odin. Or both of us. And Thor isn't around to stop them and look like a hero. In a way, that's on *you*."

I sputtered incredulously. "Me?" I demanded. I couldn't help it. I started laughing at him.

"No one had the balls to get in Thor's way," Loki argued. "He was a necessary evil. But you and your werewolf pal removed him from the equation. And rather than including the Horseman who now wields Mjölnir—because Thor's old hammer might have been enough to frighten any of these opportunistic pricks off the map—you picked the suck-head."

Alucard stepped forward, his face livid. But War latched onto his shoulders, pulling him back.

"I thought if I waited you out for the twenty-four-hours you gave me, you would bring the wolf with the hammer along, too." Loki eyed War thoughtfully. "I'll admit, this is a good bench you have, Temple. But you know what? I'm not convinced it's enough, and I would do *anything* to save my son. I would even die for it. But *pointless* suicide won't save him. Why don't you call the Horseman with Mjölnir, and we can give this a real chance at success?"

I grunted, purposely not glancing over his shoulder—where Carl was suddenly lurking. Yeah, it was probably about that time. I turned to Alucard. "Don't kill him, Alu-Carl."

The Daywalker grinned wickedly.

Loki scoffed. "What are *you* going to do? Sparkle me to death?" he muttered.

And then Loki gasped in total surprise as Carl wrapped his claws around the God of Mischief's throat and hoisted him into the air. Loki resorted to magic, throwing flames down at Carl, but the Elder used his free hand to swat it all away, only looking mildly perturbed.

"It *is* a pretty nice bench, isn't it?" I said, grinning at Loki. I let him gag for another ten seconds before clearing my throat and glancing at Alucard.

"Aw, dad," he complained, "I want to keep playing!"

I rolled my eyes.

Carl set Loki down and the God of Mischief skittered a few feet away, coughing violently. "What the hell!?" he rasped, his eyes zeroing in on the silver wire over Carl's mouth.

I shrugged. "Old family friend," I said. "You have three Horsemen and an Elder, but no Mjölnir. What are our odds of breaking into this compound?"

Loki thought about it, and he slowly began to nod. "Favorable. Maybe."

"That's good enough for me."

"Did you bring Gleipnir?" Loki asked.

"I thought you didn't need it."

"And if I don't survive first encounter with the enemy?" he replied dryly. "I doubt Fenrir will think highly of you. He is very likely in a maddened state. *I* might not even be able to control him right now. He's a prisoner in enemy territory. He won't go down—for us or these goons—without a fight."

I stared at him. "You really think he'll try to kill us, too?"

He nodded. "Precisely. Until we can calm him down, and I doubt we will get the time to do that in the middle of an abduction. We can talk him down after—if he doesn't eat us all first."

No one else spoke as Loki's words echoed with grim finality. "Or maybe we *don't* calm him down..." I said, thinking out loud. "Maybe we just need to get close enough to set him *loose*."

Loki stared at me with both fear and...a budding consideration. He took a moment to appraise each of us individually, and I saw confidence beginning to shine in his eyes. "I could agree to that, but I have one question, first."

I nodded. "Okay."

"Do you have any more team shirts?" he asked, glancing at our matching *Show-Me Your O-Face* tees. Well, Carl didn't have one because he'd told Alucard that it felt scratchy against his scales. Diva.

I turned to War. He nodded. "One left."

"Then I'm in."

"It's a small," War said, clenching his cigar between his teeth in a big grin.

Loki's excitement faded somewhat.

"I need to check on one thing before we leave to wherever we're going. You guys think you can keep an eye on him while I'm gone? Without killing or otherwise injuring him? We'll need him in fighting shape."

"I'm right here," Loki said.

Alucard spoke up. "That's the problem. We can't trust what we see with him, right?"

I nodded. Then I flipped open my satchel and pulled out a leather harness. Alucard's eyes widened in recognition. And then a truly evil smile split his cheeks.

"Why is he smiling like that?" Loki asked, splitting his attention between the item in my hand and the sheer happiness on Alucard's face.

Instead of answering, I snapped my fingers.

The Darling and Dear harness launched from my hand and wrapped around Loki in about a millisecond. He dropped to his knees, unable to move, and staring at me with wide eyes. "What the hell is this thing?" he whispered in horror. "I can't use my powers at all!"

Carl stared at it with an intent look on his face. He'd been the first victim.

War grunted. "That...is very useful. And creepy. Because it kind of looks like—"

"Bondage gear," Alucard said smugly. "Where did you find it?" he asked me.

"I don't want to talk about it," I said, repressing a shudder. "But I chose to thoroughly disinfect it before putting it in my satchel."

War cocked his head, taking the cigar out of his mouth to silently repeat my answer, trying to decipher my meaning.

"Yeah. That was probably a good call," he said knowingly. "Who would have thought, right?"

I didn't want to go anywhere near that conversation, so I appraised Loki instead. "This is for wasting my time. If one of these fine gentlemen snaps their fingers a second time, you'll experience the ball-gag option. So I would be very, very polite, because they don't know the codeword to release it."

Loki stared at me, openly terrified. "Right. How, um, long were you going to be gone, exactly? Because I really need to use the restroom."

"I hope you can hold it better than that other time you told us about," I said, turning to walk away. "No unnecessary cruelty, guys. He's harmless. I shouldn't take more than an hour."

"If it's dangerous, you should take one of us with you. Just in case," Alucard suggested.

I stopped, turning to glance back at Loki. There was no way out of the harness, so I nodded. "Want to join me, Carl?" I asked.

He nodded eagerly, and I felt a wave of relief as he jogged over to me. It wasn't that I feared he had a newfound problem with me, but it was difficult to see him so...subservient. I missed his painful attempts at conversation, teaching him new things.

But now he wouldn't even look me in the eyes.

So for him to seem excited to stand by my side felt like we were getting closer to the old days. I really wanted to rip that wire from his lips, but I knew it wasn't just wire. It was symbolic.

Maybe I could convince him to take it out.

I grinned at a sudden thought, leaning close so that no one else could hear. "I'm about to show you the biggest D in the world, Carl," I told him, grinning.

He smirked as much as the wire would allow and extended his clawed hand. I grabbed it and Shadow Walked to the Drop Zone outside Chateau Falco.

It hadn't been necessary to come here, first, but it was all about the delivery.

I pointed at Carl's tree through the hanging willow branches that surrounded us in a protective dome. "Your D, for perspective."

Then I closed my eyes in hopes that my next jump would work like I theorized—that I could travel to a place as long as I'd once been there before. The World Tree was in some strange, time-shifting realm, after all, so I couldn't be sure until I tried it.

Hell, since it was a place outside of time...

Maybe I hadn't ever been there yet.

I felt my ears pop and hoped for the best.

CHAPTER 35

*C*arl made a stunned sound from between his muzzled lips and I grinned, opening my eyes. It had worked! "The World D," I told him, pointing at Yggdrasil.

And we weren't alone.

Freya and Kára were seated near the trunk of the tree with Alice, but the three of them abruptly stood at seeing us appear out of thin air. Freya's jaw dropped when she saw a muzzled Elder, of all beings, standing beside me. She'd never met him, after all. I waved off their concern with an easy smile.

After Baldur's friend had accidentally grazed Freya with the knife in Asgard, I'd made an executive decision. Wanting to keep Gunnar's pups safe but needing to keep him out of the Loki mess so he could focus on his family—and his pups' strange new powers—I'd seen an opportunity to save three birds with one tree.

To send Freya to Yggdrasil where she would be safe from the dangers in Asgard—which indirectly protected Gunnar's pups since she was now bonded to them.

But to keep it secret from her fellow Asgardians, I'd had to be cryptic. It was the major reason I'd wanted to visit Yggdrasil in the first place. Sure, the reasons I had hinted at with Odin had also been true, providing me excellent benefits down the road that I thought would be prudent to set up, but it hadn't been pressing until I witnessed just how turbulent Asgard truly was these days. Thankfully, Loki's impersonation of Odin hadn't fucked it all up.

Codename *applesauce*.

In the confusion of the attack, I'd quietly told Freya that I needed to get her, Alice, and her most-trusted Valkyrie bodyguard somewhere safe, and that when I found a suitable place, I would say the word *applesauce*. That way the location was never mentioned where an Asgardian might overhear.

Because I had fully expected Loki to infiltrate Asgard, pretending to be someone else as he either searched for information on Fenrir—like I'd asked him to do—or tailed me in hopes of gaining some kind of leverage that he could later use against me in order to get his precious book back via multiple avenues.

That was how Loki always worked in the stories. He always found an out, and always found leverage.

I just hadn't expected him to be ballsy enough to choose *Odin* as his disguise. Sure, I had known that he could *physically* mimic anyone, but to *truly pass* himself off as Odin? In the heart of Asgard?

No way.

Loki had been imprisoned for hundreds of years, so he wouldn't have had time to catch up on every little thing that had happened in his absence. No frames of reference on current events. Trying to impersonate Odin—the god who was supposed to know everything important that happened in his kingdom—just hadn't seemed like a move with any chance of success.

He'd say something that wouldn't make sense, and everyone would instantly realize he was an imposter—especially since rumor had spread that Loki was free again.

Except…

I'd neglected to consider that Odin had *also* been gone for a long time, and that he was essentially a stranger to his own people—the perfect candidate for a switcheroo.

Still, it was remarkable he hadn't given himself away somehow.

I'd obviously underestimated Loki…or overestimated Asgardian intelligence. Perhaps both.

So, to see that Freya had successfully followed my shifty plan—without bringing all of Asgard down on her and Alice—made me ecstatic.

Except I'd told Freya to bring her most trusted Valkyrie, Kára.

Who might just be friends with Niko—the assassin with a heart of gold.

I realized that everyone was staring at me, waiting to hear why I was here with an Elder.

"I brought one of your princesses!" I called out to Alice.

She grinned, her trepidation suddenly washing away, and then she raced towards us as fast as her little legs could carry her. She hit Carl in a full-bodied hug, and I saw him grin wide enough to strain the wire over his ridged lips.

"Let's go!" she commanded him, tugging at his clawed hand—which was easily as large as her face. Carl didn't move, turning his head in my direction to get my approval. Again, no eye contact. Maybe it was just a respect thing, because I definitely didn't want him to think that he had let me down or upset me in some way.

I nodded, chuckling as I watched her immediately tug the terrifying Elder along behind her.

Freya motioned me to join her by the tree, and I realized that she was alone—which instantly set off alarm bells in my head. But Freya looked calm and relaxed, so I tried to keep my face calm as I made my way over.

"This is a *dangerous* place, Nate," Freya said. "I thought you said we needed a *safe* place."

"Is it more dangerous than Baldur growing a pair and bravely deciding to slit her throat in her sleep?" I murmured softly, watching Alice serve Carl a pretend cup of tea in a nearby patch of thick grass. They seemed to have no problem communicating. "Or your throat?"

She sighed. "I understand the necessity. I'm merely questioning the location."

"It was the best I could do on short notice, which was why I encouraged a bodyguard. The one who is now conspicuously absent..."

Freya lifted a hand to point at a hill a hundred feet away from Yggdrasil and covered in trees and bushes—a great place for an ambush. "She asked me if she was permitted to speak with you in private, but I told her I had first dibs."

"Oh?" I asked, trying not to twitch.

"I trust her over all other Valkyries, Nate, and I saw the way you flinched when you saw me standing alone. It was panic. What's wrong?"

I considered my response very carefully. "Concerned about her acquaintances."

Freya arched an eyebrow. "Oh?"

I nodded, deciding to shift gears rather than elaborate. "How is she able to own a bar? On Earth."

"Midgard," she corrected. Then she studied me for about five seconds, an amused smirk creeping over her face. "Do you not know her story? How Valkyries are chosen?"

I shrugged. "Not the real answer. We haven't talked about her past. She didn't even mention that you were in charge of the Valkyries. And what does her past have to do with her bar?"

Freya pursed her lips thoughtfully. "That is for her to explain, but I will tell you that she has only been a Valkyrie for a few years and has managed to earn more of my respect than any other in that short time. She reminds me of myself—when I was a younger, wilder, more passionate woman..." she trailed off, staring at the hill adoringly. I blinked at the goddess, wondering if I had heard correctly. "Even if that were not the case, there hasn't been much need for Valkyries lately. Especially not with Odin missing for decades."

"Have you seen him since I was last here?" I asked. "Odin."

She shook her head. "Not since he took us back to Asgard, but he didn't have more than single word responses to anything I asked him. He left Asgard almost immediately, leaving me to fend for myself. Didn't even say goodbye. At first, I thought your fear for my safety was a slight overreaction, but after his strange behavior and then sudden departure, it only took me a few hours back home to see the dark undercurrents lurking in the halls. That's when I began to like applesauce quite a bit more. I reached out to Kára, and we left without anyone noticing—they were too enthralled with their own plots and secret meetings to notice." She frowned thoughtfully, growing silent for a few moments. "I believe he is growing paranoid, because he went through my private letters before he left. At least, I assume it was him."

I sighed, not wanting to tell her the truth for fear that she would run back to Asgard to raise an army—or a search party for the real Odin.

"I should go see what Kára wanted."

"We will give you privacy," Freya said, walking over to Alice. "But give her the benefit of the doubt. If not for her, do so for me."

I thought that was a little over the top, but I pressed on, wondering how I wanted to handle the situation. Being friends with Niko was not a crime.

But it *could* be. Which was what I needed to find out.

CHAPTER 36

I found Kára seated before a pond in a cozy valley nestled between more rolling hills and looming trees. Her hair was not braided, spilling down the sides of her shaved head in a surprisingly wavy length that hung below her shoulders. She wore her armor, and her two different-colored eyes seemed to draw me in like magic, making my heart flutter at the level of happiness they showed to see me. She grinned brightly, and waved me over, practically bouncing up and down with excitement.

Despite my concerns, I found myself smiling at her general outtake on life—her *joie de vivre*—choosing to take Freya's counsel to heart. Kára had never given me a reason to distrust her, and I definitely didn't want her making decisions about my character that were based on third-party acquaintances or incomplete rumors. She'd have to assume I was a monster.

In fact, that was what I didn't want Niko doing. Ah, ye old double standard. So I took a measured breath, flashing her a smile as I decided to give her the chance she deserved. I'll admit that I was mighty curious about Freya's reference to her short tenure as a Valkyrie. I'd always thought they served for eternity.

I joined her on the grass with a sigh of relief, appreciating the soft ground over the crates in the warehouse. She was also more aesthetically pleasing than a lizard and three angry men.

"Is everything okay?" she asked. "You had your grumpy face on back there."

I nodded. "I think so. Just learned some new information that confused me," I admitted, choosing honesty. "Remember the first time we met?"

She scoffed. "We didn't *meet*. You trashed my place of business in a bar fight with Thor."

"We went outside," I argued, smirking.

"He *took* you outside, you mean."

I chuckled. "Yeah."

Kára grinned. "After your public argument with Baldur, I approached Freya about my concern for Alice. I didn't want the girl tarnished by your dangerous reputation," she teased. When I didn't laugh, her smile flickered away. "I hope that's okay."

I nodded stiffly, trying to make my smile look genuine. Because her words could be taken multiple ways. "Sure."

"Baldur is petty. He isn't one to care about collateral damage if it gets him what he wants."

I nodded, struggling to find the most natural way to slide into my questions.

"You look tense," she said, scooting up behind me without warning. Obviously, my shoulders instantly tensed even tighter. "See?" she laughed, not waiting for an answer before her strong, delicate hands began kneading my shoulders.

I groaned in surprise at her deft touch. "Wow, Kára."

"Your friend mentioned you were scheduled for a massage, but I bet I can give a better one," she murmured into my ear, making my body shiver as my hormones tried to grab hold of my decision-stick. She laughed, delighted by my response.

Alucard had been lying about the massage, but it was cute for her to remember it. Her touch was like magic, her fingers hot, surprisingly strong, and delivering the perfect pressure. "Where did you learn how to do massages?" I mumbled, impressed.

She pressed up against me from behind, rising up higher to get some leverage for a particularly difficult knot on my left shoulder blade. "I'm a Valkyrie, Nate," she whispered, grunting as her thumbs finally worked out the stubborn knot, sending tendrils of icy heat trailing across the adjoining muscles. I groaned in relief. I felt her settling back down behind me, her chest brushing down my spine as softly as fingers dancing. "A warrior this tense is liable to pull his hamstring at the first charge," she breathed. "Learning massage techniques is a necessary skill for a warrior to learn. As are many others," she purred, working her way up to the base of my neck.

Loose strands of her hair tickled my ear, and I reached my hand up on instinct to brush it away. My fingers touched her cheek and I froze like a startled deer.

Her flesh was hot and, rather than pulling away, she leaned into my touch with a pleasant humming sound.

My heart began to race again, and I wondered if I had grossly miscalculated our relationship. I carefully lowered my hand, pretending to ignore the disappointed sound in my ear.

"This is nice, isn't it?" she asked softly, her palms trailing down my neck and around the sides of my shoulders. She began to squeeze in slow, luxurious motions, working out my deltoids.

"Mmmhmmm," I managed, unable to talk as my feet began to tingle for some reason.

I felt her chest press against my spine again as she leaned her chin onto my shoulder to whisper in my ear. "I do not believe you got a massage, Nate..." she said in mock disapproval. I heard her slowly lick her lips before she continued in a smoky tone. "Or you would not be this tense," she explained, her inner thighs brushing both of my outer hips as her knees spread to bring her closer, allowing her soft, soft chest to press up against my back more forcefully. "Which means you never got your happy ending." And she nipped playfully at my ear with her teeth, her full lips brushing against my flesh before pulling away. Then she giggled. "You are tense again. Why are you tense again?" she asked, not bothering to hide her amusement.

I was panting and my tongue was tingling as my Spidey Senses suddenly gave me delayed warning that I had missed something rather obvious, forbidden, and unfairly tempting.

I scooted forward, having to force myself to do so in order to even think clearly. I twisted around to see Kára sitting down behind me, not wearing armor.

In fact, she was so good at not wearing armor that it took me a few seconds to process that she was actually wearing a thin, toga-like undergarment that ended scandalously high up on her thighs. Noticing my attention, her cheeks bloomed bright red. "This was all I had under my armor," she explained, sounding embarrassed, "and that was getting in the way of the massage. I wasn't trying to—" She cut off, and suddenly, the armor was back in place like a chastity belt.

I nodded, keeping my eyes fastened on hers. "It's okay. I didn't mean to stare. It just...caught me off guard," I said carefully. Part of me was shocked to see the armor just magically reappear. But it was a very distant thought. Magic was for nerds, and whatever had almost happened was *not* for nerds.

She smiled at me with a relieved grin. But I saw other emotions there, too. "On a related note..." she said softly, sounding both hopeful and shy, "I'm...not sure I know the words to explain how I feel about you, Nate," she admitted, and I could tell that she was being entirely honest. Despite her unintended wardrobe malfunction with slipping off her armor, I could see that she felt nervous and vulnerable and dedicated...about making the first move. "But I would like to try and *show* you how I feel..." she trailed off, holding out her hand invitingly. Her fingers were shaking. "With a kiss." She licked her full lips, and I realized they were trembling.

Kára was a figurative goddess—the fact that she literally wasn't one only made her *more* attractive, in my eyes. I experienced an internal civil war, and the North—my brain—prevailed, burning all bridges behind.

The South—my manhood—would rise again someday, but not today. And it would hold a grudge for generations.

I sighed, hanging my head and lowering my eyes. "You're making it very hard for me to do the right thing, Kára," I said, knowing that I needed to be extremely careful so as not to shatter her self-confidence, but to be true to—

"Because of Callie?" she asked, cocking her head and sounding genuinely confused.

I nodded. "Yes."

"But...I thought that was over between you two?" I looked up at her sharply. She looked just as baffled as I felt. "The way you talk about her when we spend time together made me think it was over—or close enough as to make no difference."

I shook my head, ignoring the hesitation that tried to worm into my thoughts as I remembered my most recent encounter with Callie. How strained it had felt between us—even before I'd reprimanded her. Like a wall with a single window stood between us—and the wall was growing taller as the window grew smaller.

CHAPTER 37

I could tell by the look on Kára's face that she obviously hadn't intended to meddle. In fact, she looked downright humiliated—on the verge of running away in shame. I needed to handle this carefully, but I did need to be firm. I really liked Kára…really, *really* liked her. And I didn't want to lose her because I had accidentally led her to the wrong conclusion about Callie.

"No, Kára. It isn't over with Callie. I haven't said anything bad about her to you, have I? Because even if Callie and I *were* over, I would never talk poorly about her behind her back," I said, scooting closer until our knees touched, and extending my hands in an offer to hold hers reassuringly. She had made a bold first move, and like a skittish horse, she was liable to run without a loving touch—a consolation prize of sorts. For the life of me, I couldn't recall what she thought I had said about Callie.

She let out a nervous breath, gently grasping my hands in hers. They were feverish. She took a deep breath and stared at me with her captivating dual-colored eyes. She blinked slowly, and I realized she had long, full eyelashes, making it difficult to focus. "You did not say anything cruel, Nate," she reassured me, gently squeezing my hands. "It was more in *how* you spoke when talking about her. Your mannerisms. Every time you mentioned her, you always spoke in the past tense. How you never spent time together, for one reason or another. Or you always had an excuse for not going to visit her, or you would justify her not coming to visit you. In fact, you never once told me a story where you were together longer than five minutes without it being related to some battle against a common enemy."

The look on her face told me that she genuinely didn't understand my relationship.

And I realized...that she had a point. I *had* done all of those things. And not only had I implied them...they were also *true*.

"You always spoke fondly of her," Kára assured me, "but it was more like you telling me of a beautiful sunset you had once seen—it had been marvelous, but that the sun had also *set*. And whenever you did speak of your future, I never once heard you say *we* or use her name—unless you were speaking about your duties as a Horseman. You've been back for weeks and you never once tried to visit her, even though Alucard did—several times. I actually suggested you should surprise her for a dinner. Three different times. Instead, you chose to spend four hours with me at the bar...*all three times*. I thought it was a subtle hint..." she admitted, sounding hurt and apologetic, instantly self-conscious.

I blinked at her, recalling those exact moments. Again...she was right.

"I'm sorry if it came across that way, Kára. I just didn't want to risk leaving St. Louis for too long. I had work to do," I said, the words feeling hollow, even to me.

She nodded sadly. "You said that then, too. That you were both busy with work. But we did not talk of work even once. *Any* of those evenings. Do you remember what we *did* talk about?"

I frowned, feeling guilty all of a sudden. Was I an asshole? What was I really feeling about Callie if my subconscious was out shopping behind my back?

Then I remembered what we had talked about, and I felt somewhat vindicated. But...it was a shallow vindication. "I talked about how she never called me to arrange a meeting," I admitted.

Kára nodded with a sad smile. "Yes. That she was too busy for you, too. And did you hear how your just phrased that? *Arrange a meeting*. Not a *date*. And the word *arrange*?" she asked, sadly empathetic. "It sounds like you're talking about business, not pleasure."

I nodded, realizing that she had another solid point. When I had seen Callie last night, I had definitely appreciated her beauty and her intelligence, but something had been missing that I hadn't been able to identify. Had it been our *spark*? Had we neglected it so long that it had fizzled out? Because whatever I had felt had not been limited to me—I had seen a similar emotion in Callie's eyes when she had looked at me.

As if we were watching a bridge being built between us—and that it was growing longer with neither of us attempting to cross—content to merely make doe eyes at each other from across the chasm.

"I wouldn't have made my intentions known had I thought you were still an item," Kára said. "As I admitted, I am not great with words. I'm a doer, not a talker."

I nodded. "It's not you, Kára," I said, feeling lame at the overused excuse, "but I obviously need to do some soul-searching. Maybe even…arrange a meeting with Callie," I said, smirking weakly at my choice of words, hoping to ease the tension.

She nodded sadly, staring down at our hands in silence. "I would like to hear how it goes…your soul-searching."

I nodded, finding myself thinking about what Freya had said—that Kára was a relatively new Valkyrie. But after wringing her emotions dry, I didn't feel that I had any right to ask her such a personal question. Maybe after I did some soul-searching and we put this tension behind us.

But I did need to ask her about Niko.

I squeezed her hands gently, smiling at her. "Can I ask you a question, Kára?" She nodded hesitantly. "How long have you known Niko?" I asked softly.

She frowned. "You know Niko?" she asked in disbelief.

I shrugged. "She's been the one helping me with the assassins thing. I only just learned her name."

Kára stared at me, looking like her brain was rebooting. And then she burst out laughing. "That *bitch*!" she hissed, squeezing my hands.

I stared at her, utterly baffled by her reaction. "Um…"

Her laughter finally began to subside, and she looked up at me, still shaking her head, causing her wavy hair to caress her throat…I forced myself to look away, realizing that I really needed to talk to Callie and figure out what was causing this rift between us soon. Startlingly, I felt a strange…frustration at the thought. Almost anger, like it was a job I just needed to get out of the way.

When had these thoughts started to crop up? As I considered the last few weeks, I had to admit that it wasn't anything new. I just hadn't chosen to confront these apparent demons—not even caring enough to realize that there *were* demons.

Was that the same look Callie had shown me? Not any kind of anger or dislike, but just...complacency? Growing apart? I had lost track of the number of times we had promised to spend time together, always ending the conversation with some form of *later*.

Were we subconsciously beginning to resent that in each other? Because it was obvious that it wasn't just me. Now that I was addressing it rather than avoiding it, I was beginning to realize that Callie had to feel the same way, because her mannerisms were exactly what I was feeling and portraying right now—and had been for the past few weeks, according to Kára.

I realized Kára was watching me with a deeply thoughtful look. "Are you okay? I didn't mean to upset you," she said.

Because I was frowning. I took a deep breath and shelved all thoughts of Callie for...

Later.

God damn it.

"Sorry, Kára. I got lost in my own head for a minute." I replayed our conversation. "You were saying that Niko was a bitch."

Kára smirked, rolling her eyes. "Not really, I guess. I was just caught off guard. She never told me about you, but we did speak of you often."

I frowned. "Why?"

She arched a cool eyebrow at me. "I just *showed* you why, Nate," she said dryly.

"Oh. Well, um," I stammered, feeling my own cheeks heating up. "That... I, um, don't really know what to say right now," I finally admitted.

Kára leaned forward, her dual-colored eyes pinning me in place as she squeezed my hands in hers in a forceful, but intimate way. "I told her about our conversations and asked her to give me an outsider's perspective."

I frowned suspiciously. "What did she say?"

Kára shrugged. "She only asked what you were like as a person, wanting to make sure I wasn't involving myself in trouble. Then she told me to follow my instincts. She never gave me more than that, and she definitely never let on that she *knew* you."

That…was bizarre—that she hadn't pressed Kára for intel. "We don't *know* each other," I assured her. "She's just been helping me via phone."

"Niko has a hero complex and she's fiercely dedicated to her morals. She's always trying to help people—to make up for her darker past."

I nodded woodenly, realizing I had judged wrongly. "That is great news," I finally said.

She cocked her head at a sudden thought. "Was this what you were talking about earlier? You said you learned some information that confused you. Were you talking about Niko?"

I sighed, nodding. "Yes. She went to your bar last night, running from some bad people. Old work associates."

Kára grunted. "I pity the men chasing her, but I do not know why she went to my bar. Maybe she was looking for me?"

"And she never mentioned wanting to kill me, or that she was considering it?" I asked, wanting to be entirely sure.

Kára's eyes stormed over in the blink of an eye. "If she had, she would be dead right now," she said in a cool tone.

"Right. Well, don't kill her. I haven't heard her say anything like that either. I was just making sure I could trust her. Because of her dark past."

Kára watched me in silence, considering my words. "I will not kill her. Yet. But if I hear that she means you harm…"

"Didn't you just say you were friends with her?" I asked.

She shrugged. "Yes, but not for very long. I'm just her friendly bartender. I like you more. On a personal level, I mean. I'm not speaking from…" she trailed off, suddenly blushing. "On a professional level, I am honored to know you. You inspire me, if that makes any sense."

I nodded. "I am indeed inspiring. I am also late to a fight."

"Oh?" she asked in a frosty tone.

I nodded. "But I need you here, watching over Alice and Freya."

She let out a disappointed sigh. "Fine."

I climbed to my feet, pulling her up with me. We released hands, the contact suddenly feeling much different when standing. I extended my arm. "Would you walk with me, Kára?"

She studied me for a long moment and finally nodded her head. "I would like that very much, Nate," she said, her dual-colored eyes catching the light in two different ways, like jewels in a treasure box.

She rested her head on my shoulder as we walked and…it felt nice. Not scandalous or invasive or suggestive. Just…nice. A symbol of trust and that this warrior maiden saw fit to reveal a little vulnerability when most of them were cold and heartless warriors.

"Thank you for not being cruel, and I'm sorry if I caused you harm," she murmured. "I always try to be honest, and I thought I had your situation with Callie figured out."

I nodded. "Honesty is vital," I said. "And you don't need to apologize about anything. I understand where you were coming from. I thought I had it all figured out, too. But that's life for you."

She was quiet as we came back around the hill and spotted Freya. Carl and Alice sat before her, still drinking their imaginary tea.

"Can I be honest again, Nate?" Kára asked.

"Sure."

"I hope to learn that I already *did* have your situation figured out. And I hope that you figure it out, too."

I sighed. "Either way, I'll remember to be honest about it," I promised her.

"That's all I ask." She squeezed my arm, and I instinctively flexed. She let out a surprised laugh, glancing up at me with sparkling eyes. Then she carefully extracted herself and walked over to Freya. I sighed, thinking very intently about our conversation.

Carl was already walking over to me, waving at Alice and dipping his chin at Freya and Kára.

"Let's go. I really need to let out some aggression."

He nodded, holding out his hand for me.

I waved at Alice, wondering why she was frowning thoughtfully. As was Freya. Kára was the only one not frowning. She was sitting down with her trident across her knees, smiling at me faintly.

"I'll never understand them, Carl. Never."

I grabbed his hand and Shadow Walked away.

CHAPTER 38

I stood on a hill overlooking an impressively vast castle surrounded by a tall iron fence and a Medieval style gate. We had been standing here for five minutes, now. Carl silently stared out at the rest of our surroundings, searching for hidden traps or possible assailants. This was the only building for miles and miles because they also owned the surrounding thousand acres.

After speaking with Kára and learning a little more about Niko, I felt a lot better about Niko's intentions. I assumed she had fled to Kára's bar in order to simply leave me a trail of breadcrumbs, and I was betting that if I stopped by, I would find her phone hidden near Thor's message. But I didn't have time to go on a scavenger hunt to find her.

Rather than waiting for Niko to return my calls, or for another squad of assassins to come punch my ticket, I decided to try rectifying the whole Lullaby situation in a slightly simpler manner.

"It's time," I told Carl. Then I took a step towards the castle, figuring it would take no more than five for something to happen—because I'd already seen enough curtains twitching to know I had an audience. Carl remained behind, like I had asked him.

I took a second step and a great blue dome of power suddenly bloomed to life, covering the entire gated property. Lightning slithered across the dome's surface like snakes on a frozen pond.

A protective shield, warning me not to come any closer.

I chuckled, shaking my head. I knew they had seen me standing on the hill, and like cowards, they had refused to come out, knowing *exactly* why I was here.

The Academy of Wizards.

A once-great establishment with aspirations to teach young men and women the powers of the universe, and how to use those powers to make their communities a safer, better place.

And now they posted assassination contracts on members who did not cower to their institutional dictations—as if every single wizard could possibly have the exact same creed.

Or follow hypocrisy once he or she saw it in the establishment's actions. Hubris.

I would know. I'd caught mild cases of it once or twice.

I cleared my throat and pulled up some magic of my own, using it to amplify my voice to such a degree that everyone within eyesight could clearly hear me—strong enough to even pierce their ward, which I was hoping would really tick them off.

"Come out and answer for your crimes! You, the brave, righteous professors and scholars who posted an assassination contract on my life. Face me openly instead of hiding behind your self-righteous institution, because the walls and wards aren't tall enough to hide your cowardice. Let all your students see the truth—that their own masters are merely thugs with robes, not even competent enough to stand against one man shouting at you on a hill. Tell them how we had an agreement, and that you hired third-party assassins to do your dirty work because you were too afraid to break your word where everyone could see. Too afraid to confront a man who challenged your creed. A man who held a flashlight into your dark halls and watched as the cockroaches skittered away in terror."

More curtains twitched, but no one emerged.

"I will give you one minute to send out the person responsible. I won't even attack him. I just want to see if he's brave enough to look me in the eyes. Brave enough to show his students that he is a man of character who accepts the consequences of his actions. I will even promise to walk away peacefully—as long as the cockroach steps into the light for all to see."

Nothing happened, and I laughed, letting my voice boom across the hills.

"Your decision right now is dignity or depravity. To take responsibility for all your students to see, or to show every student now hiding within your walls that you would rather use them as a shield than admit the truth. Students—take note. This is the greatest lesson you will ever learn."

I counted down in my head, confident that I already knew the answer, but hoping to be proven wrong.

The blue dome of power never even flickered, and I could see dozens of students now openly staring out the windows with wide, terrified eyes, checking to see which of their masters had upset the scary man on the hill.

Carl let out an annoyed sound, and I heard him drawing a blade. I held out my hand behind me, shaking my head. "No."

One minute came and went, and I hung my head with a sad sigh.

I looked back up at the castle, studying those young, eager faces in the windows. The only difference now was that I noticed adults also staring back at me, and the majority of them wore smug grins and haughty sneers. The look a noble would give a common peasant in the middle ages.

Disdain. Scorn. Disgust.

I shook my head sadly, disappointed in them for corrupting our youth.

They thought they could hide behind their lies and historic reputation—that their true cruelty was hidden behind the cloak of their noble institution.

Just like they thought they could hide behind their wards.

It was time to teach them an abject lesson in the futility of shields made from paper and light.

I focused on the wards themselves, studying their inner workings. In the span of ten seconds, I saw at least three different ways that I could break through them without using my wizard's magic.

Granted, I was unlike any other wizard these children had ever seen. I had access to magic from various, strange places, thanks to my parents raising me with tough love, and not permitting me to be indoctrinated by the very establishment looming before me now.

I chose one of the weaknesses and calmly walked up to the barrier.

I drew deeply on my Fae magic and lifted my hand to the ward. Then I obliterated it with a maelstrom of shadows, drawing them from every tree within one mile and attacking the dome with…perhaps a *billion* arrows of darkness—one for every dollar they had placed on my head.

The dome cracked ominously—like a frozen pond bearing too much weight. Then it simply shattered into fragments the size of my fist, disappearing before the pieces of magic had time to fall more than a foot through open air.

I stood there for five seconds, letting them see that I wasn't hunched over, that I wasn't gasping for breath, and that I hadn't used some strange artifact.

I stood with my head held high and my shoulders straight.

Then I hurled a blast of Fae fire—a living, breathing entity of flame I had made friends with once upon a time—at their outer gate. The fire raged like napalm, melting the iron to white-hot slag that finally dripped down into distorted globs on their front lawn and driveway.

I stared up at the windows.

"Behold the truth, children of magic. Your wise and noble mentors chose to bravely hide behind you rather than take responsibility. If you aren't careful, you will be molded in their image. You are who you associate with, after all. If I could leave you with one lesson, it would be this. Dynasty is not destiny. Nobility is not class. Ask yourself what kind of person you want to see in the mirror, because one day…you'll be responsible for making this place better."

I brushed off my hands, surveying the damage I'd caused.

"If the contract on my life is not removed within the hour, I will come back and burn this place to the ground. Students, it's time to call your parents and let them know that class has been canceled. Unless you choose to stand with your professors after seeing how concerned they were for your safety. In that case, I will be back very soon for a final goodbye."

I turned my back on the castle and walked back to Carl.

He nodded satisfactorily, but his gaze almost met mine for a fraction of a second.

"We're done here, Carl. Let's go pick a fight with someone our own size."

He nodded again, holding out his hand.

CHAPTER 39

We arrived back in the warehouse to find Loki shouting at the top of his lungs as War and Alucard struggled to shove him down into a large rectangular crate.

Loki saw me and cried out in relief. "Nate!"

War and Alucard glanced over at me and shrugged shamelessly.

"He wouldn't shut up, and the finger-snap trick wouldn't work," Alucard said.

War nodded. "I wanted to hit him in the mouth until he learned to keep it shut, but you didn't want us harming him. Seemed like a good compromise."

I sighed. "Get him out of there. We're leaving."

They hoisted him up and carried him away from the box. "Down on three," Alucard murmured. "One, two—"

They dropped him onto his back, and Loki gasped, losing his breath.

"Three," Alucard said. "Next time maybe don't talk so much shit. Especially about my friends," he muttered, already walking away.

I grunted, appreciating Loki's punishment much more now that I knew he'd earned it and that they hadn't been unnecessarily cruel. "Who was he talking shit about?" I asked.

Alucard was busy speaking softly to Carl and holding out his fist. Carl cocked his head and awkwardly extended his own fist. Alucard nodded approvingly and bumped his knuckles against the Elder's fist. Then they stared at each other for a few seconds. Alucard nodded, answering Carl's unspoken question in low tones.

Their strange connection was both creepy and cute, because Alucard had always antagonized Carl, poking fun at him or pranking him. To see them now bonding…it reminded me of how brothers often went through a stage of mutual hatred before becoming best friends later on in life.

War walked up to me, shaking his head in amusement as he watched them. "Loki was acting all brave and tough, talking crap about Elders. Carl, specifically. I didn't know that Alucard felt so strongly about Carl, to be honest."

I grunted, studying the two unlikely friends. "They weren't friends before. Well, Alucard didn't get along with Carl very well, anyway. He was always annoyed by Carl's utter lack of any and all social graces."

War frowned. "Well, he didn't act like it while you were gone. Pissed him right the hell off. But we didn't do anything Loki didn't deserve. I'm not a sadist."

"And dropping him?" I asked, ignoring the wheezing sound of Loki calling out my name.

War shrugged. "I could have sworn he said *three*."

I rolled my eyes, finally turning to face Loki. I covered my mouth and spoke the phrase to unbind him. The harness whipped open and I swiftly scooped it up to tuck back into my satchel before Loki got any bright ideas. I wasn't sure why the finger-snap hadn't worked for them while I was gone, but I didn't really care at the moment. It had served its purpose.

Loki muttered under his breath as he climbed to his feet, stretching out his legs, back, and arms. He found Carl standing behind him and jumped in alarm, but Carl didn't do anything. His tail did begin twitching back and forth, though.

Alucard walked up to me, holding out his phone. It was the Lullaby app, and he was shaking his head incredulously. "You fucking lunatic. You didn't even tell us you were going there!"

I shrugged, not bothering to hide my grin. "It's gone?"

He nodded. "It's not even on the app anymore. It's entirely deleted, rather than just archived or closed," he said, showing me the other filtering options on the screen.

I let out a breath of relief. At least I didn't have to worry about Niko or any other assassins coming after me anymore. It also meant Chateau Falco was safe.

"If I had known who was behind the assassinations earlier, we wouldn't have had to steal that food truck, preventing us from picking up these sweet shirts," I said, tapping on my chest.

Alucard grinned, doing the same.

I turned to Loki. "You ready to play nice? Or should I come back in another hour?"

"Yes. I'll play nice," he muttered.

I grunted doubtfully, but it was the best I was going to get from him—anything else would just be a lie.

War flung a balled-up shirt at Loki, hitting him in the chest. He caught it and stared down as he unfurled the matching shirt.

"Then welcome to the team," I said. "Now, where is Fenrir?"

"The Rocky Mountains," he said, tugging the shirt down over his head. "Ever heard of it?"

I nodded. "Yeah. Cold as hell in December."

He nodded. "It's right in the middle of nowhere. I can get us about a mile away, but we'll have to walk after that. Any closer and my Gateway might alert the guards."

I sighed. "We'll need to get some coats, first." I knew that Dean had taken to storing all the extra winter coats and snow gear in one of the unused, third-floor bedrooms at Chateau Falco. Knowing that no one had any reason to go to that area, I opened a Gateway. "Grab a coat but be quick. Werewolves are living in the house," I told them.

We all hopped through and began tearing through the closet and stacks of storage tubs. I immediately snapped up my black ski coat. It was light but warm, so it wouldn't get in my way. I tugged my satchel on over it, checking the straps to make sure it wouldn't slow me down by slapping against my hip when I ran.

After a few minutes, War and Carl still hadn't found anything to fit them, and they were both struggling with their most recent choices. War was trying to tug off a coat that was much too small for him, and Carl had his claws stuck in the sleeves of a bright pink ski jacket that I didn't recognize. I shuddered, wondering if it had been one of Indie's coats. Other than the likely demonic curse on it and the eye-gouging color, it looked identical to mine.

I froze as I suddenly heard barking from the halls beyond the bedroom door. Loud, frantic barking from two different throats, and they were getting closer—entirely too close for comfort. Shit. "Guys, we have to get out of here, *now!*" I hissed. It seemed the pups had a better sense of smell than their parents. "Loki," I snapped, running to the door. "Make that Gateway!"

He nodded and a ring of green sparks erupted on the wall opposite the door. I turned the lock, hoping to buy us some time. Loki and Alucard had already hopped through into what looked like a forest in a snowstorm, but I wanted to go through last to make sure Calvin and Makayla didn't bust down the door and follow us—because they were only seconds away.

"Calvin! Makayla! Get over here!" Gunnar's voice boomed, sounding annoyed as he chased them down—apparently hot on their heels and moving fast.

I spun, my eyes wide with panic. "Hurry!" I whispered urgently, trying to keep my voice down. But it was no use. The barks rose in pitch and volume, obviously hearing me through the door. Or smelling us. Or both.

"What do you smell, pups?" I heard Gunnar suddenly snarl, and I remembered that he thought he was playing guard dog at Chateau Falco—keeping it safe from teams of assassins.

And here we were, a team of killers behind a locked door in a room we shouldn't be in.

Carl let out a strange rattling sound from deep in his throat as he tried to snarl through his closed mouth, and then he violently shoved his hands down to force them through the sleeves. His claws sliced through the pink elbows, ripping the sleeves entirely off at the shoulder seams in the process. I grabbed him by the stupid fur-lined hood and shoved him through the Gateway.

Calvin and Makayla were right outside, clawing at the door and biting at the handle, rattling it against the hinges and frame like a goddamned tornado.

"What is it, Calvin? What do you smell?" Gunnar growled from only paces away, his boots thumping across the wooden floors of the hall.

War began waddling awkwardly for the Gateway with his arms still stuck in the sleeves, trapped behind his back like handcuffs so that he resembled a racing goose fighting for bread at the local pond.

I spotted one of my dad's old trench coats lying on the ground—a perfect fit for War—grabbed it, and dove for the Gateway just as the door exploded open behind me.

Two sleek forms blurred past me on either side, trailing chilling mist in their wake. Gunnar tackled me in mid-air, sending us flying through in a tumbling sprawl.

I spat out a mouthful of snow and tried to lift my head high enough to speak before he decapitated me. "It's me, Nate!" I rasped.

He grabbed me by the coat and yanked me to my feet, looking confused as hell. Then he noticed my crew standing a safe distance away, looking ready to fight or run. Because Calvin and Makayla were hunched low and growling at them with their teeth bared, still oozing their strange, freezing mist.

"What the hell?" Gunnar growled, turning to stare at each member of my motley crew with increasing degrees of shock on his face. They settled on Loki and he narrowed his eye murderously. "You."

Loki held up his hands. "I actually wanted you to be here, for the record." He frowned at Gunnar's empty hands. "But the hammer would have made this moment more meaningful."

"Why did you want me here?" Gunnar snarled, cracking his knuckles very slowly. "Because I can make this moment as meaningful as you want, Loki."

Loki sighed. "Because I know you're scary as hell, but more importantly...you're a new dad, and you have pups for kids. I was thinking I might be able to learn a thing or two," he said, lowering his eyes. "We're trying to save my son, Fenrir."

It sounded sentimental, but this was Loki we were talking about, so I was running on the assumption that everything he said was probably a lie.

Gunnar just stared at him, and I couldn't quite tell how he felt. "I'm going to shelve my feelings for later because it would jeopardize the mission. You should thank me for that."

The silence stretched for ten seconds until Loki realized he was being literal. "Thank you."

Gunnar nodded. "We will have a long talk later. Father-to-father, man-to-man. You won't like that. But I will like it *very* much."

Then he simply turned away, leaving Loki with a startled expression on his face. Gunnar froze to see Carl—who was still trying to tug the now-detached pink sleeves off his arms.

Gunnar opened his mouth wordlessly a few times, and then he just sat down and began to laugh, shaking his head in disbelief as he stared at the agitated Elder. "Fucking Carl," he wheezed. "You're back!"

My original crew were all staring at the strange pups and the mist surrounding them, not entirely sure what to make of it.

"Gunnar, this is no place for—"

A deep, basso howl tore through the snowy night—a long, piercing lament that I could feel in my chest. Fenrir.

Calvin and Makayla cocked their heads at the sound, whining in tandem as they zeroed in on the source. And then they fucking took off into the snowy woods.

"Motherfucker!" I hissed, pointing at Gunnar. "We have to stop them. There are a lot of bad people less than a mile in that direction!"

"Then it looks like I'm coming, too. Close the Gateway before Ashley sees us." He pointed at Carl with a big goofy grin on his face. "That was her favorite coat!" And then he was running after them.

"Gunnar?" Ashley suddenly called from beyond the Gateway, sounding as if she was out in the halls. "What on earth happened to this door—"

The Gateway winked shut, cutting her off. I shot Loki a panicked look.

"That's between him and his wife," he snapped. "In a way, it's your fault for not inviting him sooner, like I asked. You could have avoided all of this. But fate has intervened," he grinned excitedly. And then he was running after Gunnar. Alucard and Carl took one look at each other before also joining the pursuit of puppiness.

War finally tugged off the ill-fitting coat with a triumphant sound.

I flung my dad's old trench coat at him. "Hurry!"

And then I was running, too, imagining all the ways this could go wrong. And if we survived, someone had to explain this whole mess to Ashley. How her pups got dragged into a prison-break before they were even a year old.

CHAPTER 40

Gunnar had managed to catch the pups before they gave us away, but he'd had to shift into his own Alpha werewolf form to do so. It had been impressive to see. He'd been calling out their names as loud as he dared, but they hadn't listened in the slightest.

Then he had stopped running and shifted into his Alpha werewolf form —a furry, muscular, bipedal, man-shape with claws and a wolf's head.

He also had an even deadlier form, thanks to me taking him to Fae—a savage, seven-foot-tall, mountain of fangs and claws who went by the name Wulfric. But that must have been the form he chose to use when they were *really* in trouble. Like, using-their-middle-names type of trouble after their mom had resorted to calling him at work.

For this, he'd just chosen to use his dad voice.

He'd snarled.

One time.

Calvin and Makayla had skidded to an immediate halt, wilting submissively.

Gunnar had snarled again, and they had crouched down until their chins and bellies rested on the snow.

"Told you we should have had him all along," Loki had murmured, seeming marveled by Gunnar. I had found myself wondering if he felt a kinship to Gunnar because they had both birthed actual wolves for children.

I hadn't actually thought about that before—their similarities. Loki had a point, but I hadn't wanted to take him away from his pups—especially not after they'd shown their strange abilities.

I'd picked up Gunnar's phone from the pile of shredded fabric, and we were now walking side-by-side as I caught him up on everything I'd been withholding from him. He didn't ask any questions—even though he still had the ability to speak in this form, believe it or not—and he didn't once berate me. I even caught his tongue hanging out the side of his mouth, and his big hairy tail wagging.

Calvin and Makayla now remained glued to his side, choosing not to tempt fate. Because it had turned into bring your kids to work day and mommy wasn't supposed to know. I found it eerie how intently they seemed to listen to me talk, as if they could understand everything I was telling their father.

"I can make you a Gateway back home," I said, deciding to take one last chance, "before Ashley freaks out about you three disappearing. At least to send them back."

Calvin and Makayla shot me dark, accusatory looks, and Gunnar shook his head, chuckling at his pups. "She's been begging me to take them hunting. But I should let her know we're okay, so she doesn't get worried. Can you text her for me? I lost my phone back there when I shifted."

I scowled at him. "And take the blame? No way. This is your problem. I just offered a solution and you shot it down."

"Please, Nate."

"Fine." I turned my shoulders as I used his phone to text her. *Gone hunting with the pups. Be back tomorrow.*

Then I held it in my hand, waiting for the bomb to drop.

"She's probably going to be pissed at you, but I'll talk her down," Gunnar reassured me.

"What are friends for?" I said, shrugging.

We walked for another ten seconds before his personalized text notification sound went off—the Old Spice whistling jingle.

He missed a step, spinning to stare at me. I grinned, already holding out the phone he thought he'd lost when he shifted.

He snatched it away with an angry curse, and then grew silent. "Did... you read it?" he asked, sounding uneasy.

I frowned, turning to look at him. "No. Why?"

"Oh. Good. It's nothing." And then he promptly snapped his phone in half, tossing the pieces behind him.

I stared incredulously, but he refused to look over at me. What the hell had she texted him back to make him so embarrassed?

Alucard was grinning as he made inappropriate gestures with his hands and fingers in clear view of Gunnar—but he was also a healthy distance away, diminishing his bravery. Gunnar opened his mouth to put him in his place when Loki came to a sudden stop ahead of us.

"We need to crawl the rest of the way from here," he said, pointing up a slight hill in front of him. "It overlooks a valley, but there are a lot of guards and the moon is at our backs. We will be easy to spot if we're standing up. Even in this snowstorm."

Then he followed his own suggestion and began crawling.

This was it.

As we began to crawl, the snow began to fall heavier—as if some god had shaken our little snow globe to see what might happen...

∼

Loki pointed at the massive compound in the center of the wooded valley. "He's in there."

It was the only structure in sight, so I shot him a flat look. "That's condescending." He frowned in confusion. "That means talking down to someone," I explained, smirking.

Alucard suppressed a cough, and Loki shot him a brief glare before turning back to me. "On this *side* of the building. Asshole." The square, windowless building was easily the length and width of a football field, and maybe fifty feet tall.

I grunted. "The side with dozens of gargoyles and the huge hangar door? Gee. You sure it's not the itty-bitty door with the keypad?" I muttered, pointing at the normal, people-sized door near the corner of the building.

He sighed, not even bothering to argue this time. Good.

The obvious door in question was actually two adjoining concrete slabs stretching all the way to the roof. Together they took up a third of the entire side of the building. The slabs obviously slid open horizontally, rather than vertically like most hangars or garage doors.

And with the valley's limited size and too many trees for a runway, the building obviously wasn't holding any planes. Just one big bad wolf.

The pups had gotten antsy on the climb up, so Gunnar now had a hand on the ruffs of their necks to make sure they didn't run. I'd suggested a way to send them home and Gunnar had declined. I wasn't their dad. But I hoped him seeing how dangerous the situation was might change his mind. He noticed me watching and turned to grin.

I sighed. We were too close for me to do anything about it now, and I'd gotten in enough trouble trying to force him into parenting decisions. But I promised myself that I wouldn't let anything happen to them. I had given my last Tiny Balls to Alucard, but I knew Loki and War had the ability to travel in a similar manner if it came down to it. Just in case I was unable to.

I discreetly nudged Alucard, drawing his attention. I jerked my chin at the pups and murmured under my breath. "If things get hairy, get them out of here," I whispered. He nodded firmly.

Carl looked absolutely ridiculous in his hooded, sleeveless pink coat, but I realized he needed it more than any of us, being a lizard—and obviously from a place that was hotter than anywhere on earth.

War just looked like a down-on-his-luck private investigator with his trench coat and rough demeanor.

"Last time I was here," Loki murmured, pointing at the concrete doors, "they were partway open as the guards used a forklift to slide a pallet heaped with raw meat inside. They closed it as soon as the doors were clear, but I heard Fenrir's growl all the way from here." Loki nodded at the grim look on my face. "Kind of confirmed it all. And the moment those doors closed, they lit up with golden runes, so they're obviously enchanted somehow. Your guess is as good as mine."

"Is that why you tried to use the side door to sneak in?"

He nodded with a haunted look on his face.

I turned back to the valley, sweeping my gaze from end to end. The gargoyles were all lined up on the roof of the building—some walking the perimeter and others dozing, making them look like nothing more than creepy statues. Evenly spaced floodlights illuminated every inch of the building's exterior and a good distance leading up to it, making it impossible to sneak up on foot without being spotted by a gargoyle.

But the heavy snow flurries would help hide us. I could hear the wind picking up, too, serving to create brief gusts and occasionally knocking accumulated snow from the upper branches of all the trees—more visual distractions.

The compound made me think of a prison or black-ops research center. If there had been actual roads leading up to it, I would have said storage building, but there were no roads.

They must have flown the pallet of meat in on a helicopter.

About forty armed men in puffy black coats patrolled the perimeter, even walking through the thick woods further out from the building, which meant we couldn't use that for cover either. Most of them carried machine guns, but I counted over a dozen of them carrying tall, thick staffs.

Wizards.

I counted another dozen men wearing nothing but loin cloths—despite the obvious cold—wielding futuristic, sleek, black bows and what looked like military-grade quivers that resembled compact, metal backpacks.

"Why wouldn't they put him deep underground?" I mused, glancing back at the building, and wondering what the best play was. "That way he couldn't escape even if he did break free of whatever chains they have on him."

Loki turned to look at me. "Because then they would have to find a way to get him out of the hole when they want to *use* him."

I shuddered at the thought of anyone using Fenrir for their own benefit, but there really wasn't any other reason to keep him prisoner.

Direct frontal assault didn't sound promising unless we were willing to put on our Horseman Masks. But I'd already cautioned against that, because we didn't know who actually ran this place, and we now had kids with us. What if it was the Vatican, for example?

I had no problem picking a fight, but I wasn't entirely sure I wanted rumors spreading that four Horsemen had helped Loki save his son from a prison. Because it wouldn't take long for the truth to disappear and a new rumor to emerge with minor manipulations to the facts.

Loki commands the Biblical Four Horseman to destroy a Vatican Church. The Apocalypse is nigh!

We could be turning the entire world against us by putting on our Masks. War had instantly agreed, saying that the Masks were always to be used as a last resort. *Abuse their power, and they could lose their power*, he'd said

—which was news to me on an official level, but it made perfect sense on a conceptual level. The Masks were special and powerful precisely *because* they were limited and rare. Abusing any sort of magic had consequences, because magic was very particular in how it wanted to be used. It was why some wizards turned warlock—becoming addicted to magic, and slaves to their own power.

Not following the unknown rules was what had almost broken my Mask in the first place. My Mask had wanted its siblings, and when I hadn't helped facilitate that, it decided to just break on me.

Similarly, if I started walking around and picking fights with every enemy of mine while wearing my Mask, pretty soon, everyone would unite against me, collectively saying *fuck this guy*.

Because I would be abusing my power unnecessarily.

No different than a thug waving a cocked and loaded pistol in his fist everywhere he went.

Using it irresponsibly would create an arms race, and every supernatural entity would start using their strongest weapons for the mildest of offenses.

Which was one reason gods didn't too often involve themselves in mortal affairs. Because then the *other* gods would. And then the demons and angels would start measuring their haloes and horns.

Not knowing what else to do as the world turned insane, the Regulars would then start playing with their nuclear weapons.

Mutually assured destruction.

I glanced at Carl, wondering if that was what had happened to his people, why everyone had teamed up against them.

"What kind of strengths do you have, Loki? Other than illusion, of course," I finally said.

He stared out at the valley, thinking. "I can take a beating like any other god, but I'm essentially just a strong wizard. Illusion can be more useful than you know..."

"Dramatic suspense isn't necessary. Spill."

He waved a hand over us, and I saw a faint shimmer to the air, almost like a heat wave. "There. Now, if there's anything you've really wanted to do, but have always been too shy to try, tonight is your chance to let it all out."

We all stared at him blankly. "That sounded like an inappropriate invitation," War muttered unhappily.

Loki rolled his eyes. "You won't be able to notice when looking at each other, but they won't be able to identify who you really are," he said, pointing down below. "I made you all look different. It will only last a few hours, though."

I narrowed my eyes. "How did you make us look, Loki? Because this seems like an excellent way to cause some trouble, especially if we can't see what you did."

War nodded, glaring at Loki. "What if we are all women?"

Loki chuckled. "Oh, don't be so dramatic. It's just so we can get away scot-free, and not implicate ourselves in this…dubious endeavor."

Gunnar looked thoughtful, leaning towards agreeability, but the rest looked concerned.

"Who did you make us look like, Loki?" I growled.

"Spoilsports," he complained. "I simply made you look like—"

Fenrir suddenly let out a loud, mournful howl and the concrete slabs rocked at a sudden thump that made dust fall from the edges. Runes suddenly flared to life all across the surface, glowing with yellow light. The guards and gargoyles didn't even glance up at Fenrir's tantrum, though. Those nearby even shouted out taunts at him.

Gunnar snarled, desperately grasping his claws at thin air as mist wolves suddenly zipped down into the valley towards a whistling archer patrolling the woods. Gunnar spun to me with one crazy eye. "Do something!"

"I told you this was a bad idea!" I growled.

But Gunnar had already hurdled down the hill, shifting into his vanilla mountain wolf form so as to have better chances at moving stealthily—making himself a smaller target. Unless Loki's illusion made that pointless.

"I guess we have our plan," Alucard muttered. "Nice knowing you guys. Let's take out as many as we can."

CHAPTER 41

Per Gunnar's request, there wasn't much I could do that wouldn't bring every single guard down on our location, which was the exact opposite of where I wanted them looking.

"I need to draw them away from the pups," I said, thinking out loud. I scanned the valley, hoping that no one called out an alarm—

I smiled at a sudden thought. I *needed* them to call out an alarm. "Stay here and let me know if anything else goes against our favor."

I ran down the backside of the hill, out of sight from the valley, and far enough away that I didn't think the wizards below would sense me. Then I made a Gateway that opened up beyond the lip of the ridge across from my friends. I took a deep breath and drew in my magic, hurling a unique blast of air through the Gateway before closing it.

A concussive blast on the opposite side of the valley went off like a bundle of dynamite, echoing for miles. I heard men suddenly shouting, followed by the sound of automatic fire.

I made another Gateway, but this one opened up a hundred feet away from the first. This time I sent three of the concussive blasts through, followed by bolts of lightning to ignite a stand of trees. Flames roared to life, but I hurled a few more fireballs through for good measure. Then I remembered something Alice had done on my mountain in Fae, and I smiled.

I switched to my Fae magic, calling out to the snow. "I need your help," I said. Then, remembering that Loki had changed our appearances, I firmly imagined the auras of everyone in my crew—including the pups—in my head. I hurriedly formed the snow into a dozen snowmen with long arms, and foot-long spikes all over their bodies. I froze their exterior for armor and then let out a breath. "You have free reign for the next hour. Attack everyone but my team. And don't be afraid to make new friends," I said, grinning.

I watched as three rows of snowmen slowly rose up behind them, picking up branches and rocks—either for armor or weapons. Then they split up into two groups, a dozen of them staying behind to make more snow demons.

"Thank you, and I hope you have fun with this." They nodded back in perfect unison. Then I closed the Gateway with a dark smile.

I made three more Gateways in rapid succession, spacing them out and alternating between fire and lightning, but I always threw the concussive blasts of air.

My knees shook and I realized I'd used quite a bit of power in a relatively short time. And we hadn't even gotten to Fenrir yet. I shambled back up the hill to see Alucard shaking his head in awe. "Was that you?" he demanded. "The snowmen?"

I nodded, crouching low to witness the results of my hard work.

The opposite ridgeline was completely ablaze—the trees sending up thick, dark smoke as they burned from my lightning and fire. Automatic gunfire filled the air, the majority of the guards forming a line to shoot at the dozens of snowmen now zipping down into the valley like figure skaters. Bullets cracked their skin and tore through them, but they simply tackled their foes in spiky embraces.

The gargoyles had congregated above like a dark cloud, and were divebombing them, their skin too hard to be concerned about icicles.

The wizards began hurling balls of fire at anything that moved, more often than not catching the trees in the valley on fire. It was pandemonium, but I knew it wouldn't last long.

The concrete slabs on the compound rattled and quaked, blazing with light as Fenrir howled and barked loud enough to make me shudder, knowing we were about to see him up close and personal.

How the hell were we going to break him out?

I knew the snowmen would only hold them off for so long before the wizards did something to really keep them busy—like making the ground too hot for snow.

I turned to Loki. "We need to get him out, now. Do you have any idea how to open those doors?"

"No, but they're powerful. I didn't get a close look last time, but I'm guessing they're from our Vanir brethren." He surveyed the chaos below. "I know it was necessary, but with all this insanity, how the hell do you expect me to control him? Listen!" he snapped angrily. "He's losing his mind in there!"

He wasn't wrong. The whole building seemed to vibrate with his howl, and rock when he struck the door.

"I don't want you to *control* him, Loki," I reminded him, motioning everyone to follow me. "I want to let him *loose*."

Loki stared at me with a wary look on his face. I ran down the hill towards the concrete doors, trying to think of any possible way to open them. I doubted it would be as simple as pushing a button on the inside either, or I would have simply blown a hole through the wall. The door was operated by magic, so I was betting that Fenrir was surrounded by magic on all sides.

And magic didn't work by pressing a button. Thanks to the mayhem I'd caused, we made it to the door without anyone noticing us, but I knew that could change in an instant. All it would take was one gargoyle to look over his shoulder.

"War, watch our backs. We need to get Gunnar and the pups over here or *out* of here." He nodded, leaning up against the wall of the building to peer around the corner.

Alucard frowned. "Well, if he's not colorblind, all he has to do is find the only person wearing pink," he said, pointing at Carl.

I turned to stare at the two of them, frowning. I actually didn't know the answer to that. I was pretty sure Gunnar could see colors when in wolf form, but how the hell would I know?

"Carl, can you jump up and down and wave your arms?"

He nodded, and I realized he was shivering. His scales even had a dull blue color to them, and he was moving slower than normal. Not alarmingly slow, but it was noticeable.

Maybe the jumping jacks would keep him warm.

Loki lifted his hands, preparing to use some kind of magic to attack the door, so I quickly slapped his hands down. He spun, his face furious. "We don't have time to waste, Nate."

"We also only have *one* chance. Once we start attacking the door, a wizard is going to sense it and wonder what the fuck is going on back here."

He frowned, turning to study the door more closely. Finally, he nodded. "I'm almost positive this is old Vanir magic. But without knowing the right runes, or the right sequences..."

Shit. The only people who I personally knew with the knowledge of Seiðr magic was Freya and Odin. Which meant our only other option was to overwhelm it with an unhealthy amount of magic and hope we could short it out—like an electric circuit breaker.

And that was what you called courting death—because magic didn't like to mix, so you never knew what kind of reaction you might get for attempting such a thing.

But it was all we had.

"Power," I told him. "We need more power." I ran through my inventory of magic, trying to think of something that was a big one-shot strike. Even my Horseman's magic might not necessarily help. As far as I knew, the Mask merely gave me advanced combat abilities

I'd repaired the Bifröst, but that had been with the help of friends and some ingredients to power it up, and it hadn't been a one-shot strike of any kind. It had been creating something.

Here, it was just me, and I needed to destroy something. We were all heavyweights, but none of us had a nuclear button. Well, Carl did, but his lips were sewn shut—and his voice was part of his destructive power.

Carl continued to jump up and down, and I saw three wolves headed our way, hunkering low in hopes they wouldn't be spotted. They were covered in blood—all three of them. I pushed down my instant panic, hoping that none of it was theirs, and fearing to ask why the pups weren't misty anymore.

Carl stopped jumping, pointing for us to see.

I nodded. "Carl, can you do anything to blast this open?"

Carl shook his head as Alucard said, "He needs his voice to help." Just like I'd thought.

"Loki, anything?" I asked.

He shook his head. "We're just going to have to throw everything we have at it and hope for the best. It's going to get chaotic when they realize what we're doing, so someone needs to watch our backs while we work."

I saw Alucard nod grimly, turning to face War.

I stared at Alucard and then Carl. Alu-Carl...

The flashlight guy and the extreme-sun-tanning lizard.

And a strange thought came to mind. "Hey, Alucard. You get powered up by sunlight..."

"Yes, but that's not much help right now," he said pointing up at the dark sky. "Even if you did that Gateway thing on me again and found a sunrise halfway around the world, I doubt it will be strong enough to make a difference on this door. On them, sure," he said pointing at the guards around the corner.

I held up a finger, telling him to wait. Then I turned to Carl. "What about your sun? From back home?" I asked, remembering that Carl had said it would burn us alive. "Do you think Alucard could handle it?"

War shot me a horrified look, hearing my suggestion.

Alucard stared at Carl, and a smile slowly stretched across his cheeks. Carl nodded at me.

"Do you know when the sun is up?" I asked him, remembering that it had been on the other side of the mountain when we were there—sometime before dawn in St. Louis.

Carl shook his head.

But Alucard suddenly looked hopeful. "He doesn't know when it rises, but he did say that one of their days is roughly three of ours."

I let out a nervous breath. That meant the sun might be shining down on the valley with the waterfall. "Worth a shot. You want to try it?" I asked, hoping I wasn't signing his death warrant.

Gunnar and the pups skidded to a halt, and I saw that they were all staring at the door anxiously. Fenrir was growling ominously, but it no longer seemed to be directed at the distant fighting. It was directed at us—a warning growl. He could hear us.

"We're here to get you out, son," Loki said, his voice suddenly emotional. He reached his hand up to the door, as if he thought Fenrir might be able to sense it. "Please don't eat us." His hand was only an inch away, now. "I want to try and make up for—"

The exact second his skin touched the stone, wild arcs of lightning shot down from each corner of the door and struck Loki in the chest.

He flew into the snowbank as if he had been hit by a truck. And the perimeter lights on the roof all turned red as an alarm Klaxon began to wail. I flung a blast of fire up at the nearest speaker, obliterating it and muting the noise—but the speakers on the other sides of the building continued.

There went the element of surprise, ruined by Loki's first stab at redemption. If I had been the superstitious type, I would have taken it as a sign that Fenrir was not that interested in repairing their father-son relationship. But I wasn't here about that. I just needed to get him as far away from Odin—or anyone else who wanted to weaponize him—as possible.

"Let's do it," Alucard growled. "I can take it."

War glanced back. "They're coming!"

CHAPTER 42

I motioned Alucard to step to the side so that if this crazy plan worked, he would hit the door at an angle rather than blasting the concrete slabs directly into Fenrir's face.

Loki ran up to us, his hair sticking straight up, and a hole burned in the center of his team shirt. He shook the snow off his everywhere as he stared at the door with a glare. "What did I miss?"

I pointed at the corner where the guards were heading our way. "Help them out. There's nothing you can do here." He gritted his teeth unhappily, but it was true. If I wasn't making the Gateway, I'd be over there helping as well. He jogged over to War and the two spoke in low tones.

I turned back to Alucard and pointed out the joint where the two slabs of concrete met. "That's the weakest point, Alucard. Throw everything you've got at it. No pulling back." He nodded. "You have to let me know when to close the Gateway. Absorb as much as you can handle, but don't die to prove a point," I told him urgently, trying to ignore the shrieking gargoyles and shouting heading our way.

He nodded, excitedly. "This is either going to suck or be the best moment of my life," he said, staring at the magic door.

Carl and War stood side-by-side with swords in hand, waiting for the enemy to round the corner. Loki stood back a ways and was staring intently up in the air. Probably making illusions of some kind—subtle things that would keep the enemy occupied while the others hacked them to pieces. Gunnar and the pups stood behind them, looking torn on whether or not to help with Fenrir or the impending attack.

I only had one shot at this, because we hadn't gone exploring in Carl's homeland, so the only place I knew well enough to make a Gateway was the cliffs with the waterfall outside the Temple Cavern.

Alucard nodded at me, facing the concrete slabs from maybe ten feet away. I took a few steps back so the sunlight wouldn't hit me, placing me the furthest from the inbound guards, but I hadn't wanted to risk having my back to them while holding open the Gateway, so there was no other choice.

"Don't look!" I shouted, loud enough for everyone to hear.

"Oh, bring it on already! Daddy wants a tan!" Alucard shouted at the top of his lungs.

And I opened a Gateway, using my peripheral vision so as not to blind myself. Even still, I instantly averted my eyes as the Gateway screamed to life.

I felt a blast of heat sear every molecule of moisture nearby, so hot that there wasn't even any hiss of steam from the snow. I shielded my face, stumbling backwards as my exposed skin tightened and I smelled burning plastic from my jacket. "Fuck me!" I cursed, trying to get even further away.

The side of the building warped and cracked or turned white-hot, depending on what it was made of.

Alucard was cackling and screaming at the top of his lungs like a psychopath, but I could hear machine guns firing nearby. I hoped Loki was covering my friends—shielding and counterattacking the wizards, at least. If not, I would personally throw him into the Elder's homeland to watch him burn. With the crazy light from my Gateway, there was every chance the guards were firing blindly as they covered their eyes. Or they'd blinded themselves by trying to look too closely.

"Tell me when!" I shouted, hoping Alucard could hear me. I couldn't even look in that direction to see how everyone else was faring, so I crouched down, hoping that I wouldn't catch a stray bullet or blast of magic while I hid from my own Gateway.

"NOW!" Alucard screamed. I closed it in a heartbeat. I used my peripheral vision for a few more seconds to make sure I hadn't screwed anything up and that the Gateway had definitely closed.

Then I cautiously looked over, squinting against a winged, human-shaped being of pure light who was hovering about ten feet off the ground with his arms outstretched.

And he was laughing. Even the guards and gargoyles had stopped fighting to stare up at him in disbelief, those who hadn't been blinded by the light, anyway—of which there were many, now stumbling around and screaming as they clawed at their own faces. Then Alucard aimed his hands at the door, and a bar of neon-blue light struck the door with a chiming sound, lasting only a few seconds before it winked out.

The door stood, not looking remotely affected by Alucard's strike.

One of the guards suddenly laughed. Alucard flicked his wrist towards the guards and another beam of light shot from his hand, lasting the span of a blink.

I stared at his target to see dozens of men screaming in agony from grotesque proximity burns, but a group of maybe a dozen charred skeletons stood upright like statues. Then they simply disintegrated, collapsing into piles of dust and rolling smoke.

The concrete door made a strange groaning sound, drawing my attention. Then it similarly collapsed into a pile—much larger, though—of fine white dust.

Alucard lifted his arms wide, staring into the dark opening. "Who's a good boy—"

As quick as a snake, a massive wolf's head lunged out, gobbling up Alucard in one bite.

"No!" Loki shouted, running in front of me as I lifted my hands to start throwing magic at the stupid mutt. "Bad boy! Drop it!" he yelled, storming up to the opening and waving his finger demandingly.

Fenrir suddenly gagged, spreading his jaws wide as he hacked up the human lightning bug in projectile drool. Alucard struck the ground in a wet, steaming slap, rolling like a slug as his skin rapidly burned away the drool. He was still glowing brighter than I'd ever seen, but not as much as a few moments ago.

Alucard was cursing up a storm, berating the dog the moment he landed, as he struggled back to his feet.

But I didn't have time to marvel at Fenrir or check on Loki as I suddenly remembered the remaining guards—those who hadn't been incinerated or burned beyond salvation.

And the gargoyles.

But...it seemed like a lot of them—men and gargoyles—were fighting each other.

I saw Loki grinning smugly up at them before he pulled his attention back to Fenrir.

I didn't want to rely on Loki's illusions, so I started hurling fireballs as fast as I could, lighting them up as I screamed at my team to get out of the way. They tucked tail and ran from the guards, and I threw down a long, curved shield to stop the various projectiles from hitting them in the back.

Alucard had a faster solution. He buffeted his wings against the ground in a powerful sweep that ignited any of the surviving grass from under the snow—even catching War's beard on fire. The Biblical Horseman cursed and patted it out as the rest of my team scrambled my way, staying well clear of the open hangar.

Alucard landed on the ground between my shield and the surviving guards. "Morningstar is here!" he shouted.

A horizontal arc of brilliant purple light no thicker than a sheet of paper screamed through the air about waist-high, slicing every single guard in half.

But it kept right on going into the forest of our valley—ripping through every single tree with a flash of flame—before finally slamming into the snowy ridgeline with a blast of steam and debris.

For all I knew, it kept on going beyond *that*.

For a single moment, crystal-clear silence rang out as loud as a bell. Even the gargoyles hovered in stunned silence, staring down at the gory halves of their allies now painting the snow.

And then the trees began to fall, flames racing up their trunks as they toppled into each other on their way down to the ground. They hit with crashing thuds that I felt in my toes. The best part was that several of them caught a large group of gargoyles, hitting them like industrial fly swatters, and pinned them to the ground.

The evergreen branches stubbornly refused the flames for a few seconds, and then went up like they had been doused in gasoline. Luckily, we were in a valley, so we didn't have to worry about immediate fires spreading through the Rocky Mountains.

But I knew wildfires were not uncommon in the state, so I would have to take care of it—

A stone spear slammed into the ground right beside me, and I looked up to see a line of pissed-off gargoyles hefting more spears above their heads, aiming down at us.

Alucard stumbled woozily, but quickly regained his balance and swept his wings to launch him into the sky. He flew around like a drunken bat, but his aim was almost better in his practically delirious state. He released solar buckshot from his palms—each blast consisting of hundreds of tiny orbs of light—that shredded through three or more gargoyles at a time. Within seconds, it was raining hot chunks of stone down around us. I cursed, throwing another shield above our heads as I shouted at everyone to get beneath it.

War and Carl obeyed, but I didn't see Loki, Gunnar, or the pups. I cursed, shouting their names louder as Alucard zipped back and forth above our heads, finishing up the last of the gargoyles.

Then he began to fall, his glow winking out like a bad light bulb. His wings evaporated and he dropped like a limp doll.

I dropped my shield and prepared another one to try and catch him, but my head was suddenly spinning, and I lost my grip on my magic.

I heard a fleshy thump that made me cringe, and I glanced over to see Carl kneeling on the ground, holding Alucard in his arms.

The Daywalker didn't appear to be breathing.

I stumbled to my feet, watching as red-hot pieces of gravel struck Carl and his pink vest, but he paid them no more mind than if they had been light rain. I watched him brush the hair back from Alucard's forehead in a concerned, loving gesture.

I reached his side and knelt down, grabbing his wrist for a pulse. I ignored the heat of his skin, even though my knee-jerk reaction was to pull away. I felt a faint, thready pulse and let out a sigh of relief as he took a sudden breath, followed by a wheezing groan.

Alucard looked like the star of a documentary special on people addicted to spray-tans. He was so orange that it was almost a shade of brown. Except for his eyelids. Those were as white as snow.

"How did I do?" he whispered, his voice as dry as dust.

"Superstar," I told him, patting him on the chest. "Lay low while I check on everyone else," I said, suddenly remembering I hadn't seen the wolves or Loki for a while.

I also hadn't heard Fenrir make a single peep. I ran past War, who was staring into the darkened building with an unreadable look on his face.

CHAPTER 43

I skidded to a stop a few strides into the building, suddenly realizing the idiocy of running aggressively towards a chained-up monster as I felt a rumbling vibration deep in my bones.

Fenrir was growling warningly.

Luckily, Fenrir was growling as he stared down the Alpha werewolf of St. Louis, not at *me*.

Gunnar—still in his four-legged wolf form—stood before Fenrir, his body partially angled so as not to face him directly. But he held his head high, refusing to submit to the obviously superior wolf.

His lips were even curled back, matching Fenrir's growl in a cute little echo—a chihuahua challenging a Tibetan mastiff.

"Fenrir," I whispered. "What big...*everything* you have."

His eyes latched onto me and I instinctively stepped back, even though he hadn't moved.

He was fucking *huge*.

And he was lying down in deep shadow, so I wasn't even seeing his true length, mass, or height. He posed like the Great Sphinx statue in Egypt—his front paws stretched out before him and his head held high. His teeth were easily four-feet-long and his muzzle was the size of a double-decker bus. Ten feet above my head, a wide band of thick metal encircled his throat, and it was glowing with familiar golden runes—exactly like the door we had just destroyed. He had matching, rune-stamped manacles around his two front paws, and chains connected them to his rear legs deeper inside the building. The chains were so large that I could have taken a nap inside one of the links.

He had a thick coat of long, reddish-brown fur, but I noticed striated shades of white, black, and gold breaking it up.

"Shit," I whispered, my shoulders sagging. Alucard was out of juice, so how the hell were we going to break the runic enchantment on the manacles and collar?

Loki cleared his throat softly. "My son—"

Fenrir lunged with a coughing snarl, snapping his teeth three times in rapid succession—about two feet from Loki's face, slathering him with drool and blasting his hair straight back.

Fenrir's attention shifted back towards Gunnar, and I frowned, suddenly noticing a second and third set of growls coming from...

The two pups standing in front of Gunnar's barrel chest. I hadn't even noticed Calvin and Makayla. It almost looked like they were cowering, but I saw that the fur on the ruffs of their necks was sticking straight up. Their growls hadn't been audible over Fenrir.

Until he had momentarily ceased to snap at his dad, Loki.

For whatever reason, Fenrir watched them warily, almost seeming hesitant—like Gunnar should have looked right about now.

The pups cautiously advanced, keeping their heads low to protect their necks.

Fenrir lifted his head, as if trying to move his throat further away, and he snorted unhappily before letting out a huge, whining yawn that really showed off his jaws and teeth. I frowned, cocking my head. Canines sometimes yawned when they were stressed.

The pups moved closer to Fenrir's right paw, sniffing curiously.

Fenrir shifted it away, causing the pups to snarl and bark aggressively, snapping their teeth at him. Fenrir snorted again, keeping his eyes trained on them but his throat as far away from the pups as possible.

Calvin trotted over to the left paw so that they were now back-to-back between Fenrir's front legs, and I watched as that chilling Niflheim mist began to roll off their fur, accumulating beneath them like dense fog.

Fenrir let out another uneasy whine, followed by an anxious growl. Gunnar stood tall, glaring up at Fenrir in a challenging pose, daring the colossal wolf to do something stupid. For whatever reason, no matter how much I wanted to, I knew that if I opened my mouth to intervene in any manner whatsoever, something terrible would happen. Gunnar—their dad—was obviously on board with this ultimate game of poke the wolf.

I shot a concerned look at Loki, but he was staring at the pups and the mist in disbelief. He might have even looked a little pissed-off about them getting closer than he had.

Calvin and Makayla's mist connected into one large blanket of shifting fog, and Fenrir began panting anxiously, his shoulders rigid.

The pups sniffed at the manacles, snorting out frigid puffs of thicker mist that instantly iced over the metal, but then melted away just as swiftly.

And the pups didn't appear to like that.

Not.

One.

Bit.

They snarled furiously, hunkering their chests low with their rear ends in the air, and the mist really began to pour off of them, too thick for me to actually see through. Fenrir was panting louder, now, filling the space with hot air, and I realized that I was rubbing my hands together for warmth, my fingers numb from the cold mist. No wonder he was unhappy. He was probably freezing to death over there.

The mist continued to grow thicker, spilling over a wider area and even rolling over Fenrir's paws like slithering serpents. It rose over their heads and they disappeared from view—the only proof of their presence was their snarls growing louder and deeper, more confrontational.

The temperature in the room dropped by about twenty degrees as an ephemeral form began to rise from the mist—a glowing, golden set of manacles and chains that stretched back into the shadows of the building on either side of Fenrir—looking like holograms of the actual restraints.

Except, those shadows had turned white, replaced by the dense blanket of mist, and I saw another golden glow hovering just above the white fog—that had to be from the rear manacles.

It was almost like...

This glowing apparition was the *spirit* of the runic manacles and chains, breaking free from the physical representation. I couldn't even see the real restraints anymore, just the blanket of roiling mist that now entirely surrounding Fenrir, making it look like he was lying down on a cloud.

His eyes were wide and wild as he stared down at the spiritual restraints, but he didn't move a muscle, and he didn't make a sound.

The pups were entirely submerged, but I sensed movement where they had been standing, the mist shifting faster from their movement below.

I abruptly stiffened as two wolves rose up from that mist, their heads standing higher than mine, and their eyes crackling with arcs of lightning—like those storms you sometimes see up in the clouds where the lightning bolts ricochet off each other for ten or twenty seconds to produce an incredible light show in the sky.

And I realized that these new wolves were made entirely of mist, their bodies flickering with a fainter version of the piercing light in their dazzling eyes.

They lifted their heads and howled—but it wasn't a physical sound. It was more like a sound straight from the soul. Fenrir snorted, lifting his head back as if to get as far away as possible from the terrifying mistwolves.

Then they lunged forward, their jaws stretching longer and opening wider than possible, and they clamped down on that spectral chain. There was a flash of blue light, and the golden runes intensified, growing bright enough to make me squint as I sensed a desperate scream of protest emanating from them.

The ephemeral chain suddenly froze over beneath their jaws, and then that ice screamed down the length of the chain like a lit fuse, even shooting out blue sparks in a deafening series of snaps and cracks. I watched, stunned, as the ice met somewhere back in the depths of the compound with a thunderous cracking sound that made Fenrir flinch and yelp—possibly striking dangerously close to his rear. Next, the chain between the two front paws—and directly below Fenrir's muzzle—duplicated the icy ignition sequence, saving that section for last. I cringed, unable to turn away.

I held my breath as misty ice met misty ice with a sudden blast of arctic cold, and a percussive crack sent me skidding back on my ass as the spectral chain and manacles abruptly snapped free.

I stared in shock as Fenrir shook his head—looking dazed—and the mist began racing back towards where I had last seen the real pups. Almost like they were vacuuming up their mess.

The last of the mist dissipated with a muted thumping sound between

Fenrir's front paws, revealing Calvin and Makayla wobbling on unsteady paws.

They promptly passed out, collapsing into a pile. I saw their chests rising and falling, so I knew they were still alive—merely exhausted from their work.

The real chain and manacles abruptly shattered into small pieces of crushed ice, spilling down into a pile that surrounded Fenrir like a ring of salt.

I quickly and discreetly shuffled out of his direct path, wisely choosing to be out of the way when he made his dash for freedom. But Fenrir didn't move a muscle. In fact, I wasn't sure he was even aware that he was no longer restrained.

Instead, he lowered his head to stare down at the pups. He crossed his front paws, one over the other, as if to protect his favorite puppy toy. Then he lowered his nose and sniffed them curiously as he let out a nervous whine. He gently nudged them, sliding them a good three feet. They finally stirred with sleepy puppy groans and Fenrir seemed to shudder, letting out a breath of relief.

Gunnar calmly took a step closer and Fenrir looked up at him with a chilling glare.

"This is Gunnar," Loki said. "He is their father. They all wanted to help me save you from this place. To help *Nate Temple* save you from this place," Loki humbly admitted, correcting himself.

Fenrir's eyes had locked onto Loki the moment he spoke, listening to his every word. They shifted my way with startling intensity, and I seriously considered denying my involvement in the rescue.

But Fenrir dipped his head at me, blinking slowly. I mirrored the motion, not knowing the appropriate way to acknowledge his gesture, or what it actually meant. Maybe it meant *I will eat you last, tiny man-thing, but only if I'm particularly hungry.*

Then his attention shifted back to Gunnar—who hadn't moved a muscle. They locked gazes for about ten seconds before Fenrir seemed to nod and then lift his muzzle, exposing his throat ever so slightly.

I stared, almost unable to breathe. That…was almost a submissive gesture, or at least a respectful one. Gunnar repeated the gesture, and then began wagging his tail.

Loki licked his lips, shaking his head in awe.

Gunnar then calmly trotted up, hopped over Fenrir's paws, and began nuzzling Calvin and Makayla, barking proudly at the impossible feat they'd just pulled off.

Their responding whines sounded like *Daaaaad, you're so embarrassing! Let us sleep!*

"This is incredible," I breathed, shaking my head.

"Nate!" War hissed in a loud whisper from outside the building, trying to get my attention without pissing off Fenrir. I glanced back to see a grim look on his face. "We're about to have company. I can hear snowmobiles. A lot of them."

CHAPTER 44

I spun back to Loki, and then Fenrir. The pups were in no condition to move on their own. Alucard was likely still unconscious, and we had a mobile army bearing down on us.

"Fenrir," I said loudly, looking up at him and hoping he could understand me. Loki had spoken with him and he'd seemed to understand. He still had the collar on his throat, but it was no longer glowing with runes. It didn't seem to be attached to any chains, either. He turned to look at me, watching in silence. But I did notice one of his ears twitching as it swiveled, possibly hearing the snowmobiles outside. "More enemies are on their way. And you need to get out of here or this was all for nothing."

Loki pointed at Fenrir's throat. "He is no longer restrained, but that collar still has runes on it. We need to get it off."

I squinted, leaning forward. He was right. At least, I saw numerous indentations in the collar that looked like runes, but his fur was bunched over it and the building was still dark. At least they weren't glowing.

Then I realized what Loki was getting at. "All of my...rune-breakers are down for the count. This is as good as it's going to get until we can heal them. And sticking around here for the reinforcements to arrive is a great way to get us all killed."

I thought about making a Gateway, and my knees almost gave out as a wave of dizziness rolled over me. Nope. Magic was a bad idea. Then I remembered that I had given Alucard some Tiny Balls so he could get the pups out of here in the event that things went sideways.

I spun to War. "Grab Alucard's Tiny Balls. They're in his pants somewhere."

War gave me a flat look. "I fail to see how groping the vampire will help anyone. Pass."

I growled. "Magic marbles that make Gateways," I snapped, remembering that he didn't regularly work with me, so he might not be familiar with the professional lingo.

"Oh. Well, that's entirely different. I'll go grope the vampire."

I rolled my eyes, turning back around to see Gunnar carrying a sleeping Makayla in his teeth, holding her by the ruff of her neck. Loki carried Calvin in his arms. The dad-squad trotted past me with anxious looks on their faces as they heard the distant whine of snowmobiles. I was guessing we had a few minutes, tops.

I glanced at Fenrir. "Alright, big boy. You probably need to shake out those muscles—"

Fenrir stood up…and obliterated the roof in the process.

I spun and ran from the building as pieces crashed down all around me. I felt Fenrir's hot breath on my back and I instinctively clenched my butt to get it at least another inch away from him in hopes that one inch could make a difference.

Contrary to rumor, it did not make a difference.

Fenrir grabbed me in his mouth, and I fell to my back on his wet, hot tongue. I stared out through a prison of teeth that wasn't entirely closed, and saw metal beams, sheets of aluminum and steel, and other sections of the building crashing down outside of Fenrir's mouth.

I panted, suddenly feeling like I was in a steamy sauna, and ripped my coat off. I looped it around one of his teeth and held onto both ends in case he decided to tilt his head back too far and taste some magical, St. Louis long pig.

Me.

But I was pretty sure he was trying to save me.

"You know, if you had waited another ten seconds, you wouldn't have almost killed me!" I muttered. "Bad dog!"

I felt a blast of hot air wash over me as he let out a grunt that sounded like amusement.

I felt his tongue suddenly drop out from under me and I slammed into the roof of his mouth. A heartbeat later, two explosions rocked the ground outside and I landed back onto his tongue in a wizardly splat. I climbed to my feet, cursing and swearing as I wiped slobber from my face and arms, turning to see that he held his mouth open and his tongue out. It rolled out like a red carpet and Loki stood at the end, staring at me with wide, panicked eyes, having forgotten all about the puppy in his arms.

Gunnar calmly trotted over and picked up the puppy by the back of his neck with his teeth, snorting at Loki before carrying the pup away.

I walked down Fenrir's tongue with as much dignity as I could manage, wiping saliva from my satchel and carrying my dripping coat. As much as I wanted to throw it down Fenrir's throat until he choked…the frigid air was having a decidedly unpleasant effect on my soaked body.

So I turned around and glared at him, placing my hands on my hips. He had closed his mouth but still had his chin on the ground. His rear was straight up in the air, and I realized his paws were stretched out to either side of me. His massive tail was wagging back and forth, destroying the remnants of the building.

He…was play-bowing. To me.

It was a thing dogs often did with each other while wrestling and playing. They would suddenly drop down and stretch out their front paws, keeping their asses high to signal they wanted to play.

I stepped to the side in order to see past his nose and glared. "No fucking way," I told him, taking a step back and holding up my finger. "I am *not* wrestling with you."

"We are blood brothers," he whispered, his breath rolling over me in a heatwave. I flinched to hear him suddenly speak, since all he'd done up until now was growl. His voice sounded like a body being dragged through a forest of dead leaves, but it was muted and pained, as if restricted by his collar.

"Um, no. We are definitely not brothers," I said, shooting Loki a quick frown.

He licked his lips. "Yes we are, little *godkiller*."

And I saw golden light suddenly glowing from beneath his fur, just like…the veins in my arms. In fact, mine suddenly began to glow as well, responding to his.

I stared up at him with wide eyes. "Oh. I guess we are…big red dog," I said, trying to come up with a nickname, since I hadn't appreciated his *little* reference.

He chuffed, making my hair fly back. Then he spoke again, but this time it sounded entirely different. Like it was inside my head.

Anyone else stupid enough to bring Gungnir that close to me would have experienced a thousand deaths in the span of an instant. But I like your bravery, brother. You risked your life to save mine, and for that, I am forever in your debt.

I felt a momentary flutter of panic that Loki might have somehow heard him. I discreetly shook my head as I tried to think words back at him. *I had to keep Gungnir away from...your grandfather. No one here knows I have it.*

He studied me very intently, his eyes seeming to shine. *I see*, he thought at me. *You are quite interesting, little brother. I'm interested to learn why you disguise yourself as the Father of Lightning, but we can discuss that, and many other topics later, when this cursed collar is removed.*

Father of Lightning? Was he talking about Thor? Was that what Loki had made me look like?

Fenrir's eyes flicked over to the pups. *The mistwolves are in grave danger. People fear what they do not understand. I know this well. I would ask you to do everything in your power to keep them safe*, he said, and I knew it wasn't a question.

Already working on it, I reassured him. Then I heard the sound of snowmobiles—much louder, now—and I flinched. They were right over the ridgeline. *We need to go. Now.*

"Hop on," he said, out loud this time.

I blinked at him, wondering if I had heard correctly. But he was already lowering his rear down to the ground so that we could climb onto his back.

"Um," I said, turning back to Loki. "Did you hear any of that?" I asked uneasily.

Loki shook his head very slowly, but he looked incredibly interested, and he was still cupping his arms like he was holding the puppy—obviously unaware that he had been robbed. "Just that you are both godkillers. Then you called him a big red dog and stared at each other for a second," he added, not sounding impressed.

I let out a breath of relief. "Yeah. I had hoped you didn't hear that part," I mumbled, feigning embarrassment. "Reflex snark. It's real."

He nodded very slowly before turning to Fenrir. "What is he—"

"I checked everywhere," War snapped, skidding to a halt in front of me.

"Sparkles doesn't have any balls." His face instantly reddened. "Magic marbles," he said, coughing loudly. "I meant magic marbles. He must have dropped them or burned them up in his supernova impersonation."

I pointed a thumb at Fenrir. "He's offering a ride, but we should hurry," I said, my eyes again settling on the ridgeline and the sound of snowmobiles. A lot of snowmobiles.

"It's a good idea," War replied, grinning like an idiot. "I'll help Gunnar with the pups."

Alucard was lying on the ground, and I watched as Carl stepped up between his outstretched legs and grabbed the vampire's right pant leg with his left hand. Then he squatted down too scoop his right arm under the same leg and did a shoulder roll aimed towards Alucard's left armpit.

I blinked incredulously as Carl landed in a crouch with Alucard slung over his shoulder. Wow. Okay. Then Carl was jogging towards Fenrir. The wolf watched the Elder with wary respect as Carl climbed up his fur, still carrying Alucard.

Loki had already mounted, and Gunnar had shifted back to his human form. War took off his trench coat and shoved it at him, averting his eyes from Gunnar's nudity.

Great. Now we had a flasher in a trench coat. Gunnar grabbed a pup in each hand and made his way over to Fenrir, handing the puppies up to Loki.

"We're cutting it close," War said. "How are you doing on magic?"

I tapped my necklace, indicating my Mask. "I'm down to last resorts. I have enough Fae juice left to put out these fires, because I doubt these snowmobiles are carrying Forest Rangers."

He turned to me with a surprised look on his face. "Did you just think about that?" he asked.

I shook my head. "The moment they lit up," I admitted. "Someone has to do it."

"You have a surprisingly good soul, Temple."

I scoffed. "Hell no. I just don't want to get a bad rep next time I need a snowman army. Those guys gossip, and if I let their home burn down, they won't help me again."

He grinned, shaking his head. "Liar. You better hurry."

I nodded, bending low to scoop up a snowball as War walked away. I focused my mind, reaching back out to the snow to ask for one last favor. I watched as a dozen snowmen rose up in front of me, looking tired. I let out a sigh of relief and exhaustion, barely fighting back the dizzy spell that threatened to knock me down.

I pointed at War, and smiled as a dozen snowballs pelted him from behind. He cursed, spinning around with a fiery sword suddenly in his fist. I burst out laughing. Then I gave each of my snowmen a high five. "Alright. Now, this last job is for you guys, because I'm almost out of juice. We need to put that fire out, and the guys coming our way on snowmobiles want to make it a bigger fire. I want you to stop them or give them hell."

They turned to each other and nodded.

"Thank you," I said. Then I began stumbling my way back towards Fenrir, that last bit of magic making my legs shaky and unreliable. I heard a piercing screech and glanced up sharply, instinctively assuming it was Hugin and Munin as I stared up at the cloudless sky.

I suddenly saw a pair of huge talons flying at my face. I wobbled clear, already dizzy, and the talons whistled past my cheek, but a brown feathered wing hit me like a down-pillow swung by an overzealous pre-teen in a championship pillow fight, knocking me on my ass.

The brown eagle hit the ground and rebounded up into the air as headlights suddenly sailed over the rise, heralding a battalion of snowmobiles. These men wore all white and they had laser sights on their guns, because red beams suddenly appeared everywhere, locking onto the snowmen and opening fire.

Fenrir suddenly leapt over me, snapping his jaws at the frantic bird. He missed, his jaws cracking shut on empty air, but he wasted no time in tearing into the horde of snowmobiles, stomping his paws and biting down to crush them like beer cans.

Men screamed, blood sprayed, and the gunfire sounded like a drum solo at a rock concert.

But they didn't stand a chance against Fenrir. I watched his fur ripple as bullets hammered into him, but he paid them no mind. My friends hunched low on his back, holding on for dear life.

Then I saw Carl in his stupid sleeveless pink puffy jacket.

He was sprinting down Fenrir's back—away from the snowmobiles. He leapt up into the air, aiming in my general direction.

Except he was at least forty feet in the air.

His arms windmilled wildly, and I wondered what the hell he was trying to do. That's when I saw the brown eagle swooping back down towards me, the two of them racing to get to me first.

And I realized that this thing was way too fucking big to be a goddamned eagle. I tried standing, but my legs did little more than slide me back a foot. The eagle's wings flared wide as its talons stretched out to snatch me—and they were big enough to succeed.

Carl hit it from behind, swiping his claws at the eagle's face and using his other hand to grab onto a wing in an effort to either steer it away from me or rip the wing off.

The eagle screeched as Power Puff Carl's claws raked a cheek.

I screamed as the eagle's talons hit me in the chest like a taser—producing an explosion of lightning.

Fenrir howled as everything flashed, crackled, and boomed before darkness swallowed all sound and light and sensation.

CHAPTER 45

I woke up with a gasp, squinting against a bright sky. I was hanging by my wrists, my feet swinging lazily in the air. Wind whistled in my face and ears, and all I saw in the distance was a never-ending blanket of clouds.

Sky plus big fucking eagle equals Tropical Temple flavored, baby bird food, I thought to myself, suddenly panicking. *The thing is taking me to his or her eaglets for breakfast!*

I began frantically swinging my body to try and shake myself free from the eagle's grip so it would let my wrists go and drop me. I could then touch my Horseman's Mask to use my wings or try shouting for Grimm as I fell through the sky.

Except something cut deeply into my wrists, and all I heard were clinking chains. That's when I realized that I wasn't flying in the air by the eagle's talons, but that I was on a windy mountain peak above the clouds. My feet hung about five feet from the ground, since I was hanging by chained shackles around my wrists. I kicked my feet violently, trying to use my magic to break the chains, since I was no longer feeling so drained.

But it almost felt like I didn't *have* any magic—at all. I couldn't even sense it. I kicked my feet harder, my panic upgrading to full on freak-out mode.

"Calm the fuck down over there, newbie!" a deep voice growled, before spiraling into a wet, hacking cough.

I swiveled to see a hairy human body with a bird's nest for a head also hanging by chained shackles around his wrists. The blood on his massive forearms looked old and crusted, and his skin was tough and leathery and browned by the sun.

He was also a fucking giant—his toes almost brushing the ground.

Like, nine-feet-and-*it-doesn't-fucking-matter-how-many-inches-at-that-point* tall.

He had to be five-hundred pounds of solid muscle.

I kicked my feet to get a better look at his chains and saw that a pillar of rock actually rose up behind him, arcing out over his head where the chain was looped about a dozen times around the tip. Seeing his browned, beaten, lumpy form hanging like that, it made him look like the last banana dangling on the banana hanger of an apocalyptic kitchen counter.

It took me a moment of spinning to realize that I was hanging from a similar banana hanger, and that...

The mountain ended about two inches behind our pillars.

We were on the edge of a fucking cliff!

I sucked in a breath, kicking my feet wildly to turn back around before I lost my tentative grip on my sanity.

The giant swiveled his hairy dome my way to reveal a lumpy, misshapen face of leathery, sunburned skin. His *face* had calluses for crying out loud. That pretty much summed it up. He'd been here for a while.

He wore only a filthy bundle of cloth around his groin, and torso was a canvas of scars, as if a toddler with a razor had used his body to practice the alphabet. Whatever had caused them, it had happened a long time before his current predicament. His lips were cracked and bleeding, and the ear closest to me was crusted with dried blood as if someone had torn it off within the last few days.

He appraised me up and down. "At least you can talk," he muttered. "Who are you?" he asked in a tired, rasping voice, before spiraling into another hacking, wet cough—obviously not used to speaking.

"Nate Te—"

His coughing intensified, cutting me short. I winced uneasily, wondering if he was going to cough to death right next to me.

"Temple!" I shouted hurriedly, trying to time my answer between his coughs.

He finally hacked up a glob of something nasty—more solid than liquid—and furrowed his wiry eyebrows at me. "What the fuck kind of a name is Tainted Nipple?" he demanded. "You trying to make jokes and give me a bullshit name?" he roared, his pecs flexing as he tried to swing my way as if to kick me.

"No!" I snapped, swinging to avoid his wildly unpredictable attack. "*Nate!*" I shouted.

He angled his ear towards me, trying to use his shoulders to push the matted hair out of his way so he could hear me properly. "What?"

"NATE!" I shouted as loud as I could.

He grunted. "What do I care? You want to call yourself Taint, go ahead," he grumbled. "At least your mouth isn't sewn shut."

I glanced over sharply, my eyes widening. I tried to get a look past the giant, but he was just too big. "Carl?" I shouted, straining my neck.

I saw clawed feet kick out, and then a long white tail and a flash of pink. My heart soared. I wasn't alone! But my smile slowly withered. We were *both* trapped.

"What does the eagle want?" I asked, glancing over at my new pal.

He slowly turned to look at me with a furious glare. "You think you're *real* fucking funny, don't you?" he growled murderously. "Give you fire, sentenced to eternal torture, and this shit-stain thinks he can make jokes. Well, I'm not talking to you anymore."

My scalp suddenly tingled at an alarming thought. I squinted to see an even higher peak in the distance—a tiny finger of rock with a nest perched at the top. And if I could see that from this distance, it had to belong to a massive bird.

An eagle, to be precise.

My stomach began to churn for multiple reasons. *Fire*, he had said. *Eternal torture*. I slowly turned to look at the man beside me.

No. Not *man*.

Titan.

"You..." I stammered, staring at him in awe, "are Prometheus."

He grunted.

"Thanks for the whole fire thing," I blabbed, fan-girling a little. "It really gave us a fighting chance."

He gave me an incredibly dry look. "Kind of regretting it, to be honest, Taint," he muttered, glancing pointedly at his scarred torso—where the eagle ripped out his liver and ate it. Every. Single. Day.

I didn't blame him for his poor attitude, but why had the eagle grabbed *me*?

"I didn't know who you were," I said guiltily, realizing I'd offended him twice already. "My friend and I were picked up by an eagle and brought here. I wasn't being an asshole. I just didn't make the connection."

He grunted again. "I'm betting it wasn't the same eagle." He let out a breath. "I didn't see anyone bring you here, but I was busy having my liver ripped out by the cursed eagle up there. I usually black out at some point and then wake up the next morning. Woke up today and saw you two keeping me company. Tried talking to the lizard over there, but his mouth is sewn up. You're in for a real show. It's almost breakfast time," he said, glaring up at the eagle. "Hope you're immortal. Well, might be better if you're not, actually."

He fell into another coughing fit, unused to speaking this much—or at all, for that matter.

I shuddered. Almost breakfast time? Shit.

I remembered the eagle attacking us in the mountains, and the flash of lightning just before everything had gone dark. Then I remembered Loki's illusion—that he had made us all look different. Fenrir had asked why I was disguised as the *Father of Lightning*, and I'd assumed he was referring to Thor—the Norse pantheon's God of Thunder. But since we were hanging out beside Prometheus...

"Zeus," I cursed. "Why the fuck would Zeus kidnap *me*?"

"Did you give anyone fire? That really seems to chap his ass," Prometheus grumbled dryly.

"No fire," I said, wondering what I might have recently done to piss him off, other than unknowingly impersonating him—but that was probably enough right there, to be honest. I'd planned on taking the pups to the River Styx, but I hadn't actually *done* it yet, and no one knew—

"Hermes. Motherfucker."

Prometheus grunted. "He's one of the few I actually liked. Doubt he'd do anything to help Zeus."

I frowned, recalling my conversation with the Greek Messenger God. It lined up with Prometheus' comment. Hermes had carefully warned me against his fellow Olympians. Had he known what Zeus was going to do even then? Then I grinned.

He had given me a coin!

He'd also referenced the first coin of his I'd used—the one Asterion had given me to take out the dragoons so long ago. It had been more than just a coin, though.

Flip once to save another's life, flip once to save your own.

CHAPTER 46

Could it be that simple? Had he given me a golden replica? A key to my handcuffs? I scanned the ground and saw my satchel propped up against a table in a small alcove beside a wooden door that led deeper into the mountain.

But I hadn't put it in my satchel. I'd put it in my pocket!

Hanging from my wrists was going to be a problem, though, and I had no way of knowing if Zeus had emptied my pockets before leaving me here.

Only one way to find out. I kicked my feet out and began swinging. Back and forth, back and forth, building up my momentum.

"What a genius idea, Taint," Prometheus muttered.

I ignored him, swinging almost horizontal to the ground, my feet just barely missing the wall behind me. As I began my next forward pass, I latched onto the chains with my hands, kicked my feet straight up and pulled with everything I had like I was trying to pole vault.

I quickly looped my boots around the chain three times in order to support my weight, and then let out a sigh of relief.

Prometheus stared up at me, looking impressed. But I could tell my grip was precarious, so I didn't waste any time as I carefully pulled myself higher up the chain, alternating my hands. Thankfully, the links were so large that I could grip them like rings, so it wasn't as hard as rope-climbing would have been. I tried to gauge when I might be high enough to reach out with one hand and search my pocket.

Because I'd have to risk letting go of the chain with one hand to do so. My legs were still supporting my weight, but I could feel them sliding little-by-little.

I took a deep breath, let go with one hand, and shoved the other into my right pocket. My hand clasped around the coin just as my boots slipped. I yanked my hand out of my pocket and flipped the coin with my thumb, praying to Hermes for a little more luck.

There was a flash of light, and the golden coin sliced through my chains like a scalpel. I dropped to the ground like wet laundry—pins and needles instantly shooting up my ankles and shins.

I lay there for a few seconds, riding out the pain and getting my breath back. Then I let out a weak laugh. It had worked! It was just like Asterion's coin! "Boo-yah!" I crowed.

I rolled to my feet, grinning up at Prometheus. He was staring down at me with a strange look on his face, and it took me a moment to realize that it was—ironically—hope.

Something he hadn't had in a very long time.

I stared down at the manacles still on my wrists and noticed red symbols glowing on them. I tried to use my magic again, but still couldn't sense anything. Damn.

I didn't see the golden coin on the ground, but I remembered that Hermes' original coin had returned to my pocket after being used. I shoved my fingers into my pocket and grinned, pulling it out with a laugh.

I didn't know how much time I had until someone came to check on me or—

A piercing scream suddenly made my blood run cold. I spun towards the nest to see an eagle flying our way, either drawn by the sound of me breaking free, or coming over for his scheduled breakfast of Prometheus' liver.

"Get me down!" he begged, his face frantic. "Or I'll be dead, and you'll have to wait until tomorrow when I wake back up!"

I hesitated, staring at Carl and then Prometheus. If I let the Titan down, he was maybe strong enough, and tall enough, to help me get Carl down. Hell, the chains holding Carl and I were way smaller than the ones holding Prometheus, almost dainty in comparison.

But...what if the coin wasn't strong enough for his chains?

I made my decision and flipped the coin.

It zipped out and sliced through Carl's chains, and Prometheus' face darkened in fury. He'd given us fire, and I wouldn't even save him from his punishment when given the chance.

I bit back my guilt and held up my hands. "I've got an idea!" I shouted, and I sprinted over to my satchel. The eagle was rapidly approaching, only seconds away, and he looked suddenly pissed that his two new meals had somehow broken free.

I shoved my hand inside my satchel, grabbed my dirty little secret, and whipped it out with a triumphant grin.

Gungnir—Odin's legendary spear—had never actually gone missing. I knew Odin had wanted it more than anything in the Nine Realms, in order to fix the Fenrir problem once and for all.

He wanted it for protection, or murder.

If he knew I still had it, he never would have let me out of his sights, so I'd pretended that it had gone missing. Then I'd told anyone who would listen that I was traveling the world.

If he believed me about Gungnir, he'd waste his time scouring the Nine Realms for a thief.

If he doubted me about Gungnir, he'd waste his time following in my footsteps, checking to see if I'd used my travels to disguise stashing it somewhere.

Or he would use Hugin and Munin to do it for him.

And look who had been *so busy traveling* that he hadn't bothered going to Asgard to check on his own people—giving Loki the opportunity to fill his shoes? Odin.

And look who collapsed from exhaustion in my front yard, running errands for Odin all over the Nine Realms. Hugin and Munin.

So my guess had been right—either way.

I'd also known that Loki wanted it almost as badly as Odin—so he could deny his father the one weapon that could kill his son, Fenrir.

To keep up my ruse, I had duct-taped a Sensate to Gungnir and shoved it into my bottomless satchel where no one could reach it. With a Sensate stuck to it, Odin couldn't locate it via magic, and no other being could pick up on its powerful energy signature.

Making it look like I really didn't have it.

I turned and ran towards Carl and Prometheus, shouting at the top of my lungs to distract the eagle. But he was already making a direct dive for Carl since the Elder was wobbling around as if drunk, struggling to regain the proper use of his legs. I lifted Gungnir over my head and was about to throw it at the eagle when Carl abruptly spun—with surprising agility—and leapt clear of the eagle's talons, making it look like the easiest thing in the world.

He'd been faking it!

The eagle slammed into the ground with alarming force and...

Kept on sliding right between Prometheus' legs and into his pillar with an ear-splitting crack.

The pillar teetered, swinging Prometheus around like a pendulum, and his massive weight only served to make it worse. I watched, knowing there was nothing I could do but hope.

My hope wasn't enough.

The eagle was just climbing to his feet, shaking his head and tail, when the pillar holding Prometheus toppled out into the open sky.

For a single moment, Prometheus—the Titan who had blessed mankind with fire—stared at me with eternal hatred.

In that look, I saw that he hated me more than he had ever hated Zeus.

Because I'd given him hope for a brief second.

And that was the worst thing in the world to take away from someone. I knew that well, because I was the Horseman of Hope.

Prometheus had just enough slack in his chain to wrap it around the eagle's neck like a leash on his way over the edge. He yanked it tight and mounted the eagle's back in hopes that they might save each other despite the anchor of stone.

I ran to the edge, holding onto my old pillar for support as I leaned out.

"I'm really, really sorry!" I shouted as loud as I could. "And thank you for giving us fire!"

"May the gods damn you for eternity, Tainted Niiiiiippppplll-lleeeeeee..." his titanic voice boomed through the air before he and the eagle disappeared through the blanket of clouds.

I sighed, shaking my head. At least he hadn't gotten my name right. In the unlikely event that he did survive, he would stalk the earth in search of Tainted Nipple.

I turned around to see Carl staring at my feet, still averting his eyes.

"Do you think they will glide to safety?" I asked the Elder.

Carl shook his head firmly, and then fastidiously straightened his sleeveless pink coat, even wiping at a dirt stain.

"Yeah," I sighed. "Me neither."

CHAPTER 47

I used Gungnir like a staff, walking up to Carl. I scanned our surroundings, wondering what to do next. I had a pretty good idea where we were, but I found it very strange that Zeus had just left my satchel here. Why hadn't he kept it? Had he reached inside, found nothing, and just dropped it, assuming it was trash?

Why hadn't he kept it for himself?

I was betting that if we walked through the door, we would get the opportunity to ask him in person. Because since we were up so high in the clouds—right next to Prometheus' penthouse…

Good chance we were on Mount Olympus.

But if my plan to use the River Styx to protect the pups had pissed him off, wouldn't he have *personally* killed me?

And why had Hermes given me the one thing I would need to get out of the situation, as if he knew it was coming? That implied it *wasn't* about my River Styx idea. Or my impersonation. Was Zeus finally getting around to punishing me for Athena?

I sighed. Only one way to find out.

I touched my necklace, but nothing happened. I let out a frustrated breath, glaring at the strange manacles. Whatever they were, they were strong enough to hold a Titan and bar a Horseman from his powers.

But I did have Gungnir. And I had a voiceless Elder. I was betting his powers were similarly restricted or blocked, but he didn't need two handicaps, and I was about sick and tired of whatever was going on with the silver wire.

I stared at him, but he obviously refused to meet my eyes.

"I don't know what this is all about, Carl, but I'm sick and tired of that wire. And I hate seeing you act so meek and subservient around me. I don't know or care what foolish thing you're trying to prove to me. I don't know or care what my ancestors did to you, because I'm not them. I have firsthand experience with how cruel and sadistic some of them were. *But I am not them!* I refuse to be like them. From now on, you're free from any obligation you think you have to me. Your people are also free. You can burn that stupid shrine to the ground, for all I care."

I lifted his chin and leaned close, forcing him to look into my eyes or look like a fool trying to avert them all over the place. He finally did, refusing to even blink.

"The only thing I care about is my friend. I want him back. Right the fuck now, you creepy weirdo. If I'm about to die up here, I want to at least talk to my buddy again before I kick the bucket. especially if you think of something wildly inappropriate to say to Zeus. That would be perfect."

He stared at me, his shoulders quivering nervously. I carefully grabbed the wire and waited for him to nod. I lifted Gungnir to help me cut the wire, but Carl swatted it down, shaking his head. Then he touched my hand with his and nodded.

I grimaced. "You want me to rip it out?" I asked.

He nodded.

I took a deep breath, trying not to imagine the sensation I was about to give him. Then I yanked it—hard and fast like a bandage.

It slipped out of his flesh with no resistance, and Carl didn't even blink. "You okay?" I asked uneasily.

He stretched his mouth open, revealing black teeth, and then he licked his lips with his forked tongue. "Better than Peter Fireman."

I blinked at him, confused. "Who?"

He pointed a claw behind me at where Prometheus had been. "The one who called you Tainted Nipple. I refuse to use his real name since he mocked yours. I wish him to survive the fall and break every bone in his body. Then he can die in eternal agony at a later point."

I arched an eyebrow. "I think his ears were damaged, Carl."

He shook his head. "He heard the rest of your conversation without any problem. He was being an asshole purse."

I cocked my head, trying to wrap my head around the last comment. Then I chuckled. "Bag of assholes?"

"Yes," he rasped.

I wrapped my arm around his shoulder. "Good to have you back, Carl. Let's go kick Zeus' ass."

We walked for about ten minutes before coming upon a marble pavilion on a cliff. I'd been here before—or they all looked the same.

It was where I had killed Athena.

A buff older man stood in the center, watching us. He had long gray hair, a white skirt, and a wide golden belt. The buckle of the belt showed a clenched fist above a lightning bolt, and I froze, glancing down at my palm.

I felt an icy shiver down the back of my spine. It...was identical to my family crest.

I looked up at him, scowling. A suspicious thought entered my mind, and I shoved Gungnir into my satchel, not wanting him to be able to take it from me.

Because this situation looked way too easy. Zeus was just hanging out, waiting for me? Right.

Then I made my way over until we stood face-to-face.

"I wore my favorite shirt for you," I said, pointing at my chest. "Show-Me Your O-Face. O—like *Olympian*," I explained. "You can have it if you want."

He narrowed his eyes but did not comment.

I sighed. "What the hell is this?" I demanded.

He stared at me, his face unreadable. That's not to say there was no emotion. Instead, it was a storm of emotions that I couldn't identify. Well, one of them was rage. I recognized that one.

"How upset was Prometheus when you broke free?" he asked in a surprisingly calm baritone.

"He felt betrayed."

Zeus nodded. "Good. He deserves it."

"We felt much better after killing him," Carl said without a flicker of shame.

My stomach clenched. *Fucking Carl!*

I'd wanted to keep that part a secret for as long as possible. Long enough to talk my way out of whatever I had done to piss Zeus off.

Zeus' eyes flickered with lightning. And he took a very, very slow breath. "You are here to pay for your multiple crimes against the Olympians. And killing Prometheus," he said through clenched teeth.

I glanced down at his belt pointedly. Then I showed him my palm. "What if we are on the same side?"

He frowned down at it, looking surprised. Then he grunted. "Anyone can mark their flesh with my symbol."

I shook my head. "This is my family Crest. Been there for generations. Almost like we worshipped you or something."

"Be that as it may, your crimes still carry punishments. And now, you are going to do me some favors. Big favors. It seems some of my fellow Olympians have strayed, breaking my trust to pursue their own wishes. You are going to kill them for me, Godkiller."

My eyes widened in alarm. "What if I tell you I'm busy?"

"You will replace Prometheus, of course."

I nodded woodenly. "Right. Who is it I'm supposed to kill?" I asked.

He smiled. "I think you are the kind of man who needs a lesson in humility to really show you the gravity of the situation. I will keep you here for a while. It will take me some time to gather the information you will need on your targets, godkiller. I've prepared a room for you and your... friend. It even has a window."

I opened my mouth to protest and he snapped his finger.

Between one second and the next, I was back in chains in a dark stone room. The walls glowed with dozens of crimson runes that matched my manacles.

Thankfully, my chains didn't suspend me in the air this time. I even had enough slack to move around. "Carl?" I asked, searching the room.

He grunted. "I am here," he said. I saw him standing to my right, similarly restrained.

I scanned our lodgings and saw my satchel propped against the far wall, out of our reach.

A window above our heads let in the only light, but it was covered with metal bars.

"Fuck," I cursed.

"Maybe he did not like your shirt," Carl suggested.

I grunted. Then I began to laugh.

"Are you okay?" Carl asked.

I nodded, wiping at my eyes since I had enough slack in my chains. "I just remembered that I promised Gunnar I would meet with the FBI. That plan just went to hell."

Carl chuckled, and soon we were both laughing hard enough for our eyes to water.

I didn't know exactly who Zeus wanted us to kill or why, and I didn't know why his symbol was on my family Crest. I didn't know who Niko was, and I didn't know if my friends had escaped safely with Fenrir.

But I couldn't stop laughing about one thing.

"Damn you, Tainted Nipple!" Carl wheezed between laughs.

And pretty soon, we were both singing like madmen.

Sometimes that was all you could do. Learn to laugh and sing—

"Alucard can still hear me…" Carl suddenly whispered.

I turned to stare at him for a few seconds.

And then I began to smile.

*Nate Temple returns in **DYNASTY…2020**.*

DON'T FORGET! VIP's get early access to all sorts of Temple-Verse goodies, including signed copies, private giveaways, and advance notice of future projects. AND A FREE NOVELLA! Click the image or join here: www.shaynesilvers.com/l/219800

~

Turn the page to read a sample of **UNCHAINED** *- Feathers and Fire Series Book 1, or* **BUY ONLINE**. *Callie Penrose is a wizard in Kansas City, MO who hunts monsters for the Vatican. She meets Nate Temple, and things devolve from there...*

(Note: Full chronology of all books in the Temple Verse shown on the 'Books in the Temple Verse' page.)

TRY: UNCHAINED (FEATHERS AND FIRE #1)

The rain pelted my hair, plastering loose strands of it to my forehead as I panted, eyes darting from tree to tree, terrified of each shifting branch, splash of water, and whistle of wind slipping through the nightscape around us. But… I was somewhat *excited*, too.

Somewhat.

"Easy, girl. All will be well," the big man creeping just ahead of me, murmured.

"You said we were going to get ice cream!" I hissed at him, failing to compose myself, but careful to keep my voice low and my eyes alert. "I'm not ready for this!" I had been trained to fight, with my hands, with weapons, and with my magic. But I had never taken an active role in a hunt before. I'd always been the getaway driver for my mentor.

The man grunted, grey eyes scanning the trees as he slipped through the tall grass. "And did we not get ice cream before coming here? Because I think I see some in your hair."

"You know what I mean, Roland. You tricked me." I checked the tips of my loose hair, saw nothing, and scowled at his back.

"The Lord does not give us a greater burden than we can shoulder."

I muttered dark things under my breath, wiping the water from my eyes. Again. My new shirt was going to be ruined. Silk never fared well in the rain. My choice of shoes wasn't much better. Boots, yes, but distressed, *fashionable* boots. Not work boots designed for the rain and mud. Definitely not monster hunting boots for our evening excursion through one of Kansas City's wooded parks. I realized I was forcibly distracting myself, keeping my mind busy with mundane thoughts to avoid my very real anxiety. Because whenever I grew nervous, an imagined nightmare always—

A church looming before me. Rain pouring down. Night sky and a glowing moon overhead. I was all alone. Crying on the cold, stone steps, and infant in a cardboard box—

I forced the nightmare away, breathing heavily. "You know I hate it when you talk like that," I whispered to him, trying to regain my composure. I wasn't angry with him, but was growing increasingly uncomfortable with our situation after my brief flashback of fear.

"Doesn't mean it shouldn't be said," he said kindly. "I think we're close. Be alert. Remember your training. Banish your fears. I am here. And the Lord is here. He always is."

So, he had noticed my sudden anxiety. "Maybe I should just go back to the car. I know I've trained, but I really don't think—"

A shape of fur, fangs, and claws launched from the shadows towards me, cutting off my words as it snarled, thirsty for my blood.

And my nightmare slipped back into my thoughts like a veiled assassin, a wraith hoping to hold me still for the monster to eat. I froze, unable to move. Twin sticks of power abruptly erupted into being in my clenched fists, but my fear swamped me with that stupid nightmare, the sticks held at my side, useless to save me.

Right before the beast's claws reached me, it grunted as something batted it from the air, sending it flying sideways. It struck a tree with another grunt and an angry whine of pain.

I fell to my knees right into a puddle, arms shaking, breathing fast.

My sticks crackled in the rain like live cattle prods, except their entire length was the electrical section — at least to anyone other than me. I could hold them without pain.

Magic was a part of me, coursing through my veins whether I wanted it or not, and Roland had spent many years teaching me how to master it. But I had never been able to fully master the nightmare inside me, and in moments of fear, it always won, overriding my training.

The fact that I had resorted to weapons — like the ones he had trained me with — rather than a burst of flame, was startling. It was good in the fact that my body's reflexes knew enough to call up a defense even without my direct command, but bad in the fact that it was the worst form of defense for the situation presented. I could have very easily done as Roland did, and hurt it from a distance. But I hadn't. Because of my stupid block.

Roland placed a calloused palm on my shoulder, and I flinched. "Easy, see? I am here." But he did frown at my choice of weapons, the reprimand silent but loud in my mind. I let out a shaky breath, forcing my fear back down. It was all in my head, but still, it wasn't easy. Fear could be like that.

I focused on Roland's implied lesson. Close combat weapons — even magically-powered ones — were for last resorts. I averted my eyes in very real shame. I knew these things. He didn't even need to tell me them. But when that damned nightmare caught hold of me, all my training went out the window. It haunted me like a shadow, waiting for moments just like this, as if trying to kill me. A form of psychological suicide? But it was why I constantly refused to join Roland on his hunts. He knew about it. And although he was trying to help me overcome that fear, he never pressed too hard.

Rain continued to sizzle as it struck my batons. I didn't let them go, using them as a totem to build my confidence back up. I slowly lifted my eyes to nod at him as I climbed back to my feet.

That's when I saw the second set of eyes in the shadows, right before they flew out of the darkness towards Roland's back. I threw one of my batons and missed, but that pretty much let Roland know that an unfriendly was behind him. Either that or I had just failed to murder my mentor at point-blank range. He whirled to confront the monster, expecting another aerial assault as he unleashed a ball of fire that splashed over the tree at chest height, washing the trunk in blue flames. But this monster was tricky. It hadn't planned on tackling Roland, but had merely jumped out of the darkness to get closer, no doubt learning from its fallen comrade, who still lay unmoving against the tree behind me.

His coat shone like midnight clouds with hints of lightning flashing in the depths of thick, wiry fur. The coat of dew dotting his fur reflected the moonlight, giving him a faint sheen as if covered in fresh oil. He was tall, easily hip height at the shoulder, and barrel chested, his rump much leaner than the rest of his body. He — I assumed male from the long, thick mane around his neck — had a very long snout, much longer and wider than any werewolf I had ever seen. Amazingly, and beyond my control, I realized he was beautiful.

But most of the natural world's lethal hunters were beautiful.

He landed in a wet puddle a pace in front of Roland, juked to the right, and then to the left, racing past the big man, biting into his hamstrings on his way by.

A wash of anger rolled over me at seeing my mentor injured, dousing my fear, and I swung my baton down as hard as I could. It struck the beast in the rump as it tried to dart back to cover — a typical wolf tactic. My blow singed his hair and shattered bone. The creature collapsed into a puddle of mud with a yelp, instinctively snapping his jaws over his shoulder to bite whatever had hit him.

I let him. But mostly out of dumb luck as I heard Roland hiss in pain, falling to the ground.

The monster's jaws clamped around my baton, and there was an immediate explosion of teeth and blood that sent him flying several feet away into the tall brush, yipping, screaming, and staggering. Before he slipped out of sight, I noticed that his lower jaw was simply *gone*, from the contact of his saliva on my electrified magical batons. Then he managed to limp into the woods with more pitiful yowls, but I had no mind to chase him. Roland — that titan of a man, my mentor — was hurt. I could smell copper in the air, and knew we had to get out of here. Fast. Because we had anticipated only one of the monsters. But there had been two of them, and they hadn't been the run-of-the-mill werewolves we had been warned about. If there were two, perhaps there were more. And they were evidently the prehistoric cousin of any werewolf I had ever seen or read about.

Roland hissed again as he stared down at his leg, growling with both pain and anger. My eyes darted back to the first monster, wary of another attack. It *almost* looked like a werewolf, but bigger. Much bigger. He didn't move, but I saw he was breathing. He had a notch in his right ear and a jagged scar on his long snout. Part of me wanted to go over to him and torture him. Slowly. Use his pain to finally drown my nightmare, my fear. The fear that had caused Roland's injury. My lack of inner-strength had not only put me in danger, but had hurt my mentor, my friend.

I shivered, forcing the thought away. That was *cold*. Not me. Sure, I was no stranger to fighting, but that had always been in a ring. Practicing. Sparring. Never life or death.

But I suddenly realized something very dark about myself in the chill, rainy night. Although I was terrified, I felt a deep ocean of anger manifest inside me, wanting only to dispense justice as I saw fit. To use that rage to battle my own demons. As if feeding one would starve the other, reminding me of the Cherokee Indian Legend Roland had once told me.

An old Cherokee man was teaching his grandson about life. "A fight is going on inside me," he told the boy. "It is a terrible fight between two wolves. One is evil — he is anger, envy, sorrow, regret, greed, arrogance, self-pity, guilt, resentment, inferiority, lies, false pride, superiority, and ego." After a few moments to make sure he had the boy's undivided attention, he continued.

"The other wolf is good — he is joy, peace, love, hope, serenity, humility, kindness, benevolence, empathy, generosity, truth, compassion, and faith. The same fight is going on inside of you, boy, and inside of every other person, too."

The grandson thought about this for a few minutes before replying. "Which wolf will win?"

The old Cherokee man simply said, "The one you feed, boy. The one you feed..."

And I felt like feeding one of my wolves today, by killing this one...

Get the full book ONLINE!

Turn the page to read the first chapter of **WHISKEY GINGER**, *book 1 in the Phantom Queen Diaries, which is also a part of the Temple Verse. Quinn MacKenna is a black-magic arms dealer from Boston, and she doesn't play nice. Not at all...*

TRY: WHISKEY GINGER (PHANTOM QUEEN DIARIES BOOK 1)

*T*he pasty guitarist hunched forward, thrust a rolled-up wad of paper deep into one nostril, and snorted a line of blood crystals—frozen hemoglobin that I'd smuggled over in a refrigerated canister—with the uncanny grace of a drug addict. He sat back, fangs gleaming, and pawed at his nose. "That's some bodacious shit. Hey, bros," he said, glancing at his fellow band members, "come hit this shit before it melts."

He fetched one of the backstage passes hanging nearby, pried the plastic badge from its lanyard, and used it to split up the crystals, murmuring something in an accent that reminded me of California. Not *the* California, but you know, Cali-foh-nia—the land of beaches, babes, and bros. I retrieved a toothpick from my pocket and punched it through its thin wrapper. "So," I asked no one in particular, "now that ye have the product, who's payin'?"

Another band member stepped out of the shadows to my left, and I don't mean that figuratively, either—the fucker literally stepped out of the shadows. I scowled at him, but hid my surprise, nonchalantly rolling the toothpick from one side of my mouth to the other.

The rest of the band gathered around the dressing room table, following the guitarist's lead by preparing their own snorting utensils—tattered magazine covers, mostly. Typically, you'd do this sort of thing with a dollar-bill, maybe even a Benjamin if you were flush. But fangers like this lot couldn't touch cash directly—in God We Trust and all that. Of course, I didn't really understand why sucking blood the old-fashioned way had suddenly gone out of style. More of a rush, maybe?

"It lasts longer," the vampire next to me explained, catching my mildly curious expression. "It's especially good for shows and stuff. Makes us look, like, less—"

"Creepy?" I offered, my Irish brogue lilting just enough to make it a question.

"Pale," he finished, frowning.

I shrugged. "Listen, I've got places to be," I said, holding out my hand.

"I'm sure you do," he replied, smiling. "Tell you what, why don't you, like, hang around for a bit? Once that wears off," he dipped his head toward the bloody powder smeared across the table's surface, "we may need a pick-me-up." He rested his hand on my arm and our gazes locked.

I blinked, realized what he was trying to pull, and rolled my eyes. His widened in surprise, then shock as I yanked out my toothpick and shoved it through his hand.

"Motherfuck—"

"I want what we agreed on," I declared. "Now. No tricks."

The rest of the band saw what happened and rose faster than I could blink. They circled me, their grins feral...they might have even seemed intimidating if it weren't for the fact that they each had a case of the sniffles

—I had to work extra hard not to think about what it felt like to have someone else's blood dripping down my nasal cavity.

I held up a hand.

"Can I ask ye gentlemen a question before we get started?" I asked. "Do ye even *have* what I asked for?"

Two of the band members exchanged looks and shrugged. The guitarist, however, glanced back towards the dressing room, where a brown paper bag sat next to a case full of makeup. He caught me looking and bared his teeth, his fangs stretching until it looked like it would be uncomfortable for him to close his mouth without piercing his own lip.

"Follow-up question," I said, eyeing the vampire I'd stabbed as he gingerly withdrew the toothpick from his hand and flung it across the room with a snarl. "Do ye do each other's make-up? Since, ye know, ye can't use mirrors?"

I was genuinely curious.

The guitarist grunted. "Mike, we have to go on soon."

"Wait a minute. Mike?" I turned to the snarling vampire with a frown. "What happened to *The Vampire Prospero*?" I glanced at the numerous fliers in the dressing room, most of which depicted the band members wading through blood, with Mike in the lead, each one titled *The Vampire Prospero* in *Rocky Horror Picture Show* font. Come to think of it…Mike did look a little like Tim Curry in all that leather and lace.

I was about to comment on the resemblance when Mike spoke up, "Alright, change of plans, bros. We're gonna drain this bitch before the show. We'll look totally—"

"Creepy?" I offered, again.

"Kill her."

∽

Get the full book ONLINE!

MAKE A DIFFERENCE

Reviews are the most powerful tools in my arsenal when it comes to getting attention for my books. Much as I'd like to, I don't have the financial muscle of a New York publisher.

But I do have something much more powerful and effective than that, and it's something that those publishers would kill to get their hands on.

A committed and loyal bunch of readers.

Honest reviews of my books help bring them to the attention of other readers.

If you've enjoyed this book, I would be very grateful if you could spend just five minutes leaving a review on my book's Amazon page.

Thank you very much in advance.

ACKNOWLEDGMENTS

Team Temple and the Den of Freaks on Facebook have become family to me. I couldn't do it without die-hard readers like them.

I would also like to thank you, the reader. I hope you enjoyed reading *ASCENSION* as much as I enjoyed writing it.

Quinn MacKenna returns in 2019 with her Book 8 in the Phantom Queen Diaries, SEA BREEZE…

ABOUT SHAYNE SILVERS

Shayne is a man of mystery and power, whose power is exceeded only by his mystery…

He currently writes the Amazon Bestselling **Nate Temple** Series, which features a foul-mouthed wizard from St. Louis. He rides a bloodthirsty unicorn, drinks with Achilles, and is pals with the Four Horsemen.

He also writes the Amazon Bestselling **Feathers and Fire** Series—a second series in the Temple Verse. The story follows a rookie spell-slinger named Callie Penrose who works for the Vatican in Kansas City. Her problem? Hell seems to know more about her past than she does.

He coauthors **The Phantom Queen Diaries**—a third series set in The Temple Verse—with Cameron O'Connell. The story follows Quinn MacKenna, a mouthy black magic arms dealer in Boston. All she wants? A round-trip ticket to the Fae realm…and maybe a drink on the house.

Shayne holds two high-ranking black belts, and can be found writing in a coffee shop, cackling madly into his computer screen while pounding shots of espresso. He's hard at work on the newest books in the Temple Verse—You can find updates on new releases or chronological reading order on the next page, his website or any of his social media accounts. **Follow him online for all sorts of groovy goodies, giveaways, and new release updates:**

Get Down with Shayne Online
www.shaynesilvers.com
info@shaynesilvers.com

- facebook.com/shaynesilversfanpage
- amazon.com/author/shaynesilvers
- bookbub.com/profile/shayne-silvers
- instagram.com/shaynesilversofficial
- twitter.com/shaynesilvers
- goodreads.com/ShayneSilvers

BOOKS IN THE TEMPLE VERSE

CHRONOLOGY: All stories in the TempleVerse are shown in chronological order on the following page

NATE TEMPLE SERIES

FAIRY TALE - FREE prequel novella #0 for my subscribers

OBSIDIAN SON

BLOOD DEBTS

GRIMM

SILVER TONGUE

BEAST MASTER

BEERLYMPIAN (Novella #5.5 in the 'LAST CALL' anthology)

TINY GODS

DADDY DUTY (Novella #6.5)

WILD SIDE

WAR HAMMER

NINE SOULS

HORSEMAN

LEGEND

KNIGHTMARE

ASCENSION

FEATHERS AND FIRE SERIES

(Also set in the TempleVerse)

UNCHAINED

RAGE

WHISPERS

ANGEL'S ROAR

MOTHERLUCKER (Novella #4.5 in the 'LAST CALL' anthology)

SINNER

BLACK SHEEP

GODLESS

PHANTOM QUEEN DIARIES

(Also set in the Temple Universe)

COLLINS (Prequel novella #0 in the 'LAST CALL' anthology)

WHISKEY GINGER

COSMOPOLITAN

OLD FASHIONED

MOTHERLUCKER (Novella #3.5 in the 'LAST CALL' anthology)

DARK AND STORMY

MOSCOW MULE

WITCHES BREW

SALTY DOG

CHRONOLOGICAL ORDER: TEMPLE VERSE

FAIRY TALE (TEMPLE PREQUEL)

OBSIDIAN SON (TEMPLE 1)

BLOOD DEBTS (TEMPLE 2)

GRIMM (TEMPLE 3)

SILVER TONGUE (TEMPLE 4)

BEAST MASTER (TEMPLE 5)

BEERLYMPIAN (TEMPLE 5.5)

TINY GODS (TEMPLE 6)

DADDY DUTY (TEMPLE NOVELLA 6.5)

UNCHAINED (FEATHERS… 1)

RAGE (FEATHERS… 2)

WILD SIDE (TEMPLE 7)

WAR HAMMER (TEMPLE 8)

WHISPERS (FEATHERS… 3)

COLLINS (PHANTOM 0)
WHISKEY GINGER (PHANTOM… 1)
NINE SOULS (TEMPLE 9)
COSMOPOLITAN (PHANTOM… 2)
ANGEL'S ROAR (FEATHERS… 4)
MOTHERLUCKER (FEATHERS 4.5, PHANTOM 3.5)
OLD FASHIONED (PHANTOM…3)
HORSEMAN (TEMPLE 10)
DARK AND STORMY (PHANTOM… 4)
MOSCOW MULE (PHANTOM…5)
SINNER (FEATHERS…5)
WITCHES BREW (PHANTOM…6)
LEGEND (TEMPLE…11)
SALTY DOG (PHANTOM…7)
BLACK SHEEP (FEATHERS…6)
GODLESS (FEATHERS…7)
KNIGHTMARE (TEMPLE 12)
ASCENSION (TEMPLE 13)

Printed in Great Britain
by Amazon